FIRST EVIDENCE

BANTAM BOOKS

NEW YORK TORONTO LONDON

SYDNEY AUCKLAND

FIRST EVIDENCE

KEN GODDARD

FIRST EVIDENCE

A Bantam Book / June 1999

Book design by Dana Leigh Treglia.

Library of Congress Cataloging-in-Publication Data
Goddard, Kenneth W. (Kenneth William)
First evidence / Ken Goddard.
p.   cm.
ISBN 0-553-10864-6
I. Title.
PS3557.0285F57   1999
813'.54—dc21   98-46758
                                                        CIP

Published simultaneously in the United States and Canada

Bantam Books are published by Bantam Books, a division of Random House, Inc. Its
trademark, consisting of the words "Bantam Books" and the portrayal of a rooster,
is Registered in U.S. Patent and Trademark Office and in other countries. Marca
Registrada. Bantam Books, 1540 Broadway, New York, New York 10036.

PRINTED IN THE UNITED STATES OF AMERICA

BVG   10   9   8   7   6   5   4   3   2   1

To my dear sister Cat,
who has always been at everyone's side with
a healing touch and a cheerful smile . . .

and to Dell, Randee, and Nita,
my ever-delightful Pseudo-sisters, without whom
life these past years would have been far too dull.

This book would not have been possible without the technical advice of Bob, Naomi, and Terry; the character insights of Jody; and, of course, the first inspiration provided by Art Bell and his listeners during what turned out to be a fascinating late-night and early-morning discussion about evidence of first contact.

"THERE IS NOTHING THAT MAN FEARS MORE
THAN THE TOUCH OF THE UNKNOWN."

—Elias Canetti, *Crowds & Power*, "The Fear of Being Touched"
(1960; tr. 1962), opening lines.

EXCERPTS FROM THE FIELD NOTEBOOK OF
OSP DETECTIVE-SERGEANT COLIN CELLARS

CASE: OSP-09-00-6666:   VICTIM: BOB DAWSON

STATE OF OREGON
Oregon State Patrol

Region 9 Office:

Rodney Hawkins	Captain, Regional Commander
Don Talbert	Lieutenant, Watch Commander
Tom Bauer	Patrol Sergeant
Colin Cellars	Detective-Sergeant, CSI
Ruth Wilkinson	Front Desk Clerk

Medford Crime Laboratory:

Jack Wilson	Supervising Serologist
Susan Frost	Serologist
Terry Danielson	Firearms Examiner
Linda Grey	Evidence Technician

Salem Headquarters:

Ralph Sorenson	Major, Operations Commander

JASPER COUNTY, OREGON
Jasper County Sheriff's Department

Patrol Division:

Jim Downs	Patrol Sergeant
Paul Washburn	Patrol Sergeant

Clyde Wills	Deputy Sheriff
Mike Lambreau	Deputy Sheriff
Joe Beale	Deputy Sheriff

Jasper County Coroner's Office

Morgue:

Dr. Elliott Sutta	Supervisory Pathologist
Kathy Buckhouse	Lab Assistant
Randy Granstrom	Morgue Attendant

US FISH AND WILDLIFE SERVICE
Division of Law Enforcement

National Fish and Wildlife Forensics Laboratory:

Melissa Washington	Forensic Scientist (DNA)
Dr. Jody Catlin	Forensic Scientist (DNA)
Dr. Ann Tsuda	Veterinary Pathologist

MISCELLANEOUS PLAYERS

Bob Dawson	Friend of Colin Cellars
Malcolm Byzor	Friend of Colin Cellars
Yvie Byzor	Wife of Malcolm Byzor
Eleanor Patterson	President of the Alliance of Believers
Allesandra	Friend of Bobby Dawson
Jonas Breem	Resident of Jasper County
Tim Procter	Retired OSP Sergeant

COLLECTED EVIDENCE LIST

CASE NUMBER: OSP-09-00-6666
VICTIM: R. DAWSON
LOCATION: MOUNTAIN CABIN AT END OF COUNTY ROAD 2255
EVIDENCE COLLECTED BY: DET-SGT COLIN CELLARS #27
DATE OF COLLECTION: 18/11/00

CSI CC#:	OSP LAB#:	FWS LAB#:	DESCRIPTION:	COLLECTED AT:
1			body of victim	bsmt: wood floor—E of utility wall
2		11	body of dog	road cul-de-sac by cabin
3	1	1	suspected bloodstain	bsmt: wood floor—E of utility wall
4	2	2	suspected bloodstain	bsmt: N side of utility wall—E end
5	3		suspected bloodstain	bsmt: wall—between SE corner & S door
6	4		suspected bloodstain	bsmt: wood floor—SE corner
7	5	3	suspected bloodstain	bsmt: W wall next to broken window
8	6	4	suspected bloodstain	bsmt: floor below brkn window—W wall
9	7		suspected bloodstain	bsmt: wood floor just inside S door
10	8		suspected bloodstain	bsmt: broken easel—middle of main rug
11	9		matted hair & suspected blood	bsmt: middle of main rug
12	10		blood (?), water & mud stain	road cul-de-sac: by dog
13	11		blood (?), water & mud stain	road cul-de-sac: by dog
14	12		blood (?), water & mud stain	road cul-de-sac: by dog
15	13		blood (?), water & mud stain	road cul-de-sac: by tire tracks
16	14		suspected bone fragments & blood	road cul-de-sac: near tire tracks
17	15		suspected bone fragments & blood	road cul-de-sac: by dog
18			memory card	damaged digital camera—Cellars

19	16		roll of 35mm film	damaged 35mm camera—Cellars
20	17		broken hasp and lock	cabin: exterior S bsmt door
21	18		glass fragments and stone	bsmt: below bkn window—W wall
22	19		portrait & easel (blood?)	bsmt: middle of main rug
23	20		TOD (SN 0001)	scene: victim & dog
24	21		.45 SAA Colt revolver & hlstr	bsmt: W wall—N of table
25	22		.44 SAA Colt revolver & hlstr	bsmt: W wall—N of table
26	23		.45 SAA Colt revolver & hlstr	bsmt: W wall—N of table
27	24		12-gauge Remington 870 pump shotgun	bsmt: bed area—NE corner
28	25		9mm Glock semiauto pistol & hlstr	bsmt: bed area—NE corner
29	26		.44 Magnum S&W revolver & hlstr	bsmt: NE corner—bed, under pillow
30	27		empty (revolver) hlstr	bsmt: S wall—E of S door
31	28		.44 Webley-Garland revolver & hlstr	bsmt: S wall—E of table
32	29		.45 Colt SSA revolver & hlstr	bsmt: workbench area—N wall
33	30		Springfield cap&ball revolver & hlstr	bsmt: workbench area—N wall
34	31		Cooper Navy cap&ball revolver & hlstr	bsmt: workbench area—E wall
35	32		.44-40 Colt SA revolver & hlstr	bsmt: workbench area—E wall
36	33		empty (revolver) hlstr	bsmt: utility wall—W of woodstove
37	34		.44 Colt Army cap&ball revolver & hlstr	bsmt: utility wall—W of woodstove
38	35		.44 Remington cap&ball revolver & hlstr	bsmt: utility wall—E of woodstove
39	36		empty (revolver) hlstr	bsmt: utility wall—E of woodstove
40	37		.45-70 Sharps Rifle & ammo belt	bsmt: SE corner
41	38		expended lead bullet	bsmt: N log wall—E of refrigerator
42	39	5	expended lead bullet (blood?)	bsmt: N log wall—E of refrigerator
43	40		expended lead bullet	bsmt: N log wall—E of refrigerator
44	41		deformed lead ball	bsmt: S log wall—E of door

45	42		deformed lead ball	bsmt: S log wall—E of door
46	43		deformed lead ball (blood?)	bsmt: S log wall—E of door
47	44		deformed lead ball	bsmt: E log wall—by SE corner
48	45		expended hollow-point bullet	bsmt: W log wall by bkn window
49	46	9	expended hollow-point bullet (blood?)	bsmt: wood floor—below W brkn window
50	47	10	expended hollow-point bullet (blood?)	bsmt: wood floor—below W brkn window
51	48		expended hollow-point bullet	bsmt: W log wall—S of bkn window
52	49		expended hollow-point bullet	bsmt: W log wall—S of bkn window
53	50		expended hollow-point bullet	bsmt: W log wall—S of bkn window
54	51		.44 Colt Dragoon cap & ball revolver & hlstr	bsmt: floor—NW corner by W door
55	52	6	suspected bloodstain	OSP Explorer: upper driver's seat
56	53	7	suspected bloodstain	OSP Explorer: upper front pass. seat
57	54		cut ends—electrical wire	utility pole next to cabin
58	55		cut ends—telephone wire	3rd utility pole from cabin
59	56	8	torn strip of metal (blood?)	K. Buckhouse—JC Morgue
60	57		security videotape (copy)	K. Buckhouse—JC Morgue

CRIME SCENE DIAGRAM - CABIN BASEMENT

N

stream flow
retaining wall

raised deck

stairs up

grating

WEST-FACING DOOR

BATHROOM

LOG WALL

REFRIG

HW

SINK

RANGE

UTILITY WALL

WOODSTOVE

WOOD-BOX

shelf

ELEC. PANEL

STORAGE

RUG

BED

STAIRS up

WORKBENCH

RUG

TABLE

SOUTH-FACING DOOR

CASE: 0SP-09-00-6666
LOCATION: Victim's cabin ... end of C.R. 2255
DIAGRAM BY: Det-Sgt Colin Cellars
DATE: 18/11/00

CC#

25

42

CHAPTER ONE

THERE HAD BEEN NO WARNING.

No sound of an approaching vehicle echoing in the cold, crisp mountain air.

No crunch of gravel—or even dried-out pine needles—giving way under a heavy tire or boot.

No muted beeping of tripped sensors.

No creaking floorboards.

No whispered voices.

Nothing whatsoever.

Or at least nothing perceptible to any human senses.

And certainly nothing to make Bob Dawson think he might be in any kind of danger from someone—or some *thing*—trying to break into his cabin.

Which was an interesting concept in itself, because if anyone had ever bothered to ask him, Dawson would have responded—without the slightest sense of deceit or bravado—that he honestly couldn't remember the last time he'd felt threatened, much less afraid, of anyone or anything.

He'd been like that for as long as he could remember. First as a scrappy kid with lightning-fast reflexes and a seemingly permanent set of bruised knuckles and bloody nose. Then as an adrenaline-loving Army gunship pilot who made the easy transition to federal law enforcement, flying drug interdiction missions for the DEA. And now as a medically retired ex–federal agent turned bodybuilding Oregon hermit, thanks to a mysterious air crash that had never been satisfactorily explained to anyone—especially the DEA. Six months later, they were still searching the Marble Mountain Wilderness area in northern California for the remains of their supposedly shattered and burned helicopter.

But setting those minor discrepancies aside, if you were looking for someone tough, smart, aggressive, and flat-out crazy enough to take on the local school bully, the mob, biker gangs, low-flying drug runners, or just your average malicious two-bit asshole—face-to-face, single-handed, no backup necessary—then Bob Dawson was definitely your man.

If you could find him.

Which wasn't an easy thing to do, as four tired, confused, discouraged, and thoroughly pissed-off Internal Affairs investigators from the DEA would have been more than happy to testify.

Of course, they hadn't thought to look for him in a cave on a privately owned 320-acre parcel of forested land located at the far end of a rarely used logging road that had been turned over to the county when the timber industry went belly up several years ago. Which was just as well because there were hundreds of such parcels in Jasper County.

Nor had it ever occurred to them that a retired DEA agent/pilot—and especially one who had supposedly just barely survived a brutal helicopter crash—might spend the next six months handcrafting then concealing a log cabin over the top of that cave without ever bothering to mention the fact to the Jasper County Planning Department.

All of which provided ample demonstration that the DEA simply didn't know their man.

In spite of his ready smile and outwardly gregarious nature, Dawson was very much a loner, a man who valued almost nothing—other than his dog and his memories of three childhood friends—more than his treasured solitude and privacy. The seemingly endless succession of pretty and adventuresome young women who briefly crossed his path found that out quickly, too. A few days, or a week or two at the most, was all it ever took for even the most dense or inattentive of them to discover the underlying reality. In spite of all outward appearances, this ruggedly handsome, muscular, humorous, artistic, and enticingly dangerous man was a person very much out of place and out of step with the surrounding world.

Born in the wrong state, and in the wrong century. That's what everybody had told him from as far back as he could remember. Should have popped out of his mama's womb in the middle of the Texas Panhandle or the Missouri Breaks, rather than the mountains of southern Oregon. Back in the time and place where the concept of one riot, one marshal, a damsel in distress, and not even a prayer of a backup, really meant something.

Which is one hell of an ironic twist, when you stop to think about it.

From his crouched position in the far corner of his cabin, Dawson stared numbly at the torn and bloody carcass of his dog. The malamute's lifeless eyes stared back, questioning and accusing. How did we end up in this situation? Your fault or mine?

Ironic as hell, because there isn't a distressed damsel within twenty miles of this place, or at least none that I know of, and I could sure use some backup right about now.

He felt a drop of sweat—or maybe it was blood, he couldn't tell which, and really didn't care—start to slide down his cheek, and he instinctively readjusted his hands around the polished walnut grip of the ancient but fully functional revolver. Couldn't risk a slip now because his first shot had to be dead on the money. Might not be time for a second shot because whoever or whatever it was, and wherever it had gone, it was too damned fast.

Might even be faster than the damned bullet for all I know.

Dawson blinked in confusion at the thought. Then a chill ran down his spine as he turned his attention for a brief moment to the weapon he was holding in an instinctive, straight-armed, two-handed combat grip.

But he really didn't have to look. Now that his attention was focused, he knew it by feel. His treasured model 1873 Single Action Army Colt "Peacemaker." The very same make and model of revolver that Colonel George Armstrong Custer's men carried at the Little Bighorn. And loaded with ancient, balloon-head, copper-cased ammunition dating back to Custer's disastrous fight with Sitting Bull's Sioux and Low Dog's Oglala warriors: a .45-caliber, 250-grain soft-nosed lead bullet sitting in front of forty grains of FFg black powder.

Translation: a big, slow, and undependable bullet.

Shit, I should have gone for the Smith. What the hell's the matter with me?

But then he glanced across the basement, in the direction of his open bedroom, where his modern Smith & Wesson .44 Magnum revolver lay beneath his pillow, and remembered. The far more lethal weapon—with its deafening concussion, and incredibly fast and reliable hollow-point rounds—had been a good two or three seconds away from where he'd tumbled to the floor.

No, that's right, I wouldn't have made it. Good decision, he told himself as he readjusted his grip again. He was vaguely aware that his arms and wrists were starting to get tired, but he had no idea why.

Thinking about his other weapon options caused Dawson to realize that his right shoulder was pressing against the heavy octagonal barrel of his Sharps rifle—a weapon made famous by the fictional Matthew Quigley—and the shorter rounded barrel of his Sharps Military Carbine. Both weapons were chambered for the middle-finger-sized .45-70 cartridge—which meant a substantially bigger, faster, and harder-hitting projectile—and thus a serious temptation, given the unknown nature of his now-barricaded intruder. It would be easy to twist around and grab one of the unloaded rifles. But the Sharps were single-shot weapons, and slow loaders to boot. And the dozen black powder cartridges he'd carefully hand-loaded for each weapon the old-fashioned way were secured in wrapped-up canvas cartridge belts hung over the trigger guards, so he quickly pushed that option out of his mind.

Colt single action's a fine gun, long as I don't have to reload. Gotta forget about that goddamned fool Custer and stay with my instincts. Only way I'm going to get out of this room alive.

He understood now, much too late, what his subconscious mind had been complaining about all along: that he and the dog would have had a much better chance if he'd actually possessed some sense of what sphincter-loosening fear was all about. Given that insight, he might have looked up immediately from his nearly completed portrait when the dog uttered his first warning growl that, in retrospect and from the protective subconscious point of view, had sounded inexplicably wrong from the very start.

Instead, he'd waited until the instant after the dog suddenly gave out a frightened, high-pitched yelp, then looked up just in time to see his fiercely loyal canine companion being flung backward in an explosion of blood. An explosion that had splattered bright red streaks across his hands and face, and the Baroque-style painting he'd been working on, with his characteristic single-minded intensity, for the past two weeks.

He blinked in sudden awareness.

The painting.

Something about his latest artistic project had been tugging persistently at the recesses of his mind for some time now. Ever since that terrifying moment when he'd lunged for the nearest loaded handgun hanging on his wall and thrown himself backward into the nearest corner of his cabin basement, every survival instinct he possessed on full adrenaline alert.

That had been what, almost five o'clock?

He allowed his eyes to glance quickly over at the face of the ancient grandfather clock, and blinked in shock.

Two hours ago?

Christ, he thought as he readjusted his grip again, *no wonder I'm getting shaky.*

He had gone back to work on the painting a little after four in the afternoon, intending to put in a couple more hours on the critical shading, and then fix a light dinner before driving his four-wheel-drive truck down the mostly dirt and gravel access road into town. Plenty of time to link up with Colin Cellars—a long-lost childhood and college buddy whom he would be seeing in person for the first time in almost fifteen years, thanks to the persistent efforts of Jody and Malcolm—and explain exactly what kind of amusement he'd set up for the both of them with Jasper County's most infamous collection of resident fruitcakes on this particular cold and gloomy Friday evening.

Dawson had smiled in anticipation, anxious to get Cellars's opinion of his latest find—both of them, actually—although he figured he already knew what his forensic scientist buddy would think of his incredible new lady.

You never change, Dawson. That's what he'll say. The exact same thing Jody said before she walked out too, Dawson remembered with a pang of guilt. *And he'll be right. Shit.*

But reasonably certain that scientific curiosity, if not the shredded remains of their youthful friendship, would keep Colin Cellars from walking out on the scheduled lecture—or the subsequent examination of his newly found evidence—Dawson had set to work.

For over an hour, the only perceptible sounds inside the remote mountain cabin had been the sighs of the sleeping malamute and the faint whisper of fine-pointed brushes against previously dried layers of carefully blended pigments as Dawson concentrated on his work, determined to get the details exactly right.

He was good at that sort of thing: focusing every bit of his energy and attention on the intricate details of whatever matter was at hand with a degree of patience that, at times, seemed almost inhuman. He always had been, as far back as he could remember. Evidence of that God-given talent covered the walls of his log cabin basement.

The faded newspaper photos of his high school and college athletic triumphs.

The glossy image of the mangled Apache Attack Helicopter that he'd somehow kept in the air and gotten back to base in spite of the nearly severed control cables, the rapidly faltering hydraulics, the furiously whining and smoking engine, and the mostly shredded airframe.

The twelve-string guitar.

The numerous intricate pen-and-ink sketches of Western heroes, villains, horses, and lethal weaponry.

The dozens of combat handgun-shooting trophies.

And the guns themselves, hung from every available peg hook on the rough-hewn log walls of Dawson's cabin:

The single action revolvers, all dating from the mid-to-late eighteen hundreds. Each resting in its own authentic leather holster rig—many of the belts glistening with neatly aligned rows of polished .44- and .45-caliber brass cartridges in tight-fitting leather loops—which Dawson had lovingly hand-tooled and stitched himself, and which glistened from a thin protective film of gun oil. And each fully capable of delivering a lead slug on target at twenty-five yards with deadly accuracy; a slug that could tear a man's heart out of his chest or simply kill him from the hydrostatic shock of an impact almost anywhere on his body.

The modern tools of his profession that he kept near his bed: a shoulder-holstered Smith & Wesson .44 Magnum revolver, a 9mm Glock semiautomatic pistol, and a blue-finished Remington 870 police model pump shotgun with extended magazine.

And the pair of nineteenth-century Sharps rifles—the long-barreled Buffalo gun, and the shorter-barreled Military Carbine—which could reach out on long parabolic arcs and kill with even more fearsome impact in the steady hands of an accomplished expert rifleman like Dawson.

They were, by any reasonable definition, a collection of historical authenticity, discordant beauty, and unquestioned lethality. And they were Bob Dawson's pride and joy.

But what the hell good are they in a situation like this? The familiar voice whispered from some back recess of Dawson's subconscious.

He ignored the unbidden thought—the unimaginable thought, actually—as he continued to sweep his eyes across the darkened, shadowy void of his catacombed basement workroom, focusing every bit of his mental energy in a determined effort to spot the shadow before it moved again.

Should have paid more attention to the dog. Listened to what he was trying to tell me.

But how the hell was I supposed to know he was going to be afraid of a goddamned shadow? Dog's never been afraid of anything in his whole life.

The images and sounds flashed into Dawson's mind. Unable to help himself, he allowed his mind to replay the chilling memory of how—for the briefest of moments—the malamute's fearsome growl had dissolved into a terrified whimper . . . and how it had tried to turn away before . . .

Before what?

Before the impossible happened?

Before a shadow killed him?

At that moment, it occurred to Bob Dawson that he knew what the intruder was, and what it wanted . . . and he almost laughed out loud, because that didn't make the least bit of sense either.

Unless . . .

He shook that thought off, fiercely intent on maintaining his focus, no matter how long it took, and determined not to give in to the demons flickering about at the outer limits of his imagination.

And besides, he reminded himself, whoever or whatever had entered his cabin and viciously butchered his dog—and was now stalking him for whatever reason—was definitely a "he" or a "she," not an "it." Had to be because . . .

A discordant image flashed through his mind and almost caused him to void his bladder.

Get a grip on yourself, Dawson. Shadows don't . . .

At that instant, the distinctively dark shadow rippled across the far wall, almost faster than the human eye could see. The movement jarred a framed pen-and-ink drawing out of alignment and caused one of the pistol-weighted holsters hanging from a small wall peg to start swinging as the shadow disappeared into the surrounding darkness.

Along with a forty-four-ounce, 1860's era, Remington New Model cap and ball Army revolver, apparently, because the swinging holster was now empty.

Bob Dawson blinked in stunned disbelief for the second time in as many minutes.

Another droplet, definitely sweat this time, slid down the right side of his cheek as he braced his muscular shoulders against the thick, solid, and supporting corner logs. He held the heavy, familiar, and now only vaguely reassuring Colt Single Action Army revolver out in a point shoulder position, hammer thumbed back to the full-cock position, and index finger pressed tight against the trigger, as his combat-trained eyes stared over the slightly trembling but still aligned sights, searching intently—even desperately—for the target.

A target.

Anything.

But the only movement in the semidarkened room was that of the still-swinging leather holster.

Steady, Dawson muttered silently to himself. *It doesn't matter what you think you saw. Doesn't matter who or what it is, or what it's doing here. Unless it's got titanium plates for eyelids, it's going to die. Just lead and squeeze. Lead and squeeze.*

It jarred him to realize that he was still using the less focused pronoun "it" rather than the more definitive—and reasonable—"he" or "she."

Like I'm supposed to be afraid of a freaky shadow, he complained to his inner voice.

Okay, fine, but even freaky shadows aren't supposed to do things like that, his inner voice responded.

Matter of fact, they *couldn't* do things like that.

But this one had.

I'll be damned. He blinked in startled realization as, out of the corner of his eye, he became aware that the pendulum-like swings of the empty holster had dampened down to a motion that was barely perceptible.

I really am afraid.

It occurred to Dawson, in a flash of incongruous amusement, that he really ought to make an effort to get hold of Colin Cellars—who, he suddenly remembered, was probably down at the auditorium right now, waiting for him to arrive—before it was too late. Let his ever-skeptical, puzzle-solving friend in on the real surprise of the evening: how incredibly easy it was to be afraid of something that wasn't even there.

Colin had to be told, Dawson decided. Definitely had to be told, because Colin Cellars was the only person he knew who might be able to make any sense out of something like this.

And more to the point, the only person in the world he trusted enough to try to explain something like this.

The question was, did Colin still trust him?

No, probably not, Dawson thought ruefully. *And it's my own damned fault.*

Another discordant image flashed through his mind. Four teenage faces flushed from exertion and joy in having worked together, piton by piton, handhold by handhold, to defeat the much-feared Windshear route up Gravestone Peak. Byzor, Catlin, Cellars, and Dawson. The intrepid four, arm in arm at the summit, staring into the camera, teamed up in junior high school by the happenstance of alphabetical order, and virtually inseparable for the next ten years of their lives . . . until an ultimately irresistible Mother Nature tossed in her fateful monkey wrench.

Wish all three of you were here, right now, Colin old buddy. I really could use—

But then it was too late.

The shadow moved again, gun barrel and all, and the god-awful loud and blinding fireballs that seemed to erupt in all directions from Bob Dawson's ancient revolvers mercifully obliterated any sense of sight and sound.

CHAPTER TWO

"OMARR-NINE TO JASPER-TWO-BRAVO-ONE."

The single bell-like tone from his radio console that preceded the dispatcher's voice, signifying the beginning of an emergency or high-priority call, caught Detective-Sergeant Colin Cellars's attention just as he turned his unmarked Ford Explorer into the darkened and almost empty parking lot.

So he didn't see the quick, shadowy movement in the tall evergreens that lined the narrow pathway between the parking lot and the Jasper County Civic Auditorium.

Instead, Cellars quickly glanced over at the small video screen on his center-mounted communications console. The screen was blank, except for the date and the time—1856 hours—in the upper left-hand corner. So he breathed a sigh of relief as he brought the state police vehicle to a stop in the parking space closest to the curved concrete pathway.

As a regionally assigned and thereby free-roving senior crime scene investigator for the Oregon State Patrol, Cellars was technically on call for any emergency law enforcement situation in OSP Region 9 at any time of the day or night that his communications console was broadcasting its locator signal. But even so, Cellars wasn't especially concerned.

First of all, no dispatcher in their right mind was going to send a plain-clothed investigator in an unmarked vehicle into a shooting scene as the first responding officer. Not unless there were absolutely no other options. Among other reasons, it was an excellent way to get some innocent or unknowing member of the public scared or killed.

Secondly, as of two hours ago, he was officially off-duty. And official policy was very clear on the fact that off-duty officers were to be placed at the bottom of the computerized OMARR-9 list of available backup units.

But most importantly, Jasper-Two-Bravo-One was the call sign for a two-deputy patrol team. Bravo units were a rare luxury in a county where it wasn't at all unusual to have only three or four cruisers—mostly one-deputy "Charlie" units with maybe a single supervisory "Alpha" unit to oversee things—patrolling a thousand square miles of Jasper County territory during the second swing shift, which ran from three in the afternoon until midnight. As such, the Bravo units were usually held in reserve to respond to the most serious calls.

Cellars knew that Jasper County deputies were, for the most part, highly regarded by the dozen or so federal, state, and local law enforcement agencies that comprised Oregon Mutual Assistance Response Region 9 for their training, motivation, and professionalism. As such, a pair of these well-trained deputies would certainly be able to handle a routine "shots fired/unknown circumstances" call on their own without further backup.

And besides, seven o'clock on a Friday evening, even if it turns out that they do need a backup, there ought to be plenty of other uniformed state, county, and city officers out on the roads, Cellars reminded himself as he palmed the Explorer's gearshift into park and set the emergency brake. *No need to worry about . . .*

"OMARR-Nine to Jasper-Two-Bravo-One?"

There was a prolonged period of silence that was finally broken by the impatient dispatcher.

"OMARR-Nine to Jasper-Two-Bravo-One or any available OMARR-Nine units in the area of Route Twelve and Highway Two-Forty-Three?"

Cellars paused in his reach for the ignition key and turned to stare at his console-mounted speaker as he quickly traced the intersection of Route 12 and Highway 243 in his head. OMARR-9 was still unfamiliar territory for Cellars, but he'd lived in Oregon long enough to be reasonably familiar with most of the major roads. If he had his geography right, the intersection of Route 12 and Highway 243 was approximately fifteen miles from his present location. In this weather, a good twenty-to-thirty minutes away, even if he slapped the magnetic flasher onto his roof for a lights-and-siren code response, but still close enough if . . .

More silence.

Oh-oh.

Colin Cellars was starting to reach for his console mike when a deep voice erupted from the speaker.

"Jasper-Two-Bravo-One."

"OMARR-Nine to Jasper-Two-Bravo-One, I'm showing you clear for a priority-two, shots-fired call. Is that a Roger?"

"Fourteen-Bravo, that's affirmative. Be advised we just cleared Willow Creek Gorge. Turning east on Route Twelve now."

Colin nodded in understanding. Willow Creek Gorge was one of OMARR-9's infamous radio dead zones. The surrounding high mountains and stands of huge old-growth trees frequently combined to block out all UHF and VHF radio transmissions between patrol units and central dispatch. When that happened, and it wasn't always predictable, the new OMARR-9 communications and tracking gear instantly became so much computerized junk.

It was a bad situation, and everyone in Oregon law enforcement knew about it. But nothing was going to change until the state of Oregon came up with the funds to upgrade the OMARR system to satellite tracking. And everyone knew that the Oregon legislature wasn't about to do that if it meant raising taxes again. So law enforcement officers in OMARR-9 simply reminded themselves that an emergency response to a backup request from a dead zone might be a long time in coming—if at all—and marked their area maps accordingly.

The dispatcher keyed her mike, obviously aware that she was about to send Jasper-Two-Bravo-One right back into another dead zone—High Gorge—that was nearly identical in terms of poor radio contact to Willow Creek.

"Unit Jasper-Two-Bravo-One," the dispatcher replied quickly, "we have a multiple-shots-fired situation at a private residence located at the far north end of County Road Twenty-Two-Fifty-Five. Residence is described as a log cabin with an exposed basement facing south and a wood deck facing north. Resident has been seen driving a dark blue, late-model Ford pickup. Reporting party is apparently a neighbor. No further details at this time."

"What about an address?"

"We have nothing at that location in our computer files. Property is listed as an undeveloped three-hundred-twenty-acre parcel. We're checking on it now."

"Is the r-p still on the line?"

"Negative. We're trying to reconnect now. Call is number three-five-five on your locator map. Be advised, we are showing unreliable radio contact in this area."

"Fourteen-Bravo copy, we show three-five-five on our screen. Also copy limited radio contact in High Gorge. We'll check in on a land line. ETA about thirty."

"OMARR-Nine to Jasper-Two-Bravo-One, confirming ETA at about nineteen-thirty hours. OMARR-Nine out."

Smiling to himself, Detective-Sergeant Colin Cellars shut off the Explorer's engine, stepped outside into the chilling rain and fog, locked the doors, and began walking through the darkened parking lot toward the distant auditorium.

CHAPTER THREE

"SEE ANYTHING?" JASPER COUNTY DEPUTY SHERIFF MIKE LAM-breau, the driver and senior member of scout car Fourteen-Bravo, whispered to his rookie partner.

"Nothing."

"Shit."

Lambreau's curse was barely audible. They were parked off the gravel road, lights out, a good quarter mile in from the locked gate and about fifty yards back from the cabin. Plenty of distance, but the two deputies had their side windows open for better visibility, so they had to be careful. Voices had an unfortunate tendency to carry extremely long distances in this cold, crisp, and misty mountain air.

"You sure this is the right place?"

A typical rookie question, but Lambreau didn't mind. He'd been a lot like Joe Beale back when he was twenty-two years old and a brand-new deputy fresh from the Academy. He could even remember how feverishly he'd worked on his off-duty hours to polish the squeaks out of his new Sam Browne leather gear so that he, too, wouldn't look and sound like a rookie to every other law enforcement officer in the state of Oregon.

Typical new-guy stuff. No big deal.

From Lambreau's perspective, Joe Beale was just another young, strong, aggressive, quick-tempered, and moderately intelligent trainee who might possibly turn out to be a half-decent deputy someday. Might, that is, if he didn't keep getting himself into trouble with his tendency to be a little slow on the uptake and a little too belligerent on some of his citizen contacts. Notations to that effect appeared with alarming frequency throughout Beale's early training records. But Lambreau had assured the young deputy that he had nothing to worry about as long as he didn't let these typical rookie mistakes become lifelong habits.

It was, however, a matter of some misfortune—and consequence— that Lambreau chose to issue these reassurances to Beale at a local bar shortly after their first shift together as a training team.

Five drinks later, trainee deputy Joe Beale had staggered out of that bar absolutely convinced that he had nothing to worry about in terms of his future with the Jasper County Sheriff's Department. His career had been placed in the hands of training officer Mike Lambreau. And for the next eighteen weeks, it would be Lambreau's job to make sure that Beale paid more attention to his surroundings and less to the assorted character flaws of the local citizenry. Even better, training officer Lambreau had never once failed to get a trainee through probation. So in a mere four and a half months, Joe Beale would finish his probationary period and become a full-fledged deputy sheriff of Jasper County, Oregon, just like he'd always dreamed.

End of story.

"End of County Road Twenty-Two-Fifty-Five, single-story log cabin with an exposed basement, wood deck facing to the southwest." Lambreau shrugged. "Gotta be it."

"But . . ."

"Keep looking," Lambreau ordered quietly.

Beale acknowledged the order by clamping his mouth firmly shut and continuing to search the misty darkness with the handheld night-vision scope. Joe Beale might have been young, and aggressive, and occasionally slow on the uptake, but he knew better than to get into an argument with the second training officer assigned to him within a period of four weeks. The captain had explained that issue to him in a manner that left no room for misunderstanding.

For almost three minutes, the two deputies sat in total silence as Beale cautiously leaned out the right passenger-side window of the scout car to get a better view of the area surrounding the cabin.

"There's supposed to be a dark blue, late-model Ford pickup out here somewhere. Can you see it?" Lambreau finally whispered.

"No vehicles anywhere, far as I can see. Maybe it's parked around back, behind the cabin."

"Be quite a trick."

It might have been possible to work a pickup through the darkened mass of cedars, redwoods, and Douglas firs that surrounded the small isolated cabin, Lambreau decided, but he wouldn't be willing to bet a beer on it.

But even if it's possible, the senior deputy thought, *why go to all that trouble when it's just as easy—and a whole lot quicker—to park off the road and walk in?*

Just like we're doing.

Jarred by the sudden realization that he and his rookie partner might be in a much more exposed position than he'd originally thought, Lambreau quickly swiveled his head around to his left and rear quadrants, searching for any sign of movement in the surrounding darkness.

As he did so, Joe Beale set the night scope aside for a brief moment to blink and clear his tired eyes.

"I guess you're right; it's gotta be the place," the young rookie said hesitantly as he brought the scope back up to his right eye.

"But it sure would be nice to see a mailbox or an address before we go busting in there. Last thing I need right now is another pissed-off citizen in the wrong house filing a lien against my pension."

In spite of his growing concern about their situation, Lambreau was literally dumbfounded by Beale's comment, and the incredible idea that a trainee deputy would be worrying about his pension after only four weeks on the job. So much so that the senior deputy actually turned away from his surveillance for a brief moment to stare at Beale in disbelief.

Pension my ass. You ought to be grateful you're still wearing that badge, Lambreau thought as he shook his head in silent amazement.

Christ, no wonder Al Gardner's riding a desk for the next six months. You probably drove him right out of his skull.

Lambreau felt a sudden urge to take his young charge aside and explain to him exactly what he thought of a rookie who was too damned lazy to double-check the address on a felony warrant search before kicking in a door. Not to mention the fact that in doing so, he managed to land himself *and* his training officer in serious trouble.

It was a tempting idea, but Lambreau also knew that this was definitely the wrong place and the wrong time for such a heart-to-heart talk. His survival instincts were screaming for attention, and he could already feel his heart starting to pound beneath his Kevlar vest. Two clear signs, from his experience, that things were about to turn to shit real fast.

So instead, he muttered: "Right about now, I'd settle for a porch light," before quickly turning his attention back to the surrounding forest.

Something about this call definitely wasn't right. That much Lambreau was sure of. He'd been feeling that way ever since he and Beale had cut through the gate lock with their bolt cutters—standard issue for sheriff's deputies in rural counties of Oregon—driven in, and pulled off the road.

Almost fifteen minutes ago, he noted as he checked his watch. *So *what the hell's going on around here? And more to the point, where did that r-p go?*

Moments later, as if reading Lambreau's mind, Joe Beale suddenly whispered urgently: "Hey, Mike, what about the woman who called in—the reporting party? Wasn't she supposed to meet us at the gate?"

"Yeah, she was," Lambreau acknowledged, grateful to see that his young trainee was finally starting to pay some attention to their situation. "But a better question might be: 'Where does she live?' Closest thing I've seen to a neighboring house around here was that shack a couple miles back."

"Maybe she's one of those really curious-type neighbors."

"Have to be curious as hell to climb over all that barbed wire, assuming she doesn't have a gate key, then hike in another quarter mile, just to see who's capping off rounds in the middle of a forest—at what, seven o'clock at night?" Lambreau tapped his fingers uneasily against the steering wheel. "Tell you what, I don't like this situation one little bit."

"Think we could be walking into something?" Beale asked.

Lambreau could hear the tension in his young partner's voice. *Christ,* he thought uneasily, *what am I doing out here with a kid for a partner at a shots-fired call?*

"I'd say that's a real good possibility. Keep your eyes open."

"For what?"

"I don't know. Anything unusual."

"But . . ."

"Just do what you're told and keep your eyes open," Lambreau snapped . . . then immediately regretted it. He realized, much too late, that he was reacting emotionally in a situation that absolutely required calm and clear thinking.

Especially when the kid's a goddamned airhead. Last thing in the world I need right now is . . .

At that moment, Lambreau was nearly overcome by the spine-chilling sensation of suddenly feeling trapped. He whipped his head around to his left again, and thought he saw something dark—a shadow?—flash across the gap between two nearby trees.

What the hell . . . ?

"Get out of the car!"

"What?"

Joe Beale lowered the night scope and turned to stare at his training officer, a confused expression on his face. But Lambreau was already out of the scout car with his 9mm Glock in his right hand.

"Get out of the fucking car!" Lambreau ordered in a furious whisper as he stepped clear of the car door and brought the semi-automatic pistol up to eye level. He held it in an outstretched, two-handed grip while sweeping the surrounding darkness with his eyes. As he did so, he heard Beale hit the shotgun mount release and scramble out the right side of the scout car.

The sound of a four-ought buck round being rapidly jacked into the chamber of a Remington 870 12-gauge shotgun echoed through the night air.

A thin smile made a brief appearance on Mike Lambreau's lips.

All right, kid. About time you did something smart for a change.

"What is it?" Beale called out from his barricaded position—crouched against the right front bumper of the scout car. His voice crackled with tension.

Lambreau didn't answer because as far as he could tell from his position, there wasn't anything out there.

Or at least nothing that he could see or hear.

But even so, Lambreau sensed that he was terribly exposed, standing there in the open darkness. Moving at a slow and deliberate pace, Lambreau cautiously backed around to the right rear of the scout car, all the while keeping the iridescent sights of the Glock centered on the area where the flickering shadow had disappeared. Then, when he had finally worked himself around and behind, he quickly dropped down to a kneeling position with his still-outstretched arms braced over the trunk. He was vaguely aware that his index finger had taken up the slack on the Glock's sensitive double-action trigger. Ready to fire, all sixteen rounds if necessary. All he needed was a target.

Still nothing.

Frustrated and even a little unnerved by the surrounding darkness, Lambreau started to reach down to his belt for his five-cell flashlight, and discovered—to his dismay and chagrin—that he'd left it in the door rack.

Christ, he raged silently at himself, *now I'm the one making rookie mistakes.*

"Mike, what is it? What's wrong?" Beale whispered, this time sounding even more scared than before.

"Get the scope."

"What?"

"Get the goddamned night scope!" Lambreau repeated through tightly clenched teeth. He was furious at the young deputy for his seeming inability to follow a single goddamned order without asking stupid questions. But this was not the time or the place to lose his temper. Plenty of time for that later, when they got back to the station.

If we get back to the station.

The unconscious thought jarred Mike Lambreau all the way to the soles of his polished shoes.

"Okay, got it," Beale whispered breathlessly. "Now what?"

"Search the goddamned woods!"

"For what?"

The fear-induced rage in Lambreau's mind boiled over. It was all he could do to keep from jamming the muzzle of the Glock into his partner's ear and ordering him to shut up and do as he was told. Instead, Lambreau shifted the semiautomatic pistol to his left hand, moved quickly over to the right front side of the scout car, and wrenched the night scope out of the young deputy's hand.

"But . . ."

"Be quiet," Lambreau hissed, then ignored Beale, crouched

behind the protective metal of the scout car, and brought the small scope up to his face. He pulled it in tight against his right eye to keep the greenish glow from highlighting his face, thumbed the on switch, and quickly scanned across the now-visible tree line. Searching around each and every green tree trunk for a slightly lighter green figure . . . or movement . . . or anything at all that looked like a suspect.

But the only things he could see between the massive trees were rocks and brush and broken limbs.

No furtive figures.

No movement.

Nothing.

Working on instinct now, Lambreau stood up, stepped back away from the scout car, and quickly scanned the woods to his right and back quadrants. Then, after assuring himself that his back was clear, he spent another three minutes scanning the distant cabin and the surrounding woods before giving up and placing the night scope on the hood of the scout car.

"Did you see anything?" Beale whispered hesitantly, after a few moments.

"No."

The young rookie breathed an audible sigh of relief.

"Christ," he whispered. "For a minute there, I thought I was going to crap my pants."

"Don't start celebrating yet," Lambreau warned.

"Why, what's the matter?"

"We're responding to a shots-fired call. That means we still have to check out the cabin, remember?"

"Oh yeah, that's right . . . I forgot." Joe Beale hesitated, then said: "Shit. Do we really have to?"

Lambreau actually thought about the question for a few seconds before answering. "Yes, we do. That's what we get paid for."

The young rookie looked around nervously at the surrounding darkness.

"Think maybe we should try the loudspeaker and lights first?" he asked hopefully.

"Oh, yeah, no question about that," Lambreau replied.

He was still unwilling to expose himself to the portion of the surrounding forest where he'd seen—or at least thought he'd seen—the flickering shadow. So Lambreau opened the right front door of the scout car, slid into the front passenger seat, leaned across the console to switch on the driver's side searchlight, and sent the intensely bright halide beam sweeping through the trees from left to right and back again.

Once, twice, and a third time.

Finally convinced that the flickering shadow had to have been a figment of his overactive imagination, Lambreau set the beam on the distant cabin and quickly made the same sweep on the right side of the scout car—this time over his partner's ducking head—with the passenger-side searchlight.

It was only when he had both of the nearly blinding searchlights lined up on the distant cabin that Lambreau thumbed the console select switch and pulled the mike from its clip. Then he stepped back out of the car with the Glock clenched tightly in his left hand and brought the mike up against the side of his mouth.

"HELLO THE CABIN." Lambreau's deep, gruff voice boomed out over the scout car's external speakers. "THIS IS THE JASPER COUNTY SHERIFF'S DEPARTMENT."

His words echoed hollowly through the trees.

Then dead silence.

"HELLO THE CABIN," Lambreau repeated.

Nothing.

"Well, shit," he muttered as he reached back into the scout car and flipped the mike switch back to the radio setting. "Fourteen-Bravo."

"Lots of luck."

Lambreau ignored his young partner's sarcastic comment as he tried two more times to reach the dispatcher. But all he got for his efforts was intermittent static.

Wonderful, Lambreau thought sullenly. *Score one more point for the High Gorge dead zone.*

Still muttering to himself, Lambreau reached back into the scout car one more time to secure the mike back in its console mount.

That was when he heard his rookie partner's terrified scream.

CHAPTER FOUR

COLIN CELLARS GLANCED DOWN AT HIS WATCH ONE MORE TIME, then sighed.

Nineteen-forty-nine hours on a typically wet, windy, and bone-chilling evening in Jasper County, Oregon, and still no sign of Dawson or his blue Ford pickup.

Come on, Bobby, it's getting cold *out here.*

The wind shifted, and another blast of icy, rain-saturated air cut through Cellars's light down jacket and jeans, adding to the chill coming directly through the thin soles of his running shoes. He stamped his feet and shivered as a half dozen more cars turned into the dimly lit parking lot, then quickly sped toward the few remaining empty parking spaces near the walkway. Moments later, headlights switched off and car doors slammed in rapid succession as the late-arriving occupants exited their vehicles and ran for the shelter of the Jasper County Civic Auditorium.

Cellars watched closely as the late arrivers filed into the doorway under the single dirt-and-spiderweb-smeared light fixture, checking each briefly illuminated face in the hope that Bobby Dawson was among them.

But he wasn't.

Cellars closed his eyes in frustration and sighed once again as he considered his rapidly dwindling options.

One of which was to give in to the ever-present urge to pull out his cell phone and call Jody.

So what else is new? he thought morosely, feeling the familiar ache in his heart as he kept his hands firmly entrenched in his jacket pockets.

He'd been standing on the porch near the front entrance to the rustic log structure that housed what was otherwise a small, modern, and mostly underground glass-and-concrete auditorium since 1900 hours, only partially sheltered from the chilling wind and rain. Standing and waiting with growing impatience for Dawson to show up and explain exactly why it was so important that their first meeting in almost fifteen years take place at some remote town-hall evening lecture.

Forty-nine minutes . . . during which time forty-two cars and, if his count was right, sixty-six people of widely varying age, gender, and dress had arrived. Interestingly enough, at least four of these individuals bore the distinctive dress, bearing, and demeanor of covert law enforcement officers. Cellars remembered how the four men had arrived almost simultaneously in the two dark, unmarked sedans. And how the four had immediately moved apart from each other in the dark, foggy parking lot, then smoothly shuffled themselves in among the seemingly anxious and distracted attendees.

No guarantees, but Cellars would have been more than willing to bet a paycheck or two that they were feds.

It occurred to him that the DEA Internal Affairs investigators—the ones who had contacted him in Portland on three occasions with progressively less-subtle threats about the penalties for harboring a federal fugitive without ever actually confirming that Dawson really *was* a federal fugitive—might still be looking for their rogue agent and his still-missing helicopter.

But if that was the case, why was Dawson, a consummate game-player and survivalist to the core, making it so easy for them?

Not like you, Bobby. Not like you at all.

But it made for some interesting scenarios. Teams of DEA special agents combing the Marblehead Wilderness portion of the huge Klamath National Forest for the site of a helicopter crash that no one could prove had actually happened. And Internal Affairs head-hunters trying desperately to maintain a tight surveillance on one of the most elusive and eccentric individuals who had ever joined their agency.

Cellars was still smiling at the absurdity of it all when a suddenly not-so-ridiculous idea occurred to him:

Unless that's why you're late . . . or a no-show.

Because you found out they were going to be here.

Cellars was trying to imagine an even more absurd scene—four federal agents leaping up out of their auditorium seats to arrest a member of the audience for concealing the crash-and-burn site of a three-ton DEA helicopter, and making off with the evidence—when an oddly flickering shadow suddenly caught his attention.

No, make that sixty-seven, he thought, startled by the sudden appearance of the lone figure on the fog-shrouded walkway.

He hadn't seen her coming from the parking lot. One moment, the dark shadowy area between the dimly lit entrance to the rustic auditorium complex and the asphalt parking lot had been completely empty. The next moment, she was stepping up onto the porch—a dark-cloaked apparition who had appeared out of the misty darkness. Her face was visible under the loose hood of her cloak for only a brief moment before she disappeared through the log-framed doorway.

For some completely inexplicable reason, a chill ran up Cellars's spine.

It occurred to Cellars, in those next few disconcerting moments, that he had no idea how he knew the cloaked and hooded figure was feminine. He just did. But for some strange reason, he couldn't decide if that realization was enticing . . . or frightening.

Okay, he thought, *fair enough. Sixty-two members of the general Oregon citizenry, four narcs, and one apparition.*

But no matter how he counted them, still no Dawson.

Cellars had already checked inside of the auditorium (cautiously, so as to avoid any contact with the increasingly animated crowd standing outside the inner doors) twice in the last half hour, with no success. And the three phone calls to what Jody had assured him was the unlisted phone number to Dawson's remote mountain cabin only succeeded in reactivating a brief mechanical-voiced offer to leave a message that might or might not be answered right away, depending.

On what? A frustrated Cellars had wanted to yell into the phone after he hung up for the third time. But he didn't because he was terribly afraid that he might already know the answer.

A numbing crux that had hovered between the three of them, like a ghostly apparition that couldn't be grasped or fought or confronted, for the past twenty-or-so years.

She's with you right now, isn't she?

It was an absurd notion, and he immediately thrust it out of his mind before the familiar numbing images could begin to take shape again, knowing full well that neither of them had ever been like that.

Thoughtless and self-serving, perhaps. But never devious or malicious. Not intentionally, anyway.

It's funny, he thought with a sense of sadness that was still numbing after all these years. *I'd still trust either one of them with my life . . . but not necessarily with my soul.*

Which, in turn, begged the obvious follow-up question:

If that's the case, then what the hell am I doing here?

But he hadn't been able to come up with a reasonable answer to that one either, he reminded himself. Then or now.

He glanced down at his watch again and noted that it was now two minutes past eight, which meant he had a decision to make. He could go inside and find out exactly what this supposedly fascinating lecture was all about, and risk being trapped in some mind-numbing treatise on the evolution of Northwestern leaf molds. Or he could get back in his car, drive back to his remote, isolated, and newly rented hillside home, open the intriguing package—the one he'd picked up from the post office a few hours ago—to see what his electronic genius buddy, Malcolm Byzor, had come up with this time. And then—after he'd satisfied his curiosity, made something for dinner, and cleaned up the dishes—he could settle himself into his comfortable reading chair, pick up a book, and wait to see if he really was going to get a crime scene call-out on his first night working the coastal southwest region of the state. All the while ignoring the fact that he'd promised Jody he'd call.

Or he could forget about trying to keep himself occupied and simply drive out to Dawson's supposedly even more remote and isolated mountain cabin, to see if his long-lost buddy really was ignoring his phone . . . and why.

Assuming that I could actually find this supposedly handmade cabin in the dark, which—knowing Dawson—is almost certainly located on some narrow, winding, muddy, and nearly impassible mountain road with few, if any, helpful road signs to guide the way, Cellars reminded himself.

Or he could pull out his cell phone and—

The pager on his belt began to vibrate, and Cellars immediately reached under his jacket, thinking, *It's about time, Bobby.* A reasonable assumption on his part because the only person he'd given the pager and pin number to, other than the dispatcher and his new regional supervisor—a gruff and impatient captain named Hawkins, who had been unyielding on the Region 9 master vehicle key issue *and* the pager—was Dawson.

But it wasn't.

Not unless he'd relocated to the northern Virginia 703 area code.

Shaking his head in frustration, Cellars reclipped the pager to his belt, retrieved a small folding cell phone out of his jacket pocket, and dialed the familiar sequence of numbers.

"Hello?"

"It's me," Cellars grumbled. "Turn down the music."

There was a momentary pause.

"Okay, can you hear . . . hey, wait a minute, you're on your cell phone," the voice said accusingly.

"That's exactly right," Cellars agreed. "I'm standing out here on an exposed porch, in the middle of the night, soaking wet, freezing my ass off, and talking on a goddamned cell phone with a guy who, if he had any common sense to go along with his brains, would be chasing his wife around the bed right about now instead of staying up late and playing with his toys."

"Well, now that you mention it . . ." the voice began, but Cellars interrupted.

"And speaking of toys, how did you manage to find me?"

"I can always find you—or Bobby or Jody—if I really need to. I've told you that many many times. You just don't believe me."

"Okay, so you probably had microchips implanted in our heads while we were asleep. That still doesn't explain how you managed to track down my new pager and pin numbers this fast. I just got issued the damned thing this morning."

"If you'd leave your cell phone switched on, like any normal civilized person, then your friends just might not have to go to super-human lengths to track you down," Malcolm Byzor retorted. He didn't seem especially fazed by the suggestion that he might have done some illicit database snooping with his National Security Agency–owned electronic gadgetry. "What the hell do they put in the water out there in Oregon? You're getting worse than Bobby."

"Actually, I think I'm beginning to understand his point of view. People really ought to be able to go about their business on their off-duty hours without having a goddamned telephone grafted to their hip. All things considered, you ought to be amazed, not to mention extremely grateful, that I left my pager switched on."

Malcolm Byzor sighed loudly. "You know, Colin, it never ceases to amaze me how incredibly nontechnical you are for a fellow who claims to be an honest-to-God forensic scientist."

"Malcolm, as far as you and your chip-jockey spook pals are concerned, anybody who lacks a master's degree in electrical engineering is nontechnical by definition. And besides, I'm not a forensic scientist anymore. As of this morning, I'm now, officially, just a plain old Oregon State Patrol crime scene investigator. Remember?"

"Yeah, right. Detective-Sergeant Colin Cellars. Have CSI kit, will travel." Byzor snorted derisively. "Listen, buddy-boy, you may think you're a real cop, and they may think you're a real cop, but don't forget, Jody, Bobby, and I all know better. So, did you get it?"

"Get what? Oh, you mean the package?"

"You didn't open it?" The sense of stricken disbelief was audible in the engineer's voice.

"Hey, give me a break. I barely had time to change clothes and drive out here for Bobby's fun and games. It's in the back of my vehicle. I'll open it when I get home."

"Oh, yeah, that's right. Tonight's the night. Dawson and Cellars, the dynamic duo, reunited at last." There was a pause as Malcolm Byzor's steel-trap mind reprocessed the data. "So what's the deal on this lecture, or whatever it is you two are supposed to be attending? Jody claims that Bobby wouldn't tell her anything about it."

"I have no idea. He just said it was really important that I be here. 'Absolutely critical to the fate of the free world' I believe were the exact words he used. And since I haven't seen him for—what has it been?—a good fifteen years now, I figured I could take a chance and humor the guy."

"Bad mistake," Byzor commented. "You know Bobby. Same old same old."

"Yeah, tell me about it."

"So, what's our favorite crazed hermit looking like these days? Lumberjack muscles, rolled-up flannel shirts, and hair down to his waist?"

"Beats me. I haven't seen him yet."

"Why not? Jody said you were supposed to meet him there at eight."

"Yeah, that's what I thought too." There was another odd, shadowy movement off to his right that caused Cellars to pause and quickly scan the parking lot and the surrounding forest. But there was nothing to see. Or at least nothing that he *could* see. "If that really was the plan," he continued, suddenly feeling uneasy for reasons he couldn't quite understand, "then he's late as usual."

"Probably stood you up for some beautiful sensuous blonde."

"I don't know," Cellars said dubiously. "Seems to me he mentioned something about giving up on beautiful sensuous blondes."

"No, I'm pretty sure that was beautiful sensuous redheads. Blondes were out last year. I believe the relevant names were Rachael, Maureen, and Tanya."

"Okay, I stand corrected."

Cellars noted that his electronics engineer buddy was being kind and thoughtful enough not to mention Dawson's beautiful and sensuous brunette list. A list that would necessarily include the name of Jody Catlin.

Christ, this is like tossing raw eggs back and forth, waiting to see who's going to drop the first one. How long are we going to keep this up?

He looked up briefly as another car entered the parking lot. Minivan. Definitely not Dawson.

"You call her?"

"What?"

"I said, 'Did you call her?' " Byzor repeated patiently.

Cellars hesitated. He was tempted to ask "who?" But he knew there wasn't any point. Malcolm Byzor would just keep on pressing in his characteristic—and often infuriating—manner.

"No, not yet."

"Why not?"

"I don't know. Guess I figured I'd wait until after I saw Bobby.

You know Jody. First thing she's gonna want to know is how it all worked out, anyway."

"Either way, you don't call her tonight, she's going to be pissed," Byzor predicted.

"So what else is new?"

"No, I mean *really* pissed."

Cellars sighed. "Yeah, I know." He hesitated again, then decided it was a good time to change the topic of conversation. "So what's in that package?"

The high-tech angle. Old and familiar bait, but Byzor bit immediately.

"Hey, that's right. You remember that CSI laser scanner I've been telling you about the last couple of years?"

Cellars smiled, hearing the excitement in his friend's voice.

"You mean the one that you've supposedly been working on in your spare time for the last five-to-ten years? The one you told Yvie you were going to sell to the law enforcement community for a hundred million bucks—if you ever got it to work—which, if I remember correctly, was at least five or six years ago?"

"Well, you are now the proud owner of a genuine Malcolm Byzor Model 7 Crime Scene Scanner. Instructions are in the box. Take it out for a test run, then give me a call, tell me what you think."

"What happened to models one through six?"

"Never mind," the electronics engineer muttered darkly. "Hey, listen, I ran the batteries down in the computer when I was testing it outside, so you're going to need to recharge them with the AC adapter before you try to use the system in the portable mode. Other than that, everything's all set. Simple as one, two, three. Say hi to Bobby for me when he finally shows up. I've gotta go. Yvie's threatening to cut the phone line if I don't start paying more attention to whatever this silky, flimsy thing is she has on."

"My advice to you is to pat her down for concealed microchips, very slowly and carefully, and then get her out of that nightgown before she starts heaving those computers of yours out the window," Cellars warned. Then he laughed and quickly disconnected the call before his stunned friend could reply.

He had just started to slip the cell phone back into his jacket pocket when it rang shrilly.

Cellars glared at the offending instrument for three more rings, then shook his head in irritation and flipped it open again.

"I'm warning you, if you don't get that nightgown off, right now . . ." Cellars started in, and then hesitated when he suddenly realized that he couldn't hear any of Malcolm Byzor's inevitable rock and roll in the background.

There was a long pause, then:

"You want me out of this nightgown, Colin Cellars, you can come out here and take it off yourself. You know where to find me," the familiar husky voice said with brazen matter-of-factness.

"Ah . . ."

"Yeah, that's what I thought. All talk, no action. Mother was right, you men really are all alike," Jody Catlin commented with a discernible edge to her voice. "Except for you," she added as an afterthought. "You don't even like to talk."

CHAPTER FIVE

COLIN CELLARS STARED OUT INTO THE DARKENED PARKING LOT, willing himself to focus on the parked cars and the gathering mist that couldn't quite seem to crystallize into fog. He was trying desperately to keep the all-too-familiar images—the long dark hair curling over her shoulder, the intense blue-gray eyes that seemed to bore right into his soul, and the enticing curves of her athletic body—from forming in the back of his mind. But he knew it was a hopeless task, even without the familiar rasp of her voice, and the added mental enticement of the nightgown.

Fifteen years, and not a day had gone by when he didn't think of her. And Dawson.

What had she said? All you men are alike?

"And speaking of which," Jody Catlin said, "how are you and Bobby getting along up there? Has it gotten down to guns, knives, and trip wires yet?"

It was a gentle and lighthearted approach, but Cellars knew every nuance of her voice. The edge was still there. And it cut through him like a honed razor . . . even when it finally occurred to him that she couldn't possibly be with Bobby if she didn't know where he was, either.

"Well, pretty much the same as usual, I guess."

"Meaning?"

"One of us is here and the other isn't."

"He didn't show?"

Cellars started to answer when what appeared to be another incongruent shadow flashed at the edge of his peripheral vision.

What the hell?

He whipped his head around and stared into the impenetrable blackness, but again there was nothing to see.

For no good reason that he could actually define, Cellars was starting to feel uncomfortably exposed on the open porch. He shifted his position slightly to take better advantage of what little protection the overhanging roof might offer. At the same time, his right hand brushed reflexively against the semiautomatic pistol holstered securely under his jacket.

Loaded, locked, and a round in the chamber. Hammer down. Just sight and squeeze. Sight and squeeze, he repeated the training mantra to himself as he slowly unzipped the front of his jacket.

"No, not so far."

On edge now, for reasons he still couldn't quite comprehend, he turned his attention back to the mist-covered parking lot, noting the arrival of two more cars.

"Shit."

He could hear the deep sense of frustration in her voice. Perfectly understandable because he knew she'd been working on this reunion for over three years now, determined—in the way that she had always been determined—to bring the four of them back together again.

For whatever reason that possessed her to try, Cellars thought morosely. She still hadn't managed to convince him that it was a doable thing, much less a good idea.

But it had all happened so fast.

She had been living in San Francisco, teaching molecular biology for the Forensic Science Department at UC Berkeley, working her kilns, and writing mainstream articles on a wide range of scientific topics that apparently sold often enough to keep her cupboards stocked with clay, fruit, and tofu. Bobby had been flying helicopters for the DEA over the marijuana-rich forests of northern California. Malcolm had been doing God-knew-what for some truly secretive part of the federal government out in northern Virginia. And Cellars had been working trace and firearms evidence for the Oregon State Police Crime Lab in Portland when she'd called him—for the first time in several years—to tell him that Bobby's chopper had disappeared somewhere over the Klamath National Forest just south of the California–Oregon border. No fire, no explosion, no wreckage. Just plain disappeared.

Her second call had come a week later, and—if possible—was even more bizarre and shocking than the first.

Bobby was alive. According to the single eyewitness, he'd walked into the Crest View Ranger Station looking amazingly intact for a man who claimed to have survived a helicopter crash and a subsequent fifteen-mile hike through some of the most remote and rugged mountains in northern California without food or water. He'd flashed his credentials, asked to borrow a government phone, called the DEA regional headquarters office in San Francisco, identified himself, and announced that he was resigning his commission as a federal agent—effective immediately. He then put down the phone, thanked the resident forest ranger, walked out the door, and disappeared again.

According to one of Malcolm's federal law enforcement contacts, the DEA was still looking for Dawson, two days later, when he called to advise them that they could send his retirement papers to a specified post office box in Merlin, Oregon.

The DEA sent the paperwork as requested, along with a pair of agents to stake out the post office. Three days later, they were found, bound and gagged in their vehicle, in the parking lot of a local gas station. Dawson's retirement papers, all properly filled out, dated, and signed, were lying on the backseat.

But in spite of this blatantly insubordinate act of nose-thumbing, the name of Robert Dawson never appeared on the FBI's nationwide NCIC "wants and warrants" list. Clearly, the DEA wanted to keep their resolution of their missing helicopter and rogue agent strictly in-house.

Jody had called one more time, three weeks later, to let him know that she had accepted a job with the National Fish and Wildlife Forensics Laboratory and had moved to Ashland, Oregon. She had also suggested they really ought to get together again sometime, now that they were all living in the same state.

But she never explained who she meant by "they," and he was still too hurt and saddened to ask. So they left it at that, and Cellars made a determined and mostly successful effort not to think about what might or might not be going on down there in the mountains and forests of southern Oregon.

Until the anonymous letter with the announcement and application for a newly established position in the Oregon State Patrol showed up in his mailbox. Position available: senior crime scene investigator, detective-sergeant rating, extensive experience in CSI and evidence handling required. Assignment: work full-time on a series of unresolved kidnappings and missing persons—all with homicidal overtones—in the southern coastal region of the state. Drawbacks: no partner, no support, long hours, no overtime, and minimal opportunities for interaction with the regional supervisor. Advantages: minimal interaction with the regional supervisor and a series of interesting puzzles to solve.

In other words, they were looking for a loner who wouldn't mind working several seven-day weeks in a row, and wouldn't be distracted by the demands of friends, family, or inquisitive supervisors.

Acting completely out of impulse, Cellars filled out the application and sent it in.

Four weeks later, he found himself sitting in an interview room in Salem, Oregon, trying to explain to the selection committee why a senior forensic scientist with fifteen years of field and lab experience with the Oregon State Patrol might find the idea of working out of a Jeep—and trying to cover the entire southwestern region of the state as a one-man, free-roving, CSI response team—an interesting if not reasonable proposition.

Whatever he'd said—Cellars could no longer remember any part of the interview—must have been convincing because he signed the papers that afternoon without ever being able to escape the uneasy sense of being caught up in a karma-driven riptide. "Go with the flow, see where it takes you," Malcolm Byzor had advised. "And besides," the electronics engineer had added with his ever-frustrating sense of logic, "what else are you going to do with your life?"

The familiar voice pulled him away from his memories.

"What?"

"Have you tried to call him?" Jody Catlin repeated patiently.

"Sure. Three separate times."

"And?"

"No answer, just a mechanical recording. Can't even tell if it's really Dawson."

"Maybe he's running late or—"

"Otherwise indisposed," Cellars finished, then immediately regretted it.

There was a long silent pause that seemed to last forever. Then: "I thought we all agreed that we were going to try to be civilized about this."

"We did . . . and I am," Cellars muttered.

"Oh?"

"It's a matter of perspective."

"Go on."

"He said he'd meet me here sometime between seven and eight. I've been standing around in this freezing wind and rain for over an hour now. I'm waiting for a onetime friend whom I haven't set eyes on for fifteen years—a guy who, in his more lucid moments, has always been convinced he's some kind of composite reincarnation of Peter Pan, Wyatt Earp, and George Armstrong Custer—to show up and introduce me to a bunch of his Jasper County neighbors whom *he* describes as being a little eccentric. I'm cold, wet, tired, and hungry; my feet are freezing; and I'm absolutely convinced that even if I stay out here another hour, the chances of his ever showing up are remote at best."

"What would you say to another fifteen minutes?"

This time in a much softer voice, no edge. Bringing back memories.

"Listen, Jody . . ."

"Come on, Colin, give me a break. It's taken fifteen goddamned years just to get all of us back in the same state."

"Last time I checked, Malcolm and Yvie were still living in Virginia," Cellars reminded her gently.

"Yeah, but with those two, it's always a virtual reality anyway. Doesn't matter where they live. In fact, knowing Malcolm, he's probably video-recording this entire conversation as we speak."

"It wouldn't surprise me at all," Cellars agreed.

"But Bobby promised me he'd be there," she went on quickly. "And I know he wants to talk with you face-to-face, really bad. Finding that rock has twisted him around like you wouldn't believe. I mean, it's like he's become obsessed by the damned thing."

"Rock? What rock? What are you talking about?"

"Didn't he tell you?"

"Tell me what?"

"That's just it, I don't know. He won't tell me either. He just keeps repeating the same thing over and over again. The DEA doesn't understand. The whole thing's too big . . . and too dangerous. Better I don't know."

"What?"

"Colin, please, you need to hear this from him firsthand. I don't know what's going on, but I think Bobby's in serious trouble, and you're the only one he trusts to help."

"Me?"

"That's right, you."

"If Bobby thinks I can keep four pissed-off DEA agents from taking him into custody the moment he sticks his head up around here, then he really has lost his grip on reality," Cellars commented.

"Listen, he knows the DEA is trying to tag him, but he doesn't care. You know Bobby."

"But—"

"Listen, he promised me he'd be there to meet with you, no matter what. But if he doesn't show in fifteen minutes, *please,* call me back immediately. I'm counting on you."

The phone went dead in his ear.

Then, before he could do or say anything else, a dark shadow suddenly flashed across the floorboards at his feet.

CHAPTER SIX

"EXCUSE ME—"

Colin Cellars had already started to react to the rapidly moving shadow by turning his right shoulder and hip away from the logical source as his right hand instinctively brushed his jacket back and away from the rubberized grip of the holstered pistol—when the tenor of the woman's voice registered in his mind.

"—would you happen to be Detective-Sergeant Cellars?"

Catching himself in time to keep the semiautomatic holstered, Cellars stared wide-eyed into the familiar face of an elderly woman with curly white hair and a three-strand pearl necklace clearly visible under her thick shawl. Familiar in the sense that he immediately recognized her as one of the early arrivals. She had caught his attention right away because in the dim light, she'd looked an awful lot like Barbara Bush. He also remembered being intrigued by the visible display of enthusiasm and excitement on her finely wrinkled face as she hurried up the wooden steps to the auditorium, as if she could barely wait to see or hear whatever was on the program for this evening.

It occurred to Cellars to wonder if Northwestern leaf molds might be more interesting than he had ever imagined. But then an uneasy sense of foreshadowing caused him to hesitate and glance around the area one more time before answering.

"Uh, yes, ma'am," Cellars responded cautiously as he slowly brought his right hand out from under his jacket and turned to face the woman.

"Oh, thank goodness!" She clapped her gloved hands in delight and reached out to grasp his hands in a surprisingly firm grip. "I'm Eleanor Patterson, your host for this evening. And I can't tell you how delighted I am to see you. I told Jane and Lorrie that the man standing by himself out here must be you, but they were so sure you'd be arriving with Robert."

"Robert?" Cellars asked in confusion.

"Oh yes, that dear boy. He was so excited when he told us you agreed to be our guest speaker for this month's meeting."

"I—*what?*"

"Here now, it's hardly fair for me to be out here talking with you all by myself when everybody is so anxious to hear your presentation. And besides, we need to get you inside before you catch a chill." She ignored Cellars's questioning look as she grabbed his arm and firmly escorted him in through the door. The sudden blast of warm air caused him to wince. "He talks about you all the time, you know."

"He does?"

"Oh, yes," She smiled mysteriously. "You'd be amazed at some of the things he's told us about you."

"I would?"

"According to Robert, we understand you're quite the Sherlock Holmes of the Oregon State Patrol."

"Ah." Cellars gritted his teeth and smiled weakly.

"Here, let me help you with your—"

She grabbed the zipper edge of his jacket with one hand, started to pull it over his shoulder, then hesitated, her eyes widening in surprise as they focused on the suddenly exposed badge and holstered pistol.

"Oh my. I guess you wouldn't want to—"

"That's quite all right," Cellars said hurriedly as he quickly pulled off his jacket, removed the badge case, holstered pistol, and handcuffs from his belt, wrapped them tightly in the jacket, then smiled reassuringly. "I don't think I'm going to be needing them tonight . . . unless Robert shows up," he added under his breath.

"Oh, I certainly hope not. We've all been waiting so anxiously for you to get here," the elderly woman exclaimed as she glanced down at her wristwatch. "Oh dear, we really do need to get going. You know, everybody is just absolutely dying to hear all the fascinating things you're going to be telling us this evening," she added as she took his free right arm in a firm grasp.

"Yeah, me too," Cellars mumbled.

"I beg your pardon?" She turned, a quizzical look forming on her face.

"I was just saying that Da—, uh, Robert never did tell me what he'd decided on for a lecture title."

"What, you mean he didn't even send you one of his delightful flyers?" The elderly woman looked properly shocked as she quickly escorted him into the noisy auditorium, down the left side aisle, and over to the center podium. The decibel level in the room dropped noticeably as the still-standing members of the audience moved quickly to claim the few vacant seats in the first few rows.

"Flyers?" Cellars barely heard the question. He was staring out at the animated faces of the audience, most of whom were still engaged in whispered discussions with their neighbors, trying desperately to remember exactly what Dawson had told him about the lecture. Absolutely nothing about who would actually be *giving* the lecture, or on what. That much he was certain about.

Colin, please, you need to hear this from him firsthand. I don't know what's going on, but I think Bobby's in serious trouble, and you're the only one he trusts to help.

Jody Catlin's words, echoing in his mind.

He promised me he'd be there to meet with you, no matter what. But if he doesn't show in fifteen minutes, please, *call me back immediately. I'm counting on you."*

Cellars shook his head in frustration.

I should have called her, damn it. Bobby must have—

"Oh, that Robert." The woman interrupted his thoughts as she rolled her eyes skyward and sighed heavily. She released his arm to fumble quickly in her tote bag, then came up with a folded piece of paper. "Here, you can have this one." She thrust the paper into his hands, and Cellars, distracted by his failed promise to Jody, absent-mindedly put it into his shirt pocket. Then, without another word, she stepped up to the podium.

"Ladies and gentlemen," she began, looking out at the audience with an expression of excited anticipation in her eyes.

The auditorium went instantly silent.

"These are exciting times for us, here, in the Northwest. And indeed, for the world. Only a few years ago, those of us who were forced by circumstances to battle ignorance, indifference, and ridicule all by ourselves first came together as a group—to share our experiences and our faith—and I am truly gratified and encouraged by our progress. And," she added with a conspiratorial wink, "by our potential to accomplish so much more in the very near future."

She paused to look around the auditorium, as if challenging anyone to dispute her account of the situation.

"We gained strength, slowly and surely, through our growing numbers and our reinforced beliefs. And through the wonders of talk radio, we have learned that we are not alone. That there are many thousands like us, secure in our beliefs and our faith that we, as an intelligent and dominant species, are not alone in this great universe. But like many others here tonight, I remain convinced that it wasn't until that fateful day, almost three months ago now, when Robert first appeared among us—seeking our guidance and offering his own view of the government forces that seem so determined to control and conceal these wondrous events in the history of our planet—that we, as a group, truly began to make significant progress in our own sense of awareness and empowerment.

"In effect, we found our voice, and we will use that voice to send our message to the world!"

Her emphasis on these last words, and the resulting applause, caused Cellars to remember the folded flyer he'd put into his shirt pocket.

"And in that spirit," she continued, smiling brightly, "I can't tell you how excited I am to introduce our guest speaker this evening. As we all know by now, Detective-Sergeant Colin Cellars spent the last fifteen years working in the Oregon State Police crime laboratory up in Portland, where, I'm told, he investigated hundreds of crime scenes and collected thousands of items of evidence. But ever so fortunate for us—as residents of Jasper County as well as members of this audience," she smiled cheerfully, "I understand that he was just reassigned to the southwestern region of Oregon this very week so that he can personally investigate what our state officials are now describing as"—she paused, giving the entire audience a conspiratorial wink and knowing look—"crimes of a *special* nature."

Voices began to murmur appreciatively, and a few people clapped, as Cellars drew the folded piece of paper out of his shirt pocket and began to unfold it with a sense of impending doom. But the woman quickly went on, and the room immediately grew silent again.

"I also understand that this is Detective-Sergeant Cellars's first day at his new assignment, so I'm sure he has many other things that he really ought to be doing right now instead of meeting here with us. And I know it must be especially exciting for him, after all these years, to be reunited with Robert, his childhood friend."

The cheerful murmuring threatened to burst out of control again, but the woman maintained a firm grip on her audience.

"So given all of that," she smiled brightly, "I think we can all agree that we are especially fortunate tonight that Detective-Sergeant Cellars has graciously offered to share with us his expertise—"

Cellars looked up from the open flyer in stunned disbelief.

"—on how to properly preserve and collect evidence at the point of first contact with our alien visitors."

Before Cellars could say or do anything, he suddenly found himself propelled up to the podium by a fragile but surprisingly firm hand, then watched with a sense of total abandonment as his silver-haired hostess quickly took her reserved seat in the front row.

If anything, the room grew even more silent than before. Cellars realized that he could now hear the patter of the rain on the thick-shingled roof high overhead.

Well, Bobby, you really did it to me this time.

It occurred to Cellars, at that moment, that it wouldn't have mattered if he had called Jody, like he'd promised. She wouldn't have said anything. *Not about something like this,* he thought as he stared down at the familiar inverted-teardrop-shaped head with the flattened-out eye slits—a sketch that took up a good quarter of the brightly colored flyer. *No way in the world, because she knows me too well. I wouldn't have come. Not for another one of Bobby's bullshit games.*

But now that I'm here—

Realizing he was trapped, Cellars sighed inwardly as he raised his head to face his audience. He was trying to decide which way to go, knowing full well that whichever way he chose, Captain Rodney Hawkins, his new supervisor, wasn't likely to be pleased if word about this talk ever got back to the regional office. And in any case, he was still going to have to wing it.

Hell with it, he decided with a mental shrug. *If I'm going to piss the guy off my first day in his region, I might as well have fun doing it.*

"Good evening, ladies and gentlemen." Cellars smiled good-naturedly. "I get the impression that the fellow you all seem to know, with some degree of fondness, as Robert—I usually just call him

Bobby or Dawson—went to a great deal of effort to set the stage for my talk here this evening. And knowing Robert Dawson, as I most certainly do, I can hardly wait to hear his excuse for why he couldn't be here tonight to share the podium with me. All I can tell you is it ought to be a very interesting one, because this is exactly the kind of moment that our mutual friend absolutely savors."

Cellars paused to look around the audience, and was momentarily distracted by the intriguing features of an absolutely gorgeous dark-haired young woman seated at the far end of the third row.

Jody?

No, not Jody Catlin, Cellars quickly realized. From a distance, the similarities were there—her hair, her eyes, her facial structure. But this woman was younger, her features more—what?—Asian? Mediterranean?

More like what Jody looked like in college, fifteen years ago, only . . . older, Cellars realized with a start.

His eyebrows furrowed for a moment in confusion, trying to remember.

Did I see her coming in?

But he knew he hadn't. Couldn't have, because he knew he would have reacted immediately if he'd seen someone who looked so much like Jody walking up that path from the parking lot to the auditorium.

So where did she—?

Then he remembered. The dark-cloaked and hooded figure whose face he hadn't seen. Whose sudden and unexpected appearance out of the misty darkness had caused a chill to run down his spine.

The apparition.

He wanted to keep on staring at her. To try to understand what it was about this beautiful young woman—who looked so much like an inexplicably younger but more mature Jody Catlin—that had caused him to react like that. But then Cellars remembered where he was, quickly recovered, and refocused his attention back on the audience as a whole.

"You see," he went on smoothly, "my good buddy Dawson never got around to telling me that I was actually going to be making a presentation tonight. Which, as it happens," Cellars added quickly when murmured sounds of concern began to emerge from the audience, "may work out to your benefit. You see, had I known about it, I would have almost certainly brought along a tray or two of gory crime scene slides. And I would have then spent the next hour or so making a very determined effort to sidestep the primary topic that—judging from Bobby's distinctive artwork on this flyer—clearly brought you here in the first place."

Cellars held up the flyer, and watched with a sinking feeling in his stomach as several members of the audience began to nod at each other and smile hopefully.

Christ, he thought, *these people really do want to believe.*

"But since I didn't know that I was going to be speaking to you tonight—much less have any sense of the topic—I haven't had time to dream up an hour's worth of stagecraft that just might have sent you home believing that you'd actually been given a glimpse of the Holy Grail." Cellars paused to shrug his shoulders. "So, in view of all of that, I'm going to do something that I'm certain our mutual buddy Dawson would have never expected me to do."

The audience held their collective breath.

"What I'm going to do is walk you right through it, step-by-step. Just like you've been promised."

CHAPTER SEVEN

THERE WAS A LONG MOMENT OF STUNNED SILENCE IN THE JAS-per County auditorium ... immediately followed by a buzz of whispered excitement as people throughout the audience turned to whisper to each other.

Cellars waited patiently until the murmurs died down to a muted hum.

"But before I do that," he said as he allowed his eyes slowly to sweep the auditorium, "I want you all to have a clear understanding of why I've been assigned to work in this area."

As if of one mind, the room went deadly silent.

"As you all undoubtedly know," Cellars went on, "an unusually large number of people have been reported as either missing or 'possibly kidnapped' in Jasper County over the past eleven months. At the risk of alarming some of you who may not have been keeping up with the articles in the papers, I believe the number is now something in the neighborhood of twenty-four. And while this is certainly a large number for a county with a population of approximately one hundred thousand, it would not be an *unusually* large number . . . *if* the count included people under the age of twenty-one. Which is to say, teenage runaways.

"Unfortunately"—he paused for effect—"it doesn't."

This time the buzz was short-lived as almost everyone in the audience quickly whispered their "I told you so's" to their neighbors, then turned their attention back to the podium.

"Mrs. Patterson"—Cellars turned briefly to nod in the direction of his hostess—"mentioned the term 'crimes of a special nature.' Implying, I assume, that many—if not all—of these missing persons might be related, in some manner, to the relatively large number of 'alien contact' reports we've received from residents in this county during that same period of time."

"What do you mean by 'relatively large number'?" a voice from the back of the auditorium demanded.

Cellars hesitated.

"According to the briefing I received in Salem, there have been over two hundred and twenty reports of visual sightings—of UFOs, glowing lights, and what are described as distinctly nonhuman intelligent beings—and forty-nine reports of actual UFO abduction in Jasper County during this same period of time. Which, as I understand it, is approximately as many as the rest of the state combined," Cellars added in what he hoped was a reasonably neutral voice.

This set the murmuring off again. Cellars waited until the auditorium returned to order, then nodded in the direction of an older man in the front row who was frantically waving his hand.

"Yes sir?"

"Sergeant Cellars, I've been informed by a reliable source in the Oregon State Patrol, who understandably wishes to remain anonymous, that all but two of the missing person reports, and approximately eighty percent of the UFO reports, if you will, are clumped into three forty-five-day time periods. As a forensic scientist, which

I believe Robert said you are, just how would you interpret that data?"

"As a forensic scientist?" Cellars smiled. "I wouldn't."

The man blinked in surprise. "Good Lord, man, why not?"

"One simple reason," Cellars replied evenly. "Evidence. Or more to the point, the lack thereof."

"That these people are missing?" The elderly man looked incredulous.

Cellars shook his head. "No, evidence that these reported UFO sightings and contacts actually occurred."

"But—"

"Let me assure all of you," Cellars went on smoothly, "that in spite of the interesting mathematical clumping of—as you correctly put it—twenty-two of the missing individuals and approximately eighty percent of these reported alien sightings or contacts, we in the Oregon State Patrol are not treating these missing person situations as *special* crimes. We are, however—because of the unusual number of missing persons—treating them as a possible *serial* crime situation. And because one of the best ways to deal with a serial criminal is to assign one or more officers to work all of the cases—and, more importantly, examine all of the evidence—a senior crime scene investigator has been assigned to this area for that specific purpose.

"And, as you may have guessed by now"—Cellars smiled patiently—"I am that investigator."

A flurry of hands rose from the audience.

"Uh, yes sir." Cellars pointed to one of the closest waving hands.

"Officer Cellars"—a man who appeared to be a thirty-to-forty-year-old lumberjack said as he rose to his feet—"are you saying that the OSP thinks we have a serial kidnapper living in this county?"

"No, not at all." Cellars shook his head firmly. "What I'm saying is that we have an unusual number of missing person reports in a relatively small area—reports that occurred within three relatively short time periods—that *may* all be related to each other. And if that is the case, we want to find out how and why."

"So, in other words, someone in the government is finally going to take all of these abduction reports seriously?" The muscular man cocked his head with a curious smile as he sat back down.

"We are certainly taking all of the missing persons and possible kidnapping reports seriously," Cellars replied cautiously. "I'm not sure what you mean by 'abduction reports.' If you're including all of those supposed UFO sighting and contact reports in with the missing persons, then—"

"But there's a clear correlation between the two sets of data. You said so yourself," a young man with long, bushed-out hair and a distinctively reedy voice in the back of the auditorium protested.

"No, I said there's an interesting mathematical *clumping* of two sets of numbers," Cellars corrected. "One set is hard data—twenty-four Jasper County residents are definitely missing or unaccounted for. There's no doubt about that. But the other is simply a tally of eyewitness reports, every one of which was unsubstantiated by other eyewitnesses *or by any physical evidence*," he emphasized. "And as far as I'm aware, no one in the OSP has any reason to believe that the two sets of numbers are related—directly or otherwise—in any manner."

"So we're back to the way it's always been," the lumberjack spoke out loudly. "Nobody in the government believes us—"

"Or if they do, they're not about to admit it publicly," another member of the audience added sarcastically.

"Yeah, right, exactly," the lumberjack nodded. "So what you're really telling us, Officer Cellars, is that nothing's changed. If we're going to prove what's really been going on around here the last several months, we're going to have to do it ourselves . . . without any help from the OSP or anyone else in the government."

"But that's exactly why Robert invited him here," Eleanor Patterson protested. "To help us do it ourselves."

"That's right, Sergeant," the reedy voice piped up. "You said you're going to walk us right through it, step-by-step. So what does that mean, exactly?"

"What it means, exactly, is that you need the evidence," Cellars said matter-of-factly. "Because without it, no one in any position of authority, much less the general public, is *ever* going to believe any claims of alien contact, or alien abduction, or any other out-of-this-world interactions that a few people—perhaps people like yourselves—claim to have experienced."

"And you really are going to tell us how to collect that evidence, right? That's what you just promised us, isn't it?" the reedy voice demanded.

"Yes, that is exactly what I'm going to do," Cellars replied. "Unless I get called out to respond to another kidnapping or missing person report—or to assist at a homicide crime scene—during the next hour or so, I'm going to stand up here and do exactly that. Spend as much time as you wish explaining exactly how you would go about recognizing, documenting, preserving, marking, collecting, and packaging that physical evidence. How you would set the scene perimeter, and prepare the sketch. Basically, teach you everything you need to know about the step-by-step process of a professional crime scene investigation.

"And if you listen carefully this evening, and maybe take a few notes, every one of you will walk out of this auditorium with all of the information you need to properly document what we, in law enforcement, would call a crime scene. *And* in doing so," Cellars added with emphasis, "demonstrate beyond any shadow of a doubt that direct physical contact did in fact occur between the scene, the victim—which is to say our witness, who has presumably survived the encounter more or less intact—and our most intriguing John Doe suspect."

Almost everyone in the audience was smiling widely now. Several were nodding their heads excitedly at each other, and most had begun to take frantic notes. That made it easy for Cellars to pick out the DEA agent types, all four of whom appeared extremely annoyed by the way things were turning out. It also gave him time to glance over at the stunningly attractive dark-haired young woman who sat quietly at the far left side of the auditorium with her hands in her lap and an oddly contemplative look on her face.

The young woman whose mere presence brought back a torrent of youthful memories and emotions.

It occurred to Cellars that he would have been perfectly content simply to stand there at the podium and stare at this lovely apparition from his past for the rest of the evening. But, instead, he pressed on, determined to make his point.

"To begin with, you need to be aware of one basic and irrefutable bit of logic upon which all crime scene investigations are based. To put it very simply: It is virtually impossible for a suspect, a victim, and a crime scene to come into contact with each other—and I should note here, in most cases, this means violent contact—without the exchange of physical evidence taking place. The items of evidence we're talking about may be very large and obvious to the casual observer, such as a footprint or a tire track impression in soft soil, or a projectile lodged in a body. Or they may be very small and difficult to find without special equipment and expertise, such as a latent fingerprint, or a hair, or a fiber, or even some microscopic portion of blood or dust. But in any case, they will be there. They have to be."

Cellars observed with some satisfaction that everyone in the audience (with the notable exception of the four visibly pained DEA types and the enticing young woman) was now scribbling furiously.

"So what does all this mean? Very simply, if alien visitors from another planet, galaxy, or universe have, in fact, landed on our planet, and have, in fact, made contact with members of the human race, then there *must* exist, somewhere, physical evidence of that contact. The trick, of course, is to find it."

Cellars smiled pleasantly.

And then, for the next fifteen minutes, he proceeded to walk them through it, step-by-step, explaining exactly how to set a perimeter and conduct a methodical crime scene search. And how each typical category of located evidence—paint, glass, soil, residue, hair, fiber, blood, tissue, bone, or impression mark—had to be properly documented, marked, packaged, tagged, and preserved for later examination by a scientific expert.

"But the thing is," he went on, ignoring several frantically waving hands, "even if one of you does manage to observe such a contact, and even if that individual does manage to conduct an immediate, proper, and thorough crime scene investigation—roping off the crime scene perimeter, taking dozens of overall and close-up photographs, making a detailed sketch, photographing and casting the impression marks from the landing points, collecting soil samples to locate exhaust debris, or perhaps even scraping some metal off the ship for elemental analysis as we just discussed—it won't do him or her the least bit of good."

"What do you mean?" the young man with the reedy voice cried out, a look of absolute distress appearing on his face. "You just said—"

"I said it won't do any of *you* any good," Cellars repeated with a sympathetic smile, "because of one simple fact: You are all advocates."

"But—"

"I get the distinct impression that most if not all of you here tonight sincerely believe that alien visitors have made contact with earth, and that human contacts with these aliens have, in fact, occurred. And I gather that some of you even claim to have been personally involved in such a contact. That's all very well, and I'm not here to ridicule anyone, or doubt their word. But you must understand that it won't do any of you the least bit of good to locate and properly collect evidence of that contact if you can't get that evidence analyzed and interpreted by recognized and unbiased scientific experts—people such as you would find in a police crime laboratory.

"But the problem is, no crime lab director in his or her right mind is going to accept, much less examine, physical evidence collected by an unsupervised advocate."

"Why not?" an anonymous voice demanded from the back of the auditorium.

"Why not? It's very simple: Advocates such as yourselves are widely considered to be people who want to believe—and convince others—so badly, so desperately even, that you wouldn't hesitate to fake or alter or switch your evidence to make your point."

Cellars held up his hand to still the sounds of protest that seemed to fill the audience.

"I know this isn't what you wanted to hear. And I understand why," he said softly when the auditorium finally quieted down. "Believe me, I do. But there's something else you have to understand. These crime lab directors we're talking about are very accustomed to police officers and prosecutors—not to mention virtually every defense attorney who handles one of their cases—questioning everything they do. That's the nature of the game. But that is also why they will absolutely insist that every conclusive statement in every official lab report issued from their laboratories be based upon solid physical evidence. Not conjecture. Not fantasy. Solid evidence. And given their pragmatic nature, these crime lab directors are not about to expend their limited resources, or risk their hard-earned reputations for that matter, examining evidence that lacks a reliable chain-of-custody. They simply won't do it."

"But . . . but, what can we do? How can we convince these people that visitor contacts *are* occurring, night after night, right in their own backyards, if these crime lab people won't even look at our evidence?" the reedy voice demanded.

"It's not going to be easy," Cellars conceded. "First of all, from my perspective, what you really need is for your evidence to be discovered, preserved, documented, and collected by someone who doesn't have a personal interest in the outcome." He was speaking in careful, measured words to his now-silent audience, making a determined effort to keep his eyes from focusing on the enticing features of the dark-haired young woman at the far end of the third row. "In essence, I suppose, someone like myself."

"Why you?" another voice demanded out of the darkened middle of the audience.

"Not me, specifically," Cellars corrected with an easy smile. "Someone like me. Someone who conducts crime scene investigations on a professional basis. Someone who knows how to recognize and properly collect, document, and preserve physical evidence in all of its extremely varied forms. And more importantly," he added with deliberate emphasis, "someone who would present that evidence— the scientific facts, if you will—with professional indifference as to the outcome, not caring if it helps the prosecution or the defense. Or in this case," he shrugged, "the advocate or . . . what? The disbeliever?"

"So which are you?" the enticing young woman at the far end of the third row asked in a voice that was amazingly soft and gentle, and yet caught his attention immediately over the noisy audience.

"I beg your pardon?" Cellars replied.

"Which are you?" the young woman repeated. "Believer or disbeliever?"

"Actually, that's a different question entirely," Cellars responded after a moment's hesitation.

"Yes, I know." Her smile was soft, intriguing, and from Cellars's thoroughly distracted point of view, almost overwhelmingly seductive. *Just like Jody.*

Maybe Malcolm's right, he thought, forcing himself to ignore his tumbling emotions and focus on the task at hand. *Maybe I do need to start going out more.*

"If you're asking me whether or not I believe it's possible that intelligent alien life-forms exist, and whether or not it's possible—or even probable—that they've made contact with humans on this planet, I suppose I'd have to start out by making the obvious point. The odds in favor of other life-forms being out there in the first place are astronomically huge. What are we talking about? A minimum of at least fifty billion galaxies, each of which contains something in the order of fifty to one hundred billion stars, right?"

Several heads in the audience nodded.

"So if we accept that almost-impossible-to-contemplate number of stars that could, at least in theory, possess a planet with the orbit, atmosphere, and nutrients necessary to support and nurture intelligent life, are we then supposed to believe that our own star, good old Sol, is the only one among these five thousand billion billion stars that actually managed to pull it off? If you'll allow me to set aside the irresolvable issues of religious faith and dogma for the moment, and indulge myself in a moment of pure understatement, I'd have to say that's a pretty unlikely proposition. Perhaps even unthinkable."

"So you *do* believe there's other intelligent life out there?" the reedy voice pressed.

Cellars stared out at his inquisitor for a moment, hesitating because he knew this was the critical junction point. The point at which he was absolutely committed.

"Yes, of course I do. As a scientist, how could I not? But at the same time," he added quickly, "as a forensic scientist, I have a professional obligation to seek out and evaluate the evidence in an unbiased manner before coming to a conclusion. And just what is that evidence—the irrefutable facts—that we possess to date? Well, first of all, we certainly know that the distances between these stars are huge in terms of our own lifetimes. So regardless of the presence or absence of things such as wormholes, I think we can all agree that the process of actually traveling to our planet from another solar system or galaxy has got to be a technically difficult—or at the very least, technically advanced—process.

"Secondly, and perhaps equally important, we know intuitively that any species possessing the technical capability to get here from some distant planet, galaxy, or corner of the known universe, is certainly going to be far more technically advanced than we are. Which means it's highly unlikely that they would view us as any kind of serious threat.

"And given that pair of theorems, I personally find it very difficult to believe that any intelligent creature who possesses the technical capability of getting here within their lifetime in the first place, would really care if he or she or it was observed by a lesser creature such as ourselves during its visit. Take our own biologists, for example, who are constantly going out into the wilds to collect specimens of so-called lesser species. Do they really care if they are seen by the ants, spiders, or even the local birds and mammals during their excursions?"

"They could have their reasons . . . like not wanting to corrupt our cultures or our civilizations," the reedy voice suggested.

"Yes, of course," Cellars acknowledged. "The altruistic anthropological approach. But if that is the case, and they really do care about not being seen, then why would they find it so technically difficult to avoid detection by a 'lesser' species such as ourselves?"

"Maybe they just do. Maybe things just go wrong every now and then, like they do with us," another hidden voice called out.

"I agree. No reason that I can think of why Murphy's Law wouldn't apply to an alien traveler as well as to the rest of us." Cellars smiled, but then his expression turned serious.

"And, in fact, that might be a good thing to hope for. We tend to view ourselves as pretty intelligent and reasonably benevolent beings. But when you stop to think about it, we really are a pretty nasty species when it comes to dealing with our neighbors. We've got relatively advanced brains, and opposable thumbs, and we're pretty good at making and using tools. Three simple little advantages. But with them, we've been able to completely ransack every other species on this planet. And I'm not necessarily talking about one-on-one. A white shark or a grizzly bear in its own environment can certainly do a number on an individual human, especially if that individual had the misfortune to leave one of his or her primary advantages at home. But as a species, we are definitely the top dog on Mother Earth. We always win. Which is a pretty terrifying concept when you stop to think about how many more advantages a visiting alien species might possess."

Cellars looked around. His audience was dead silent.

"So what do I believe?" He paused for a moment. "I honestly

don't believe that we're alone in this greater universe. Given the al-most-incomprehensible expanse of the universe that we know about just through the Hubble Telescope, the idea that our own Earth is the only inhabited planet seems, to me, to fly in the face of any sense of rational thinking.

"But," he went on quickly, "I also believe—just as strongly, I assure you—in the almost-limitless capacity of humans to con each other. Out of maliciousness, out of greed, out of a desire for recognition, or just for the pure hell of it."

He paused once more for effect.

"So, in my mind, what it all comes down to is the evidence. Which is why I can always hope that I'll be that lucky crime scene investigator who gets to work the first contact scene, and collect that first piece of confirmatory evidence."

"But you're a government official," the same hidden voice protested. "If you did find this piece of evidence, and the government ordered you to cover it up, you'd have to do it, wouldn't you?"

"I am a police investigator and a forensic scientist, which, I suppose, does make me a government official," Cellars conceded. "But government employee or not, my primary job is always to tell the truth to the best of my ability, period. Nobody, and I do mean *nobody*," Cellars said emphatically, "could ever force me to conceal or lie about any evidence that I might ever collect at a crime scene."

"But . . ." the persistent questioner tried one last time.

"Trust me," Cellars said with a gentle, reassuring smile. "It isn't going to happen. My ancestors were immigrants from Scotland and Ireland. Which, I'm told, makes me a thickheaded Scotsman with a stubborn streak."

The audience responded with appreciative laughter.

"But in any case, I can honestly tell you that I don't care if the order comes from a law enforcement superior, the governor, or even a federal judge," Cellars went on evenly. "It simply isn't going to happen."

"You must drive your wife absolutely crazy," the white-haired elderly woman with the three-strand pearl necklace commented loudly, to the delight of the audience.

"I'm sure that I would drive my wife crazy *if* I was married," Cellars said, speaking to the audience at large. "But I might add here that Mrs. Patterson has revealed the one major drawback to the career of a crime scene investigator. As you might imagine, it's pretty difficult to maintain any kind of permanent relationship—as a husband, father, or even a steady boyfriend—when you're constantly getting called away at one o'clock in the morning. And especially when you end up being gone for twenty or thirty hours at a time, and hardly ever show up for anniversaries and birthdays, much less casual dates."

"You don't have a steady girlfriend either?" His elderly host looked properly horrified.

The image of Jody Catlin—her dimpled features breaking out into laughter—as she took up slack on the safety line flashed through Cellars's subconscious. *I need to call her,* he thought, feeling the familiar tightening in his chest. *I really do.*

He shrugged and shook his head.

"Oh dear."

A sudden shift in the expression of the enticing young woman at the end of the third row caught Cellars's attention. It was fairly obvious that she was reacting to something he'd just said. But before he had a chance to think back over exactly what he *had* said, Mrs. Patterson continued on in a thoughtful voice: "Well, I suppose that *would* explain why policemen can be so grumpy at times."

The entire audience erupted into laughter. Even the four DEA-types managed to lose their dour expressions for a few moments.

Once the laughter died down, and he could make himself heard, Cellars continued with a wide smile on his face.

"You know, I'm probably giving you all a very warped impression of crime scene investigators in general. But, to tell you the truth, even if I stayed up here and rambled on for the rest of the evening,

I don't think I could ever top *that* comment. So perhaps this might be a good time for me to stop while I'm more or less ahead, and spend the rest of our time this evening trying to answer any questions you might have about evidence or crime scenes or whatever."

"But before you do," Mrs. Patterson interrupted as she stepped up to the microphone, "I'm pleased to announce that we have cookies, brownies, and hot coffee or tea in the back. So if we all can take no more than ten minutes for a quick trip to the bathroom and refreshments, and be back in our seats by"—she glanced down at her watch—"eight forty, I'm sure Sergeant Cellars will be happy to answer all of our questions."

The auditorium immediately erupted into a buzzing frenzy as the sixty-some members of the audience began to work their way toward the rest rooms and the tables of food. Cellars was following in the wake of Mrs. Patterson, who seemed quite adept at clearing the way up the stairway, intent on calling Jody before he lost his nerve again, when he felt a hand on his arm.

"Excuse me, Detective-Sergeant Cellars?"

For reasons he couldn't even begin to comprehend, he knew who it was even before he turned around.

It's her voice, he realized as he turned and found himself staring into a pair of violet eyes that seemed hypnotic in their intensity. *She sounds exactly the way I thought she'd sound. Just like Jody . . . only different.*

"Yes?"

Incredibly, even though there was at least a foot of empty space between them, Cellars was absolutely convinced that he could feel the heat emanating from her body. But it was her eyes that drew his attention. Deep pools of shimmering violet.

"I have to talk with you," she said in an urgent, whispery voice.

Cellars blinked, feeling his heart beginning to pound in his chest. "You do?"

"Yes, it's very important." Her hypnotic eyes held his for a brief moment before she suddenly swiveled her head around.

Following her gaze, Cellars saw that two of the DEA-types were working their way toward the podium from either side of the auditorium.

"Uh, look, maybe we can get together for a cup of coffee after I, uh, finish answering everyone's questions?" Cellars suggested. It was all he could do to keep himself from walking right out of the auditorium with this enticing young woman, right then, and never looking back.

Christ, what's the matter with me? I'm acting like a lovestruck teenager with a woman I've never even met.

"Yes, please, that would be wonderful." Her violet eyes widened in gratitude beneath a suddenly beaming smile of such magnitude that it nearly sent Cellars into cardiac arrest. "It's very important," she repeated. "It's about Robert."

"Robert?" Cellars blinked in shock. "What about—?"

But he never got to finish his question because the tightly wrapped jacket on the chair next to the podium suddenly began to ring shrilly.

Still caught up in a whirlwind of emotions that now—incredibly, and once again—included Bobby Dawson, Cellars turned and stared at the offending jacket, realizing that he must not have turned the cell phone off after he'd finished talking with Jody.

Muttering to himself, he turned back to the nearly irresistible young woman, and said, "Excuse me for just a moment, please."

Then, feeling vaguely light-headed and dizzy, he walked over and removed the cell phone from the wrapped jacket, flipped it open, put it up to his ear, and whispered a terse acknowledgment. As he did so, he noticed that both of the DEA-types had paused in their forward movements and were watching him intently from a distance of about twenty feet.

He listened carefully for almost thirty seconds, all the while keeping his eye on the two solemn-faced men, until finally he asked, in a resigned voice: "Where?"

After another twenty seconds or so, he closed the cell phone, glanced briefly at the incredibly beautiful young woman, shook his head, stepped up to the podium, and then leaned forward to speak softly into the microphone.

"Ladies and gentlemen, if I could have your attention, please."

The amplified sound of Cellars's voice caused virtually everyone in the auditorium to stop talking, turn around, and face the podium.

"I'm very sorry, but it seems that I won't be able to answer any more of your questions this evening. That ringing phone you may have heard a few moments ago was one of those call-outs I told you about, and I do have to leave right now."

"Ha, see, I knew it!" the reedy voice called out triumphantly from the top of the stairway. "Just like I told you! They've been listening in the whole time, and now they don't want him talking to us anymore."

Cellars stared up at the young man for a long moment before the words finally registered.

"I wish it were that simple," he said in a tired voice, making a determined effort not to look again into the captivating eyes of the young woman who stood by the podium with a stricken look on her face. "Believe me, I really do."

CHAPTER EIGHT

THE RAIN HAD STARTED UP AGAIN. THE COLD, DRIZZLING KIND OF rain that made the paved roads treacherously slick with nearly invisible sheets of oil-saturated water, turned gravel roads into aggregate slush, and dirt roads into rutted lanes of slippery mud that were nearly impassable without the dual benefits of high clearance and four-wheel drive.

In other words, standard wet weather driving conditions for southwestern Oregon.

The back road leading away from the auditorium looked as if it hadn't been regraveled in recent memory. But the dispatcher had advised that a county road crew was responding to a washed-out bridge on the main road, and traffic was already backed up for a quarter mile in both directions. So Cellars took the back road out, concentrated on the illuminating path of his headlights, dropped the Explorer into low-four to negotiate a couple of tricky soft spots, then waited until he had the Explorer safely back on asphalt before he reached for his console mike.

"Oregon-Nine-Echo-One to OMARR-Nine."

The response came back immediately—the words only mildly distorted by the new encryption software that supposedly made the Oregon law enforcement communications system secure from outside scanner monitoring.

Secure from everyone except people like Malcolm, Cellars thought, wondering if his high-tech buddy really was capable of monitoring OMARR transmissions from Virginia as he often claimed.

"Oregon-Nine-Echo-One, go ahead."

"Oregon-Nine-Echo-One. I'm en route on your call from the county auditorium. Requesting additional information on missing Jasper County deputies."

"Roger, Oregon-Nine-Echo-One. Hold one."

Moments later, the dispatcher was back on the air.

"Oregon-Nine-Echo-One, at eighteen-fifty-six hours we had a reported shots-fired situation with unknown suspects in the proximity of a private residence located at the far north end of County Road Twenty-Two-Fifty-Five off of Highway Two-Forty-Three. Residence is described as small log cabin with the front porch facing north, and an exposed basement facing south. Reporting party is not identified at this time. May have been a neighbor."

The dispatcher paused.

Something about that description tugged at Cellars's subconscious. But before he could figure out why, the dispatcher's voice regained his attention.

"Oregon-Nine-Echo-One, be advised that Jasper-Two-Bravo-One was dispatched to that location at eighteen-fifty-eight hours. Location is a radio dead zone. There was no further contact with missing deputies until nineteen-forty-two hours, at which time the emergency transponder assigned to Jasper-Two-Bravo-One was activated for approximately ten seconds. Jasper-Two-Alpha-Four and

Two-Charlie-One were dispatched to the location at nineteen-forty-three hours with an estimated ETA of twenty-fifteen hours."

Eighteen-fifty-eight hours? That's right. Jasper-Two-Bravo-One. The guys who almost missed that call.

Cellars nodded. A cold prickling sensation started down his spine as he remembered sitting in the auditorium parking lot and starting to reach for his mike when the deep-voiced member of the scout team finally checked in.

"Have you had any contact with the responding Jasper units?" he asked, speaking into the mike as he glanced down at the date/time display on his console: 2046 hours. Approximately thirty minutes since a patrol sergeant and a deputy had presumably arrived at the scene. Plenty of time for one of them to find a land line and call in.

"Oregon-Nine-Echo-One, that's a negative. But be advised," the dispatcher went on in her professionally calm and controlled voice, "at twenty-thirty-four hours, Jasper-Two-Bravo-One's empty cruiser was located in a parking space behind the Rusty Bar in Whitehurst. The Jasper County Watch Commander is at the scene now along with responding OSP units."

"Any sign of the deputies?"

"Negative. The cruiser was found parked and locked. We're issuing an all-points bulletin right now. The Jasper County Watch Commander has requested that you respond to the scene of the initial call-out, relieve Jasper-Two-Alpha-Four and Jasper-Two-Charlie-One, and direct them to report to the Rusty Bar location. Your assignment is to remain at the scene to search for any evidence relating to the missing deputies or the original shots-fired call. Also be advised the initial shots-fired scene is located in a radio dead zone. Request that you contact the resident of the cabin immediately upon your arrival and report in by land line. Repeat, report in by land line. If you are unable to do so, and require assistance while at this location for any reason, activate your emergency transponder immediately."

"Oregon-Nine-Echo-One, ten-four. I'm on my way."

The site of the initial call-out was the end of a dirt road that branched off from a rarely used strip of crushed rock, gravel, and asphalt that the US Forest Service had built several years ago in an effort to keep the logging trucks from sliding down the steep mountain slopes during the rainy season. There were only three turns, and all three were clearly marked, so it shouldn't be difficult to find, the dispatcher had said reassuringly.

To Cellars's amazement, the scene was easy to find, but it had nothing to do with the signs.

The roads probably had been clearly marked at one time. At least that would have explained the fresh dirt surrounding what appeared to be recent signpost locations that Cellars had managed to find with his flashlight at the last two intersections. But as it turned out, the missing signs hadn't mattered at all.

As Cellars pulled his vehicle off to the side of the road, about twenty yards behind and on the opposite side of the road from the two Jasper County Sheriff's cruisers, he told himself that law enforcement officers at a crime scene must find something inherently soothing about rotating red-and-blue emergency lights. That was the only reason he could think of for why the sweeping beams of brightly colored illumination had been clearly visible for the last three miles.

Although, in fact, there was another—equally plausible— explanation why the occupants of these two vehicles might not have gotten around to shutting off their emergency lights when they first arrived at the scene. But Cellars didn't want to think about that other explanation right now.

Not when he was a lone responding officer coming into a radio dead zone where the first responding pair of Jasper County deputies had disappeared, and the second pair was nowhere to be seen.

And especially not when the follow-up pair hadn't responded to any of his radio calls.

He'd even tried his cell phone—thinking he might be able to get a patch through to one of the relay towers—before giving up in frustration and sticking the maddening device in the glove compartment.

Come on, guys, where are you?

Cellars quickly scanned the two cruisers parked in parallel along the side of the dirt road, looking for any sign of broken glass, bullet holes, or other signs of violence. At the same time—staying alert for any sign of movement in the surrounding darkness of the tree line— he put the Explorer into reverse gear, left the engine running, and brought the mike back up to his mouth.

No High Gorge "dead zone" excuse now. The radio transmitter in his Explorer was powerful enough to reach any vehicle or portable radio receiver within a quarter mile, in spite of the surrounding trees and mountains.

"Jasper-Two-Alpha-Four or Jasper-Two-Charlie-One, this is Oregon-Nine-Echo-One. I'm ten-eight at your location. Please acknowledge."

Nothing.

Muttering to himself, Cellars shifted the mike to his left hand. Then he slowly drew the .40 caliber model P229 SIG-Sauer semi-automatic pistol from its holster and set it on his lap, his fingers wrapped loosely around the rubberized grip and his index finger resting against the trigger guard.

"Repeat. Jasper-Two-Alpha-Four or Jasper-Two-Charlie-One, this is Oregon-Nine-Echo-One. Do you read me? I'm driving a white, un-marked Explorer, and I'm parked at the end of the dirt road in front of the cabin. Please acknowledge this transmission."

Again nothing.

Shit.

It was only after Cellars finally satisfied himself that—apart from being empty—both vehicles looked perfectly normal, that he concentrated his attention on the tree line.

That was when he spotted the first uniformed figure—or what looked like a uniformed figure in rain gear, in the intermittent sweeps of red-and-blue light—crouched with arms extended in a barricade position in the trees about thirty yards to his left. Cellars couldn't see the gun, but he didn't have any doubt it was pointed in his direction.

What the hell . . . ?

Then he remembered.

Oh yeah, that's right. I'm the one who's responding in plain clothes and an unmarked vehicle.

Shifting his attention away from the barely visible figure for only a few seconds at a time, Cellars continued his search of the darkly shadowed tree line. Now that he had a better sense of what he was looking for, it only took him another twenty seconds to locate the second figure in a similar barricaded position on the opposite side of the road. Perfect placement for a lethal cross fire.

Cellars knew that any suspicious movement on his part could easily cause a fusillade of 9mm rounds to come exploding through his windshield, so he carefully kept his right hand in place on his lap as he thumbed the mike switch again.

"Oregon-Nine-Echo-One to the uniformed officers at my ten o'clock and two o'clock positions. I advise you again, I am a plain-clothes crime scene investigator for the Oregon State Patrol. If you are operating on this frequency, please acknowledge immediately."

As Cellars watched, feeling the tension start to build in his chest and shoulders, the uniformed figure to his left brought what looked like a portable radio up to the side of his face.

"This is Jasper-Two-Alpha-Four to the subject in the white Explorer. Turn off your engine, toss your keys out the driver's side window, and exit your vehicle with your hands over your head. Do it now!"

The voice coming out of his console speaker was tight with tension—almost to the breaking point—and it jarred Cellars's self-protective instincts.

Subject? Christ, this isn't right. Jasper-Two-Alpha-Four's a patrol sergeant, and he knows he's got me boxed in. What the hell is he afraid of?

Then an unnerving thought occurred to Cellars.

What if he doesn't belong in that uniform?

Unconsciously, Cellars's right hand tightened around the grip of his pistol and his index finger slipped in against the cool, soothing curve of the trigger as his mind sought the security of the firing range mantra.

Loaded, locked, and a round in the chamber. Hammer down. Just center on the target and squeeze the trigger. Sight and squeeze. Sight and squeeze.

Exactly as he'd been trained, except this wasn't the firing range, and there were two of them in a perfectly executed barricade and cross-fire position, and he knew the windshield on his Explorer wouldn't do much to stop or deflect an incoming 9mm hollow-point. Not at these angles. If the shooting started, the only chance he'd have would be to duck, slam his foot on the accelerator, and try to keep the vehicle on the road long enough to get some distance from the cross fire before he hit a tree.

Shit.

"Jasper-Two-Alpha-Four, this is Oregon-Nine-Echo-One. I repeat, I am a crime scene investigator for the Oregon State Patrol. I have been dispatched to assist Jasper-Two-Alpha-Four or Jasper-Two-Charlie-One at a shots-fired call involving two missing deputies. Also be advised I am not shutting off my engine and I am not stepping out of this vehicle until I see at least one uniform in full view."

There was a pause. Then:

"Oregon-Nine-Echo-One. Identify yourself."

Cellars blinked in momentary confusion, then nodded in understanding.

Right. Same problem. We don't know each other. And two missing deputies means two missing portable radios that anybody could be using right now. Perfectly understandable.

"This is Detective-Sergeant Colin Cellars. Call sign Oregon-Nine-Echo-One, assigned to Oregon State Patrol Region Nine."

"Who's your supervisor?"

"Captain Rodney Hawkins."

"Describe Captain Hawkins."

Cellars hesitated, then shrugged internally.

What the hell, it's not like he can hear me up here.

"Six-one, brown and bald, lousy disposition. Your typical captain."

This time the pause was considerably longer.

"Oregon-Nine-Echo-One, how are you armed?"

"With an OSP-issued forty-caliber SIG-Sauer semiautomatic pistol."

"Where is it?"

"In my right hand, on my lap."

Another pause.

"Oregon-Nine-Echo-One, be advised that I'm about ready to have a coronary out here, and you're not helping things much. You can leave your pistol on your lap, your engine on, and the transmission in reverse gear; but I want you to toss your ID into the trees to your left, then keep both of your hands on the steering wheel of your vehicle until I tell you it's okay to move them. Is that understood?"

I understand you know all of us OSP-types carry .40-caliber SIG-Sauers, and you probably know what Captain Rodney Hawkins looks and acts like, but yet you're still spooked . . . which means I don't like this situation one little bit.

But the only other option was to duck and jam his foot on the accelerator, and Cellars didn't like the odds on that any better. If he ran into one of the surrounding trees in the first fifty yards, they'd have him cold.

"Ten-four," Cellars acknowledged as he reluctantly released his comforting grip on the heavy semiautomatic, reached inside his jacket for his photo ID, tossed the thin badge case into the woods to his left, then placed his gloved hands lightly on the steering wheel.

He remained in that position, ignoring the figure to his right as he watched the rain-gear-garbed figure to his left begin to move cautiously through the trees.

Moments later, the dark figure of a Jasper County Sheriff's patrol sergeant, with his uniform and badge visible under his opened rain jacket, stepped out of the tree line and began walking toward the driver's side of the Explorer. Cellars noted with some degree of relief that the sergeant had reholstered his Glock . . . but kept his gloved hand firmly on the grip.

Nice gesture, but it probably wouldn't take you more than a half second to draw and put a couple of rounds right into my head, Cellars guessed. He didn't relax or move his hands from the steering wheel until the patrol sergeant came up to the side of the Explorer, leaned forward, and handed Cellars back his badge case.

"Feel free to do whatever you want with your hands. I'm Sergeant Jim Downs, Jasper County Sheriff's Department. Don't suppose you were thoughtful enough to bring along a couple extra pairs of shorts in one of those CSI kits of yours?" he added conversationally.

Cellars looked up at the uniformed officer, who still had a worried expression on his face.

"No, but it's a hell of an idea," he replied. But before he could say anything else, another chill swept up his spine as he realized that the patrol sergeant's eyes were still sweeping the surrounding tree line. Searching for . . . what?

Cellars wasn't sure he wanted to know.

CHAPTER NINE

IT WAS A MATTER OF COMMUNICATION, OR LACK THEREOF, JAS-
per County Patrol Sergeant Jim Downs explained as he introduced
his fellow deputy—a young officer named Clyde Wills, who, if anything, looked even more nervous than Downs. No one had gotten
around to notifying the other agencies in OMARR-9 about the new
OSP "Echo" designation for a civilian-clothed detective-sergeant-type
CSI officer. Typical bureaucratic screwup.

Which, in a way, was actually comforting, Cellars decided. It
was always easier to deal with known evils than to have to keep
looking over your shoulder for the ones that come out of nowhere.

"Thing is, you had that asshole Hawkins pegged dead on,"
Downs went on. "Good thing, too, or I just might have shot you
out of pure spite." Then the sound of a cracking branch caused his
head to jerk around and his hand to drop down quickly to the grip
of his holstered Glock.

They were standing together in the middle of the road next to Cellars's Explorer, the light beams from their flashlights forming slowly moving circles of intensely bright light about their boots. The lights on the two Jasper County cruisers had been turned off, and everything else around them was dark.

Jesus Christ, Downs, what the hell's the matter with you? Cellars wanted to ask. But some instinct told him to hold back. Better to let the veteran officer broach the subject on his own terms.

"I guess I ought to confess that I was only going on a lousy first impression," he said instead. "Hawkins and I got into an argument over why he refused to issue me a Region Nine master vehicle key. Is the guy really that bad?"

From Cellars's uneasy point of view, the Jasper County patrol sergeant's frank comment about an OSP captain was almost more unnerving than his visibly shaken demeanor. Not that there was anything unusual about a couple of sergeants from different agencies sharing their less-than-charitable opinions of each other's brass, Cellars reminded himself. But in his experience, such intimacy usually required a certain amount of trust based on a reasonably clear understanding of personal alignments and loyalties. That way you didn't have to worry too much about an especially candid comment coming back to haunt you someday.

But if Downs had any such concerns, they weren't evident in his words or his attitude.

"Man's a climber . . . usually over the backs of his fellow officers," the patrol sergeant responded, making no effort to mask the bitterness in his voice as his eyes continued to scan the surrounding darkness. "He used to work for us a few years back. Made it all the way to detective-sergeant in record time before he transferred over to OSP. My training sergeant—Tim Procter, hell of a good instructor, really worked at teaching new recruits their street smarts—made the mistake of being the first guy to get in his way."

"What happened to him . . . if you don't mind my asking?" Cellars added, wanting to keep Downs talking. He figured that was the only way he was going to find out what was going on around here.

"Typical chicken-shit deal. Hawkins caught him in the back of a shopping center working on a homework assignment when he was supposed to be writing a report. Got him busted down to patrolman, and then rode his ass until Tim finally said to hell with it and pulled the pin. Last I heard, he was shaking doorknobs for some drugstore chain in Medford."

"Yet another example of law enforcement wasting good training officers," Cellars commented.

"Exactly." Downs nodded in agreement. "But that's Hawkins's MO. He likes to focus on the loners. Guys who don't bother with the mentor system or ass-kissing their way up the ladder. Guys who like to be left alone to do things their own way. And once he gets you in his sights—" Downs shook his head. "Probably nothing much you can do. He's smart, no doubt about it. Word on the street is that he's looking to be the youngest major in the history of the OSP, which means, knowing Hawkins, he's gotta be looking around real serious-like for another target right about now."

"Wonderful, just what I need."

"Hey, for what it's worth, if he ever does focus in on you, you'd better watch your back—and go for his throat the first chance you get, 'cause you can bet your ass *and* your pension he'll be going for yours."

"Sounds like a hell of a guy."

"Man's a peach. Him and his stinking cigars. Hope he chokes on one of the damned things someday," Downs responded in a deadly cold voice, then quickly turned his head in the direction of another— more distant—crackling branch. "Let me put it this way: I'm real glad he's yours and not ours anymore."

"That's a real comfort." Cellars shook his head in amazement. He was beginning to get an uneasy feeling that this entire Region 9 transfer deal might have been a serious mistake on his part. And that didn't even begin to take into account the situation with Dawson . . . and Jody.

Oh yeah, Jody. He felt a familiar twinge of deep-seated guilt as he remembered his promise to call. *I ought to be getting on the phone to her right now, letting her know that Dawson didn't show.*

So what the hell am I doing here instead?

The question also reminded Cellars that he'd been sent out on this call for a reason. Time to get his mind back on business. He stuck his flashlight under his left armpit and reached into his jacket pocket for his pen and field notebook.

"These missing deputies of yours. You happen to know their names?"

"Yeah, sure. Mike Lambreau and Joe Beale."

Cellars nodded as he quickly begin to write. He'd already noted the five hash marks on the patrol supervisor's sleeve, which gave him some hope that the twenty-year veteran field supervisor might be able to put some useful perspective on the call. But it quickly became obvious that, if anything, Downs and Wills knew even less than Cellars.

"Dispatcher sent us out here to check on things when they didn't report in," the patrol sergeant explained. "Soon as we got here, the first thing we saw was two sets of tire tracks, coming and going, and a lot of blood alongside the road."

"Blood?" Cellars's head came up.

"Yeah, right over there." Downs used the beam of his flashlight to indicate a general area about twenty feet in front of the two parked cruisers.

"But no bodies or anything else suspicious?"

Cellars got the immediate impression that Downs seemed to hesitate before shaking his head.

"The tire tracks consistent with your scout cars?" Cellars asked.

"Yeah, could be." The patrol sergeant shrugged. "The way the county budget's been heading downhill the last few years, we usually end up with whatever's on sale. Kind of hard to see the tread pattern anyway with all this rain we've been having, but I guess maybe the general pattern, tire width, and wheelbase might tell you something. Suppose we could always check the garage records . . . if we really had to," he added in a softer voice.

"I'll take the measurements and photos," Cellars promised as he made a series of notations in his field journal.

"Oh hell, there ain't no need—"

"It's not a problem, I'm already out here," Cellars said, then went on before the sergeant could protest any further. "Tell me more about the blood."

"Really not much to tell, other than there's a hell of a lot of it out there. A couple of big pools, about ten feet apart, and a lot of splattering off to the right." Downs gestured with his flashlight again, this time indicating a general area to the side of the road. "Kind of hard to see in the dark. We tried to stay out of the area as best we could, just in case."

"In case of what?" Cellars paused in his note-taking again.

The two deputies glanced at each other.

"In case it turned out to be human, I guess." Downs shrugged uneasily.

"You don't think it is?"

Downs looked down at his feet and shrugged again. "I don't know. My guess is, it's probably from a couple of deer. Not exactly unheard-of around here for a fellow to jacklight a doe or two when nobody's looking, and then pack the carcasses out in his trunk."

"You think your deputies might have done something like that, figuring nobody would ever come out here to double-check the scene?"

"It's a possibility," the patrol sergeant acknowledged.

"Especially with Lambreau and Beale," Wills added.

"Yeah, that's a fact."

"Thing is, though," Cellars said, "dispatch said they found your missing cruiser down the mountain at a local bar."

Jim Downs's head came up quickly.

"Oh yeah? You remember which one?"

"Rusty Bar. Something like that."

"That's their hangout," Wills commented, which drew another frown from Downs.

"God damn their lazy, good-for-nothing hides," the patrol sergeant muttered, suddenly looking a little more relaxed as he glanced around at the surrounding tree line again. "And to think I damn near had a coronary out here, all because . . ."

"But the dispatcher didn't mention anything about finding blood on the vehicle," Cellars added.

"Doesn't necessarily mean anything."

"Yeah, that's right, rain could have washed it off," Wills added quickly.

A little too quickly, Cellars thought. It was becoming more and more obvious that the two deputies really wanted to believe in their poached deer theory.

And want me to believe too. Interesting. Especially since it stopped raining, what, over an hour ago?

"Which reminds me," Cellars went on. "Dispatch said to tell you that they want you guys to report back to the bar ASAP. I'll stay out here, look around some more, and do some CSI . . . see if I can make some sense out of those blood patterns. If I find something, I'll call it in. Oh yeah, and that reminds me of something else," he added. "You know where I can find a land line? They wanted me to report in soon as I got here."

Downs and Wills looked at each other again.

"Cabin's probably the only place around here," Downs finally said as he glanced over at the illuminated structure. "We were going to check it out, ask if we could use the phone. But it didn't look like anyone was home, and then—"

The patrol sergeant hesitated, as if uncertain about what else he could—or should—say.

"We got distracted," Clyde Wills finished helpfully.

"Oh really?" Cellars cocked his head curiously as he looked up from his notes again. "By what?"

The younger deputy blinked and his mouth dropped open. "Uh . . . the dog."

"The dog?" Cellars's eyebrows furrowed in confusion. "*What* dog?"

"Uh, well . . ." Completely in over his head now, Wills could only turn and look to his supervisor for help.

From Cellars's perspective, Jim Downs now looked thoroughly embarrassed. He started to say something, hesitated again, then glared at his younger partner before turning back to Cellars.

"We found a dead dog over there in the trees," he gestured again with the beam of his flashlight. "It wasn't any big deal. It's just that we were a little spooked when we saw all that blood, because the first thing we thought was that something had happened to Mike and Joe. But then we found the dog, and it looked like he probably got gored by one of the bucks—"

No, not bucks, Sergeant, Cellars thought. *Does. Jacklighting a couple of does. That's what you said.*

"—so we figured maybe the dog hurt one of them, then Mike and Joe showed up, spotted all the ruckus, probably tried to help the dog by shooting the deer, then decided what the hell? when they saw the dog was dead anyway, and a bunch of perfectly good deer meat was going to go to waste."

"And then we saw your headlights—" Wills added, getting caught up in the story again.

"And you know the rest," Downs added quickly. "I guess I was kinda spooked when you told us that Mike and Joe were still missing. But if they left their cruiser down at the Rusty Bar—" The patrol sergeant shrugged as if to say "what can you do?"

Which doesn't even begin to explain why you ignored my radio calls, or why you were perfectly ready to drop me if I so much as twitched before you saw my photo ID, Cellars thought but didn't say. *What the hell is going on around here?*

"Yeah, the only crime scene we have to worry about now is going to be in the watch commander's office tomorrow morning," Wills added.

"That's about it." Jim Downs smiled as if a weight had suddenly been lifted from his supervisory shoulders. "So I guess what we're saying is there's no point in your staying out here by yourself just to work a couple poached deer. Leave that sort of thing for the state game wardens."

"Yeah, you're probably right." Cellars nodded thoughtfully, deciding there wasn't much point in mentioning that state police officers in Oregon *were* the state game wardens. "But like you said, a guy like Hawkins is probably staying up nights just waiting for a new guy like me to do something stupid—like disobeying a directed CSI assignment from OMARR-Nine. All things considered, I think I'm a whole lot better off if I stay out here and do my job."

"Yeah, but if you call in and explain . . ." Downs started to say, then stopped.

Cellars nodded patiently. "That's exactly what I plan to do once I check in with the owner of that cabin."

"But what if he's not home?" Wills interjected nervously.

Cellars smiled. "That's the advantage of having a tech background . . . and the right equipment in my truck. If the owner's not home, it won't take me more than a couple minutes to patch into the phone line."

The younger deputy looked stunned.

"Hey, don't worry about it," Cellars said reassuringly. "I don't get lonely working by myself. In fact, to tell you the truth, I've gotten to the point that I kind of like it. You guys go ahead down to that bar and check in with your watch commander. I'll be fine up here. And while you're at it, when no one's looking, don't forget to take a look in the trunk of that cruiser."

"Okay, if that's the way you feel about it." The patrol sergeant had a resigned look on his face. "We'll let OMARR-Nine know you're still up here."

Cellars stood and watched as the two uniformed deputies walked toward their cruisers. As he continued to stand there, the two men began to argue in low pitched voices . . . but the faint sound of intermittent raindrops starting to strike the surrounding trees and the vehicles quickly ended the argument. As Cellars reached back into the Explorer for his rain gear, Downs accelerated around in the narrow cul-de-sac and drove off in a spray of mud and gravel.

Deputy Clyde Wills brought his cruiser around in a more careful maneuver, came to a gradual stop alongside Cellars, and rolled down his side window just as the OSP crime scene investigator was finishing putting on his protective rain gear.

"What's the matter with him?" Cellars asked as he opened up the back of the Explorer and began pulling out his thick, waterproof CSI equipment cases.

"I don't know," the young deputy answered evasively, keeping his eyes pointed in the direction of the rapidly disappearing taillights. "I guess he's still worried about Mike and Joe . . . and about leaving you here by yourself."

Cellars paused in his efforts to turn and stare curiously at the young deputy.

"And just why would he be worried about that?"

"Uh, well . . ." Wills seemed unsure about how to broach the topic. "Look, just take my word for it," he blurted out, glancing up at Cellars briefly. "You really don't *want* to be out here by yourself."

"I don't? Why not?"

A look of almost complete frustration seemed to overwhelm the young deputy as he dropped his hand onto the shift lever. For a brief moment, it looked as though Wills was going to shove his cruiser into drive and take off down the dark muddy road after his supervisor. But then something in his expression changed, and he hesitated with his hand on the shift knob, seemingly transfixed by something he expected to appear at the outer edge of his headlight beams.

"Because," he said with a catch in his voice, "the shadows around here can really start getting on your nerves."

It was a stunning admission by a young and seemingly aggressive law enforcement officer who, from Cellars's perspective, looked
muscular, well trained, and otherwise perfectly capable of dealing
with any kind of routine felony situation, with or without a partner. It also reminded him of the comment Sergeant Jim Downs had
made just before leaving his barricaded position to approach the
Explorer. The one about getting ready to have a coronary.

Cellars blinked and continued to stare at the young deputy for a
long moment.

"Listen, Wills," he finally said, "I don't want you to take this
wrong, but the thing is, I haven't been afraid of shadows since I was
a kid."

Which isn't completely true, Cellars thought, feeling a mild pang
of guilt when he remembered his reaction to the shadows on the
deck outside the county auditorium earlier that evening.

The young deputy turned his head to stare directly at Cellars,
so that his face was illuminated by the glow of the Explorer's interior lights. And for the first time, Cellars could clearly see the fear
in his eyes.

"That so?" the young officer responded nervously as he palmed
the gearshift into the drive position. "Well, just wait. After a couple
of hours out here, you will be."

CHAPTER TEN

THE DOG WAS DEAD. NO DOUBT ABOUT IT.

It had taken Cellars almost ten minutes to work his way carefully along the side of the road. Ten minutes of kneeling every few steps and using the beam of his flashlight as a guide to keep from leaving his own shoeprints in the barely visible pools of watery blood. Or in the barely visible tire tracks that looped around and then disappeared in the gravelly slush created by the departing patrol sergeant's rapidly spinning tires.

There hadn't been much in the way of scene protection. But then too, Cellars decided—as he turned his flashlight off, set it aside, switched on the small, battery-operated headlamp strapped securely to his hat, then used the much dimmer circle of light to help frame and focus his first shot—it wasn't like this really was a crime scene.

More like a canine hit-and-run, he thought, as he carefully depressed the shutter button on the high resolution digital camera.

In doing so, he never saw the discordant shadow separate itself from the thick trunk of a forty-foot fir and move toward him.

The black and thus essentially invisible shadow was less than fifteen feet away, and coming in fast, when the sudden intensely bright glare of the high-powered electronic flash unit burned the full frontal view of the sprawled malamute into Cellars's retinas.

It took a couple of seconds for the images to register.

Jesus Christ.

The hair stood up on the back of Cellars's neck.

He reacted to that subconscious warning by whirling around . . . and in doing so, accidentally hit the digital camera's shutter release with his index finger again, sending another intense burst of white light in the direction of the surrounding trees. Caught off guard by the unexpected flash, Cellars first blinked . . . then tossed the camera aside, dropped down to both knees, and grabbed for his SIG-Sauer and flashlight, certain that he had seen something move in the pattern of falling rain off to his left.

Less than a second later, he had his left arm up in a defensive position with the flashlight pointing outward, and the wrist of his right hand—the one holding the SIG—over his left, placing the semiautomatic pistol in a parallel alignment with the flashlight. As he swung the beam-guided pistol to his left in a flat arc, his finger tightened on the trigger.

But there wasn't anything there.

Cellars took another few seconds to swing the flashlight beam and aligned pistol in a full 360-degree arc.

Still nothing.

That was when the words of the frightened Jasper County deputy flashed in his mind.

Because the shadows around here can really start getting on your nerves.

Okay, I can see your point, Cellars thought ruefully as he slowly stood upright and reholstered the SIG-Sauer. It occurred to him, as he snapped the hip holster's thumb strap shut, that this was the second time this evening he'd reacted to a shadow by reaching for his gun. It wasn't an encouraging trend.

How does that old saying go? There's nothing wrong with being paranoid if they really are out to get you?

Then he remembered the camera.

He found it sticking out of the mud, right next to a large, jagged chunk of rock. Some careful wiping with a handful of tissues enabled Cellars to confirm his bleak expectations. The power switches were still locked into the ON positions, but the display screen on the back of the computer-chip-controlled electronic camera and the ready lights of the powerful flash unit were both blank.

Wait a minute, maybe—

He tried replacing all of the batteries in the camera and flash, but that didn't have any noticeable effect. Then, working on the unlikely theory that a damaged memory card just might have short-circuited the entire system, he exchanged the barely used card with a new blank one from his shirt pocket. But that didn't help either. The digital camera and strobe remained just as inert as the rock they had apparently struck.

Cellars stared down at the scarred plastic case of the expensive, high-tech camera and shook his head in disgust. He had a spare 35mm camera and flash unit in his CSI kit, along with a half dozen rolls of color film, so it wasn't a question of being out of business. It was more a matter of injured pride—a situation that wouldn't improve much when he turned in his damaged equipment report.

It took Cellars another fifteen minutes to work his way back to the Explorer, return the damaged digital camera and flash to its protective kit, then assemble and load his backup 35mm camera system. In doing so, he added a short extension tube in what would probably be a futile effort to shield the lens from the steadily increasing rain. Then, realizing that he would be in serious trouble in terms of scene documentation if he lost his backup camera too, he dug through the camera kit and came up with a rarely used neck strap that he attached to the camera body. He adjusted the neck strap so that the camera hung securely at mid-chest level.

Finally, he picked up his flashlight again and readjusted the focal ring.

Okay, he thought, *enough of this bullshit. Now where was I?*

Oh yeah, the dog.

This time, the tightly focused beam of light revealed the enormity of the malamute's terrible wounds.

Beneath the rain-matted fur, Cellars could clearly see where the dog's chest had been torn open—a three-inch crevice at the widest point—revealing ripped intestines, splintered ribs, a lung partially severed from its brachial tube, and a red mass that looked to be the remains of his heart. The malamute's eyes were wide-open, and its teeth were bared in what might have started out to be a fearsome snarl . . . before the loyal and protective creature realized what it was confronting.

Buck deer, my ass.

Cellars examined the wounds more closely, noting the sharp cuts through the skin and organs, and the presence of mud and gravel deep in the chest cavity. An interesting observation, he decided as he took a couple of quick close-up photos with the flash held out to the side and below the camera to get more light into the wound, because the dog was facing away from the road.

Kind of hard for a car to spray rocks into a wound like that when the dog's facing the wrong way. So what does that mean? Cellars used his flashlight to examine the surrounding blood splatters more closely. *The dog flipped over after it was dead, and after the departing cruisers of the two missing deputies sprayed the mud and gravel into the wound?*

Deciding there had to be a more logical sequence of events, Cellars carefully retraced his steps back to the Explorer. There, he unpacked the small, hand-calculator-sized TOD device that his inventor buddy, Malcolm Byzor, cheerfully described as his patented vampire gauge.

The installation of a 9-volt battery brought the device to life. Cellars set the display screen to Carcass #1, the scanning timer to AUTO, and then he carefully removed the plastic caps protecting the three sharp inch-and-a-half-long probes and the external air temperature sensors. Another keyed-in command zeroed the instrument.

Finally satisfied that all was well—at least with this particular piece of equipment—he carefully worked his way back through the increasingly slippery mud and knelt beside the dog again. He used the tips of his rubber-gloved fingers to find the largest muscle mass on the animal's exposed hindquarter. Then he firmly pressed the device against the dog's hind leg until the three hypodermic needle–like probes were completely buried into the solidified tissue. Once he was satisfied that the device was securely in place, he thumbed the START switch. A series of red numerals started to flash across the small screen as the computer-chip-controlled device began to measure and compare the cooling rate of the muscle tissue against the ambient air temperature.

Malcolm Byzor had designed the TOD gauge to calculate the approximate time of death for illegally poached deer, then store up to a dozen such calculations in its internal RAM chip. The device had proven to be accurate within a plus-or-minus-five-minute window over the first eight-to-ten hours, much to the dismay of Oregon deer hunters, who could no longer depend on their gift of gab and the known variability of *rigor mortis* to talk their way out of an early-hours shooting ticket. There was a lot more muscle mass on a deer, but Cellars figured the device ought to work reasonably well for a dog too. Assuming, of course, that the cooling rate factors for dog tissue were reasonably close to those of deer, and that the dog was still cooling down and hadn't already stabilized to the surrounding temperature.

Satisfied that he had done all that he could for the moment with the dog, Cellars left the device in place and went about the process of photographing and collecting samples from four of the largest of the surrounding blood pools.

It was difficult work. Each sample required the placement of a sequentially numbered, dated, and initialed bright yellow plastic evidence locator tag; a close-up photo in addition to the overall shots; and the appropriate notations on his scene sketch and collection notes. Only then was he able carefully to absorb the blood—along with as little water as possible—onto a clean one-inch-by-one-inch square of white cloth. To accomplish all of this, he had to switch back and forth from his camera and pen, and then repeatedly clean a pair of Teflon-coated forceps before absorbing the next sample. The dark mud and reflective drops, puddles, and streams of water effectively concealed a great deal of the partially coagulated blood in the area surrounding the dog, so Cellars ended up taking several more samples than he might have otherwise.

In doing so, he discovered some small chips of what looked like bone partially buried in the mud . . . which required more tags and photos and properly labeled collection envelopes.

Twice during the long process, he thought he spotted another flickering black shadow. The first time, he swept the area again with his flashlight and found nothing. The second time, he simply ignored the tingling sensation down the back of his neck and went back to work.

In better weather conditions, Cellars might have clipped the stained cloth squares onto the locator tag to air-dry while he worked other areas of the scene, then placed them in individual manila envelopes. But the rain would have leached most of the blood out of the squares long before they dried, so he had to carefully place each square in an open glass vial so that it could air-dry. And then mark each vial so that he could later associate the blood sample with a correctly labeled envelope.

All of that took more time.

He was transferring the last of the twelve cloth squares into a wide-mouthed vial—working slowly and carefully not to get any blood materials on the outside of the vial where it might contaminate other evidence items—when he happened to glance down at his watch.

Cellars blinked in surprise.

Oh shit, I was supposed to have called in over an hour ago.

He stepped back away from the Explorer and looked around. The heavy raindrops were still falling, creating a muted hissing in the background that effectively blocked out most of the other forest sounds. The drops were still intermittent, but they seemed to be increasing in size and intensity.

Another dilemma in the making.

Cellars wanted to believe that Downs and Wills—the two patrolling Jasper County deputies—had reported in to the OMARR-9 dispatcher as soon as they got back into radio contact. And in doing so, had advised anyone who might care to know that OSP Detective-Sergeant Colin Cellars was out here by himself and doing just fine, thank you. That being the case, he just might be able to finish working the scene before the infamous Oregon rain started up again in earnest and wiped out any remaining evidence of the two missing deputies. But at the same time, he knew better than to ignore a primary safety directive, especially one that could easily result in yet another officer being dispatched to the far north end of County Road 2255 to see if everything was okay.

Yeah, wouldn't old Hawkins just love to hear about something like that?

Then he remembered how the Jasper County patrol sergeant had left the scene. Like the veteran officer couldn't wait to put some distance between himself and Cellars, both physically and officially.

Because I embarrassed him.

Embarrassed both of them for that matter.

So what were the chances that Sergeant Jim Downs, legitimately concerned about two of his missing deputies, and thoroughly embarrassed over his own failure to make a land line check-in to OMARR-9, would go to any serious effort to cover for an OSP trooper?

Sighing to himself, Cellars repacked the camera, flash unit, and CSI gear, put the heavy CSI kits back into the Explorer, collected and repacked the TOD device, and spent several minutes filling a backpack with several items of his more specialized electronic gear. Then he switched on his flashlight again and started walking toward the dark mass of trees and brush that stood between the road and the barely visible silhouette of the distant cabin.

CHAPTER ELEVEN

A SHOULDER-WIDE GAP BETWEEN TWO HUGE DOUGLAS FIR trees turned into a narrow, well-worn pathway cut through tightly packed brush that looped around to the right, made two sharp lefts, and then dead-ended in a head-high mass of blackberry vines.

As Cellars retraced his steps back to the last turn, he located a substantially narrower gap between a double-trunked scrub oak that opened up into a continuation of the pathway. He had to remove his pack to squirm through the gap, but the new path remained shoulder-wide until the second right turn, where it dead-ended again.

All the while, the crackling sounds of breaking branches somewhere in the surrounding darkness continued to force him to stop and wait and listen.

It wasn't until the third cut-back, when Cellars found himself facing yet another seemingly impassable barrier of thorny blackberry vines, brush, and tightly clumped evergreens, and impatiently started to turn back and retrace his steps again, that it occurred to him what he might have walked into.

A carefully worked out maze.

Moments later, he had the backpack off again and was down on his hands and knees, scraping away a thick matting of pine needles.

"Well, I'll be damned," he whispered to himself as the flashlight beam reflected off the bright green plastic tie-tag that read: Fogelman's Nursery. He shifted the flashlight around, searching for other such labels in the clustered arc of eight-to-ten-foot young evergreens, then blinked in surprise when the light beam reflected off what appeared to be a series of roughly parallel lines.

A minute or two of careful maneuvering revealed five strands of anodized barbed wire—almost invisible against the dark browns and greens of the surrounding flora—looped around the thicker tree trunks and secured with heavy-duty staples to form a supporting web that kept the natural barricade of evergreens and tightly packed brush in place.

Cellars immediately shut off his flashlight and remained there, crouched and immobile in the darkness, until he was reasonably certain that the intermittent crackling noises emanating from the surrounding forest were still occurring in a reasonably random manner.

As he did so, one word kept flashing through his mind.

Trap.

It took Cellars five more minutes, working slowly and carefully, to remove his night-vision goggles and an infrared-filtered flashlight lens from his backpack, install the new lens, and secure the twin-tubed goggles over his face. This time, when he turned his flashlight back on, the resulting bright green beam lit up the surrounding brush and trees . . . and more importantly, exposed a movable portion of the barrier that led into another narrow pathway. This one ran for a good thirty feet in a straight line before turning right in the direction of the cabin.

Far more wary now, Cellars moved forward one slow and cautious step at a time with the IR-filtered flashlight in his left hand and the .40-caliber SIG-Sauer in his right.

In spite of the enhanced vision provided by his night-vision goggles, Cellars still wouldn't have seen the trap if his eyes hadn't already been conditioned by the discovery of the straight-lined segments of barbed wire. As it was, the thin strand of fishing line stretched across the pathway—approximately five feet above and parallel to a pair of three-inch-diameter branches lying across the pathway—was barely visible, even when he touched it with his gloved hand.

Nice, he thought. *Very nice indeed. Low enough to catch most humans right across the head, but high enough so that most animals would walk right under it . . . especially with their heads down and sniffing while they felt their way across the logs. And I would have walked right into it because I was already ticked-off and impatient from hitting the first three dead ends.*

The important question: What was at the end of the line, an alarm or a device?

A quick but cautious search revealed that one end of the fishing line was tied around a tree trunk, and the other ran through a small pulley nailed to the opposite tree before disappearing into the forest. Cellars tried to follow the line with the beam of his flashlight, but finally gave up when he realized that he'd have to leave the relative safety of the pathway and work his way through the tangle of branches, rocks, brush, and tree trunks to get the answer.

Yeah, right. And stumble right into a bunch of treble hooks. I don't think so.

He paused to consider his options.

Everything about this entire situation—the remote location, the isolated cabin, the trip wire, not to mention all the money and effort that had been put into funneling unexpected guests into one easily controlled and monitored pathway—strongly suggested a dope lab or a pot ranch. And if that was the case, Cellars reminded himself, treble hooks hanging at eyeball level, sharpened *punji* sticks in dug-out footfalls, and more trip wires leading to home-made claymore mines armed with nails and dynamite might be the least of his problems. He could also be walking in on a bunch of paranoid drug dealers strung out on home-brewed methamphetamine and clutching military assault rifles in their sweaty, trembling hands.

Which could easily explain the two missing deputies, and the torn-open dog. But not the abandoned and empty cruiser at the Rusty Bar. Or the fact that no one had gone after Downs and Wills when they were at the scene.

Unless the pot growers or crank-heads were long gone before they arrived, Cellars reasoned, *in which case all I have to do is be careful.*

It took Cellars almost ten minutes to reach the end of the narrow, winding, man-made trail, during which time he'd been forced to pause twice to work himself around similarly rigged trip wires. Once there, he stood motionless at the edge of the tree line for another minute, searching every inch of the visible cabin exterior with the night-vision goggles and IR-filtered flashlight beam for any sign of movement.

Nothing moved. Or at least nothing that he could see.

Then, when he finally couldn't think of anything else to do, he removed the night-vision goggles, put the normal, unfiltered lens back on his flashlight, placed all the gear back into his backpack, then stepped away from the protective cover of the trees and approached the cabin.

———

From the moment he stepped onto the dark wooden porch, Cellars had the sense that the cabin was empty. But even so, he made a point of moving slowly, and watching where he placed his feet, as he worked his way over to the left side of the front doorframe.

Once he had the left side of his body pressed firmly against the rough log wall of the cabin, Cellars placed the SIG-Sauer in a protective ready-to-fire position against his chest. Thus prepared, he reached across with his left hand to pound the back end of his flashlight sharply against the thick wooden door, and yelled out:

"OREGON STATE PATROL. IS ANYONE AT HOME?"

He paused and waited, listening intently for the sound of voices or footsteps.

Nothing.

He tried again.

"THIS IS THE OREGON STATE PATROL. I REPEAT, IS ANYONE AT HOME?"

Still nothing.

Okay, be that way.

Alert for the first sound of movement, Cellars extended the flashlight as far away from his body as possible, brought his gun hand up to the left side of his face to protect his eyesight, and thumbed the light on.

After the muted greens of the night-vision goggles, the bright white glare of the flashlight beam was nearly blinding. But Cellars forced himself to keep his eyes open as he swung the beam—and the .40-caliber SIG-Sauer—around in a rapid 180-degree arc and quickly back again.

No wide-eyed druggies, no dogs, no moving shadows.

Nothing.

After breathing a sigh of relief, Cellars carefully worked his way off the porch and around to the far right—west—side of the cabin. As he did so, he immediately became aware that the ground sloped sharply downward at a thirty-to-forty-degree angle, and that the cabin was actually a two-story structure with a top floor and a basement that opened to the rear.

There were steps leading down to a small door at the northwest corner of the basement, but the door was shut—and presumably locked. He continued to move downhill in a steady and careful manner, consciously digging his heels into the soft earth to keep from slipping as he held the SIG-Sauer in a ready-to-fire position over his left wrist, the barrel aligned parallel to the flashlight beam.

It was only as he approached the back door and saw the exposed wood that he realized the bolt latch mechanism had been ripped loose from the doorframe. The door itself was hanging partially open.

Bingo. Just what I needed: some probable cause.

After making a quick sweep with the flashlight beam across the tree line that surrounded the back of the cabin, Cellars quickly adjusted the lens to a wider focus and positioned himself so that his right shoulder and hip were pressed against the rough log wall. From that position, he slowly moved his right foot forward and cautiously nudged the broken door. The hinges squeaked in protest, but he continued on until most of his right shoe was within the doorframe. Then, in one single movement, he swung the door open with his foot, yelled, "POLICE!" and lunged into the room with the flashlight beam and SIG-Sauer sweeping the room in unison.

The first thing he saw in the flash of diffused light was the overturned easel, chair, and stretched canvas lying in disarray on a ten-by-sixteen-foot rug lying in the middle of the twenty-five-by-forty-or-so wooden plank floor.

Then the dark stains on the rug . . . and all of the guns hanging from pegs all along the log walls.

And then, as he continued to swing his flashlight to the right, a sprawled body lying on its back next to a large dark stain.

Cellars's heart sank.

It was going to be a very long night.

CHAPTER TWELVE

THE LAND LINE CALL-IN OPTION TURNED OUT TO BE A MOOT POINT. The telephone line to the cabin had been cut and removed between the second and third utility poles, leaving a one-foot section dangling at the top of each pole. The rest of the line was nowhere in sight.

Cellars made that discovery after spending almost fifteen minutes trying to get a dial tone—first from one of the phone outlets inside the cabin, then from the outside utility box. And he didn't have pole-climbing cleats or a chain saw in his vehicle, which effectively narrowed his options down to two:

The first was tempting. He could leave everything the way it was, get into his Explorer, and drive back down the mountain to get help. But in doing so, he would lose at least an hour of valuable time, not to mention control of the scene, and the body. Or he could work his way back to the road, get into his Explorer, take out his CSI kits, haul everything back to the cabin, and do what he got paid to do . . . which was work the crime scene.

Unfortunately, it wasn't much of a choice, which didn't do much to improve Cellars's rapidly failing sense of humor.

However, on the way back to the Explorer, he did discover that the trip lines had been rigged as alarms—actually connected to a series of cowbells hung on the cabin basement ceiling—rather than booby traps, which was actually reassuring in an odd sort of way.

At least I'm not going to have to worry about running into one of the damned things and blowing my ass off, he thought, gasping for breath as he stumbled out of the tree line toward the cabin for the third time that evening. In addition to being heavy, the waterproof cases were awkward in the narrow pathways, and tended to catch on closely interwoven tree branches, especially when he tried to carry one in each hand and a smaller one under one arm.

On the previous trip, he'd carried two of the cases and the flashlight with his left hand and arm while keeping the SIG-Sauer out and ready in his right. It had seemed, at first, a reasonable precaution, given all the bizarre circumstances of the evening so far. But four exhausting trips through that long, narrow, winding, and increasingly slippery maze was at least one more than Cellars thought he was up to on this particular evening. So on the final run, he'd returned the SIG-Sauer to its holster and resorted to the much dimmer headlamp as a source of light in order to keep both hands free for carrying and tugging.

Besides, whoever shot that poor bastard is probably long gone . . . just like those missing deputies.

It was a thought that caused Cellars to pause in reflection, as well as to catch his breath.

Course, for all I know, it could have been the deputies who did the shooting. The missing ones or *the follow-up pair. Which would certainly explain the way Downs and Wills acted when I showed up unexpectedly.*

All of that was assuming, of course, that a bullet had, in fact, ended the victim's life. The basement was full of guns, there were several apparent bullet holes in the log walls, and the room still smelled of burned gunpowder. But the face of the victim—a middle-aged male with shoulder-length blondish gray hair in excellent physical condition, apart from being dead—had been torn into an unrecognizable mess. And the patterning of the blood spatters that covered the nearby internal utility wall and the surrounding wood flooring had looked a lot more like the results of a small explosion, or a very severe beating, than impacting bullets.

Or maybe a very severe beating followed by a shooting by a pair of deputies who lost control of the situation? Or just simply lost control, period?

Whatever the case, it was going to make for some interesting explanations once the Jasper County Sheriff's Department found their missing deputies, Cellars decided as he stacked his hard-won CSI equipment kits together outside the south door of the basement and looked around uneasily at the surrounding tree-filled darkness.

The idea of a pair of rogue deputies roaming around loose—and possibly very directly concerned about what a lone OSP sergeant might find during an unexpected crime scene search—was making Cellars a lot more uneasy than the intermittent forest noises. Especially since he was now depending on Sergeant Downs and Deputy Wills to notify OMARR-9 as to his status at the scene.

Be interesting to know the approximate time of death on this guy, and how that matches up to their arrival at the scene, Cellars thought. *Especially if those other two deputies stay missing for a while.*

With that thought in mind, Cellars took the necessary few minutes to unpack the TOD device again, clean off the probes, reset the display to read Carcass #2, and verify that the timer was still set on AUTO. He slipped a small pair of sharp scissors into his shirt pocket, stood up, and started toward the body, when a loose board under his foot creaked.

But the sound also sounded a great deal like a squeaky hinge, a thought that immediately sent a chill racing up Cellars's spine. He whirled around in the direction of the south basement door, his eyes widening and his left hand coming around in a deflecting motion as his right hand closed around the rubberized grip of the SIG-Sauer. But even as he instinctively dropped down into a more stable and defensible kneeling position—his right knee on the edge of the dark rug and the elbow of his left arm braced against his ribs—as he centered the pistol sights on the doorway, he knew there wasn't anyone there.

Just a loose nail.

Nice going, Cellars, he thought as he lowered the pistol and took in a couple of deep, steadying breaths. *A couple more knee-jerk reactions like that and you're going to end up being a prime candidate for a rubber room, just like Downs and Wills.*

But even so, he remained where he was for a few more seconds, listening and waiting for his pulse and respiration rates to steady, before he finally returned the semiautomatic pistol to its hip holster.

Then, still muttering to himself, he knelt beside the body, readjusted the headlamp to a closer focus, and reached into his pocket for the scissors. The sharp blades sliced through the thick denim easily, creating a four-inch square flap that he folded back to reveal a patch of pale white hairy thigh. After probing with his fingers to confirm that he was well clear of bone, he firmly pushed the sharp probes of the TOD device deep into the victim's congealed thigh muscle.

Okay, Malcolm, he thought as he switched on the device, *one more set of calibration values for you to calculate. If you can make this thing work for a deer, then you ought to be able to make it work for a dog and a human. Give you something else to do instead of worrying about my technical orientation.*

That task out of the way, and still feeling far more exposed than he cared to, Cellars decided the next item of business on the agenda would be to get the lights in the cabin turned on. After that, a few overall photos to document the condition of the scene as close to the time of the incident as possible, and a quick cursory search for any fragile or perishable evidence that might need special attention. And then, when all of that was done, he'd begin the long, laborious process of sketching the scene and locating, documenting, marking, packaging, and tagging all of the relevant evidence items.

All the while keeping his eyes and ears open for the ever-possible return of the suspect.

After readjusting his flashlight to a tighter beam, Cellars began to search the basement cautiously, using the beam to try to keep from disturbing or destroying any more evidence than he had already unknowingly done with his initial entry when he had first tried to find a working light switch.

He wasn't any more successful on his second attempt. After locating four nonfunctional light switches, he turned his attention to the wall outlets . . . and got exactly the same result. Nothing. He redirected his search to the electrical panel where he discovered that all of the circuit breakers and the main breaker switch were in their proper ON positions, but the two 120-volt lines branching out from the 240-volt feeder cable were both dead. A trip back outside revealed a nonfunctioning electrical meter . . . which, in turn, finally led him to the answer when he worked his way back to the service utility pole at the end of the road and focused his flashlight on the barrel-like step-down transformer mounted just below the crossbar. The fuse holder connecting the transformer to the main electrical distribution lines was empty.

Cellars's first thought was that the fuse must have been blown out by a lightning strike. But a quick search of the area around the base of the pole failed to reveal any fuse or fuse fragments, and another quick check with the flashlight revealed that the lightning arrester—mounted on the opposite side of the transformer from the fuse holder—was still intact. It was only then, as he continued to search around the transformer with the flashlight beam, that he realized that two of the three lines to the house were also missing.

Okay, so much for the lightning theory. Pretty obvious that somebody deliberately removed the fuse, and then cut and made off with the two power feed lines. But why would anybody go to all that trouble just to cut power to a single residence when it was a hell of a lot easier just to shut down the main breaker switch in the distribution box, then pull out the individual circuit breakers?

No reason Cellars could think of, other than an irrational—and unlikely—desire to make the responding crime scene investigator's life more difficult, a theory which even he had to admit was carrying paranoia to unreasonable lengths. And besides, in spite of his growing frustration with this increasingly bizarre scene, he really couldn't think of a single reason why a murderer would take the time to be that clever or malicious.

But whatever the case, restoring electrical power to the cabin was definitely out of the question. One, because he didn't have the proper wire. And two, because even if he could find the missing segments, he wasn't about to risk frying his ass by trying to rig a fuse bypass on a hot distribution line carrying what had to be a minimum of four thousand volts.

Even if I knew how to do it safely and had the right equipment. Which I don't, thank God.

Cellars continued to stare up at the empty fuse holder for a long moment before finally shaking his head and forcing himself to focus on the issue at hand.

Okay, so much for a better light source. Just means I've got to be careful with my flashlight batteries. Only one extra set in the truck. Better get going.

The next step was to make a cursory search of the scene, in order to locate and protect the most fragile evidence. But as Cellars knew all too well, at that stage of the investigation, the people most likely to damage or destroy the evidence were the other officers at the scene. And since it wasn't likely that there would be any other officers showing up in this isolated part of the county for the next few hours, he figured scene control wouldn't be much of a problem.

Accordingly, Cellars made the perfectly logical decision to shoot the overall photos at the same time he conducted his search for evidence, combining two jobs into one, and thereby—ideally—getting everything done before sunrise.

It took only a few moments, with the flashlight held awkwardly under his arm, to reassemble his backup camera system. Then, deciding that he'd better be careful with his batteries, he turned the flashlight off and set it aside. Comfortable with the familiar feel of his equipment, he flicked the power switch of the flash unit to ON and was kneeling beside the camera case, reaching around for the diffuser to go over the flash lens before he set the flash to maximum power, when he realized that the thyristor was powering up awfully slowly.

Uh-oh, better start out with new batteries.

He had the whining flash unit in his hand, getting ready to turn it off and replace the batteries, when he heard what sounded like a soft shuffling noise over in the far northwest corner of the dark basement near the smaller northwest exit door. He jerked his head around and started to reach for his flashlight, but immediately realized it was too far away. So instead, he hit the shutter button on the camera.

The intense burst of white light that, for a brief instant, lit up the otherwise dark basement caused Cellars to blink . . . but his eyes had already started to widen in shock as his brain processed and identified two fleeting images on the far wall to his right: a dark shadow, and an old-fashioned revolver coming halfway out of its wall-hung holster.

Reacting instinctively, Cellars flung the camera and flash aside and reached for his own holstered pistol as he screamed, "FREEZE RIGHT THERE!"

But by the time he had his SIG-Sauer up at eye level in a two-handed grip, the basement was completely dark again, and the two images—along with his night-adapted vision—were long gone.

At that moment, he heard the sharp CLICK of a hammer being drawn back to its full-cock position.

Oh shit.

Without truly realizing what he was doing, Cellars centered his two hands on the apparent direction of the sound and tightened his index finger around the trigger. The SIG-Sauer roared, sending a .40-caliber copper-jacketed bullet streaking across the basement as the heavy semiautomatic pistol recoiled sharply in his hands.

Cellars hardly noticed the recoil. He was too busy reacting to the billowing white flash that seared his retinas, and the incredibly loud concussion that felt like a pair of ice picks piercing his eardrums. But even so, he still heard the incredibly high-pitched and definitely inhuman scream that erupted from the far corner of the basement—then a loud gunshot, a loud clattering sound, and an oddly quiet clattering sound—as he continued to center and squeeze the trigger. Three more eye-blinding-and-ear-jarring explosions sent three more .40-caliber hollow-points ripping through wood, glass, and plasterboard at hip to chest level.

Immediately after the fourth shot, knowing he was dangerously exposed, Cellars rolled to his right on the hard basement floor. From a prone position, he sent two more hollow-points into the basement corner, high and low, then immediately twisted back to his left.

He lay there with the SIG-Sauer extended out in both hands, only vaguely hearing the metallic ricocheting of the expended brass cartridges over the severe ringing in his ears as his flash-blinded eyes searched desperately for a target—or any movement at all—in the almost-total darkness.

Six gone, one in the chamber, three in the magazine. Two and two, then you've got to reload, he reminded himself, reluctant to reload if he didn't have to because the sound of the magazine release would be audible throughout the enclosed basement.

But other than the severe ringing, and the shadows of six bright flashes still etched on his retinas, he saw and heard nothing.

He remained in that prone position, arms extended out, finger tight on the trigger, breathing softly and moving only his eyes, as he mentally counted out a hundred seconds.

Still nothing.

Every instinct told him to remain where he was—flat on the wooden plank floor, minimally exposed, and ideally invisible—and let his opponent make the next move. But after another hundred-second count, Cellars finally convinced himself that he had to do something. So, moving as slowly and quietly as he possibly could, he reluctantly released his two-handed grip on the SIG-Sauer and used his left hand to lever himself up to a kneeling position while keeping the pistol out and ready in his right.

It took him almost another five minutes, moving slowly and carefully on his hands and knees and trying very hard not to make a single sound, to locate his flashlight. Once he had it in his hand, he slowly stood up with the pistol ready to fire. Then he extended the flashlight out and away from his body at about chest level, aligned the flashlight and pistol in what he believed was the direction of the northwest basement corner, and switched the flashlight on.

The idea of this basic police tactic was that anyone in the basement with murder in mind would immediately fire at or below the flashlight beam, which would give Cellars about one second to return fire before the assailant discovered his or her mistake.

The flashlight beam missed the corner by a few feet to the left. He quickly readjusted, painting the corner with the light beam as he tensed against an expected bullet. But the corner was empty. Or at least as much of it as he could see.

He knew he had already exposed his position, so he quickly scrambled out onto the rug and lunged forward onto the smooth wood planks. As he did so, he rolled the flashlight away from his body—with the beam pointing toward the narrow corridor—then twisted around in a parallel position to the west wall with the SIG-Sauer extended out, ready to shoot.

But the corridor was empty.

Uh-oh.

Realizing that he had been effectively deafened by the shrill ringing in his ears, and probably wouldn't have heard anyone moving around into a flanking position, Cellars quickly whipped the flashlight beam around. He tensed again as the light beam swept through the basement, expecting to see some deranged soul lunge up with the old-fashioned revolver in his hand at any moment.

But he completed the 360-degree turn without seeing any movement at all.

It occurred to him, then, that the suspect must have escaped into the kitchen or bathroom area on the other side of the cabin's interior utility wall.

Shit, how am I going to get back around there without him seeing me coming?

He did it by quickly turning the flashlight off, then—intent on staying as low to the floor as possible—slowly and cautiously crawling his way back across the rug and overturned easel in the direction of the body until his hand brushed against the victim's leg. From that position, he was able to reach out and feel the interior utility wall. It took him a few moments to work himself into an upright position, using the wall as a shield.

Then, with his left hand extended out and away from his body as far as possible, Cellars switched his flashlight on with his left thumb and swept the beam to his right, around the stairwell and into the bed and dresser area in the far northeast corner of the basement.

Nothing.

Reassured that he wouldn't have someone coming up behind his back, Cellars quickly swung the flashlight beam to his left to search the open kitchen area. After verifying that the kitchen area was unoccupied, he finally—and ever so slowly and carefully—worked his way in through the first door to the double-entrance bathroom area.

It too was empty.

Must have gone back the other way. Shit.

Cellars realized, then, that the interior utility wall effectively made the basement into a circular track. He quickly turned off his flashlight.

Great. Now what? We could end up following each other around in a circle all night in this damned place.

He forced himself to remain calm.

Okay, we can circle forever, but eventually, one of us is going to step on a loose board . . . so it might as well be him.

Working as carefully as he could, Cellars slowly pulled the far bathroom door open, set himself with his left shoulder tight against the left doorframe, slipped his badge case out of his belt with his left hand, and then tossed it out to his left in the narrow corridor.

The badge clattered noisily on the wooden plank.

But there was no other sound of movement.

Then, steeling himself for the shot, he quickly switched his flashlight on again, and swept the beam through the narrow corridor to his left. As he did so, he immediately saw a discarded cap-and-ball revolver lying on the floor next to the small exit door. He quickly checked the door and discovered that it was bolted shut from the inside.

What the hell?

As he moved cautiously out into the narrow corridor, Cellars observed a shattered window, what looked like fresh blood splattered against the adjoining wall, and the splintered impact points of three of the .40-caliber hollow-point slugs in the basement wallboard just below the window frame. He played the flashlight beam across the floor, and located, as well as dozens of pieces of broken glass, two of the mushroomed slugs, and what looked like a small gray stone.

But no suspect.

It took Cellars another five minutes to verify that he was alone in the basement. The methodical search finally brought him back to the broken window in the northwest corner of the basement.

About two thirds of the windowpane had been blown out, leaving an irregular hole that was too small for a human but plenty big enough for a small animal like—what? A house cat? Bobcat? Raccoon?

He tried to remember exactly how the inhuman scream had sounded, and the actual shape of that chilling dark shadow. Feline-like? More like what he imagined a startled cougar might look and sound like, Cellars decided, but that didn't make any sense.

For one thing, the hole in the window was too small for a cougar to escape through. And besides, he reminded himself, a cougar wouldn't—and in fact, couldn't—reach for a gun. At least not in any meaningful way.

Must have been a raccoon.

A raccoon would explain the impression he had that someone was pulling the old-fashioned revolver out of the holster. A raccoon could have been sitting on the wooden shelf next to the holster and playing with the revolver grip when Cellars triggered the flash. A raccoon could have pulled the revolver out of the holster, then dropped it, causing it to go off.

But how would a single action revolver go off accidentally if it wasn't cocked?

Some portion of Cellars's subconscious warned him that he was trying to rationalize something he simply didn't understand. But he decided to ignore the warning and worry about the problem at some later date. At the moment, he had far more pressing concerns.

Like how I'm going to explain six shots fired at an unverified target right in the middle of a homicide crime scene, he thought as he quickly reloaded the SIG-Sauer with a full ten-round magazine. He slid the partially loaded magazine into his left hip pocket, holstered the weapon, and used the flashlight to search for his discarded camera and flash.

He found them next to the door. The lens of the flash was shattered, and the force of the impact had caused the relatively heavy 6-volt battery to break through its trapdoor plastic closure in the base of the camera. Using his headlamp as a light source, and pieces of evidence tape to hold the flash lens and battery closure in place, Cellars managed to get everything reassembled, but it turned out to be a wasted effort. Both of the computer-chip-controlled devices were dead.

Great, he thought as he repackaged the camera and flash, set the sealed case outside the doorway, and looked around at his other neatly aligned CSI kits. *Now what am I going to do for a camera?*

At that moment, it occurred to Cellars that one of the heavy waterproof cases looked out of place. He stood there for a moment, blinking in confusion.

Then a flash of recognition made him smile.

CHAPTER THIRTEEN

TRUE TO THE LINEAR THINKING OF ITS INVENTOR, THE MALCOLM Byzor Model 7 Crime Scene Scanner was a virtual model of efficient design, labeling, and packaging.

Underneath a Velcro-sealed protective cover on one side of the deep, double-sided shipping case, Cellars discovered a dozen identical electronic devices labeled "Laser-Source/Sensor." They looked, to any casual observer, like someone had mounted half of a blue-green Ping-Pong ball to the face of a small, rectangular aluminum box the size of a deck of cards. The twelve devices were fitted into foam-core slots in a three-by-four grid. Apart from the snap-open nine-volt battery enclosures on the back sides, all twelve devices were completely devoid of any other lights, dials, buttons, or anything that even remotely resembled an ON/OFF switch.

Under an identical Velcro-sealed cover on the other side of the case, Cellars found a thirteenth device. This one was identical to the other twelve in all outward respects except for the box and hemi-sphere being about three times the size, a label that said "Primary Receiver," a recessed OFF/ON switch on the base, and about twelve feet of shielded cable that was connected to the back of a new 600 Mhz Mac PowerBook computer.

Cellars shook his head in amazement as he stared at the state-of-the art computer.

Jeez, Malcolm, you really do know how to spend the government's money, don't you?

The powerful notebook computer came with a built-in Zip drive, an AC adapter, an extra rechargeable 15-volt lithium-ion battery, twenty-four blank 2-gig Zip disks, a roll of wide double-sided tape, a separate cardboard box containing thirty 9-volt batteries, and a pair of protective goggles. Like the other devices, these components were all clearly marked with bright green letters and symbols as to iden-tity, function, and connectivity.

No wonder you don't have time to pay attention to your wife's nightgowns, Cellars thought as he peeled open a Velcro enclosure la-beled MANUAL. *You're too busy playing with little bitty stencils and cans of spray paint.*

The manual turned out to be four single-spaced pages of instruc-tions and two more of self-explanatory diagrams, most of which— to Cellars's amazement—were fairly easy to follow.

According to the instructions, a single fully charged nine-volt battery would power the miniaturized blue-green lasers in each of the Laser-Source/Sensors for three hours—sufficient scan time for twelve rooms if the operator followed the recommended minimum of fifteen minutes per room. The idea was to mount the Laser-Source/Sensors on the walls and ceiling—using squares of double-sided tape—in such a manner that every relevant area or item in the room was in a clear line of sight of at least two of the devices. Simple enough in concept, but proper communication and linkage be-tween the devices also required each unit to be in line of sight of at least two other units and the Primary Receiver. That particular device, Cellars noted, took four of the rectangular nine-volt batteries.

Once all of the devices were properly aligned and communicating with each other, the Primary Receiver would signal the computer to set the time/scan interval and begin scanning. According to the instructions, the end result would be a three-dimensional electronic replica of the room and contents, accurate to plus or minus a tenth of a millimeter, and viewable—with or without a reference grid in the background—from all sides of the room and in all three dimensions. The resulting 3-D image could be viewed on the PowerBook screen, or—if everything was properly aligned, the instructions noted—as a reverse projection in a room of at least the same size.

Cellars was impressed.

There was a long section starting at the end of the third page that explained how the computer program would overlap scan feeds from each device at thirty-second intervals to determine the most accurate three-dimensional fix for each data point. The details might have been interesting to another electrical engineer or computer geek, Cellars decided, but he really didn't care how the scanner worked. Only that it did. The details of how and why could wait for a less stressful rainy day.

As it turned out, getting the Laser-Source/Sensors properly aligned in the dark was the tricky part. It took Cellars almost an hour and about forty squares of double-sided tape before the switched-on Primary Receiver finally signaled the PowerBook computer that the devices were linked and communicating. The computer responded by displaying the message:

LSS UNITS INSTALLED: 12

LSS UNITS LINKED: 12

LSS UNITS NOT RESPONDING: 0

SYSTEM READY.

WARNING: HIGH POWER LASER SCAN HAZARDOUS TO
VISION
DO NOT OPERATE SYSTEM WITHOUT PROTECTIVE GOGGLES!
PRESS ENTER KEY TO BEGIN SCAN

Okay, Malcolm, let's see if seven really is your lucky number.

After making sure the goggles were securely in place over his
eyes, Cellars knelt outside the south doorway to the basement and
pressed the laptop's ENTER key.

The results were visually dramatic.

In the first instant, dozens of crisscrossing thin blue-green lines
burst out of one large and twelve small plastic hemispheres, visually
connecting the LSS units to the Primary Receiver and each other.
Then, as Cellars watched in fascination, twelve cones of bright blue-
green light began to sweep across the room in a seemingly frantic
and randomized manner.

The flashing light show continued for almost fifteen seconds.
Then, without warning, the entire system suddenly shut off.

Now what the hell?

To no great surprise, Cellars quickly discovered that the Mac
PowerBook was ready with the answer:

ROOM 1 SCAN TERMINATED
SYSTEM ERROR: LOW BATTERY
PROBLEM UNIT: MAIN PROCESSOR
SOLUTION 1: REPLACE BATTERY
SOLUTION 2: INSTALL AC ADAPTER
SOLUTION 3: INSTALL DC ADAPTER
PRESS ENTER KEY TO RESTART SYSTEM

Low battery? But I just . . .

Then he remembered Malcolm Byzor's last comment. *Hey, listen, I ran the batteries down in the computer when I was testing it out-*

side, so you're going to need to recharge them with the AC adapter before you try to use the system in the portable mode.

Oh no . . .

Hoping against all logic, Cellars quickly switched the Power-Book over to its standby mode and exchanged batteries. But he had no real reason to think his ever-practical buddy might have wasted a few amps of perfectly good battery power . . . and as it turned out, he hadn't. The backup battery was completely discharged.

It didn't take Cellars long to confirm what he already expected. Neither the batteries, the power adapters, or the Zip drive of his own far-less-powerful PC notebook computer were compatible with the PowerBook. And he didn't have any way of patching the Mac's software programs over to the PC.

Well shit, now what am I going to do? All I've got are a dozen or so spare nine-volt batteries and I'd need, what, at least a hundred of the damned things wired in parallel to come up with enough amps to put a fifteen-minute charge in one of these 15-volt computer batteries. And probably more than that 'cause I'd lose a lot of juice in the wire, assuming I could ever figure out the wiring in the first place. Which means I can't charge the batteries without a source of AC power, and the only dependable source of AC power anywhere near here is at least a half hour drive down the goddamned mountain. And if I do that, I might just as well drive the rest of the way back to the station and pick up another camera. In which case, I lose control of the scene . . . unless maybe I can figure some way to climb up that telephone pole and—

Hey, wait a minute. What *DC adapter?*

He found the DC adapter buried under the foam padding where, as best he could tell, it would have only been found by another electrical engineer.

It took him another five minutes to secure the inside basement stairs door, the broken window, and the exterior door with evidence tape. A reasonable if temporary solution to the scene control problem, Cellars decided, assuming that there wouldn't be any more scary-shadow-generating raccoons breaking through the tape and trying to make off with the evidence.

He was still muttering to himself—mostly about screaming shadows that went around grabbing old-fashioned revolvers, and electrical engineers whose linear thought processes completely ignored the impact of Murphy's Law on their more technically challenged buddies—as he hiked back through the maze to the Explorer with the DC adapter in his pocket, the PowerBook and flashlight in one hand, and the SIG-Sauer in the other.

Basically daring anyone—or anything—to get in his way.

It took only a couple of minutes to connect the battery-loaded computer to the Explorer's multipurpose cigarette lighter with the DC adapter, then start up the engine to ensure a steady current flow. But it would take at least a half hour to put a decent charge on the PowerBook's battery. And Cellars wasn't about to leave the Explorer—his only easy way back down the mountain—in the middle of a remote and isolated road with his keys in the ignition and the engine running, while he hiked back and forth through the forested maze like a demented elf. So he spent the time carefully transferring the stiff, bloody, and mud-splattered carcass of the malamute into one of the bright yellow heavy-duty zippered plastic body bags he kept in the vehicle for just such a purpose.

By the time he got the bagged carcass secured in the back of the Explorer and finished dictating the first phase of his CSI report, the computer screen was showing a half charge on the battery.

Good enough, he decided as he wrapped the PowerBook in another one of the body bags. As he did so, he tried not to think about why he was going to need another bag in a few minutes. Then, resigned to his task, he secured the vehicle before loading up the notebook computer, flashlight, and SIG-Sauer for the hike back to the cabin.

This time, the miniaturized blue-green lasers continued their intricate light show for the entire fifteen minutes before the fully energized PowerBook finally shut everything down and flashed the cheerful message:

SCAN OF ROOM 1 COMPLETED

DO YOU WISH TO SCAN ANOTHER ROOM? (Y/N)

God, I hope not, Cellars thought, trying not to yawn as he quickly shut down the computer, disconnected the shielded cable, and peeled the Primary Receiver and LSS units off the ceiling and walls. The system components went back into their precisely measured slots, and the wadded-up squares of tape went into Cellars's jacket pocket. Only then did he glance down at his watch: 0145 hours.

It was time to get going.

Okay, I've got the scene recorded . . . or at least I hope I do. Forget the close-up photos. Tag and bag the obvious—including the blood on the wall by the broken window and all the crap on the floor that I added to the scene, he reminded himself. *Mark everything on the sketch, bag the body, seal the place up, then head for home. Leave everything else for daylight, when I can come back with some help.*

It was a reasonable plan under the circumstances. But even so, it still took Cellars the better part of another half hour to transfer all of the spent bullets, casings, glass fragments, assorted debris, and blood samples into evidence bags after marking their descriptions on the bags and their locations on his sketch. It took two more trips back to the Explorer before he had all of the evidence packages stowed and secured in the two padlocked evidence lockers—one of which was insulated and temperature-controlled for perishable items—bolted to the floor behind the front seats of the Explorer.

The body was easier in the sense that it only represented one large evidence bag. The first step was to remove the TOD device and safely secure it back in his CSI kit—reminding himself as he did so that he would have to download and record the time-of-death results in his CSI report once he got back to the station. The trick then was to slide the unzipped bag under the body in such a way as to minimize the loss of trace evidence adhering to the victim's skin, hair, and clothing. Given the weight and rigored condition of the corpse, it would have been a difficult task in a lighted room with one or two medical examiner assistants to help. Working by himself, Cellars could only lift, shove, pull, bend, grunt, curse, and pray.

It was a quarter 'til three in the morning when he finally managed to pull the long zipper closed.

Nearly exhausted, and still facing the worst part of the job, he sat on the floor to rest while he changed batteries in his headlamp and contemplated the nature of the fates that led him to this particular moment in his life.

Should have taken another path, he told himself as he dropped the depleted AA batteries into his jacket pocket. *Become a hermit or an artist like this poor guy.*

Smiling cheerfully at the pleasant thought of having nothing better to do all day than to sit out on the porch of an isolated mountain cabin and paint, Cellars reached forward and picked up the stretched canvas that had been lying facedown on the basement floor all evening.

The first thing he noticed was the blood—splattered across the painted surface with sufficient force to have turned the blood droplets into elongated streaks.

But then his eyes were drawn to the haunting image of the young woman.

His first thought was that it was a portrait of Jody as she might have looked when she was about twenty-seven or so—which was as incomprehensible as it was stunning. But then he saw the violet eyes and he knew better.

My God, she's . . . the one at the auditorium.

And the focal point of the painting: a thin gold necklace bearing a single stone that hung just above the deeply curved hollow of her full, partially exposed breasts. A stone that looked very much like the one he'd found on the floor by the shattered basement window.

But it wasn't until his eyes drifted down to the signature at the bottom edge of the painting that the true enormity of the situation hit him like a baton blow to the solar plexus.

R. DAWSON.

Dawson?

Stunned and horrified, Colin Cellars slowly turned his head, causing the bright beam of his headlamp to shine brightly on the yellow plastic body bag in the far corner of the basement.

CHAPTER FOURTEEN

WHAT THE HELL'S THE MATTER WITH ME? COLIN CELLARS thought, almost overwhelmed by numbness and depression as he slowly worked his way through the dark upper main floor of the cabin with his night-vision goggles and IR-filtered flashlight, searching for some clearly identifiable remnant of Bob Dawson's life. Something he could use to make a positive ID.

Ideally, a wallet with a driver's license.

Or a file cabinet filled with legal documents or correspondence.

Or even the remains of an addressed envelope in the trash can.

Just something with Dawson's full name on it.

Anything at all.

But apart from the characteristic firearms collection, and the all-too-familiar signature at the bottom of the haunting portrait, he still hadn't found a single piece of evidence to suggest that the body encased in the yellow plastic body bag down in the basement was

Dawson's. Even the picture frame on the night table next to the single bed in the basement was empty.

It was a tiring and frustrating search; but to some degree, Cellars knew he was just going through the motions. Everything about the scene spoke to the obvious conclusion that the dog, the contents of the cabin, and the body on the basement floor all belonged to his long-lost friend.

I know Bobby's living in some remote mountain cabin, within an hour's drive from the auditorium where we're supposed to meet. I wait for an hour. He doesn't show. Then I get called out to a supposed shots-fired scene at an isolated mountain cabin. And what do I find? Nineteenth-century revolvers hung all over the wall, and a loner-type victim with weight-lifter muscles and long blond hair lying dead on the floor. Christ, what did I need, a flashing neon sign? Was I really that dense?

Then another equally chilling and depressing thought occurred to him.

Or was it that, deep down inside, I really didn't care?

That was a question that Colin Cellars really didn't want to think about at the moment.

The realization that he'd been blind to the possibility that Dawson's failure to appear and his own subsequent discovery of a body matching all of the appropriate descriptions might somehow be related was deeply troubling. But in spite of all that, there were still several things about the scene that bothered Cellars.

Things that didn't make any sense at all.

Like the bullet patterns in the wall, for a start.

If he had read the scene right, Dawson had been working on the painting—as evidenced by the broken easel and the two opened and squashed tubes of paint—when he was caught by surprise by an armed assailant coming in through the small northwest basement door. The directional pattern of the blood splatters on the rug and the painting suggested that he'd been hit right away—presumably in the head because a cursory search hadn't revealed any other significant wounds on the body.

Or the splattered blood could have come from the dog, Cellars reminded himself. The malamute clearly lived at the cabin. He'd found bags and cans of dog food in the storage shelves, and there were doglike hairs visibly consistent with the malamute all over the basement. Even more relevant, he'd found numerous doglike hairs clumped in with a mass of coagulated blood on the rug between the painting and the woodstove.

But if the dog was killed in the cabin, then why did the killer go to all the effort to drag him through that tree maze and toss him out on the road. Just so the responding deputies could find him?

That didn't make any sense to Cellars either.

But in any case, wounded or not, it was pretty obvious that Dawson had gotten to at least one of his treasured revolvers—a deduction Cellars based on the two sets of bullet holes on opposite sides of the basement. The bullet holes, and the empty holster hanging on the utility wall next to the electrical panel that was within a few feet of his body. And it was equally apparent to Cellars—assuming that the four widely spaced slugs buried in the opposite log-wall corner next to the exterior door were, in fact, linked to this shooting scene—that Dawson had gotten off at least four shots before being cut down by another burst of gunfire. These rounds had turned his face into an unrecognizable mess of torn and bloody tissue.

From the perspective of a once-close friend, it was a numbing and gut-wrenching sequence of events. But from the more hardened view of an experienced crime scene investigator, it was also a perfectly reasonable and logical accounting of the available evidence.

The trouble was, Colin Cellars hadn't been able to shake off the uncomfortable feeling that the entire scene read better as a mirror image of reality—a feeling enhanced by the fact that several crucial items of evidence were clearly missing.

It was the spacing of the bullet holes in the two opposing walls that first caught his attention. The four widely spaced slugs in the southeast corner next to the south door, and the three tightly spaced slugs in the north wall just to the right of the refrigerator. The first pattern suggested an individual firing wildly, and maybe even blindly, in a desperate attempt to save his life. The second was far more indicative of a cool, calm, and thoughtful killer placing his shots with deadly and icy control. All very fine as far as Cellars's reasonable and logical accounting of the evidence was concerned.

Except for one little problem.

During their junior high and high school years, Cellars and Dawson had spent a goodly portion of their free time shooting .22 rifles and pistols at a wide variety of pop cans and paper targets. And in all of those hundreds of hours of target shooting, Cellars couldn't remember a single instance when Dawson—a cool and deadly shot even then—had ever put more than a single bullet outside the black at fifteen yards. Much less throw a pattern of four where the closest pair of bullet holes were more than thirty inches apart.

So unless you really changed a hell of a lot in these last fifteen years, Bobby, you had to be the guy in the corner next to the south side door placing your shots . . . which would explain the empty holster on the wall over by the door. Which means whoever was shooting at you had to have come in at you through the other basement door in the northwest corner, or from the inside stairwell.

But if that really was the case, then how did you end up on the far side of the room?

And more to the point, where's your gun? And the other body? I know you didn't group those three shots into that wall just for the hell of it.

There weren't any visible blood splatters or drag marks on the dark wooden floor planks between the two sets of bullet holes. So the only thing that even halfway made sense was the possibility that one of the wildly fired shots had caught Dawson a glancing blow to the head as he was either running to or crouched down in the exterior door corner of the basement. That could explain the relatively small amount of blood on the wall about three and a half feet above the floor.

So then what, Bobby? Assuming you're still alive at that point, but not putting up much of a fight, the killer drags you over to the opposite side of the basement. Stands you up by the utility wall. Puts three or four rounds right into your face from point-blank range, execution style, spraying blood all over the wall and doorway. Lays you out on the ground all nice and neat. Pulls everything out of your pockets. Collects anything and everything in the cabin that might help the policy identify you. Collects the guns you both used. Cuts and removes a couple dozen feet of telephone and electrical cable. Tosses the dog out on the side of the road. And then just walks away?

What the hell kind of sense does that make?

None, as far as Cellars was concerned.

First of all, in his experience, killers who wanted to conceal the identity of their victim, and had the time to do so, almost always used one of two very basic techniques. They either cut off the victim's fingers and head, and then got rid of those readily identifiable parts separately, or they simply transported the entire body to some remote location for a quick burial. In rare instances—usually when they weren't worried about a timely police response—the killers might set the body and the surrounding scene on fire with gasoline or diesel fuel in an attempt to destroy all of the relevant evidence. But Cellars couldn't think of a previous case in which the killer had gone to the effort of destroying the victim's facial features and removing all items of identification from the residence, then simply walked away leaving the body with all ten fingerprints intact.

Nothing to gain except time . . . and only a few hours of that at the most. So why go to all that effort? Or more to the point, if you are going to go to all of that effort, why not just set fire to the place . . . or set a booby trap and take the cops out too?

Or maybe that's exactly what they did, Cellars thought, remembering the missing deputies.

And then there was the missing evidence to consider. The lengths of telephone and power line cables. The transformer fuse. The two revolvers, at least one of which should have been lying in reasonably close proximity to Dawson's body. And all of the personal notes and documents and memorabilia—not just the items of identification—that tend to accumulate if you own a car or property, or lead any kind of reasonably normal life.

Not to mention a point of entry for the killer, Cellars reminded himself. All of the other windows and doors—including the north-west corner basement door—had been locked, and the south basement door had clearly been broken out from the inside.

But more than anything else, Cellars's sense of skepticism kept bringing him back to the primary flaw in the scene reconstruction so far: Robert Dawson himself. A man whose lightning-fast reflexes, incredible ability to focus, and inherent belief that people *were* out to get him had kept him alive through God knew how many fire-fights with fanatical insurgents, trained mercenaries, and desperate drug smugglers through his military and DEA careers. Quite a few, if Jody's occasional letters were to be believed.

So is that what it took to put you down, Bobby? Two lucky head shots from somebody who sneaks into your cabin and surprises you and your dog. A dog you told me could spot a deer or a hunter at five hundred yards?

Cellars didn't buy it. Couldn't buy it.

There had to be another answer. Something that made more sense.

And something that explained the portrait of the violet-eyed young woman who looked so much like Jody Catlin.

The idea that suddenly formed in Cellars's mind had sent him back outside to his CSI kits for the night-vision goggles and IR-lens cap. A few minutes later, he was back upstairs on the upper floor of the cabin, searching for some document, some personal item, some form of identification that would add credence to the only idea that made any sense. The idea that the dead body in the yellow plastic body bag had to belong to someone else besides Bobby Dawson.

But the entire upper floor of the cabin looked like no one had ever lived there. There was nothing in the kitchen—no refrigerator, stove, table, dishes, or silverware. No furniture at all in the living room. And only a queen-size wooden bed frame and mattress, a pair of small bedside tables, and a large empty dresser in the one main bedroom. In fact, there wasn't a single item of a personal nature anywhere at all on the upper floor. Or at least nothing that he'd been able to find.

This is weird, he thought as he moved around the empty rooms. *Really weird.*

Even the orientation of the stairs—the way the upper landing was right against the eastern log wall, with the doorway opening right into the main bedroom—didn't seem to make sense.

He was still searching the main bedroom of the cabin, slowly and methodically pulling out the drawers of the empty dresser—to see if anything was taped to the undersides—when a chillingly familiar sound reached his ears.

The sound of a loose board creaking.

Downstairs, in the basement.

Cellars froze in place even as his subconscious mind began to count.

One thousand and one, one thousand and two . . .

Moving his feet very slowly and carefully, he turned away from the dresser and set the flashlight on the mattress so that the bright green beam—invisible to anyone lacking night-vision goggles—highlighted the open stairway door. Then he crouched behind the rear bed frame, keeping his eyes on that open doorway as he reached down with his right hand to quietly release the SIG-Sauer's holster thumb strap. Listening all the while for any other sound.

Nothing.

One thousand and seven, one thousand and eight . . .

He had his mouth open now, consciously controlling his breathing—slow, steady, shallow breaths—as he slowly pulled the SIG-Sauer from his hip holster. His index finger instinctively slid across the smooth edge of the trigger guard. There was still a residual buzzing in his ears from the previous shooting incident down in the basement, but he ignored it, forcing it into the background.

Still listening. No other sounds.

One thousand and fifteen, one thousand and . . .

Creak.

Softer this time, but closer . . . at the base of the stairwell.

Cellars cocked his head, listening intently now as he carefully brought the SIG-Sauer around into a two-handed grip, both of his arms extended and resting on the firm mattress.

A third creaking sound . . . barely audible, but incrementally closer.

Moving up the stairs?

Cellars settled his chest in tight against the edge of the mattress, then dropped his head down—intent on providing a minimal target—as he carefully aligned the iridescent sights of the SIG-Sauer on the open doorway. His right index finger pressed snugly against the cold metal of the trigger.

Loaded, locked, and a round in the chamber. No safety. Just sight and squeeze. Sight and squeeze.

Come on. . . .

Then, unexpectedly, a completely different sound reached Cellars's ears. A sound that caused him to bring his head up and blink in shock.

The distinct, and slightly metallic sound of a long, heavy-duty zipper being slowly drawn open.

Body bag.

Some rational portion of Cellars's brain was trying to warn him that the two sounds sounded too far apart for only one suspect, but the more aggressive portion of his psyche wasn't paying attention. His eyes had already widened with rage.

Then, before he could catch himself, Cellars grabbed the flashlight with his left hand, scrambled around the bed on his hands and knees, and dived through the stairway door and onto the upper landing. He landed flat on his chest, screamed, "POLICE!" as loud as he could as he twisted to his left in the night-vision-enhanced bright green stairwell, and aimed the flashlight beam and pistol down the stairs. He started firing the moment he saw the dark, greenish black shadowy figure whirl around and lunge toward the bottom stairway door.

The erupting bright green fireballs overwhelmed the photon absorption capability of the night-vision goggles and caused the greenish black figure to disappear briefly from sight. By the time the electronic goggles reattenuated to the ambient low-light levels, and he could see down the stairway again, the splintering door was already bouncing back from the outward thrust of a rapidly disappearing greenish black arm and the more sharply focused impacts of three expanding .40-caliber hollow-point bullets.

Missed.

Cellars cursed.

Then, knowing that there had to be at least two of them in the basement now, Cellars dived down the stairway on his chest, scrambling with both legs and his left arm to propel himself downward. The impact of his ribs, elbows, and knees against the bare, hardwood edges of the steps forced grunts and gasps out of Cellars's lungs. But he ignored the pain, concentrating instead on keeping his head and pistol up and away from the stairs, his eyes open, and the fingers of his right hand tight around the rubberized grip of the SIG until he reached the landing. Then, bracing himself with his left hand on the wooden flooring and his right foot against the second step, Cellars used his legs to heave himself through the splintered doorway.

The door slammed open, struck some obstacle, and bounced back sharply, catching Cellars across the side of his head and knocking the night-vision goggles down around his nose and mouth as he landed on the wooden floor of the basement.

Effectively blinded by the dislocated goggles, Cellars instinctively rolled to his right and flattened out into a protective prone position, with the SIG-Sauer extended and ready. He still couldn't see anything, but the sound of the south basement door swinging open on its squeaky hinges was unmistakable. And the sound gave him enough of an alignment vector to send the first of three more hollow-point rounds streaking through the open doorway and into the darkness.

The repeated detonation of the .40-caliber high-velocity cartridges in a closed environment left Cellars visually stunned and almost completely deafened. He remained down in his prone position— frantically struggling with one hand to get the goggles back up and over his eyes—as he tensed for the impact of a bullet, knife blade, club, or bare hand.

But the expected attack never came.

Moments later he had the goggles back in place, but his field of vision remained black and featureless. He had to thumb the power switch off and on twice before the structure and contents of the basement finally reappeared in a burst of bright green radiance—an effect that caused Cellars to twist around with the SIG-Sauer in a double-handed grip, ready to fire. But a quick visual sweep of the basement confirmed what he already half expected: no dark greenish black figures anywhere in his immediate proximity.

For Cellars, it was a moment of almost overwhelming relief, immediately followed by an equally intense emotional wave of anger and frustration.

Both . . . gone?

He couldn't believe it.

More to the point, he refused to believe it. Still dazed from the accumulative effects of shock and adrenaline, and distracted by the shrill buzzing in his ears, Cellars scrambled to his feet and staggered toward the outside doorway, with the SIG-Sauer still out in a two-handed grip, searching for a target.

But when he got outside, all he saw in his bright green field of vision were rocks and trees . . . and rapidly falling rain. No dark running figures. No lurking shadows.

Nothing.

Shit!

He briefly considered trying to follow them, on the reasonable theory that their footprints would be easy to track in the mud. But even with the advantage of the night-vision goggles, he knew his chances of spotting them among several hundred surrounding trees before they saw him were poor at best. And if they did see him first . . .

Cellars didn't want to think about that part.

Better to collect the body, take off down the hill, and come back with a lot of help, he decided as he thumbed the magazine release on the SIG-Sauer. The partially emptied magazine dropped into the palm of his hand. He stuck it into his left jacket pocket, then reloaded the pistol with the last full magazine from his belt pouch.

No point in trying to be a dead hero.

Buoyed by that encouraging thought, Cellars went back to searching the basement and immediately discovered that the body bag had been moved. It had ended up lodged against the partially opened stairwell door. He was kneeling beside the partially opened bag, intent on searching the body one more time before zipping it back up and carrying its gruesome contents out to the road, when he heard, somewhere out in the distance, the sound of an engine trying to turn over. It was a sharp, hesitant sound. Like someone was trying to jump-start—

Oh Jesus!

The Explorer.

CHAPTER FIFTEEN

COLIN CELLARS LUNGED TO HIS FEET WITH THE IR-FILTERED flashlight in one hand and the SIG-Sauer in the other. He hesitated at the doorway, and looked back in dismay at the unsecured basement he was about to abandon. But there wasn't anything he could do about a broken door lock in a couple of seconds, and he knew full well that an unprotected crime scene would be the least of his problems if he lost all the rest of his evidence.

It was that last thought, coupled with the distant sound of a second grinding attempt to provide the necessary power to the Explorer's heavy-duty starter, that sent Cellars running for the all-too-familiar opening in the trees.

The visibility provided by the night-vision goggles, and the fact that he had already made over a dozen such trips in the last few hours, gave Cellars a definite advantage in his effort to sprint his way through the forest maze of blackberry vines, tree trunks, and brush. But the falling rain made the thick, underlying leaf mat extremely slippery, and he fell three separate times . . . the last time hard enough to dislodge the goggles again. It cost him precious seconds to get them back over his eyes. In doing so, he was still sprawled on the ground, in the last segment of the maze, when he heard the Explorer's engine roar into life.

The thought of having all of his hard-earned evidence—and his vehicle—disappear down the mountain road without him had the effect of reenergizing Cellars's nearly exhausted body. He was back up on his feet and pulling himself through the double-trunk scrub oak when the Explorer's rapidly accelerating tires sent a wave of gravel splattering into the tree line.

Oh, no!

Drawing on the last of his reserves, Cellars burst through the last barrier of transplanted nursery trees just as the Explorer completed a U-turn in the middle of the cul-de-sac and started to accelerate down the road with its lights off.

Cellars blinked in disbelief.

A few hours ago, he might have stood there in the road and opened fire at the driver of his stolen vehicle without a moment of thought or hesitation. But that was long before he worked and hiked and ran himself into a state of almost total exhaustion.

More aware of his physical limitations now, Cellars took two staggering steps to his left and braced himself against the rough-barked trunk of another scrub oak. Then he brought the SIG-Sauer up in a two-handed grip, aligned and centered the sights on a point just above and in front of the Explorer's left-side mirror, and started squeezing the trigger.

The weapon recoiled sharply . . .

One . . .

. . . sending the first bullet streaking across the road and into the darkened forest just inches ahead of the rapidly moving vehicle.

Two . . . three . . .

The Explorer drove right into the trajectory of the second and third bullets, which blew out the driver's side window and punched two starred holes through the middle of the windshield.

Four . . . five . . . six . . . seven . . .

The Explorer seemed to turn away slightly from the exploding glass, narrowing the angle of impact for bullets four through seven—which punched through the side engine panel, completely obliterated the left rear passenger's side window, and turned the front windshield into an abstract pattern of crusted and starred bullet holes.

Eight . . . nine . . . ten . . . eleven.

Forced back to the left by the lack of road, the Explorer accelerated into the oncoming turn. It was just about to drop down and ultimately disappear around the relatively sharp bend to the right when the eighth round hit the rear door, and the last three rounds exploded through the rear window—the first two in line with the driver and the third in the general direction of the front passenger seat.

The SIG-Sauer's smoothly recoiling slide locked open against the empty magazine, but Cellars had been counting shots for a purpose and he was already starting to reach for the partially loaded magazine in his left jacket pocket. Working out of instinct and training now rather than any conscious thought, he thumbed the magazine release, allowing the empty magazine to drop at his feet. Then he fed the partially loaded magazine into the open base of the hot and smoking weapon, and released the slide, forcing a new round into the chamber.

He was reaching down for the empty magazine at his feet when he vaguely heard—over the intense high-pitched buzzing in his ears—the distant muffled sound of breaking glass and crunching metal.

Then silence.

Yes!

He pushed himself away from the supporting tree and started to run toward the distant bend in the road where the Explorer had disappeared. But the energy-sapping combination of wet clothes and icy penetrating wind, in addition to his already exhausted condition, proved to be too much . . . and his legs simply refused to cooperate. So instead, he limped and staggered down the middle of the cold and dark mountain road, looking like a bewildered and exhausted marathoner as he followed the reflective trail of shattered safety glass. He had to stop four separate times to catch his breath and to readjust the night-vision goggles—leaning forward and supporting himself with his hands on his knees each time until his head cleared—before he finally saw where the Explorer had veered off the road into the trees.

By then, Cellars had regained enough of his strength and awareness to realize that he had to be careful.

He approached the Explorer slowly, with the SIG-Sauer extended up and out at eye level, using a succession of trees for cover. He was very conscious of the fact that he only had four rounds in his pistol, and two more in his backup magazine. But that was plenty, he reassured himself. Just as long as he held his fire until he had a clear target.

But when he finally worked his way over to the rear driver's side of the vehicle, he discovered it was empty.

He immediately dropped down beside the left rear tire, using it—and the mass of the Explorer—to protect his back while he quickly scanned the road and surrounding trees back the way he'd come. Much too late, he realized that he'd been stupid and careless in making himself an easy target.

But you had to have hit one of them. The driver at the very least, his subconscious protested. *Why else would he have crashed the car?*

It didn't make any sense, but Cellars knew he couldn't worry about that now. He had a much more pressing problem: the fact that the suspect or suspects who had nearly gotten away with his vehicle and all of his collected evidence could be hiding nearby. Or equally frustrating, long gone in any one of a dozen different directions.

It took Cellars almost fifteen minutes—slowly and methodically working his way around in a full circle while continuing to stay low and using the Explorer for protection—to convince himself that they had to be long gone. In doing so, he discovered that gas was leaking from somewhere in the engine compartment. Likely caused by one of his errant bullets, or the impact with the tree. Either way, it wasn't anything that he could resolve at the moment, so he ignored it.

Instead, he stood up again and slowly began to move away from the vehicle, the SIG-Sauer up and ready, trusting the night-vision goggles to help him spot and react to any threatening movements.

It was an act of faith—or foolish bravado—as much as anything else, because he hadn't found any outgoing footprints in the splatters of mud that covered a goodly part of the surrounding asphalt. And he hadn't found any sign of freshly broken limbs or branches, or freshly dislodged rocks in the adjacent tree line. Even worse: If anyone *was* moving around in the darkness in this immediate area, it wasn't likely that he'd be able to hear or track that movement over the severe buzzing in his ears.

But even so, he continued to stand there, exposed and vulnerable, as he slowly turned in place, scanning the surrounding tree line one more time over the sights of the SIG-Sauer . . . and saw nothing.

Okay, enough of this shit, he thought as he shook his head, trying without success to clear his ears. *Time to hit that emergency transmitter and get some help up here.*

The OMARR-9 emergency transmitter was a high-power, low-band system designed for the specific purpose of sending a unit ID and a corresponding distress signal to any and all listening receivers within a five-hundred-mile radius of any radio dead zone. The high signal-to-noise ratio and the relatively low frequency of the resulting radio waves allowed the signals to bend and bounce off of almost anything—mountains, trees, clouds, and in theory, even overflying airplanes. As such, it was an extremely handy and powerful backup

to routine radio and land line communications, even if most of the
sworn officers in the state of Oregon chose to look upon the system
as the embarrassing equivalent of yelling, "Mommy, help!"

But the rule of thumb in electronic communications was frus-
tratingly simple: There were always trade-offs, and you never got
something for nothing. And in this case, the trade-off was significant. Because the emergency transmitter radio waves were able to
bounce repeatedly in almost any direction prior to being detected,
it was almost impossible for the OMARR-9 dispatchers to track the
signal back to its source. If they didn't know where the officer calling for help was supposed to be in the first place, then the system
wasn't going to do much more than send every available officer within
receiving range into rapid and random motion.

But they know exactly where I am, Cellars thought, *so all they
have to do is send a couple of units up the mountain to find out what's
going on. No problem.*

No problem, that is, until he returned to the Explorer and discovered, to his absolute amazement, that the driver's side door was
tightly locked.

What?

He immediately stepped back and quickly examined the other
three doors. They were locked also. No real problem, because all he
had to do was reach in through the shattered side window and unlock the door, but even so, he couldn't understand why . . .

That was when he noticed the radio console.

Whoever had driven the Explorer away, and then escaped after
the crash—apparently through one of the broken side windows, although Cellars couldn't see how *or* why—had taken the time to
pound the radio and the emergency transmitter into useless bits of
shattered plastic and chipboard. Apparently using the spare flashlight mounted on the front passenger-side door, he decided, noting
the tubular-shaped indentations in the console and the broken bulb
and lens of the flashlight lying next to the radio. To no great surprise,

he also discovered that the spare bulb in the base of the flashlight was also broken . . . probably as a result of the violent hammering.

Wonderful. Just wonderful.

A quick examination of the driver and front passenger seats under the enhanced illumination of the night-vision goggles—the best Cellars could do because he'd left his other flashlight back on the floor of the cabin basement, and the interior lights wouldn't come on—was inconclusive. There was a small stain on the top and upper rear portion of the driver's seat that might have been blood.

A quick check of the glove compartment confirmed another suspicion. The cell phone was gone. That discovery, in turn, caused Cellars to make a more thorough search of the Explorer's interior . . . whereupon he discovered that his digital camera case was also missing.

Why would a couple of homicide suspects take the time to steal a cell phone that's completely useless up here, and a heavy-as-hell camera case with a broken camera? Especially when at least one of them is wounded, and they're being chased and shot at?

Cellars shook his head in bewilderment. *I don't understand any of this. I really don't.*

He stood there for a long time, continuing to stare at the locked doors, the slightly stained driver's seat, and the mostly empty window frames, all offering persuasive—albeit conflicting—evidence that he must have hit *someone* with all of those shots.

That thought triggered the realization that, somewhere down the line, he was going to have to explain why he'd shot at his own vehicle. And to do that, he was going to need some evidence. The bloodstains were the obvious—and potentially most useful—choice. But he'd left his evidence collection kit back at the cabin, so he simply used his pocketknife to cut out two big squares of seat material bearing the stains. These he placed in separate plain white envelopes from the Explorer's glove compartment. He put the two envelopes in his shirt pocket.

Then it occurred to Cellars that there might be a very good reason

why these people had gone to so much effort to keep him from calling for help.

Accordingly, he quickly went around to the back of the Explorer,
unlocked and opened the rear door, and rummaged through one of
his canvas satchels until he found his spare box of .40-caliber pistol
ammunition and a roll of duct tape. Then he sat down in the mud
again with his back braced against the left rear tire of the Explorer,
and let the steadily falling rain pour down his face and clothes and
hands while he slowly and methodically reloaded ten rounds into
each of the three SIG-Sauer magazines.

It was only after he had the fully loaded pistol and extra magazines resecured in their holster and ammo pouches and checked the
surrounding area one more time with the night-vision goggles that
he was able to summon up the strength to pull himself to his feet.

He found the source of the gas leak. One of the .40-caliber
rounds had punched through the left front engine panel in front of
the driver's side door, and ricocheted off the engine block . . . and
fragments of that bullet had apparently punctured the fuel line in at
least three places.

Knowing that it was a temporary solution at best, Cellars used a
half dozen strips of the sticky tape to stop the dripping and secure
the fuel line—as much as possible—away from the hot engine block.
Then, feeling much more secure, he took the time to brush most of
the glass fragments off the driver's seat before turning the key in the
ignition.

To his utter amazement, the Explorer's engine started right up
the first try.

It took Cellars ten minutes to get the Explorer back to its previous spot at the end of the cul-de-sac, then disable it by locating and
pulling three carefully selected fuses. Then another fifteen to return
to the cabin, confirm that Dawson's body was still where he'd left it,
pick up the hammer and bag of 16-penny nails he'd discovered during his initial search, and finally work his way back to the outer-
most of the two disconnected utility poles.

In a relative sense, the process was pure simplicity. Cellars drove the first pair of nails halfway into the wood on opposite sides of the wet utility pole at knee level, then alternated them at roughly one-foot increments—left side, right side—until he held the last nail in place with the outstretched fingers of his outstretched arm. Finally, he secured his lineman's equipment belt around his waist, looped the end of a makeshift rope-climbing harness around the pole, tied a barely remembered bowline knot from his Boy Scout days, leaned back against the rope to double-check his memory, and began to climb.

Twelve more nails—left, right and left—put him within easy reach of the severed telephone line leading down the mountain road. He leaned back against the rope harness—more cautiously this time— and got to work with a pair of wire strippers and the alligator connectors to a lineman's phone.

Two minutes later, he brought the phone up to his ear.

Dial tone.

Smiling to himself for the first time that evening, Cellars quickly punched in a memorized number and waited.

One ring.

Two rings.

Come on, people, answer the damned . . .

"OMARR-Nine, how can I—"

The line went dead.

Colin Cellars stared down at the silent phone for a long moment. Then he shifted his gaze to the telephone line that looped its way across to four more identical poles before finally disappearing from sight down the road toward town.

You bastards.

It took Cellars another fifteen minutes to climb down the pole, repack his lineman's gear into the back of the Explorer, and make one more trip back to the cabin. He was exhausted, and shivering from the wet and the cold, but he hardly noticed. Everything he did now—every physical effort, every moment of contemplation—was now fueled by a cold rage that would tolerate no further lapses . . . in concentration or in effort.

He used up a goodly portion of that rage, and his remaining energy, hauling all of Dawson's treasured weapons—sixteen handguns of assorted calibers and eras, and the amazingly heavy Sharps rifle—out to the Explorer. Once he had them stacked on and around the front passenger seat, he stood in the drizzling rain for a long moment, uncertain and uneasy about leaving the loaded weapons in the essentially windowless vehicle. But he wasn't about to leave them in the unsecured cabin, and he didn't know what else to do, so he finally said, "To hell with it," and started walking back to the cabin one last time.

Once he was there, he took one last look around the basement, to confirm he'd either collected or documented everything that appeared to be relevant. Then, after taking in one last deep, steadying breath, he drew the SIG-Sauer out of its holster with his right hand, and reached down with his left to grab the canvas web strap at the head end of the body bag.

The effort nearly brought him to his knees. But failure was not an option at that point, so Cellars simply blinked, shook his head, and staggered forward toward the doorway. He made it out the door and almost halfway to the tree line—a good forty feet—before he collapsed and had to catch himself to keep from burying the muzzle of his pistol in the mud.

The maze was more of a challenge, mostly because the rigored body wouldn't bend easily around a couple of the tight turns or fit through the double-trunk scrub oak. Cellars was forced to lift the body bag upright around the turns and actually heave it up over a wire-supported barrier of smaller trees adjacent to the impassable oak.

He found the energy to pull himself over the same barrier, then collapsed to his hands and knees, dizzy from exhaustion and gasping for breath as he forced himself to concentrate on the basics: Head up, pistol out of the mud, look and listen.

Goddamn you, Dawson. Should have known you'd still be a pain in the ass, even when you're dead, Cellars thought morosely, blinking his eyes and shaking his head as he stared at the crumpled body bag that was now a pale green in the electronic optics of the night-vision goggles.

He made the last twenty yards on his butt, two yards at a time. Holding on to the body bag's head strap with his left hand, the SIG-Sauer with his right, and thrusting himself backward with his heels dug into the mud. Dragging the increasingly heavy body bag through the mud and the rain. Grunting and cursing. Alternately hoping for one more shot at the bastards, and praying that they'd leave him alone until he got Dawson's body settled into the back of the Explorer.

Fifteen minutes later, Cellars shut the back of the Explorer, staggered over to the driver's side door, pulled himself into the seat, shut and locked the door, set the SIG-Sauer down on the adjacent front passenger seat next to the other pistols, and started the engine. He could smell gas again, but he didn't care.

Then, after the engine caught, and was rumbling more or less smoothly, he looked down at his watch.

It was 4:13 in the morning.

CHAPTER SIXTEEN

OSP PATROL SERGEANT TOM BAUER TOOK ONE LOOK AT THE NAME imprinted on the official OSP credentials in his hand, blinked, and looked up at the wet, muddy, and exhausted figure standing next to his scout car.

"*You're* Detective-Sergeant Colin Cellars? The new roving CSI officer from Portland? One of the guys we've been looking for all over the damned county?"

Well, so much for Downs and Wills reporting in my status, Cellars thought.

"I'm Cellars, and I am the new roving CSI officer for Region Nine," he acknowledged, in no mood to put up with an inquisition from a fellow sergeant at five o'clock in the morning. "But I don't know anything about that last part. The dispatchers knew where I was working. They're the ones who sent me there in the first place."

He'd started looking for a telephone as soon as he reached the highway at the base of the mountain, and he'd been heading toward a distant gas station when he noticed the scout car in the parking lot of a used furniture store. He'd parked on the directly opposite side of the parking lot from the scout car, wanting to give the patrol officer plenty of time to see him coming. It had been that kind of night.

"You'd never know it, the way they've been calling for you the last hour," Bauer commented. "And you say your radio's out of commission?"

"That's right."

Bauer reexamined the photo on the laminated OSP ID card, took a sip from his thermos cup of steaming coffee, and looked back up at Cellars.

"If you don't mind me asking, Cellars, just where the hell *have* you been all night?"

Given the mind-boggling events of the past eight hours, Colin Cellars's first instinct was to respond to the mildly accusatory question with a mildly sarcastic variation of "you wouldn't believe me if I told you." But the all-too-serious tone of the uniformed patrol sergeant's voice, and the expression on his face, caused him to hesitate.

"I've been working a homicide scene, up on the mountain." He gestured with his head back in the direction he'd just come.

"You mean that shots-fired call out on Twenty-Two-Fifty-Five? You say *you've* been working that scene?"

Bauer didn't exactly accuse Cellars of outright lying. He didn't have to. The expression on his face and the tone of his voice took care of that nicely.

"That's right," Cellars repeated, nodding his head slowly. "I've been working *that* scene. All night. All by myself. Which is probably why I'm tired and grumpy in addition to freezing cold and soaking wet. You have a problem with that?"

"Not me," Bauer replied evenly, "but there's a dozen or so scout cars up in the north sector, not to mention one thoroughly pissed-off captain out at the Rusty Bar, who just might see things a little differently."

Cellars's eyebrows furrowed in confusion. "What the hell are you talking about?"

Bauer started to say something, then simply shook his head.

"Here," he said as he handed his console mike out the window. "I think you're going to want to hear this directly from the source."

Cellars stared at the patrol sergeant for a long moment before bringing the mike up to the side of his mouth.

"Oregon-Nine-Echo-One to OMARR-Nine."

The response was immediate.

"OMARR-Nine to Oregon-Nine-Echo-One, what is your location?"

Cellars looked around for the closest street sign. "I'm at Highway Two-Forty-Three and Washboard."

There was a long pause.

"Echo-One, please repeat your location."

Bauer shrugged as if to say "I told you."

"I'm standing here next to"—Cellars leaned down to look at the patrol sergeant's name tag, then smiled pleasantly as Bauer raised his thermos cup in salute—"OSP Sergeant Bauer, in the parking lot of Margraff's Furniture at the intersection of Highway Two-Forty-Three and Washboard."

"Echo One, you're not showing on our locator board. Please check your unit transmitter status. We've been trying to contact you for the last—"

"I've been up in a radio dead zone, at the north end of County Road Twenty-Two-Fifty-Five, for the last eight hours," Cellars interrupted. "And the reason you're not picking me up now is because I'm transmitting on Sergeant Bauer's radio. My entire radio console, including the unit transmitter, was destroyed by the fleeing suspects . . . and probably also by one of my own bullets when they attempted to steal my vehicle," he added as an afterthought.

Bauer paused in mid-sip to stare at Cellars while the radio speaker remained silent for another long count.

"Echo-One, please confirm you've been up at the north end of County Road Twenty-Two-Fifty-Five for the last eight hours, and that you fired a shot at a fleeing suspect at that location."

"Echo-One to OMARR-Nine, correction, be advised that I fired a total of twenty-four shots—"

Bauer choked, spraying hot coffee all over the dash of his scout car as he turned to stare up at Cellars in disbelief.

"—at fleeing suspects at that location," Cellars finished. "Also be advised that the reported shots-fired situation at the residence at the far north end of County Road Twenty-Two-Fifty-Five *is* a homicide situation. I repeat, *is* a homicide situation. The victim has been tentatively identified as the resident: a male Caucasian, six-one, muscular build, approximately thirty-six years old. Two suspects, unknown descriptions, last seen heading southbound on County Road Twenty-Two-Fifty-Five in the direction of Highway Two-Forty-Three about thirty minutes ago. One or both may be wounded or injured. No further at this time."

"OMARR-Nine to Echo-One, verifying two homicide suspects, unknown description, last seen heading southbound on County Road Twenty-Two-Fifty-Five about thirty ago. One or both may be wounded or injured," the dispatcher repeated. "How are the suspects armed?"

Cellars hesitated.

"Echo-One, unknown if or how suspects are armed."

Sergeant Bauer shook his head slowly as the expression on his face shifted to compassionate sympathy for a fellow officer.

The OMARR-9 dispatcher seemed to share Bauer's viewpoint.

"Echo-One," she spoke quietly, as if hesitant to deliver bad news, "be advised that Captain Hawkins has requested that you report to him at the Rusty Bar immediately."

Colin Cellars sighed, then brought the mike up again. "Echo-One to OMARR-Nine, please advise Captain Hawkins that I am en route to the morgue with the body of the victim, ETA approximately ten.

After I drop the victim off, I'm heading back to the station to log my evidence and file my report on the homicide scene. I'll contact him there."

"Echo-One, also be advised—"

But Cellars didn't give her a chance to finish her admonition. "Echo-One, out," he interrupted, and handed the mike back to Bauer.

As Cellars stood there, trying to collect his thoughts, Sergeant Tom Bauer stepped out of the scout car with his thermos bottle and stared in disbelief at the bullet-hole-pocked windshield and shattered side windows of the Explorer. Then he walked across the parking lot to the back of the Explorer with Cellars at his side. No words were necessary. Cellars reached into his pocket, pulled out his keys, unlocked and pulled open the rear door.

Bauer stared at the body bag for a good twenty seconds. Then he unscrewed his thermos, poured a full cup of the steaming liquid into the metal cap, and handed it to Cellars . . . who accepted it gratefully.

"Any good advice?" Cellars asked as he sipped at the hot brew.

The veteran patrol sergeant stared at him reflectively.

"Twenty-four rounds, huh?"

Cellars nodded.

"Hit anything?"

Cellars shrugged and then motioned with his hand at the severely punctured front windshield, the shattered back and side windows, and the back and side panels of the Explorer.

"Anything else?" Bauer asked hopefully.

"Might have hit one of the suspects back at the victim's cabin. And probably hit whoever was trying to drive off with this thing before they hit the tree. Little bit of fresh blood in each instance, but no bodies."

"Except for this one." Bauer gestured with his head at the body bag in the back of the Explorer.

"Right."

"Must have been one hell of a crime scene investigation," the patrol sergeant commented, for lack of anything better to say.

"Yeah, it was," Cellars acknowledged as he handed the cup back to Bauer. "Trouble is, I don't think it's over yet."

———

The night shift attendant at the Jasper County Morgue was sound asleep and in the middle of a perfectly satisfying dream when the sighs of the sensuous young woman were suddenly replaced by the jarring sound of a fist pounding on the outside door.

"Help you?" the attendant asked sleepily, staring at the unfamiliar figure on his security monitor.

"Yeah, Detective-Sergeant Colin Cellars, OSP. Open up."

"Uh, what's this about, Sergeant?" The attendant looked over at his main computer monitor as he clicked on the REFRESH button. "I don't have any incomings listed on my screen."

"I've been out of radio contact—" Cellars started to explain impatiently when the phone next to the attendant's computer monitor rang loudly.

"Uh, excuse me a second," the attendant said quickly as he cut off the external speaker switch and reached for the phone.

"Morgue, how can I—"

The voice on the other end of the line interrupted. The attendant blinked, then listened carefully for a full thirty seconds before mumbling "Yes sir, I understand . . . Yes sir, I'll tell him . . . Yes sir!" before hanging up.

"Uh, Sergeant Cellars?" the now-wide-awake attendant inquired as he switched back to the external speaker.

"I'm still here."

"Come on in, Sergeant," the attendant replied as he reached over to release the electronically controlled security gates. "Guess we've been expecting you after all."

———

The white-gowned, rubber-gloved morgue attendant was standing anxiously outside a set of electronically operated double doors and holding on to a glistening stainless-steel gurney as Cellars pulled forward into the morgue's drive-in receiving area. The attendant remained in place while he waited for the massive roll-up door to rattle back down into a closed and locked position, then started forward with the gurney just as Cellars shut off the engine and stepped out of the Explorer.

"Randy Granstrom, night shift attendant," the young man said with a tired smile as he brought the gurney to a stop next to Cellars and extended a gloved hand.

"Hi. Detective-Sergeant Colin Cellars, OSP," Cellars responded in a gruff and tightly controlled voice as he handed his credentials over for inspection. The image of Bobby Dawson lying in a body bag behind his back was not helping his mood—or his temper—in terms of putting up with bureaucratic bullshit.

"Uh, yes sir, welcome to the Jasper County Coroner's Office, Sergeant." Granstrom glanced at Cellars's new photo ID card and quickly returned the badge. "Sorry about the mix-up. We've got orders to be pretty careful about who we let in here late at night . . . especially when we don't know they're coming. Not like anybody's really gonna break into a morgue and make off with one of the stiffs," the young attendant added hurriedly, "but you know how it goes. Rules are the rules. I just do what they tell me around here."

"Good. Glad to hear it," Cellars commented, as the two men walked around to the back of the Explorer.

"Oh, and speaking of which, before I forget, Captain Hawkins said to tell you that he wants you to report to him out at the Rusty Bar, ASAP, soon as you get to—"

The young attendant stopped in mid-sentence and blinked, apparently noticing the condition of the Explorer for the first time.

"Jeez, it looks like you had . . ." The young man paused and blinked again as his eyes focused on the shattered back and side windows, and the visibly fresh bullet holes in the front windshield of the Explorer. ". . . a rough evening?"

"I've had better," Cellars muttered as he pulled open the back door.

"Uh, you know you're leaking gas?" The morgue attendant was squatting and looking under the Explorer.

"Yeah, I know. Don't worry about it."

Something in the tone of Cellars's voice caused Granstrom to quickly stand up. He took one look at the cubed fragments of safety glass that covered most of the Explorer's back compartment, shifted his gaze to the exhausted yet thoroughly pissed-off expression on Cellars's face, and wisely decided he'd asked enough questions that were none of his business for one morning.

It took Cellars and the morgue attendant less than two minutes to work the body bag onto the stainless-steel gurney and wheel it through a couple of mechanical double doors into the refrigerated main storage room.

"Uh, do you have a case number on this one?" the attendant asked as he looked up from his clipboard.

"Not yet. I'll call it in as soon as I get to the station."

Not standard procedure, but Granstrom obviously wasn't about to argue. Not without someone else in the room to back him up.

"Uh, how about a name?"

Cellars hesitated.

"Dawson, D-A-W-S-O-N, first name Robert," he finally said.

"And the spelling of your name?"

"Colin Cellars, C-O-L-I-N C-E-L-L-A-R-S, OSP, badge twenty-seven."

The attendant nodded as he carefully filled out the names, date, and other pertinent information on the toe tag and body receipt in block letters. Then he handed the two forms back over to Cellars for his signature.

"That it?"

"That's all I need," Granstrom said reassuringly as he quickly attached the waterproof tag on the exposed right big toe with a practiced series of movements. "Soon as you get me that case number, I can—"

"Oh, shit," Cellars suddenly remembered, "I forgot about the damned dog."

"Dog?" Granstrom blinked in confusion.

"Yeah, listen, do you have any place I can store a dog carcass for a few days?"

"Uh, well, is it part of your case?"

"I don't know. Probably not," Cellars admitted. "But I was going to see if I could get one of the pathologists to take a quick look at it. Maybe give me some idea of what killed it."

"Gee, I don't know." The morgue attendant hesitated. "The thing is, my boss would be real upset if he ever found out I put a dead dog in one of his refrigerator units. Don't know why he'd care—after all, dead's dead—but you know how some guys are."

"Overly bureaucratic?" Cellars suggested with a slight smile.

"And then some." Granstrom shrugged, then looked off into space for a few moments before apparently coming to some kind of decision. "Hey, listen, I'll tell you what. You just drop it off here and I'll find someplace to put it temporarily until you can work something out with the docs. I won't log it into the system. Just leave them a note, letting them know what's going on . . . and telling them that you'll be contacting them tomorrow morning. How does that sound?"

"Sounds just fine to me."

Cellars and the morgue attendant dragged the stiff carcass of the malamute out of the back of the Explorer and dropped it at the edge of the driveway. It took Cellars a couple more minutes to fill out the additional set of tags.

"Okay," he said as he handed the signed forms back to the kneeling attendant, "I'm going to go check in at the station, get you a case number, log in my evidence, then get started on my report. After that, I'm going to try to get a couple hours of sleep. So it may be a while before anyone gets back here to do a trace evidence search on the victim . . . or the dog."

"Hey, no problem," the morgue attendant said. "Today's my

Friday, and as soon as I go off duty, I'm heading south for a few days of sun and surf. And besides," he added with a forced attempt at cheerful camaraderie, "I don't think Mr. Robert Dawson here is going to be in any particular hurry to go anywhere else this morning anyway. Know what I mean?" he asked, looking up with a hopeful smile.

Only to discover that a coldly silent Detective-Sergeant Colin Cellars was already walking toward the door.

CHAPTER SEVENTEEN

THE OSP STATION WAS LOCATED TWO BLOCKS OFF OF STATE HIGH-way 243 and about five miles west of Interstate 5 that ran north all the way from Tijuana, Mexico, to Vancouver, British Columbia. It was a relatively new facility. Sparkling blue-and-white metal siding, blue-tinted and triple-paned thermal glass in all the windows, fresh paint on the driveways, and a silvery chain-link fence that encompassed a huge asphalt parking lot at least three times the size of the main station and the separate building that housed OMARR-9.

It was 0635 hours on a cold and rainy Saturday morning, and the parking lot was mercifully empty of scout cars and patrol officers. This allowed Cellars to card-key his way in through the security gate and back the Explorer up against the Property Unit loading dock without having to answer a lot of irritating questions. Like "What the hell happened to your vehicle?" "Did you know you're leaking gas?" and "Did you know that Captain Hawkins is looking for you?"

The image of Bobby Dawson lying in the back of the Explorer in a zippered body bag sat heavy on his mind.

The Property Unit loading dock had been designed so that investigators returning to the station with a car full of evidence could back right up to an extrawide security door that led into the evidence preparation room. The room itself was equipped with a pair of stainless-steel and Formica-topped layout tables; two desks; two computer terminals with attached printers; bright lights; securable drying cabinets and temporary evidence lockers; and an impressive collection of evidence marking, packaging, and tagging materials. In addition, near the exterior door, some thoughtful designer had added an explosion-proof cabinet for the storage of flammable arson evidence, and an array of fire safety equipment that included a safety shower, a wall-mounted fire blanket, and a large, red, push-button fire alarm.

After he finished wrapping another piece of duct tape around the leaking fuel line patch, Cellars started unloading the Explorer. Light-headed and nearly exhausted, it took him six separate trips to transfer all of Dawson's weapons, his CSI gear, and all of the evidence items into the prep room. The weapons and loose items of evidence filled four of the temporary storage lockers. He secured the steel doors, pulled the keys, dropped them into his pocket, and walked down the empty bright hallway to the main office. As he did so, he ignored the radio traffic being broadcast over the small ceiling speakers distributed throughout the station.

An older woman—heavyset, gray and brown hair, in her mid-fifties—was sitting at the front desk and jerked her head up from her magazine, seemingly startled by the presence of an unfamiliar figure inside the station.

"Oh . . . hello. You startled me." She smiled uneasily when she saw the glazed-eyed expression on Cellars's face. "Can I help you?"

"Hi. I'm Detective-Sergeant Colin Cellars."

"Ruth Wilkinson. Can I help you?" she repeated.

"I hope so." Cellars looked around the empty office as he held out his ID for the woman to examine. "First question: Where is everybody?"

"They're all out in the field working a missing deputy case, so I guess I'm it here until the day shift—did you say *Cellars*?" The woman blinked in surprise as the name registered. She immediately took another closer look at the ID card in her hand. "You're—"

"Nine-Echo-One? The new roving CSI officer from Portland that everyone was looking for all night?" Cellars suggested, working hard to mask his impatience. All he wanted to do was to finish up at the station, go home, go to bed, and try to blank out the haunting image of Bobby Dawson in a body bag . . . at least for a few hours.

"Boy, did you ever cause a ruckus around here the last few hours," the clerk commented as she handed the badge case back to Cellars. "I heard over the radio that they'd found you, but I sure wasn't expecting to see you here. I thought they wanted you to—"

"Meet them out at the Rusty Bar? With a body starting to turn ripe in the back of my vehicle, and gasoline leaking all over the place? I don't think so. First things first," Cellars replied with a discernible edge to his voice.

"Body . . . in the back of *your* vehicle?"

Cellars closed his eyes for a moment, willing himself to stay calm and controlled.

Not her fault, he reminded himself. *She doesn't know.*

So instead of venting his rage and frustration at a woman—and a member of the department—whom he'd already startled with his unexpected appearance, he simply said: "A coroner's investigator and a transport gurney would have been helpful. Unfortunately, they didn't know where I was either, much less that I needed them to respond to a homicide scene."

"Oh dear." Wilkinson looked stricken. "The Ha—I mean Captain Hawkins," she corrected quickly, her face coloring, "is really upset. I mean *really* upset. I don't know about everyone else out there, but

I do know that *he's* been trying to track you down all night. Driving everybody around here"—she looked around hurriedly—"absolutely crazy," she finished in a hushed voice.

"That so? Well, maybe he'll calm down a little bit, ease up on everybody now that he's found me," Cellars suggested. He didn't quite manage to keep the sarcasm out of his voice.

"I wouldn't count on it," she replied.

"Not exactly the nice, easygoing, and understanding type, I take it?" The expression on Cellars's face was still that of a man looking for someone—or something—to take apart at the seams, but he could feel himself beginning to relax.

Keep on talking to her, he told himself. *Not her fault.*

The front desk clerk looked as if she didn't know what to say. "Have you, uh, ever met the captain?" she finally asked cautiously.

"Briefly, yesterday afternoon," Cellars replied, barely masking a yawn with the back of his hand. "Personally, I thought he was kind of a shithead, if you'll excuse the expression, but we may have just gotten off to a bad start."

"Oh dear," Wilkinson repeated, looking—if anything—even more stricken as she quickly thumbed through her notes. "I don't know that I can help you improve your, uh, relationship with Captain Hawkins. But as long as you're here, I do have some messages for you. First of all, the captain was very insistent that if you did happen to come by here first, for whatever reason, I was supposed to remind you"—she looked up at Cellars with a sympathetic expression on her face—"that he's very definitely expecting you to report to the Rusty Bar immediately."

"When did he tell you that?" Cellars asked with unfeigned indifference.

"Oh, let me see." She looked at her notes again, then checked her watch. "I'd say about a half hour ago."

"Here at the station?"

"Oh no. The captain called in—"

"From the Rusty Bar?"

"That's right." Wilkinson nodded her head agreeably.

"Okay, you can consider me properly notified. Anything else?"

"I think . . . yes, here it is," she said, a triumphant smile appearing on her face as she found the notation in her notebook. "A young woman stopped by to see you last night . . . at approximately twenty-three-thirty hours. And now that I think about it, she was very insistent also. Said that she needed to talk with you right away, and that it was very important."

Jody, wanting to know about Dawson. Oh shit. It was a call he'd been dreading ever since he'd discovered Dawson's body. Cellars felt his stomach start to churn. But then he remembered . . . there was another possibility.

"Did she leave a name?"

"Uh, no, she didn't."

"Do you recall what she looked like?" he pressed, desperate to know because the very last thing in the world he wanted to do right now was to call Jody and tell her about Bobby Dawson.

"Well, let me think." Wilkinson hesitated. "There's been so much going on all night. I do remember she was a very attractive young woman. In terms of a description, I'd say she was about five-six, maybe a slender build—although I'm not certain about that, she was wearing a heavy jacket—and very dark hair."

"What about her eyes?"

"I'm sorry?"

"Do you remember what color her eyes were?"

"Oh. Uh, no, I'm sorry I don't." The front desk clerk hesitated again, then her head came up. "But there is something else I do remember."

"What's that?"

"She was absolutely terrified about something."

"Oh?" Cellars blinked. "Did she say why?"

"Actually, she really didn't ever say she was scared," Wilkinson said hesitantly. "But you could see it in her face . . . and her hands. They were trembling almost uncontrollably. In fact, I don't think

I've ever seen anyone so visibly shaken about . . . whatever it was. I asked her if she needed help, or if she wanted to talk with another officer . . . but then she said something very strange."

"What was that?"

"That she was in some kind of terrible trouble, and that you were the only one who could possibly help her. I *think* she even said something like, 'They're going to kill me.' "

"Did she say who 'they' were?" Cellars was alert now, in spite of his numbing fatigue.

Wilkinson shook her head. "No, she didn't. After she said that, she just had this terribly scared look on her face. Then she turned and ran out the front door." The clerk smiled uncertainly. "At first I kind of thought she might be one of those women who was being— I don't know—overly dramatic, as a way of getting an officer's home address or phone number."

"Did she ask for my home number?"

"No, she just kept repeating that she had to speak with you." Wilkinson shrugged her shoulders, looking slightly embarrassed. "I suppose the idea occurred to me because she did mention that she met you at some kind of lecture—"

Thank God.

"I think I know who you're talking about now," Cellars said, with a heartfelt sense of relief. "She sounds like a young woman I did meet at a lecture last night." He hesitated. "If you don't mind, if she calls again, would you please ask her to leave her name and a contact number so I can call her back as soon as possible . . . and as-sure her that if she really is in serious danger, we'll get an officer out to her immediately."

"I'll be happy to," Wilkinson said as she wrote in her notebook, "and I'll be sure to let her know that you're involved in a very com-plicated investigation, so it may be a while before you can get back to her." Then she looked up from her notebook. "And if Captain Hawkins calls again?"

Cellars was thoughtful for a long moment. "The Region Nine

master vehicle keys," he finally asked. "Do you know if there are any spares around here?"

"No, I don't think so." The front desk clerk hesitated. "I'm sure there's one in the watch commander's office. But he's out in the field with Captain Hawkins, and I don't have access to that either."

"And you don't have a vehicle key yourself?"

"Good heavens, no."

Cellars smiled. "What about a phone number for the Rusty Bar?"

"No, not offhand, but I can certainly get it for you." She started to reach into her desk drawer for a phone book.

"That's all right." Cellars shook his head as he reached for the phone on the clerk's desk and quickly punched in a memorized number.

"OMARR-Nine, how can I help you?"

"This is Oregon-Nine-Echo-One. Can you patch me in on a land line for Oregon-Nine-Alpha-One at the Rusty Bar?"

"OMARR-Nine to Echo-One, that's not a problem, but be advised that all land line calls patched through this location are recorded on the master tape."

"Echo-One, understood. Thank you."

Ten seconds later, Cellars sat in the chair next to the clerk and listened to the phone ring. Once. Twice.

"Rusty Bar."

"Can I speak to Captain Hawkins?"

"Sure, just a second."

A few moments later, a gruff voice came on the phone.

"Hawkins."

"This is Cellars. I understand—"

"CELLARS? Where the hell are you?" the voice demanded.

"At the station. I understand you want to see me." Deadly calm. The image of Bobby Dawson drifting in the back of his mind.

"You're goddamned right I want to see you. Get your ass over here, right now!"

"I can't."

There was a brief pause.

"What do you *mean* you can't?" the voice finally demanded. "I just gave you a direct order."

"Yes sir, I understand that. But I've got a steady gas leak in my CSI vehicle, coming out of the main fuel line. Left a trail all the way from the morgue. Lucky I made it to the station. You don't want that vehicle back out on the road until we can get it fixed."

"Sergeant, I don't care if you're pissing gas all over the god-damned town. I want to see you at this location in fifteen minutes, or I'll have your stripes."

"I understand that, sir, but I'm afraid I'm going to have to make an 'officer-at-the-scene' judgment call on this one. In my consid-ered opinion, it's definitely not safe to drive my assigned vehicle any farther through the middle of town. One spark and we're liable to end up with a line of fire a couple miles long . . . not to mention one hell of a fireball when my vehicle explodes," Cellars added calmly. "Among a lot of other problems, the fire department would probably go nuts trying to put out all the secondary fires."

"I don't give a—" Hawkins started in, then hesitated as he seemed to reconsider his comments. There was another much longer pause.

"Sergeant," the enraged station commander finally managed to get the words out, "are there any other OSP vehicles at the station at this moment?"

"Yes sir. Five total that I saw: three scout cars, an unmarked de-tective unit, and one of those new Expeditions."

"Good," Hawkins growled in a deadly cold voice. "Now listen to me, Sergeant. Listen to me very carefully. I want you to go out to the parking lot and get into one of those vehicles and proceed to the Rusty Bar immediately. And I mean *right now*. And if I don't see you here in—"

"I'm sorry sir, but I can't do that either," Cellars interrupted.

"*What?*" The word erupted from Hawkins's throat. From Cellars's coldly amused perspective, Captain Rodney Hawkins sounded as if he was within moments of completely losing control of his temper.

"There's no one at the station except for Mrs. Wilkinson and me," he replied calmly. "And she doesn't have a Region Nine vehicle key."

"Then use your own goddamned key, you stupid—!"

"I can't," Cellars interrupted again.

"What did you say?" This time the voice on the other end of the line was barely audible—as though Hawkins's throat had suddenly become tightly constricted.

"I said I can't, sir," Cellars repeated calmly.

"Why not?"

"I don't have a Region Nine vehicle key, sir."

"Why the hell not?"

"You insisted that I didn't need one, because I'm still driving a Region One CSI unit, sir. We discussed that yesterday afternoon, when I first reported in. Remember?"

Cellars smiled—a cold and deadly smile—as he held the phone away from his ear.

"What did he say?" Mrs. Wilkinson finally asked in a hushed whisper.

"Not much of anything," Cellars said indifferently as he gently hung up the phone. "I think he was too busy throwing the phone across the bar."

"Oh, dear God." The clerk's hands rose to her mouth.

"Don't worry about it," Cellars said reassuringly. "I'm sure he'll see the humor in it someday."

Ruth Wilkinson shook her head adamantly. "Oh, no, I don't think so."

"And in the meantime," Cellars added as he got up from the chair, "if Captain Hawkins does happen to come by here in the next couple of hours, you might let him know that I'll be in the evidence prep room, logging in my evidence and working on my report. I'll be easy to find."

CHAPTER EIGHTEEN

ONE OF THE ADVANTAGES OF HAVING THE EVIDENCE PREP ROOM all to himself was that it gave Cellars plenty of room to spread his evidence out on the two six-foot-by-eight-foot stainless-steel and Formica tabletops. He had just laid his collected evidence items out on the tables—placing the blood-related evidence on the stainless-steel tabletop—when he heard a car equipped with a powerful engine accelerate into the parking lot and come to a tire-screeching stop outside the secured door to the Property Unit dock.

Okay, Rodney, he thought, a cold, malicious smile forming on his face as he stood up from the tables and walked toward the door, *here we go. Hope you enjoy it.*

Cellars stepped outside the evidence prep room door and onto the dock just as Captain Hawkins came storming around the back of a sparkling white watch commander's scout car with a glowing cigar clenched tightly in his teeth. As he did so, another uniformed

OSP officer—this one wearing a pair of silver lieutenant's bars on his shoulders and seven hash marks on his sleeve—stepped out of the white scout car and then stood there, staring at the Explorer parked a few feet away with a stunned look on his face.

"Cellars, you insubordinate son of a bitch," Hawkins yelled, ripping the cigar out of his mouth and pointing like a glowing torch when he spotted Cellars on the raised concrete dock. "You patched that call through OMARR-Nine on purpose! You knew exactly what you were doing!"

"Yes sir, that's correct," Cellars conceded.

"By God, if it's the last thing I do on this earth, I'm going to see to it that you—"

Hawkins stopped in mid-sentence, suddenly speechless as he, too, saw the shattered side windows and starred windshield of the Explorer, and the bullet holes in the side panels.

"What in the living hell happened to your vehicle, Sergeant?" Hawkins demanded when he finally found his voice again.

"I was forced to shoot at it," Cellars explained calmly as he walked down the stairs to the dock and approached the uniformed station commander. "Several times, in fact."

"You . . . *what*?"

"Actually, to be more precise, I was forced to shoot at two fleeing homicide suspects who were in the process of stealing my vehicle—and my evidence," Cellars corrected, staring directly into the station commander's eyes with an expression that should have caused any observant law enforcement officer to go on full alert. "I was able to intercept them at the road before they got too far. And I probably hit the driver because he ran the car into a tree. You'll notice the fender damage." He gestured toward the front of the Explorer. "But then they—"

"That's it!" Hawkins screamed in rage as he flung the cigar aside. "Lieutenant Talbert, you are my witness. As of this moment, Detective-Sergeant Cellars is officially—"

"Oh, shit," Cellars said as he watched the cigar bounce under the Explorer.

Both Talbert and Hawkins turned to follow Cellars's gaze. At that moment, a sheet of flame erupted under the Explorer with a loud WHOOSH. As all three officers staggered backward, the billowing flames quickly spread across the asphalt to the adjacent white scout car. Within moments, both cars were ablaze.

"WHAT THE HELL?" Hawkins screamed, then turned to stare at Cellars in furious disbelief.

"You idiot! You just set fire to my vehicle with that damned cigar, and I hadn't even processed it for prints yet!" Cellars yelled out over his shoulder as he ran toward the dock stairs.

"ME?"

"I told you, it had a gas leak!"

"WHAT?"

But Cellars was no longer paying any attention to Hawkins. He was up on the Property Unit dock now and running as fast as he could toward the door to the evidence prep room.

Hawkins turned to his watch commander, hands outstretched and eyes wide with shock, and yelled: "Talbert, do something!" At almost that same moment, Cellars reached the door to the evidence prep room, yanked it open, reached around, and then slammed the palm of his hand against the fire alarm button.

The effects were immediate. Red lights started flashing throughout the parking lot and loading dock area, and a fire alarm bell began to ring loudly. The lights and alarm seemed to jar the stunned lieutenant into motion. Talbert broke into a mad dash toward the nearest fire extinguisher about fifty feet away.

"NO, NO, NOT THE FIRE ALARM, GODDAMN IT!! GET AN EXTINGUISHER AND GET THIS FIRE—" Hawkins started to scream at Cellars . . . but at that moment, the Explorer's half-empty gas tank exploded. The resulting shock wave sent Hawkins tumbling backward into the dock stair railing just as the fiercely burning Explorer launched itself into the air . . . and came back down on top of the station's fenced-off step-down transformer. The crushed transformer immediately erupted in a blinding inferno of white sparks, causing all of the station and parking lot lights suddenly to go dark.

Seconds later, as the station's emergency backup generators kicked in, and yellow emergency lights began to flicker on throughout the station and around the loading dock, the watch commander's car exploded, sending burning gasoline and car parts in all directions.

Varying portions of Captain Rodney Hawkins's uniform jacket and pants were already on fire by the time Cellars reached his unconscious supervisor with the fire blanket he'd pulled from the evidence prep room. Cellars worked quickly to drag Hawkins clear of the flaming debris and get him wrapped into the oxygen-suppressing blanket. But it was Lieutenant Talbert's timely arrival with the fire extinguisher that actually saved Hawkins—and Cellars—from some potentially lethal burns. And it was the noisy arrival of the fire and rescue crews into the darkened parking lot that ultimately allowed Cellars and Talbert to stand back and watch while the paramedics took over, checked Hawkins's vital signs, cut away his partially melted clothing, and applied some preliminary first aid.

The two officers continued to watch in rapt fascination as the fast-working medical team strapped the unconscious station commander onto a gurney and heaved it into the back of the ambulance. Then they stepped back out of the way as the ambulance roared into life, announcing its imminent departure with a loud and blinding display of eardrum-piercing sirens and flashing lights.

———

Fifteen minutes later, Talbert and Cellars sat at a table in the amber-emergency-light-illuminated lunchroom, staring out the parking-lot-side window and watching the firemen poke around the still-smoldering remains of the scout car and the Explorer.

"Tell me, Cellars, things ever get this exciting up in Region

One?" the watch commander inquired calmly as he poured from a pot of rapidly cooling coffee into a pair of official OSP mugs.

"No, not that I can recall," Cellars replied as he sipped gratefully at the lukewarm but still revitalizing brew. "But it occurs to me that I might have lived a sheltered life up there."

"Good." Talbert nodded contentedly as he added a couple packets of diet sweetener to his cup. "I'd really hate to think that this was the sort of thing you do to your new supervisors on a routine basis."

Cellars eyed the watch commander cautiously, his survival instincts overriding his general sense of exhaustion. "Are you suggesting I might have set this whole deal up just to cause Hawkins some grief my first day on the job?"

Talbert stared into his coffee cup for a long moment.

"No," he finally said, "not really. I figure you might have set a few things into motion. Like that tape-recorded conversation on the patched line, for example. But I really don't think you're clever enough—or maybe the better description is 'lucky enough,' " he corrected after a moment, "to turn a leaky fuel line into a two-alarm blaze, a destroyed transformer, and a medivac response for your target. Especially when the entire situation ultimately depended on the thoughtless son of a bitch doing something incredibly stupid with a lit cigar."

"Glad to hear you feel that way . . . I think."

"Because if I did," the watch commander went on, "then I'd probably feel obligated to put you in for some kind of meritorious service award. Maybe even a promotion. And I really hate to do that for a guy the first day on the job. Sets a bad precedent, if you know what I mean."

"Ah," Cellars said noncommittally.

"My guess," Talbert went on in a conversational tone, "is the bastard walks out of the hospital in less than a week with a mild concussion, some pretty tender second-degree burns, and maybe—if he can't talk his way out of it—a departmental reprimand for being careless in a no-smoking zone. Not to mention a real serious hard-on for your ass," the watch commander added meaningfully.

"Whereupon he goes back to being the station commander . . . and my direct supervisor?" Cellars smiled slightly, as if the idea was something mildly pleasant to contemplate.

"Oh, yeah." Talbert nodded. "In addition to being a first-class prick, the man's definitely a survivor. You never want to forget that."

"Any suggestions?" Cellars was still on a cautious alert. Everything about Talbert suggested a man who was very self-confident, and very much in command—of himself and his circumstances. In other words, definitely not a man to screw with.

"Sure. Next time you get him flat on the ground like that, take the time to plant a stake in his heart. We'll pass a hat around the department to cover your legal fees."

"Ah."

"Which brings us to the question of vehicles."

"I guess I'm probably going to need one," Cellars said.

"Yes, you will. Otherwise, you'll still be hanging around the station when Hawkins shows up, and that doesn't strike me as being a tremendously good idea . . . for everyone concerned."

"I'll go along with that."

"Thing is, I'd be happy to lend you mine—I hardly ever get to leave the station anymore anyway—but it looks to me like it's going to need some major bodywork." Talbert gestured with his mug in the general direction of the glowing mass of blackened and twisted sheet metal and broken safety glass that only an hour ago had been a brand-new, shiny white watch commander's scout car.

"Hope you weren't too fond of it."

"Oh, I was. Matter of fact, it was a damned sweet little ride for a guy with twenty-nine years on the job, a bad back, and a lousy disposition. And I don't mind saying it really pisses me off to see it looking like that. Thing is though, I just don't see how I can blame you for its current condition. Not directly, anyway, unless I really put my mind to it," Talbert added as he reached into his shirt pocket, pulled out a key, and tossed it onto the table. "You know what that is?"

Cellars glanced down at the familiar key. "A Region Nine master vehicle key?" he ventured.

"That's right," Talbert nodded approvingly. "And as you might expect, it's cut to fit every OSP vehicle out in that parking lot, including that brand-new four-wheel-drive Expedition you can just barely see over there in the far end of the lot. The one I was holding back for our new Search and Rescue Team . . . which happens to be my pet project."

"Looks like a nice one," Cellars offered.

"It is. Top-of-the-line vehicle. Just what those fellows are going to need if we ever get the rest of the funding to put the team together. But even so, I'd be mighty tempted to slap a watch commander's insignia on it right now . . . except for the fact that I happen to know that the damned thing rides like a brick with all that off-road gear, and I've gotten pretty soft the last couple of years.

"So here's the deal," Talbert went on, not bothering to wait for any comment from Cellars. "You're going to hook one of our computers and printers up to an emergency power plug in the evidence prep room. Then you're going to write and file your CSI report, drop off your evidence at the lab, load your gear up in my brand-new Search and Rescue vehicle, go home, get some sleep, and then report back in to OMARR-Nine sometime later today ready to do your job. In the meantime, I'm going to use my temporary signature authority to order myself a brand-new sweet ride, and you're going to do me the tremendous favor of staying the hell away from this station for the next couple of weeks until everything settles out. How does that sound?"

"Like the best deal I've heard since I joined up," Cellars said seriously.

"Good. Maybe you really are as smart as some of those people up in Portland say."

"I guess I'd settle for not being quite as stupid and thick-headed as some of the others probably say," Cellars offered.

"All right, fair enough." Talbert nodded agreeably. "In that case, I suggest you get that report on my desk within the hour, then get the hell out of here before I change my mind and make a serious effort to try to see Captain Hawkins's side of this whole goddamned fiasco."

"Only thing is," Cellars added reluctantly, "I may have a problem."

Talbert stared at Cellars for a long moment.

"There's no maybes about it, Cellars," he finally said. "You definitely have a problem. Probably more than one would be my educated guess." Talbert hesitated, and then sighed in resignation. "Okay, let's assume for the moment that you're not deliberately trying to fuck with me. What's bothering you now?"

"The victim out at the shooting scene at the end of County Road Twenty-Two-Fifty-Five."

Cellars had spent a goodly part of the time while they watched the paramedics working on Hawkins to give Talbert a quick thumbnail sketch of the circumstances surrounding the homicide scene he'd just worked. The watch commander hadn't seemed overwhelmingly concerned at the time. But Cellars figured that the presence of the fire department hosing down a raging fire involving two OSP vehicles in the middle of the station parking lot—while a fire and rescue team was working to stabilize and medivac the station commander who had sustained a head injury and serious burns—might have been a little distracting. And besides, he hadn't given Talbert all of the relevant information.

"Yeah, what about him?"

"I know the guy. He and I went to school together about fifteen years ago down in Southern California," Cellars said, the image of Dawson in the zippered body bag still hovering in the back of his mind.

"So you figure that puts you in a conflict-of-interest situation? A *legitimate* conflict of interest?" Talbert turned to face Cellars, watching him very carefully now.

"Maybe." Cellars shrugged. "He and I were real close when we were kids, until we got into a pretty serious beef—"

"Let me guess," Talbert interrupted. "Over a girl, right?"

Cellars hesitated, then nodded. "Yeah, it was. How'd you figure that?"

"Girl or a car. Kids that age, had to be one or the other," Talbert commented. "Go on."

"Anyway, we were supposed to be getting back together again, after fifteen goddamned years—at a lecture down at the County auditorium—to work things out. But he didn't show . . . and then I got called out to the scene—"

"And found your buddy DOA."

"Yeah."

"You said that kind of hesitant-like," Talbert said suspiciously. "Almost like there's something else you haven't gotten around to mentioning?"

"That lecture at the auditorium I told you about?"

"Yeah, what about it?"

"I was the one giving the lecture."

"So?"

"The topic was collecting evidence at an alien contact crime scene."

"You mean aliens as in—?" Talbert raised his eyes skyward.

Cellars nodded.

Talbert closed his eyes and sighed again, giving the perfect impression of a man in the process of developing a world-class headache. But then, after another few seconds, the veteran watch commander opened his eyes and stared directly at his newly assigned CSI officer.

"Is there anything else about this entire evening that you feel a need to tell me?"

Cellars nodded. "Yeah, one more thing. The girl. She's still in the picture."

"You mean the girl who was a problem fifteen years ago when you and your buddy were a couple of horny teenagers? Or the woman you were both still in love with as of yesterday evening?"

The pained expression on Cellars's face gave Talbert his answer.

The watch commander spent a few more seconds staring at his CSI officer.

"But you didn't actually shoot this ex-buddy of yours while you were capping off rounds at fleeing suspects and OSP vehicles right and left, correct? That's not something you're holding back on me?"

Cellars met the watch commander's appraising gaze squarely. "No, I didn't shoot Bobby, accidentally or otherwise."

"That's nice to hear," Talbert said in a manner that suggested—from Cellars's suspicious point of view—an unlikely degree of almost complete indifference.

Neither man said anything for a few moments, until Cellars finally broke the silence.

"You going to ask the next question?"

"What's that?"

"Am I willing to take a polygraph?"

The expression on Talbert's grizzled face never flickered.

"As a matter of fact, no, I wasn't. But seeing as how you brought the subject up . . ." Talbert cocked his head in a questioning manner.

"The answer's yes, anytime you want. Just tell me when and where," Cellars replied calmly.

"That's a pretty open-ended offer."

Cellars shrugged indifferently. "I haven't got anything to hide . . . or at least nothing that I can think of at the moment. My life's not that exciting."

"I might argue with you on that last point," Talbert replied after a moment, "but I appreciate the offer. Let's hope I don't have to hold you to it."

Talbert continued to sit there in the faint amber light, staring out at the darkened parking lot for almost a full minute, seemingly lost in his thoughts.

Then, finally, he turned his attention back to the newest member of his station command.

"You want to know what I think?"

Cellars nodded. "Yeah, sure."

"I don't think there's any question but what you've got at least one legitimate conflict-of-interest problem floating around somewhere in this whole mess. And under anything resembling normal circumstances, I wouldn't hesitate to assign another CSI officer to the investigation of your friend's death right now . . . just to play things safe.

"But the thing is," he went on, "everybody up in the Portland office tells me that you're the best CSI officer in the department. In fact, they're a little curious as to why you'd walk away from a cushy crime lab job just to work crime scenes, which everybody agrees—presumably even you—consists mostly of hard work, long hours, dirty clothes, lousy memories, and aching knees."

Talbert eyed Cellars, who shrugged agreeably.

"But the general consensus," Talbert went on, "is that if anyone's going to find a link between all these suspicious disappearances throughout Jasper County during the last eleven months, you're the one who's going to do it. And the investigation you were sent out on most definitely involves missing Jasper County deputies. What's more, you've already worked the goddamned scene and presumably collected all the evidence, so it doesn't make a hell of a lot of sense for me to send somebody else back up to that cabin to look for evidence that isn't there. And even if it did make any sense, I don't have any more CSI officers to send because they're all out in the street looking for four missing Jasper County deputies."

"Four?" Cellars blinked in confusion. "I thought—"

"Downs and Wills. They never showed up at the Rusty Bar."

"But—"

"The last we heard from them, they said they'd just gotten down to the bottom of the hill, and that they were going to check out some kind of lead in the northwest corner of the county."

Cellars wrinkled his eyebrows in confusion. "What lead is that?"

"I don't know. They didn't say. Presumably something they found up at that scene."

"As far as I know, the only thing they found up there was a dead dog . . . and a bunch of shadows that scared the shit out of them," Cellars added cryptically.

"What?"

"I'm just telling you what they said . . . and how they acted."

"Scared of shadows?" Talbert asked skeptically.

Cellars shrugged. "Definitely scared of something."

"And you said you never got a clear view of the suspects you were shooting at," Talbert reminded.

"That's right," Cellars conceded. "But don't forget, my shadows managed to hot-wire a locked OSP vehicle, drive off with it down the road, destroy my radio and emergency beeper, and steal my cell phone."

The watch commander nodded, then remained silent as he seemed to be considering this new information.

"You know, that's really interesting," he finally said. "Especially when you consider that when Downs checked in with OMARR-Nine, he said that you were almost done with your CSI work up on the mountain . . . and that as soon as you were done, you'd be driving over to the north end to help them follow up on that lead."

"What?"

"A story that gets even more interesting," Talbert went on as he watched Cellars's face closely, "when you take into account that was several hours before we found deputy Clyde Wills's scout car— empty and abandoned—out at the northwest corner of the county. No sign of him or Sergeant Downs."

Cellars looked stunned. "I—I'm sorry, I don't understand what's going on around here."

Talbert continued to stare at Cellars, as if trying to make up his mind about something.

"Neither do I, Sergeant," he finally said in a deadly calm voice.

"Fact of the matter is, I don't think anyone around here has the slightest idea what this is all about. But the one thing we *do* understand is that we've got four missing deputies and a dead body all linked to a remote cabin up in the High Gorge. A body that you tell me belongs to a long-lost buddy that you haven't seen for fifteen years because you've been fighting over a girl. A girl—or woman— who's still in the picture, as I believe you put it. And just to make things a little more interesting," Talbert added when Cellars remained silent, "right now, as far as we know, you may have been the last person to have seen at least two of those deputies . . . dead or alive."

Cellars blinked, speechless, as the implications of Talbert's words hit home.

"So maybe you'll understand, now, Sergeant, why there's a whole bunch of people—in the OSP *and* the Jasper County Sheriff's Department—who are really anxious to read that CSI report of yours. Just to find out exactly what it is you claim to have been doing up on that mountain for the past eight hours."

CHAPTER NINETEEN

FIFTEEN MINUTES LATER, DETECTIVE-SERGEANT COLIN CELLARS—now increasingly hungry in addition to being thoroughly confused, angry, frustrated, tired, and depressed—sat down in the dim amber light of the station's evidence prep room and stared at the pile of collected evidence.

There was still a lot of work to be done, but none of it amounted to an emergency situation. The scene had been worked and the evidence collected. The victim had been turned over to the county morgue. And the evidence was now within the secure confines of the OSP substation. In effect: The suspects were long gone, there was no hot trail to follow, the body of the victim wasn't going anywhere, and neither was the evidence. All of which meant that Cellars ought to have been able to take his time—and maybe even go home and get a few hours of sleep—before completing all of the evidence-related steps that a team of two or three homicide investigators would have normally divided among themselves.

Had this been anything resembling a normal homicide investigation.

But it wasn't.

Not when Bobby Dawson is lying in a goddamned morgue freezer, four Jasper County deputies are still missing, and the primary investigator is rapidly becoming the chief suspect, Cellars thought glumly as he continued to stare at the mound of evidence items, willing himself not to reach for the phone.

The temptation to call Jody and Malcolm—to tell them that Bobby Dawson was dead—was almost overwhelming.

I owe them that, he kept telling himself, over and over again.

But you don't know for sure it's Bobby, some unrelenting entity in the back of his mind argued. *So why cause your friends all that grief when all you've got is circumstantial evidence?*

Yeah, right. A half-finished portrait of the Jody-like woman with his name at the bottom. The remote mountain cabin. All the Custer-era guns. What the hell more do you want?

"I want an answer . . . and I want proof," Cellars answered his own question out loud, knowing with a sinking heart that what he really wanted—the love of the girl/woman who had haunted his dreams and his waking moments all these years—was about to slip away from his grasp forever.

Unless you can find the evidence.

That last thought seemed to reenergize Cellars.

Determined to finish this part of the investigation before he made any effort to resolve his other problems in life, he began to lay out the collected items into organized groups on the two tables so that he could mark, package, tag, and log them into a computerized evidence list.

Assuming I can find enough power around here to run the computer and *the printer,* he reminded himself.

He first tried to plug one of the evidence prep computers and

printers into the orange-plated backup power socket, but the fluc-
tuating current from the emergency generators turned out to be too
much for the surge protector. Then he tried hooking his battery-
powered notebook computer into an emergency-generator-powered
printer, and got essentially the same results. He thought, briefly, about
typing his report into his notebook computer, then leaving the entire
thing on Talbert's desk with an explanatory note. But his survival
instincts told him that he might be pushing his luck with a watch
commander who had been amazingly supportive so far, all things considered. So, instead, he rummaged through the desk drawer, and went
back to the evidence table with a pen and a pad of old-fashioned report forms in hand.

A quick phone call to Ruth Wilkinson got him the assigned case
number: OSP-09-00-6666.

The amber emergency lights gave off enough illumination to do
the job. But as Cellars quickly discovered, the color shift made it
difficult to make out specific identifying characteristics . . . especially when it came to the presumed bloodstains from the expended
bullets.

At the scene, he had absorbed all of the suspected bloodstains
onto one-inch-square pieces of clean white cloth that he'd placed in
open glass vials to air dry. Now, at the station, working with a pair
of Teflon-coated forceps and a bottle of cleaning solution, he transferred each of the dried cloth squares into a small manila envelope.
He labeled the envelopes with the date, the assigned OSP case
number, his initials, and the identifying scene item numbers CC-3
through CC-10, and CC-55 through 56; and marked the same identifying numbers and other related information on the ten evidence
tags. Then, after sealing each envelope with lengths of red tamper-
proof evidence tape, and placing his initials and date across the
seals, he stapled each evidence tag to its corresponding envelope.

The sample of matted hair and dried blood from the basement
rug was marked, packaged, and tagged CC-11.

The blood-, water-, and mud-soaked squares collected from the cul-de-sac near the dog carcass, and the fragments of bone found nearby, were marked, packaged, and tagged CC-12 through CC-17.

The memory card from his damaged digital camera was designated CC-18, and the roll of film from his damaged 35mm camera CC-19.

The broken hasp and lock from the exterior basement door of the cabin was scribed with the item number CC-20 before being packaged and tagged.

The small rock and glass fragments beneath the window were designated CC-21.

The blood-splattered painting of the haunting, violet-eyed young woman—who was supposedly terrified and desperately looking for him, according to the front desk clerk, Cellars reminded himself—was CC-22.

The TOD device was secured in its transport carton, sealed, and tagged CC-23.

He hesitated at the thirteen holstered handguns of varying makes, models, and eras, the two empty holsters, the pump shotgun, and the Sharps rifle. Proper evidence protocol required that all weapons be inscribed with the assigned case and item number on the smooth metal surfaces beneath the wooden grips and/or stock. This often provided useful information to investigators, especially when a weapon seized in one case turned out to have already been inscribed from a previous case.

But Bobby would kill me if he ever found out I did that to one of his guns, much less his entire collection, Cellars thought, setting aside as irrelevant the fact that he had just delivered his friend's body to the morgue earlier that morning.

Accordingly, Cellars took a certain amount of comfort—and no little self-satisfaction—in ignoring the protocol. Instead, he simply recorded the serial numbers of the weapons, and marked the item numbers CC-24 through CC-40 on evidence tags that he attached to the trigger guards of the weapons and buckles of the holsters.

Using a fine-tipped metal scribe, he took the time to methodically inscribe the corresponding scene item numbers CC-41 through CC-43 on the base of the three lead bullets he'd carefully dug out of the cabin wall by the refrigerator. And then did the same thing— carefully inscribing the numbers CC-44 through CC-47—on the four misshapen lead balls he'd removed from the log wall by the exterior door. As he did so, he noted that bullets CC-42 and CC-46 (and the surrounding fragments of wood) appeared to be contaminated with small amounts of blood and/or tissue. As best he could tell without digging away at the protective and concealing pieces of wood, the other five bullets all appeared to be clean. He made note of that on his evidence list.

He repeated the protocol with the mushroomed hollow-point bullet he'd dug out of the basement log wall by the window, and the two mushroomed hollow-points on the floor next to the glass fragments and stone. The first bullet was marked CC-48, and the last two CC-49 and CC-50. As he completed his notes on those items, he recorded the fact that the two mushroomed projectiles from the floor also appeared to be contaminated with blood.

The other three bullets he'd found buried in the log wall opposite the stairwell—presumably the ones he'd fired at the fleeing greenish shadowy figure lunging down the stairs—were inscribed CC-51 through CC-53.

Each inscribed bullet was then placed in its own marked, sealed, and tagged evidence envelope.

The cut ends of the telephone and electrical wires were labeled CC-57 and CC-58.

The tabletop was beginning to get crowded, so he started to put the tagged evidence packages and submittal/chain-of-custody forms into a large cardboard box for transportation to the lab. But he hesitated when he remembered that all of Dawson's revolvers were loaded.

You and your goddamned paranoia, Cellars muttered, feeling himself starting to nod off as he fumbled with the oiled cylinders.

Surprised you didn't mount a loaded Civil War cannon out in your front yard while you were at it.

He managed to remove all the cartridges from the "modern" revolvers, but he gave up on trying to extract lead balls and loose powder in the cap-and-ball models, and finally was forced to remove the entire cylinders. Which, in turn, forced him to take another few minutes to block print written warnings for the crime lab staff, to the effect that the separated cylinders with the shiny primers stuck tightly on the exposed nipples were still loaded.

Then he went back to packaging and tagging the rest of his collected evidence.

It was only when he got to the nine expended .40-caliber casings he'd collected from the cabin basement floor that he realized he wasn't sure which ones were which. He knew he'd fired six rounds at whoever—or whatever—had been reaching for the holstered revolver on the wall, and three more at the shadowy figures fleeing through the exterior basement door. And his crudely hand-drawn sketch of the basement floor showed the relative locations of the nine casings. But he had no idea which ones were which.

Doesn't matter, he told himself. *They're all .40-caliber Winchester-Western casings, and presumably all from the same batch of ammunition. They were all fired through the same pistol. I'm the one who fired them. I've admitted that I fired them. Hell, I'm even documenting the fact that I fired them. And in any case, everybody knows the damned things bounce all over the place in an enclosed space, so what does it matter where they were found?*

It was a perfectly reasonable rationalization. But Cellars also knew that if he were the CSI officer investigating a questioned shooting by another officer, he would have meticulously documented the observed location of every impacted bullet and every expended casing . . . simply because you never knew what trivial piece of evidence might turn out to be important.

And since I'm the one who may end up being accused of an improper shooting—or worse, he remembered, thinking how Talbert had all but told him he would be in the crosshairs for an IA investigation once they found those missing deputies, or his fleeing suspects.

It occurred to Cellars, at that moment, that he hadn't collected the expended casings he'd fired up at the top of the stairs, or the ones out at the cul-de-sac. In fact, he'd completely forgotten about them.

Shit.

He thought, briefly, about going back out to the scene . . . or better yet, getting Talbert to take him back out there. The idea appealed to him. *Let him see what that cabin is like for himself. Maybe, if I'm lucky, we might even run across one of those goddamned shadows.*

But then he thought better of the idea.

No. To hell with it, he decided. *It's not like I'm denying I fired the shots. The IA guys don't believe me, they can go back up there and collect the damned things themselves. I've got more important things to worry about.*

Like Jody . . . and Malcolm, he thought morosely.

The idea of being the target of OSP's Internal Affairs team was unsettling enough. But the logical follow-up to that situation, the possibility that someone might actually accuse him of being involved in Dawson's death, and that word of such an accusation would almost certainly reach his treasured friends—especially Jody—was truly numbing.

Cellars shook his head in frustration.

Enough of that. Gotta figure out how to make sense out of the evidence I did collect.

He stared down at the small pile of hand-marked manila envelopes, trying to remember the sequence of events.

Okay, let's work through it logically. I should have marked the location of the first six casings on my sketch right away. But I didn't because I got distracted by that portrait, and started searching the rooms upstairs for some proof that it might not be Bobby's cabin. Then I fired those last three rounds at the bastards when I lunged out of the stairwell and onto the basement floor, so those casings got mixed in with the first six. And

I never got any overall photos at the scene, because I broke the damned camera right away, so then I used . . .

Cellars smiled.

. . . Malcolm's scanner.

It took him about five minutes to pull the PowerBook and the linked Primary Receiver out of its case, and another two or three to confirm that there was still enough power in the battery to get the notebook computer up and running, and the proper data file selected. Finally, the display on the screen read:

DATA FILE SELECTED: CC_JOHNDOE_CABIN

CHOOSE DISPLAY:

SCREEN Y

3D PROJECTION Y

SELECT CHOICE & HIT ENTER KEY

Cellars selected "SCREEN," hit the laptop's *ENTER* key, then recoiled backward as a burst of bright laser light erupted from the Primary Receiver.

Shit, forgot to turn the damned switch off, Cellars muttered, shielding his eyes as he lunged forward, grabbed the Primary Receiver, and turned the laser-light-emitting hemisphere away from his face. He quickly flicked the recessed ON/OFF switch to the OFF position, and then sat there at the desk, trying to blink away the faint streaks of light that seemed to have been burned across his retinas.

That was when something out of the corner of his eye caught his attention.

He turned his head just in time to see one of the manila evidence envelopes on the desk stop moving.

CHAPTER TWENTY

CELLARS REMAINED WHERE HE WAS FOR A GOOD THIRTY SEC-
onds, a cold chill running up his neck as he continued to stare—
stunned and disbelieving—at the evidence envelope in the dim lights.

It was a standard, tape-sealed, medium-sized nine-inch-by-six-
inch manila envelope, bulging in the middle. And it was lying immobile at the far corner of the desktop. Just as it had been doing
thirty seconds ago.

Except Cellars was certain—absolutely certain—that thirty seconds ago, that specific envelope had been lying in the middle of the
desktop.

Right where he'd put it.

The chills were pouring over his shoulders and down his arms.

Cellars could feel his heart pounding. His fingertips were numb,
and he was trying to ignore the warning alarms that were screaming
in the back of his mind. But even so, he continued to sit there in

the chair, staring at the tagged evidence envelope. Waiting to see if it would move again.

But it didn't.

So finally, slowly, and ever so cautiously, he stood up in the chair and leaned forward over the desk until he could read the marking on the evidence tag.

Item CC-21. Rock and glass fragments located beneath broken window, NW corner of cabin basement.

Cellars shook his head slowly.

I must be losing my mind, he thought. *Rocks and glass fragments don't move. They just flat don't.*

He started to reach for the envelope, hesitated, then picked up his pen and used the tip of it to flip the envelope over cautiously.

Nothing. Just his initials and date marked across the red evidence tape.

What the hell?

Cellars could feel his heart pounding even harder now, to the point that he was starting to feel dizzy. But even so, his protective senses immediately attempted to rationalize the situation.

Dawson's dead. Jody doesn't know. I've got to tell her. I've been shooting at shadows the whole goddamned night. I'm tired, exhausted, probably even in some degree of shock. Which would explain why I'm starting to see things. Talbert's right. Definitely time I go home and get some sleep.

He stared at the wayward evidence envelope for a few more seconds, daring it to move again.

But it didn't.

Which is exactly what I'm going to do . . . just as soon as I finish up my scene report and drop all this evidence off at the lab. Then *I can go home, get some sleep, and try to forget about all this shit for a few hours.*

It was a very appealing thought.

He stopped by the lunchroom to pour the last dark dregs from the coffeepot into a paper cup. He took a cautious sip of the cold and bitter brew, winced, then tossed the rest down the sink, deciding there had to be a better way to stay awake. Returning to the evidence prep room, he spent another forty-five minutes typing and printing out a single-spaced narrative report of his crime scene investigation.

He held the printout of the four-page report in his hands for a long moment, staring at the cover page, knowing that several of the paragraphs—as written—would make little sense to Talbert or Hawkins . . . or a review board, for that matter.

What the hell, he shrugged as he signed the cover sheet in the appropriate block and initialed the other three pages. *It's all true. Or at least I think it is. Let them sort out what makes sense.*

He dropped the signed report off at the watch commander's in-box, waved a tired good-bye to Talbert—who was standing in the doorway arguing with a couple of utility repairmen who didn't seem to be making much progress in replacing the blackened and mangled transformer—and walked out into the dark cloudy sky and drizzling rain to his new CSI vehicle.

There he discovered, much to his amazement—when he started up the engine and the radio console lights came on—that it was nearly ten-thirty in the morning.

———

The evidence clerk at the Medford Crime Lab popped her head out of the evidence storage room in response to the ringing bell.

"Hi, I'm Linda Grey," she said as she closed and secured the heavy metal door behind her before walking up to the counter. "Don't believe we've met."

"Colin Cellars." He shook her extended hand. "New CSI officer for Region Nine."

"Oh that's right. Detective-Sergeant Cellars. We heard you were coming down here from Portland to work on those kidnapping and unexplained disappearance cases. Welcome to Medford, Sergeant."

"Colin will do just fine, but thanks." Cellars smiled wearily. "I almost hate to ask, but have you folks gotten in much evidence on those cases?"

The evidence clerk shook her head glumly. "Hardly anything."

"Well," he said with a tired sigh as he reached down for a large cardboard box and placed it on the counter, "I think it's fair to say that we're going to take a different approach to the problem from now on."

Linda Grey stared at the box that was brimming over with tagged evidence packages. And blinked in surprise as Cellars bent down again and brought up a second box . . . and then the long-barreled Sharps rifle.

"Anything else down there?" she asked cautiously as she leaned forward and looked over the counter.

"No, that's it . . . for now. But I suspect there'll be more coming."

"Okay, I'm convinced," she nodded, a wide grin appearing on her dimpled face. "Looks like Jack was right. Things really are going to start picking up around here now that you're working the scenes. Why don't you come on in," she added as she unlocked the door next to the evidence counter, "and we'll get all this sorted out."

"Jack? You mean Jack Wilson?" Cellars asked as he entered the evidence layout room and carefully closed the door behind him.

"That's the fellow," Grey said as she put both boxes on the lay-out table and began removing the items from the box and sorting them out on the four-foot-by-eight-foot Formica surface. "Number two head honcho around here. He said you might stop by some-time."

"Is he around right now?"

"No, all the scientists are out at a staff meeting at the range. They probably won't be back until after lunch." She glanced up at the clock on the wall. "At least a couple of hours or so from now."

"No problem. I'll catch him next time," Cellars said, watching as she gingerly started to remove the first holstered pistol from the bottom of the first box. "The rifle and all of the pistols are un-loaded," he said quickly, "but I didn't have the tools to pull the black powder rounds in the cap-and-ball revolvers, so I just re-moved the cylinders and marked them 'LOADED.' "

"Gotcha." The evidence tech nodded as she reached into the box and carefully placed the three red-tagged metal cylinders off to the side of the table. "I think I'll let the firearms people handle these things from the get-go."

"Good idea," Cellars agreed. "Also, you might advise them that based on what we know about the victim, all of the weapons are probably in first-class shape—at least as far as test-firing goes," he added thoughtfully. "But the suspects probably had access to them, so—"

"Advise them to be careful?" Grey finished.

"Yeah, I think that would be a good idea."

"Okay, so noted. Let's see what we've got here." She looked down the submittal form that Cellars had filled out, comparing the item descriptions to the tagged packages that she'd laid out in order of tag number. "All the blood and tissue work looks pretty straight-forward." She continued reading. "You want the revolver in CC-Fifty-Four tested to see if it has a faulty firing mechanism?"

"I want to find out if it can go off accidentally from a half-cock position," Cellars explained.

"Okay, that shouldn't be any problem. Hey, wait a minute, it says here you want all the weapons test-fired and compared against all of the *non*-forty-caliber hollow-points and casings. Is that right?"

She looked up at Cellars, who nodded.

"You mind if I ask why?"

"A couple of reasons, actually. First of all, I'm pretty sure that none of those revolvers are chambered for a modern forty-caliber auto-loading round. And secondly, I'm the one who did all of the forty-caliber hollow-point shooting," he explained.

She looked back down at the submission form for a brief mo-ment. "*All* of it?" she whispered, a startled look appearing on her face.

He shrugged self-consciously. "I'm afraid so. Not one of my bet-ter days."

"I guess not," Linda Grey commented as she quickly scanned the list again. "Boy, I guess Jack knew what he was talking about. Things really are going to get a little more interesting around here," she said— mostly to herself—as she continued down the list. Then her eyebrows rose. "Uh, what about this notation on CC-Twenty-One? 'Request lab identify any unusual characteristics about item contents'?" She looked up at Cellars curiously. "You want to expand on that?"

Yeah sure, he thought, *tell me why an inanimate object suddenly becomes mobile. That ought to start some interesting discussions about the sanity of CSI officers around here.*

"No, that's all right. I'd just like . . . uh, Jack to take a look at it for me. I left him a note in that envelope stapled to the tag. I'll talk to him about it later."

"Okay, I'll make sure he gets the case file." The evidence tech shrugged agreeably as she continued to read the submittal form. "Uh, what about this roll of thirty-five-millimeter film?"

"There may be one exposed frame on the roll," Cellars explained. "I'm not sure if it's going to be relevant to anything, but I'd like to take a look anyway. You think you could get me a blowup of it? Maybe by tomorrow afternoon?"

"Let me check." The clerk reached for a nearby phone and quickly punched in a memorized number. Moments later, she replaced the handset into the receiver, then shook her head.

"Sorry, but it looks like you're oh-for-two on special requests around here today. According to Matt, our processor went belly up last night. He says we're probably looking at forty-eight hours—at best—to get a replacement board down from Portland." She saw Cellars wince.

"You know," she went on, "if you need it in a hurry, you could always take it to Frodshams. They're out at the shopping center, about ten minutes from here. We've got a blanket contract with them for stuff like this. All you have to do is give them your badge number and drop it off. In fact," she added, "hold on just a second. Hey, Mary?" she yelled out over her shoulder.

A reddish blond head poked in through the counter window. "Yeah, what's up?"

"Are you still going out to Frodshams this afternoon to make a film run?"

"Heading out there right now."

"Great. Here, I've got one more for you." Grey picked up the evidence envelope containing the film canister and made some quick notations on the back of the evidence tag. Then she handed the package to her assistant. "Tell them to put a one-hour rush on it, four-by-six print." Grey turned to Cellars. "That way you can see if there's anything worthwhile on the negative before you go to the trouble of having it blown up."

"Sounds like a great idea."

"Okay, got that taken care of," the evidence technician said, making some notes on the evidence submittal form as her assistant disappeared around the corner. Then she looked up at Cellars. "Anything else?"

"No, I think that ought to do it just fine for now."

"Okay, here you go."

Cellars signed the offered chain-of-custody form in the "Released By" box, watched Grey sign in the adjacent "Received By" box, then waited patiently for her to bring him a Xeroxed copy for his file.

"Thank you very much, Linda," Cellars said sincerely. "I can't tell you how much I appreciate your help on all this."

"Hey, no problem, that's what we're here for," the evidence technician replied cheerily. "And if there's anything else you need while you're here, all you have to do is ask."

"Well, as a matter of fact, there is one more thing." Cellars hesitated. "You wouldn't happen to have a fast modem port that I could hook my notebook computer into for outside e-mail traffic, would you? Either that, or just a plain phone line? Either one would be fine."

"I know there's a modem port out in the front office . . . but why don't you just use one of our computers instead? Be a lot easier than setting yours up."

"That would be great."

"Consider it done." The evidence tech smiled as she reached for the phone again. "I'll set you up with the ladies in the front office, and I'll be sure to tell Jack you stopped by. I assume I can let him know we'll probably be seeing you around here again pretty soon?"

"Oh yeah," Cellars nodded sleepily, "I think that's one thing you can definitely count on."

CHAPTER TWENTY-ONE

AS PROMISED, LINDA GREY QUICKLY HAD CELLARS SITTING IN front of a desktop computer in an isolated office by the front desk.

He thanked the cheerful evidence technician again and waited until she closed the door behind her. Then he quickly called up the resident e-mail program. Entering the code ~INTERNET allowed him to type in Malcolm Byzor's e-mail address. Then he started writing the message he'd been dreading for the last couple of hours.

MALCOLM,

BAD NEWS: BOBBY'S DEAD, OR AT LEAST I THINK HE IS. I FOUND HIM—OR A BODY MATCHING HIS GENERAL DESCRIPTION—DOA LAST NIGHT IN WHAT I THINK IS HIS CABIN. THE BODY HAD SEVERAL GUNSHOT WOUNDS TO THE FACE, BUT I DON'T THINK THERE'S MUCH DOUBT ABOUT IT BEING BOBBY. ESPECIALLY SINCE I FOUND A PARTIALLY FINISHED PORTRAIT

OF A WOMAN WHO LOOKS A LOT LIKE JODY USED TO LOOK IN
COLLEGE—ONLY A LITTLE OLDER—WITH HIS SIGNATURE AT
THE BOTTOM. LOT OF CONFUSION AT THE SCENE ... AT
LEAST TWO SUSPECTS ... TOOK OFF WITH MY OSP VEHICLE ...
SHOTS FIRED, THAT SORT OF THING ... AND I MAY BE IN DEEP
SHIT OVER THE SHOOTING. STILL TRYING TO CONFIRM A LOT
OF DETAILS. I'LL TELL YOU MORE ABOUT ALL THAT LATER.

IMPORTANT: JODY DOESN'T KNOW ABOUT BOBBY YET. I'M GO-
ING TO GET SOME SLEEP AND THEN CALL HER TONIGHT. NOT
SURE WHAT I'M GOING TO TELL HER, BUT I GUESS I'LL THINK
OF SOMETHING.

COLIN

Cellars paused to reread the message. Then, not knowing what
else to say, he clicked on the SEND tab. Moments later, the computer confirmed that the message was on its way.

Relieved that he at least had one of the bad news messages out of
the way, he shut down the computer with a tired sigh, got up out
of the chair, and headed toward the door.

If anything, the sky seemed to be getting even darker as Cellars
pulled out of the Medford Crime Lab parking lot. He could hear
ominous rumblings in the distance, a sure sign that another southern Oregon lightning storm was imminent. It also meant the roads
would be predictably slick and the drivers distracted.

*Okay, it's almost noon. Time to get something to eat, stop by the
photo shop to see if there's anything on that negative, then go home and
get some sleep.*

He found the photo shop and a deli nearby that advertised deli-
cious egg sandwiches. He ordered one, determined that the adver-
tising was right on the mark, ordered another, then sat at a window
table and slowly ate them both while he watched the rain. Then,

feeling much better with his stomach full, he walked over to the photo shop.

"Hi, I'm Sergeant Cellars," he said, offering his badge and credentials for identification to the clerk at the counter. "I'm checking to see if a rush order is completed."

The clerk reached into the bin labeled "COMPLETED RUSH." "Okay, let's see here, OSP . . . Cellars, badge 27." She glanced over at Cellars's badge again. "Yep, that's you. Here you go." She handed him a photo packet that he quickly opened.

It was better than he expected, but not by much. The flash on the camera had still been set for narrowly focused close-up shots, the weak batteries hadn't charged the thrystor fully, and he'd only roughly aimed the camera in the general direction of the noise. The outlines of the basement interior were clearly visible in the center of the dark photo. But the area he was interested in—the area in the upper right corner of the photo where his more sensitive retinas had caught what he thought was the fleeting image of a dark shadowy arm reaching for the revolver—was almost completely black.

"Not what you had in mind, I take it?" The white-coated technician's voice startled Cellars. He hadn't heard her come up beside him.

"No, not really." He stared glumly down at the photo. "I was hoping I'd pick up more over in this area here." He pointed at the darkened corner.

"Hold on a second. Let me take a look at the negative."

She carefully laid the short strip of negative on the light table and used a magnifier to examine closely the single exposed frame.

"Well, I wouldn't want to get your hopes up," she said as she straightened up from the magnifier. "The negative's pretty thin in the corners, and especially on that side. But I think there might be something there. If you want, I can try a long exposure. You'll lose everything in the center—"

"I don't care about the stuff in the center," Cellars said quickly. "Just that one corner."

"In that case, I'd say we go for a full five-by-seven or eight-by-ten enlargement of just that corner," she suggested. "Trouble is, we're pretty backed up on routine developing right now, so I probably won't be able to get to it until tomorrow afternoon. If you want to come by then, maybe you can stand by the enlarger while I work on it. Point out what you're after, so we don't waste the state's time and money. That way too," she added with a conspiratorial grin, "you can be the one who testifies in court."

"The idea doesn't appeal to you, I take it?"

"Just thinking about it almost makes me cry," the girl confided in a soft voice, looking around to make sure no one could hear her.

"In that case," Cellars smiled tiredly, "tomorrow afternoon would be just fine."

"Okay, Sergeant Twenty-Seven, you've got yourself a deal." The photo technician winked as she slipped the negative back into the plastic holder. "I will see you then."

———

In spite of his near exhaustion, Cellars found himself humming as he hurried back to the Expedition. Bobby was dead, and Jody still had to be told, and the rain was starting to fall faster—indicative of the storm to come—but he refused to allow the weather to dampen his spirits any further. The one thing keeping him going was his unwavering determination to find the evidence necessary to bring the killers of Bobby Dawson to justice. And he had every reason to believe—or at least hope—that at least some of the necessary elements were finally starting to fall into place.

All he had to do now was go home and get some sleep. Tomorrow would be a better day.

Slow and easy, and watch yourself going through the intersections, Cellars reminded himself as he started up the Expedition and slowly backed out of the parking space. *Last thing you need right now is a traffic accident.*

But the traffic was light, and the few drivers on the roads were amazingly cautious. Which made it relatively easy for Cellars to negotiate the two stoplights, three stop signs, and the blinking yellow yield-to-oncoming-traffic light that led to a final right-hand turn in front of his newly rented house.

He made the turn, parked in the driveway, got out, locked the Expedition, walked up his driveway, and stepped up onto the porch.

That was where he discovered the sensuous young woman with the jarringly familiar features and enticing violet eyes waiting for him. Cowering in the far corner of his porch, cold, wet, and shivering, and looking past his shoulder with widened eyes as if she were terrified out of her mind.

CHAPTER TWENTY-TWO

"OH SHIT!" WILDLIFE FORENSIC SCIENTIST JODY CATLIN MUT-tered as she stared at her computer monitor.

Melissa Washington looked up from her open case file.

"What's the matter?"

Jody sighed and rubbed her tired eyes. "I don't know. I think I screwed up."

"Well, it's 'bout time you 'fessed up, girl. Took you long enough."

Jody turned to stare at her lab partner. "Excuse me?"

"Hey, now, don't you go '*ex-cusin' me*' like that, Miss Ah'm-pissed-off-at-the-world-but-Ah-ain't-gonna-talk-about-it." The dark-complexioned forensic scientist held up her hands in mock surrender. "Hasn't anybody ever explained it to you, sugar? Mankind is *not* a mystery."

"What?" Jody Catlin's eyebrows furrowed in confusion.

"Hey, I'm just telling you the well-known facts of life. They've always been that way, and they aren't ever gonna change, no matter what we do. So we might just as well learn to live with it."

Jody opened her mouth to say something, stopped, shook her head, and started over again.

"Melissa, I was referring to a PCR extraction I just screwed up. I have no idea what you're talking about."

"A PCR extraction?" Melissa tilted her head skeptically. "That all we're talking about here? A bunch of mismatched chemicals?"

"You don't think two hours of work right down the drain is anything worth getting upset about?"

"Well, I guess it's as good a reason as any to get upset," the forensic scientist allowed. "But you sure wouldn't see me getting down in the dumps about it. At least not the way you been acting lately. That's why I figured it just had to be something more interesting."

"Such as?"

Melissa sighed in exasperation as she first rolled her eyes heavenward, then fixed her lab partner with a steady gaze.

"What would you say is the one topic of conversation that is just absolutely guaranteed to get the womenfolk around here riled up?"

"Men?" It wasn't really a question.

"There you go." Melissa nodded approvingly. "About time you brought up the subject, 'cause everybody around here's been wondering . . . only they're all too polite to ask."

"Meaning you're not?" The edge of a smile started to appear on Jody's solemn face.

"Sugar, when you grow up with three older brothers in the District, you find out real quick that tryin' to be subtle isn't gonna get you anywhere," Melissa explained matter-of-factly. "Especially when you're trying to figure out why men do stupid stuff all the time."

"Trust me, you don't want to get me started on that topic."

"That bad?" Melissa inquired hopefully.

Jody Catlin was the new Ph.D. geneticist and senior DNA analyst in the National Fish and Wildlife Forensic Lab's Genetics Section. She'd been on board for several months now, taking on some of the lab's more interesting—which usually meant more difficult—DNA cases. But so far, Jody had kept to herself and no one in the unit knew much about her. True to her irrepressibly inquisitive nature, Melissa intended to change that situation without any further delay.

Jody shrugged indifferently. "Depends on your point of view. At the moment, I lean toward the theory that given the slightest opportunity, men are just naturally inclined to be testosterone-poisoned shitheads. Unfortunately," she added with a halfhearted grin, "that doesn't say much for those of us who tend to be attracted to the bastards."

"Definitely a lady after my own heart." Melissa nodded in cheerful agreement. "You musta grown up with my brothers too." Then she cocked her head and raised an eyebrow. "Or do I detect a sense of something a little more personal in the way of background here?"

In spite of her foul mood, Jody couldn't keep herself from laughing. "You don't even try to be subtle, do you?"

"Like I said, it never got me anywhere." Melissa crossed her arms and smiled unashamedly. "So give, girl. Tell me all about this heartless bastard."

"Neither of them is heartless." Jody Catlin's eyes briefly took on a distant and sad expression. "Just God-awful stubborn. Trouble is, they've been that way ever since they were twelve."

"They?" Melissa Washington's dark brown eyes lit up expectantly. "Sugar, are we talking *two* boyfriends here?"

"Depending on your definition." Jody nodded her head slowly. "Colin, Bobby, Malcolm, and I. We were close friends all through high school and college, until . . . until things got complicated." Her voice drifted off.

"I knew it!" Washington clapped her hands with unrepressed glee. "Everybody else around here—or at least all the women," she corrected, "the men don't have a clue, as usual—they figured you just had to be one a' those dedicated professor types. Too busy studying or working or whatnot to let a man cause you any grief.

And the boss won't let us dedicated curious types anywhere near the personnel files," she added with a dimpled grin, "so that made figuring you out a little more difficult. But I had faith in you."

"You did, huh?"

"You damn right I did. First time I laid eyes on you, girl, I just knew you were bringing some *history* to this job. 'Course I didn't expect it to be anywhere near this good. Four high school and college friends, all buddy-buddy like, until suddenly it got complicated. My, oh, my." Melissa rubbed her hands expectantly. "Sugar, if this story is even half as good as I think it's gonna be, I just might have to stop taping my afternoon soaps."

"It's been fifteen years since we split up, and only a few days since we've tried getting back together again. And as best I can tell, it's not even starting to work, so don't get your hopes up," Jody warned.

Melissa grinned. "Like my mama always says, ain't nothing good ever comes easy."

"And, to make it even worse," Jody went on, "it was one of them who sent me this tissue sample to figure out . . . which isn't helping my sense of humor," she added grimly as she turned back to glare at her monitor screen.

"Can't ever lose your sense of humor," Melissa commented as she moved her chair over next to Jody's monitor. "Only thing that keeps us . . . hey, what's that?" She pointed at the screen.

"That's my problem. I don't know."

"Let me get in here now, take a closer look at that." Melissa moved in closer, her attention now completely focused on the base-pair sequence graph being displayed on the monitor. "Shouldn't you be having a few more base pairs in that string . . . like at least a couple hundred instead of three?"

"Uh-huh."

"So the sequencer started cutting, kicked out three bases . . . C - A - T . . . and then hit what? A compression?"

"Looks that way," Jody acknowledged.

"Never seen anything like it. You?"

Jody shook her head.

"It looks like the restriction enzyme got so far . . ."

"And then hit the molecular equivalent of a brick wall," Jody finished.

"Yeah, right." Melissa nodded. "But what about all this mess over here?" She pointed to a series of smaller peaks that tailed off into a flat line on the farside of the monitor screen.

Jody shrugged her shoulders. "I don't know. Looks like some of the enzyme got through . . ."

". . . cut two more bases . . . A - T . . . then hit another wall?"

"Actually three walls, one after the other," Jody muttered, tracing her finger along the sloping series of peaks.

"Three compressions? Just like that? Wham, bam, thank *you*, ma'am?"

"Uh-huh."

"Seems to me I remember this sweet-talking sales rep telling us real serious-like how you can't hardly get compressions anymore with this new fancy Model 577 Sequencer."

"He lied."

"Yeah, no shit. So now what?"

Jody sighed tiredly. "Start over with another extraction, I guess."

"You got enough sample?"

"Maybe enough for one more try. It was a tiny piece of tissue he said he scraped off a rock, and it was already starting to degrade. Not much in the way of DNA."

Melissa looked down at her watch.

"Tell you what," she said. "You tell me some more about these thickheaded boyfriends of yours and I'll give you a hand with it. If nothing else, keep you company for a while."

Jody hesitated a brief moment, then grinned.

"Okay, fair deal. Which one do you want to hear about first?"

"Oh hell, girl, let's get right into it. Start with the most God-awful stubborn one of the whole bunch, and we'll work our way up from there."

"The most stubborn one?"

"That's right. The one who never gives in or gives up, no matter what."

Jody sighed again, then smiled sadly. "Well, I guess that narrows it down to the basic two. Take your pick. Bobby or Colin?"

CHAPTER TWENTY-THREE

"THEY'RE GOING TO HURT ME," SHE WHISPERED SOFTLY.

Her name was Allesandra. Cellars had managed to get that much out of her. She was huddled deep into his overstuffed reading chair now. Still wet, still shivering, her face pale, and her arms wrapped tightly around her denim-clad legs. Waiting for him to finish dead-bolting the door. Her eyes following his every movement.

"Who? The DEA?"

Cellars had the SIG-Sauer out in his right hand as he pulled the outer edge of the closed drapes aside, watching for movement out on the street.

"No, not them." She hesitated. "They're different. They just want Bobby because of some stupid helicopter they can't find."

"Who then?"

She hesitated again. "I don't know. I've never actually seen them.

Only their . . . shadows." She said the last word softly, as if she was afraid that someone—or something—would hear her.

"But you *do* know they exist, these shadowy people?" he pressed, intermittently turning away from the window, watching for the first sign of a flickering shadow inside the house. "And you *do* know they want to hurt you?"

She hesitated, then went on in a hushed voice. "Yes, of course. I'm sure of it now."

"Why?"

She blinked, looking confused.

"Why would they want to hurt you?" Cellars stepped back and away from the window for a moment, watching her closely now.

"Because they think I know something. Something to do with Bobby."

"Bobby?"

She nodded. "I think he has something that belongs to them. Something they want back very badly. And now they think I have it . . . or know where it is."

"They think you have *what*?"

"That's the problem, I don't know. I really don't." She looked up at him imploringly. "I told them I didn't, but they wouldn't listen. They didn't believe me." Her hands and shoulders were starting to shake again.

"It's always possible that you may know something, but not be aware of it," Cellars suggested as he checked the window again. "Walk me through it. Have you ever seen these people, face-to-face?"

"Oh God, no!"

"But you say you talked to them."

"On the phone, yes."

"How many times?"

"Uh . . . three, I think. Yes, three times."

"And when was the last time?"

"Last night. When I got home. They—"

"What did they sound like?" Cellars interrupted.

"What? I don't understand—"

"Male? Female? Deep voice? Foreign accent? Anything like that."

"Oh, uh . . . male, definitely. Very deep voices."

"You keep saying, 'they.' How many of them are there?"

"I . . . uh . . . don't know. At least two or three, I think, because I keep seeing—"

"Their shadows?"

She nodded, closing her eyes and swallowing hard—like she was about to throw up at any second.

"Okay, let's forget about them for a while," Cellars said, afraid that he was going to lose her—to shock or panic—if he didn't change the subject. "Let's get back to Bobby. What exactly did he tell you about all this?"

"Bobby said . . ." She seemed to choke on the words. "He said, if anything ever happened to him, I was to find you, tell you what he was doing. He said you'd know what to do."

Her teeth were chattering now. It seemed to Cellars, as he momentarily turned his attention back to the window, that it was all she could do to get the words out.

"Has something happened to Bobby?" He asked the question reflexively, only vaguely interested in her answer now. Something flickered in the trees across the street. Something dark . . . and shadowy. He slipped his index finger inside the trigger guard of the SIG-Sauer.

"I don't know."

"Then why did you want to see me last night? At the lecture, then later at the station?" he asked, continuing to press as he kept his eyes focused on the trees across the street. Another shadow flashed between two trees in the cloudy darkness, about thirty feet to the right of the first. Two of them now, circling the house, watching and waiting? Or maybe just his imagination, fueled by the oncoming storm, his general state of near exhaustion, and the adrenaline surging through his veins?

Okay, maybe I am just imagining things. And maybe Dawson in that body bag, and the shitheads who cut the power and telephone lines, and stole my goddamned cell phone and camera, are just illusions too. So what does that mean? That I'm losing my grip, and that it's time to get fitted for an extralong-sleeved jacket and a nice rubber room?

It occurred to Cellars that he really ought to call for backup—911 or just dial in to the station, Talbert's office, get somebody out there. But what was he going to tell them . . . or Talbert? That he was barricaded inside his house with a beautiful young woman because a pair of flickering shadows were stalking them?

And just what are these shadows doing that seems so threatening to you, Officer Cellars? Moving real fast? Pulling guns out of holsters? Stealing police vehicles? And killing people? Oh really?

Yeah, right.

"He was supposed to meet me the night before last, to show me . . . whatever it was. That's what he said." She was talking in a raspy, whispery, distant voice. As if in shock . . . or rapidly heading that way.

"Do you have any idea what it might have been?"

"No." She shook her head slowly. "At first I thought, maybe, after all this time, he was finally going to show me what he'd found that made him believe in us . . . and in them," she added with a shudder. "And I still think maybe he was. And it's probably what they want . . . what they think I have now. But he never did say," she added wistfully. "All I know for sure is that whatever it was, he was really excited about it. Really anxious for me to see it. But then he never showed up . . . and he didn't call."

"Sometimes he's like that," Cellars commented absentmindedly, blinking his eyes and concentrating because it looked like the two flickering shadows had suddenly merged into one.

"I know, he almost never calls. But then last night, when he didn't show up at the meeting, I just knew—" She shivered again.

Then, suddenly, a clattering outside caused her head to jerk up and her eyes widen in shock.

"Just a cat. No problem."

"I . . . God, I don't know . . . I mean, that lecture, and your being there, it was just about all he'd ever talk about the last couple of weeks. And then, when he heard—"

She screamed loudly as a sudden nearby explosion rocked the house.

"Relax, it's okay," Cellars said soothingly, even though his own nerves were becoming increasingly frayed. "It's just lightning . . . the storm's coming in."

As if responding on cue, a strong burst of wind rattled the windows, causing Cellars to jerk his head around.

The young woman cowered down in the chair, whimpering.

"What did he hear?"

It took her a moment to respond.

"What?"

"I said, what did he hear?"

Cellars was moving now, keeping the SIG-Sauer tight against his leg and an eye on the darkened hallway as he checked each window, one by one. It was still getting darker outside, and he couldn't see any of the flickering shadows now.

"He—he said you'd been transferred down here, which he thought was great, because—"

A burst of wind rattled the windows again, causing her to squeal in fright.

"Because what?" Cellars pressed as he walked past her, his index finger still on the trigger of the SIG-Sauer, checking the hallway. If they weren't outside anymore, then—

"Because he was sure the two of you could figure it all out," she whispered.

"Figure what out?"

Cellars stood over her now, staring down at her. She looked up with wide, frightened eyes.

"I—I don't know. Whatever it was that he found several months ago. The thing that brought him to the Alliance in the first place."

"The Alliance?"

"The Alliance of Believers."

"You mean the people I talked to last night? The people who be-lieve in alien contact?" Cellars felt the familiar chill starting up his spine.

She nodded.

"But you don't have any idea—any idea at all—what this thing he said he found several months ago might be?"

"No, I don't. I wish I did. I mean, everybody wanted to know, but he never would tell us. All he said was it had something to do with . . . *them*." She swallowed hard.

"Them?"

"You know, the—"

She screamed loudly again as another lightning bolt exploded— this time directly overhead—causing the house to rock on its founda-tions and all of the lights in the closed-off house to go out instantly.

"Oh, God, they're coming," he heard her moan as the room went dark.

"Okay, that does it," Cellars snarled as he grabbed her by the arm, yanked her up out of the chair, pulled her down the hallway and into the master bedroom, pushed her toward the bed, and slammed the door behind him.

"What—?"

He could barely see her, sprawled on the bed, but the intense warmth from her arm still lingered on his hand. Alarm bells were going off in the back of his mind, but he ignored them.

"Don't worry, you're fine. Nothing's going to hurt you. Just stay there," he admonished as he holstered the SIG-Sauer, then grabbed up a duffel bag from the closet.

He worked quickly, filling the bag from the closet shelves, a chest of drawers, and the adjacent bathroom. He started to zip up the bag, hesitated a moment, then went into the closet for a couple more items before closing the duffel bag. He quickly adjusted the shoulder straps, slung the bag over his shoulders, drew the semiau-tomatic pistol in his right hand, and reached for her with his left.

"Come on," he whispered urgently, "we've got to get out of here."

"But we can't! They're . . . out there."

He could sense the beginning of hysteria in her voice as he pulled her up off the bed, feeling the incredible warmth again moving up his arm.

"I know, but we can't stay here. Too many ways in. I can't watch them all."

"But—"

"It's okay, trust me," he whispered against her ear, using the thumb of his gun hand against the farside of her face to bring her in close. "Whoever or whatever these people are, they bleed just like us—so that makes them vulnerable, too."

The warmth from her face—in fact, from her entire body—threatened to envelop him; but he resisted, knowing they had to get out of the house . . . and into the Expedition . . . before they were trapped.

She started to say something when another lightning bolt caused both of them to flinch and duck as the house shuddered.

Whatever she'd intended to say, it apparently wasn't an issue anymore. She didn't resist as Cellars cautiously opened the bedroom door, made a quick check of the almost-dark hallway, then held tightly on to her hand as he headed for the front door.

The wind drove both of them backward as Cellars pulled open the door. But he persisted, ducking his head and yanking her through the doorway as they staggered toward the Expedition parked in the driveway.

"Where are we going?" she screamed against the wind, but he ignored her as he looked around, then unlocked and pulled open the front passenger door.

"But—"

"Get in the car! We're getting out of here," Cellars yelled as he pushed her into the seat, slammed the door, looked around one more time, and ran around to the driver's side.

He kept the SIG-Sauer in his lap until he had the engine started and his seat belt fastened. Then, after making another quick search of their surroundings, he swiftly holstered the pistol and jammed the transmission into reverse. Moments later, they were accelerating down the street, the wind rocking the heavy vehicle as Cellars kept his foot on the gas, glancing up at the rearview mirror after each turn.

They were a good four miles from Cellars's newly rented house before either of them spoke. Cellars finally broke the silence.

"Where do you live?" he asked, keeping his eyes focused on the road ahead and the rearview mirror, and trying to ignore the persistent memory of her radiating warmth.

"Why? Where are we going?" she asked hesitantly. Her enticing features were still pale and drawn, but she looked better than she had only ten minutes ago.

"I'm taking you back home. Getting you out of all this, before things get any worse."

"But I—can't go home."

"Why not?"

"They were in my house last night. I could tell, as soon as I got home from the lecture and walked in the door. That's why I turned and ran . . . all the way to the police station. And that's why I stayed there so long," she added in a shuddering voice. "I couldn't go back home. Not by myself."

"Where did you go?"

"What?"

"Last night . . . and this morning. Where did you go if you didn't go home?"

"I—I stayed at a friend's house last night."

"Okay, where does he or she live? I'll take you there."

"She's not home now. She had to go to work, but—"

"What's the matter?" Cellars asked when she remained silent for several seconds.

"I guess we could stop by her work. She said she'd give me a key if I wanted to stay with her for a while, but—" She hesitated again.

"But what?"

"I'm afraid," she said softly, staring down at her shoes.

"You mean to be by yourself?"

She nodded her head. "I'm sorry, I know it sounds stupid—a grown woman afraid of shadows . . . and voices over a phone. And I don't mean to drag you into my problems. I just thought—"

"That you could stay with me until your friend gets off work?"

"Either that, or . . . help me find Bobby?" she added hopefully.

Cellars kept his eyes focused on the road for several more seconds as a rush of conflicting thoughts tumbled through his mind.

No, you really don't want me to do that. You really don't. Not the way he is now.

But what if she can positively ID him? Distinguishing marks, whatever? Do I put her through all that, just so I can be sure?

Jesus.

"Look," he finally said, "I'll be happy to help you try to find Bobby. But the thing is, I was out at that crime scene all night, and I'm really tired right now. Probably too tired really even to think straight," he added, forcing back a yawn. "So what I'm going to do right now is check myself into a motel room. Ideally, a room with a single door and windows that lock shut, so I can get some sleep. You're welcome to come with me. I'll get you your own room. Check it first, make sure it's empty, then let you lock it from the inside so you don't have anything to worry about. But I've got to—"

"No, I can't." She shook her head firmly. "I'm sorry."

"Look, you don't have to worry about me. I'm not going to try to—"

She put her hand on his arm, and he could feel the warmth immediately radiate up into his shoulder and down his spine.

"It's not that," she whispered, her voice barely audible. "And please don't take this wrong. I'm not trying to come on to you. I just don't know if I can stay by myself. Not right now. Not after what I . . . saw."

"Okay," Cellars gave in, trying—unsuccessfully—to concentrate on the rearview mirror, and to ignore the almost-dizzying effect of the warmth as it spread to his hips and legs and groin. "One room, one door, two beds."

In spite of her visible fear, her eyes almost seemed to twinkle with amusement as she turned to stare at him.

"It's all right," she whispered. "Whatever they have is fine. Bobby said I could trust you completely."

"Yeah, well, Bobby didn't necessarily know what he was talking about," Cellars muttered mostly to himself as he turned the Expedition in the direction of the Jasper County Windmill Inn.

CHAPTER TWENTY-FOUR

FORENSIC SEROLOGIST SUSAN FROST'S EYEBROWS FURROWED in confusion as she stared at the diffusion plate.

"Oh no, not again."

Jack Wilson, supervisory serologist for the OSP's Medford lab, happened to be walking by with a handful of case files.

"What's the matter?" he asked as he looked over his subordinate's shoulder.

"Look at this. Exact same results as last time," she replied as she held up the gel plate so that her supervisor could see for himself. "Definitely negative for human, and no match to anything else in our database."

"Where did the blood come from?" Wilson asked as he set the files on the lab bench.

"Uh, let's see, LAB-five and LAB-six." Frost looked down at her lab notebook. "Bloodstains from wooden floor and log wall next to a broken window. CSI officer's item numbers CC-seven and CC-eight."

"CC?" Wilson blinked in surprise. "This is one of Colin's cases?"

"Colin?"

"Colin Cellars," Wilson explained. "Used to be one of our senior examiners up in the Portland lab. I'd heard he transferred down to Region Nine to work CSI on some of those 'suspicious disappearance' cases. Be nice to have him around. So what's this one on?"

"Looks like a simple, straightforward homicide out at a mountain cabin," Frost said as she picked up the lab case file.

"With shots fired by the investigating officer? Doesn't sound very simple to me," Wilson commented as he started reading the narrative summary. "Knowing Colin, he probably collected half the cabin as evidence."

"Close," Frost nodded. "We logged in fifty-five items."

"Fifty-five items, into *serology*?"

"No, thank God." Susan Frost shook her head, smiling. "I've got plenty enough to do as it is. We only got eleven bloodstains; seven mixed blood, hair, water, and mud samples, and four bullets with possible blood or tissue. Looks like everything else went to firearms, latents, and criminalistics."

"So how many do you have a problem with?"

"Counting those last two"—Frost ran her right index finger down through her notebook—"a total of seven."

"Seven?"

"Yep. 'Bloodstain from wall by the stairs, bloodstain from wall by shattered basement window, bloodstain from carpet by stairs, two blood samples extracted from lead bullets, and two more stains from the seats of an OSP Explorer,' " Frost recited from her notes.

"According to the narrative here, there's supposedly a dead dog involved in this whole mess," Wilson noted. "Maybe that's your source."

"Possible, but I don't think so. Several of the other samples screen positive for canine. Five total, as I recall. One of those also tested positive for human." Frost looked up from her notes. "But those last seven all came up negative to everything."

"Degraded samples?" Wilson suggested.

"Possible." Frost shrugged. "Could have been older stains, not associated with the homicide. That might make some sense."

"Yeah, except that Colin should have recognized that at the scene and said something about it in his work request."

"You would have thought so," Frost agreed. "So what do you think I should do? Keep on working with these unknowns or concentrate on the samples I know I can do something with?"

"I don't know. What else would you try?"

"Well, I could always run another antisera series with more concentrated extracts, but we don't have a lot of stain." Frost hesitated. "Maybe we ought to go directly over to hemoglobin screening with the LC/mass spec."

"Fine, except that our hemoglobin database is still pretty small," Wilson reminded. "As I recall, I don't think we've got more than a couple dozen nonhuman samples total."

"Yeah, I know. I've got to get back over to the wildlife lab in Ashland someday. We've got an open invitation to share their data and their reference samples, but I've been so busy lately—"

"Hey, what about the victim's blood? Didn't we get a sample from the autopsy?" Wilson was thumbing back through the case file, a perplexed look on his face.

"Uh, no, I don't think so. In fact, as I recall, I don't think we've gotten anything in from the autopsy yet."

"I don't see anything here in the file," Jack Wilson agreed as he handed the case file back to Frost. "May not have happened yet." He paused for a moment. "Look," he finally said, "you can't do much with the human stains until we get the victim's blood for comparison anyway. So why don't you just go ahead and send those seven unknowns over to Ashland? If it is animal blood, they ought to be able to track it down at least to family level. And besides," Wilson added as he pointed to the stack of fourteen case files he'd placed on the bench top, "it's not like we don't have anything else to do around here."

"Those are ours?" Susan Frost had a stricken look on her face.

"Not ours, yours," Wilson said, smiling sympathetically. "I left my half back on my desk."

Frost groaned.

"Hey, remember what they always say about job security in a crime lab."

"Yeah, yeah, I know, if it wasn't for the criminal mind . . ." Frost nodded as she made some quick notations in her lab notebook. "Okay, bunnies and guppies lab it is."

"And by the way," Wilson added, "if Colin happens to call in on this case, ask him to stop in and say hi. Tell him one of his old Portland buddies would like to know if he's managed to get himself into trouble down here yet."

CHAPTER TWENTY-FIVE

HE DIDN'T KNOW WHEN IT HAPPENED.

He remembered them checking into the hotel. The clerk giving Allesandra an appraising look that turned into a wide grin when she asked for an emergency toilet kit. And paying cash for a room that was almost exactly what he'd asked for—a top floor room at the end of the hall, adjacent to the emergency stairs, no adjoining room door, a single fireproof metal door at one end and a pair of small, solidly mounted windows at the other—except for the two double-sized beds that turned out to be one queen. But he was too tired to care.

He remembered the look on her face as she sat on the bed and watched him secure the door and windows with Malcolm Byzor's most recent Christmas gift. A set of electronic security devices with replaceable adhesive bases that formed protective seals between doors, windows, and walls. Once activated, each device would scream out a warning if the slightest attempt was made to break the seal.

He remembered her shaking her head when he asked her if she minded if he took a shower first . . . and her smile when he offered her the opportunity to rummage through the contents of his duffel bag, and first choice of anything she found that fit.

He remembered how he'd come out of the bathroom feeling wonderfully clean and blissfully exhausted.

And he remembered placing the SIG-Sauer on the dresser closest to the door . . . and getting into bed . . . and hearing the shower turn on as his head sank into the pillow.

But that was all he remembered. Until the moment he came awake with the sense that he was completely enveloped in an incredibly soothing and sensuous warmth. A warmth that had something—everything, actually—to do with the naked body that was wrapped around his back . . . and front . . . and everywhere in between in a manner that didn't seem real . . . or even possible.

Then he remembered bringing his hands up to her incredibly warm breasts. And kissing her unimaginably warm lips. And a sensation of being drawn into an inconceivably warm and sensuous whirlpool that seemed, in some inexplicable manner, to separate every single cell of his body and every fragment of memory in his mind, and merge them—in a seamlessly erotic manner—with hers.

He remembered thinking—if that was the right word—that it was sex at its most primitive and basic form: the merging and fusing of two gametes into one mass churning with life and purpose.

But then he stopped thinking . . . or doing . . . and just . . . became.

———

He awoke eons later—but only three hours according to the alarm clock on the nightstand—to find her sitting up in the bed and watching him.

"What are you?" he whispered groggily.

Her smile seemed to release a flood of sensations and memories that nearly overwhelmed his consciousness. "Don't you mean 'Who are you'?" she asked, her full lips widening out into a dimpled grin.

Cellars shook his head. "No, I don't think so."

"I'm a person who is very frightened," she answered matter-of-factly in her amazingly soft and sensuous voice.

"Of what?"

"Of them. Of you. Of Bobby."

"But Bobby's dead," he protested, feeling his mind start to drift as the warmth from her body seemed to flow toward him from under the sheets.

"Yes, I know, that's what you said. But it's all right. I'm sure he doesn't mind."

He couldn't understand how she could manage to look so sad, and happy, and irresistibly sensuous all at the same time.

Another name from his distant—and increasingly irrelevant—past tried to fight its way up through the jumbled mass that now served as Cellars's consciousness.

"Jody?" he mumbled.

"What?"

"Did Bobby ever mention a woman named Jody?" he asked, clinging desperately to his sense of awareness . . . and of himself.

"Don't worry about her. She's fine, too."

"But—" he tried to protest. But then Allesandra brought her deliciously warm hand down against the side of his face in a gesture that instantly soothed his soul and sent him gliding back into his gloriously sensuous dreams.

CHAPTER TWENTY-SIX

IT WAS A TERRIBLE DREAM.

He had been running from place to place, being chased by lethal shadows, desperately seeking help, or a way out—for minutes or hours, he couldn't tell—but it didn't matter. Nothing mattered except finding it.

But he didn't know where it was.

No that's not true, a soft whispery voice corrected. *You know where one of them is. Two, actually, if the truth were known. But where is the other one? Tell me. I have to know.*

But he couldn't, because he didn't even know *what* it was, much less where. But she was right. He understood that now. If he didn't find it, they'd kill him *and* her . . . just like they killed Bobby. No reprieve. No mercy. Just a simple matter of evidence.

So he ran, trying desperately to keep some distance away from them—the shadowy creatures—while he continued his search for something he couldn't define, much less describe.

But he couldn't stop, and he couldn't escape—no matter what he did—because they knew where he was.

And they knew where he was going.

And there was nothing he could do about it because . . .

It's all right, she whispered, her warm hands soothing, caressing, enveloping. *I'm here with you. I won't let them harm you. Help me.* Then he was lost again, disconnected and diffused within an all-encompassing meld of pure radiant energy.

Please help me . . .

But he couldn't.

And then the shadows began moving again.

———

"Uhhh!"

He lunged upright, covered with sweat and trembling, only vaguely aware as he did so that his hands were up in a defensive posture. Ready to deflect or strike out at . . . something.

But then his eyes opened, and he realized immediately that there was nothing there. Nothing at all.

Where am I?

He looked around, blinking uncertainly.

Hotel room? What am I—?

Memories flooded his consciousness, some of them incomprehensible. And dreams—only they really weren't dreams. More like nightmares made up of terrible, chilling, and unbelievable images. And one set of images in particular. The lethal shadowy creatures. The ones who were coming for him . . . out in the open and visible . . . but only for the briefest of moments before they disappeared back into the depths of his subconscious.

No, wait! Come back! I want to see you. To see what you look like. Please.

Come back.

But the terrifying images wouldn't reappear, no matter how hard he tried. And in some dark, indefinable sense, Cellars realized that he really didn't want them to come back. Not ever. Because if they did, then she would have to . . .

She?

Allesandra.

More memories, incredible ones . . . but much less defined than the others, and fading fast. Drifting back into the depths of his mind, just like the shadowy creatures.

He whipped his head around, searching for her. But the room was empty.

He lunged up out of the bed, naked and trembling, and stumbled into the bathroom. But it was empty too.

Gone. But—

A flashing red light out of the corner of his eye caught his attention. He turned his head and saw one of Malcolm Byzor's security devices blinking merrily next to the doorknob.

Still sealed and locked? But then how—?

He turned, went over to the window, pulled open the drapes, and then stared uncomprehending at the two flashing devices on the window locks.

Must have let her out and then rearmed the devices. No other way she could have gotten out. But why can't I remember her leaving?

Then he saw the gray sky.

What time is it?

He turned back toward the bed, then stopped and blinked in surprise when he saw the red numbers on the alarm clock: *8:58 AM?*

In the morning?

He stumbled back to the bed, sat down on the rapidly cooling sheets, and reached for the phone.

"Front desk. How may I help you?"

"This is Room Six-Thirteen . . ."

"Yes, Mr. Cellars. Good morning."

"It *is* morning?" he asked hesitantly.

"Oh, yes, sir. Eight fifty-nine, in fact, on what is apparently going to be another wet and dreary Oregon Wednesday. Will you be checking out this morning, or staying with us for another night?"

Wednesday?

He stared down at the phone in disbelief.

"Uh, Mr. Cellars?"

What the hell happened to Tuesday?

At that moment, someone knocked lightly at the door. Cellars's head snapped up.

Allesandra?

"Excuse me just a moment, please," Cellars spoke into the phone. Then he tossed the phone on the bed, grabbed for his jeans, which were folded neatly on a nearby chair, pulled them on, and stumbled to the door.

He started to reach for the doorknob—to yank the door open—but then the flashing red light caught his attention again.

Shit, Malcolm's security lock. Gotta disarm it first.

Another knock at the door, this time more insistent. In his mind, Cellars could see her standing outside the door, impatient to get back inside. Impatient to—

"Just a second, I'll be right there!" he yelled as he fumbled with the disarming mechanism. Finally, he was able to open the door without setting off a very loud alarm.

"Where have—" he started to say, then blinked in surprise when he saw the uniform . . . and the cart.

"Your breakfast, Mr. Cellars." The bellhop smiled pleasantly as she stepped around the serving cart.

"My . . . what?"

"Your breakfast, sir." The bellhop looked down at the order slip. "Fruit, cereal, hot coffee, wheat toast, and marmalade. Nine o'clock sharp. As you ordered, sir."

"How did you—" he started to ask, but stopped when he realized that the question made no sense.

Not knowing what else to say or ask, Cellars stepped back out of the way . . . and stood there in the doorway as the bellhop placed the plates on the open table, then walked briskly back to the door.

"Everything's been taken care of, sir," she said brightly. "Have a good morning."

"Yes, thank you—" he whispered, then closed the door.

He continued to stand there for a few moments, staring blankly into the room . . . until he remembered the phone he'd tossed on the bed.

"Hello?"

"Mr. Cellars?"

"Yes, I'm sorry, I . . . I will be checking out . . . this morning . . . but I may be back," he added as he tried desperately to collect his thoughts.

"That will be perfectly fine. We have plenty of rooms this time of year. Was your breakfast delivered satisfactorily?"

"Uh, yes, fine. Thank you."

"Excellent. Then all you need to do is leave your room key on the dresser."

"But my bill—"

"Is paid in full, sir. Would you like a copy delivered to your room?"

"Uh, no, that's all right. I'll pick it up when I leave."

Paid in full? But I only—

"Fine. Checkout is at eleven, but there's no need to hurry. Enjoy your breakfast and please do come back and see us soon."

"Yes . . . I will," Cellars said hesitantly as he hung up the phone.

He found the SIG-Sauer, the extra magazines, his badge, credentials, and the rest of his clothes and duffel bag gear in the dresser drawers. He checked the pistol, verifying that it and the extra magazines were still fully loaded. Then he got dressed, sat down, and ate the breakfast—realizing as he did so that he was definitely hungry, but certainly not starving—and was still sitting at the table, staring out at the darkening clouds when he remembered.

Bobby.

I was supposed to be back there . . . yesterday?

Oh, shit.

He grabbed for the phone and quickly punched in a familiar number.

"Watch Commander's Office, Talbert speaking."

"This is Cellars, I—"

"Cellars? Where the hell are you now?" the watch commander demanded.

"I'm in a hotel. Fell asleep. I'll explain later," Cellars said quickly, having no idea how he was going to explain any part of the last thirty hours. "What's the status on the Dawson autopsy?"

"What are you talking about?" There was a definite edge to Talbert's voice, suggesting that his patience was long past the point of wearing thin.

"You know, the DOA victim up at the cabin. Dawson. Robert Dawson. I dropped his body off at the morgue yester—uh, I mean Monday morning." Cellars shook his head, still trying to make sense out of it all.

There was a long pause at the other end of the line.

"There is no body at the morgue related to your investigation," Talbert finally said. "No body identified as Robert Dawson. No body, period."

"What?"

Cellars felt the familiar cold chill start to spread up his spine again.

"Get your ass down to the morgue, right now," the watch commander ordered. "I'll meet you there."

CHAPTER TWENTY-SEVEN

"HOW YOU DOIN'?" MELISSA WASHINGTON ASKED AS SHE WALKED into the National Fish and Wildlife Forensics Lab's PCR room.

Jody Catlin looked up from her pipettor and rack of microtubes with an expression of pure frustration on her face.

"Oh my, that bad, huh?"

Jody just shook her head irritably, and went back to her pipetting.

"Let me guess," Melissa said over her shoulder as she sat down at the control terminal for the 577 Sequencer. "Neither one of them good-for-nothing boyfriends of yours ever did call, right?"

"How'd you know?"

"Listen to me, sugar," Melissa went on as she called up the base sequence data on her gel. "My mama told me all I need to know about men a long time ago. Gave me a list of all their positive traits—and you know it wasn't a big list to start with. But believe me, calling us womenfolk up when they say they're gonna just isn't anywhere on it."

"Yeah, that's the truth," Jody agreed, nodding grimly.

"Hey, now, what's this here?"

Jody looked up from her pipetting. "What's the matter?"

"I think we got ourselves twisted up with our file names." Melissa rekeyed the file retrieval sequence, took one look at the screen, and shook her head. "I'm trying to call up the base-pair sequence off the gel I'm running here, but all I'm getting is that three-compression mishmash you ran the other day."

"What?"

"I'm telling you, girl, this is definitely your old file, not my new one."

"But how can that be?" Jody asked as she stood up from her chair with a puzzled look on her face.

"Hey, don't ask me, I'm just the gel jockey around here. Gonna have to get one of them extrasmart tech support types in here to figure this one out."

"Wait a minute," Jody said as she leaned over next to Melissa, "let me try something." She used the mouse to open another window, and then keyed in her file name from the previous day. Moments later, the familiar three-compression base sequence appeared on the screen.

"Well I'll be . . ." Melissa whispered as Jody switched back and forth between the two files.

"Look, it's exactly the same thing I ran into the other day," Jody said. "Two completely different samples, but exactly the same result." She thought about that for a few seconds. "We've both run other gels in between these two, and the internal standards all came out fine, so it can't be the sequencer, right?"

"Okay, so?"

"So that means it's got to be the extraction."

"Honey, I understand what you're saying, but I'm tellin' you, I *know* I ran that extraction right."

"There's only one surefire way to resolve this," Jody said. "We'll rerun both sets on the same gel, but this time we work the extractions together."

"Sounds good to me. Hold on a second, let me get my evidence."

Melissa disappeared out the door. Two minutes later, she came back in the PCR room with a handful of tagged manila envelopes. "Okay," she said, "let's get to it."

"I'll log the data," Jody volunteered as she opened her lab notebook and reached for a pen.

"You ready?" Melissa inquired as she set the frosted evidence envelopes in a neat pile.

"Go to it."

Melissa picked up the top evidence envelope. "Okay, first item."

"Agency?"

"OSP."

"Agency Case Number?"

"Zero-nine-zero-zero-six-six-six-six."

"Four sixes?"

"Correct."

"Item number?"

"Got three numbers on this one: Ours, a Medford Crime Lab number, and a CSI number. Our LAB number is three, OSP number is LAB-five, and the CSI officer is CC-seven."

"Victim?"

Melissa turned the evidence tag sideways.

"Dawson. D-A-W-S-O-N. First name Robert."

The sound of breaking glassware caused Melissa to turn her head to stare at her lab partner.

"What did you say?" Jody Catlin whispered, her eyes and mouth wide-open in shock.

CHAPTER TWENTY-EIGHT

CELLARS AND TALBERT STOOD BACK AS DR. ELLIOTT SUTTA, THE supervising pathologist for Jasper County, opened refrigerator drawer number twenty-eight and pulled the long, roller-and-beam-supported stainless-steel tray out to its fully extended position.

It was empty.

Sutta and Talbert turned to stare wordlessly at Cellars.

"Randy Granstrom," Cellars said. "Young fellow, blond hair, blue eyes, five-eight, one-sixty, maybe twenty-three or twenty-four."

"Yes, Randy's been working with us for over a year now," the supervising pathologist acknowledged in a soft, raspy voice that spoke of too many years hovering over formaldehyde-soaked bodies. "Usually swing or graveyard shifts. He's off this week. Traveling down south, I understand, to see some friends."

"He was here last Monday, at about five-thirty in the morning, when I delivered the body here," Cellars said emphatically.

"Randy was here at that time," Sutta agreed. "But when Lieutenant Talbert called me this morning, I immediately checked our computer logs and our videotape security library. According to our computer logs, the body of a thirty-two-year-old female was brought in by the paramedics from a traffic accident at one-forty-three that Monday morning," he recited from memory. "The next delivery was at ten-thirty-seven that Monday morning, a seventy-nine-year-old man from the Lone Pine Rest Home. According to those same records, there were no deliveries between those two times, a fact that I was able to confirm by examining the dates and times on the security tape," Sutta added, giving Cellars a sympathetic look.

"Granstrom and I took two body bags out of the back of my Explorer. One containing the victim and one containing the dog."

"A dog?" Sutta interrupted. "What dog?"

"A dead malamute I found at the scene," Cellars explained. "It probably belonged to the victim. I didn't have any other place to put it, so I—"

"You brought a dead dog into my morgue?" Sutta had an incredulous look on his face.

"Like I said, I didn't have any other place to put it," Cellars repeated. "But getting back to the victim, Granstrom and I put it on a gurney and rolled it into this room at about five-forty-five in the morning. I filled out the forms and tags while Granstrom logged the body into your computer system. I watched him do that. I also watched him put the toe tag on the body . . . the right big toe. Then I personally helped him transfer the body onto *this* specific refrigerator tray—second row up, five from the end, drawer number twenty-eight," he finished emphatically, pointing down at the stainless-steel tray.

Dr. Elliott Sutta opened his large hands out over the empty tray in a helpless shrug. "I don't know what to tell you, Sergeant. I certainly wasn't here that morning, but—"

"What about the other drawers?" Talbert interrupted.

"I personally checked every one of them," Sutta replied. "We have twenty-seven bodies in-house at the present, none of which even remotely match the description of your victim, Sergeant Cellars. However, you are certainly welcome to conduct your own search. I won't be the least bit offended." Sutta gestured with his hand at the array of individual refrigerator units that were arranged in a three-high-by-sixteen-across grid along the back wall of the cold-storage room. The look on his face suggested that he was still more disturbed by the idea that a dead dog had been brought into his morgue than the fact that one of his human bodies might be missing.

It took Cellars and Talbert a little less than fifteen minutes to search the other forty-seven drawers, and another ten to make a fast-forward review of the tape from last Monday.

Cellars reset the tape to 0545 hours, then let it run forward on regular PLAY speed. As the three men watched silently, the monitor continued to display the image of an empty entry bay. No white OSP Explorer. No young blond-haired morgue attendant. No body bags. No dog. And absolutely no Detective-Sergeant Colin Cellars. For five long minutes, the only thing that changed on the entire display screen was the last digit on the recorded date/time clock.

"We'll be happy to make you a copy of that tape," Sutta offered as Cellars—still looking stunned and disbelieving—reached forward and shut off the VCR.

"Thank you," Cellars whispered. "I'd appreciate that."

"Who changes the tapes, Doctor?" Talbert asked.

"That would be Bucky, our lab assistant," he said. "She—"

"Speaking of the devil," a woman in her mid-forties came into the office with an evidence-tagged plastic bag in her gloved hand.

"Ah, here she is, just in time as usual." Sutta smiled approvingly. "Bucky, this is Lieutenant Talbert and Detective-Sergeant Cellars from the OSP."

"Pleased to meet you guys," the blue-gowned woman smiled as she took off her right-hand glove and shook the offered hands.

"I was just explaining to these officers," Sutta went on, "that among many other things, you are responsible for maintaining the tapes on our video monitoring system."

"That, and everything else around here—except the johns, thank you very much"—she shrugged cheerfully—"which definitely includes lost and found." She handed Sutta the tagged plastic bag. "Found this in drawer twenty-eight this morning when I was doing my disinfecting."

"Speaking of lost and found," Cellars said. "Do you happen to know what Randy Granstrom did with the dog I dropped off—?" Then he blinked. "Excuse me, did you say drawer twenty-eight?"

"Yes, that's right." The lab assistant nodded.

A puzzled expression appeared on Dr. Elliott Sutta's face as he glanced at the contents of the plastic bag and handed it over to Cellars.

Both Cellars and Talbert examined the contents more closely. It was a twisted strip of metal, about a half inch wide, an inch and a half long, three eighths of an inch thick, and sheared off at both ends.

"Any idea?" Talbert asked.

Cellars shook his head, then looked up at the lab assistant. "You say you found this when?"

"Oh, I'd say about seven-forty-five this morning," she said. "I get here at seven sharp, sometimes a little earlier, and usually start cleaning up in here at about seven-fifteen or so. Try to get everything shipshape before the doctors arrive. But I sure don't know anything about any dog," she added as she glanced uneasily over at Sutta.

"And you always disinfect every tray, every day?" Cellars asked.

"Sure, every one that doesn't have a body on it. And every day except Saturday and Sunday. Those are my days off."

"And how do you know that—know which drawers not to open?"

"Oh, that's easy. I just skip every one with a name tag on the door. Doesn't always work, though. Sometimes the graveyard shift guys forget to put the tag on the door. But what the hey," she shrugged, "it's not like I'm gonna faint at the sight of a dead body or anything. I just close it up and go on to the next one."

"So there wasn't any tag on drawer number twenty-eight this morning? No tag that read Robert Dawson?" Cellars asked.

"No, definitely not." She shook her head emphatically. "I mean it's not like I'm looking for things to do around here. If there'd been a tag on the door, I would have skipped it. You can bet on that."

"What about yesterday morning?" Cellars pressed.

"You mean was there a tag on drawer twenty-eight yesterday morning?"

"That's right. A tag with the name Robert Dawson, block-printed in black ink."

"Ya got me." She shrugged her muscular shoulders. "Hey, I just look for the blank ones. Names don't interest me. In fact, like the doc says"—she gestured with her head at Sutta—"better I don't pay much attention to names around here anyway. That way I don't get in any trouble, telling people who and what I saw."

Then she saw the frustrated look on Cellars's face.

"Hey, I guess that's not what you wanted to hear, huh?"

"No, not really," Cellars admitted. He stared down at the bag in his hand. "Where exactly did you say you found this?"

"Oh, that was on the tray—" She thought for a moment. "—way in the back. About where the head would be. Didn't see it at first, until I pulled the drawer all the way out . . . and there it was." She smiled. "You think it means something?"

"I wish I knew," Cellars said. Then he turned to Sutta. "This may sound like an odd question, but do you have the capability to draw a blood sample around here?"

"You mean from a live patient?" Sutta smiled.

"Yes."

"It's not something we would normally do, but I suppose we could work something out. Mind if I ask who the patient is?"

"Me."

Sutta blinked. "You want me to draw a blood sample from *you*? Right now?"

"That's right, if you don't mind."

"How much of a sample would you need?"

"I don't know. What does it take for a full tox-screen workup these days?"

Sutta thought for a moment. "I suppose twenty cc's would be more than enough."

"Okay, twenty cc's it is." Cellars nodded agreeably. "Where do I sit . . . or do I have to lie down?"

Ten minutes later, Sutta removed the piece of cotton from Cellars's inner arm, replaced it with a small Band-Aid, and handed him a pair of purple-capped vials. "This ought to do it," he said. "If not, come on back. We'll lay you out on one of the tables and put a tap in."

"Appreciate it, Doctor. I really do." He carefully placed the vials next to the plastic bag containing the twisted piece of metal, turned the tag over, and started writing on the back. Then he turned to Sutta's lab assistant. "I'm sorry, your full name is?"

"Kathy Buckhouse. Kathy with a 'K', B-U-C-K-H-O-U-S-E. 'Cept everybody around here calls me Bucky."

"Okay, Bucky," Cellars said with a sigh, "if you'll just sign on the back there, agreeing that you turned this evidence over to me today at about"—Cellars looked at his watch—"ten-forty-five hours, I'll get you a receipt and put you in the chain-of custody."

"Evidence? Hey, does that mean I get to testify in court?"

"You might," Cellars said as he grabbed a pad of paper off a nearby desk and quickly wrote out a receipt. "Let's just hope, for my sake, that I'm not the one you're testifying against."

CHAPTER TWENTY-NINE

JODY CATLIN STARED AT THE PHONE IN HER HAND.

"What's the matter, girl?" Melissa Washington asked.

"I don't know. I just called Colin's cell phone, and someone answered . . . or at least I think they did, because I'm sure I heard it click . . . but then no one said anything."

"You sure you punched in the right number?"

"I . . . think so."

"Hey, if it don't work once, try it again, that's my motto."

Jody held her phone book open, slowly punched in the correct sequence of numbers, then brought the phone up to her ear.

Then she blinked, and a confused expression appeared on her face. "What?"

Melissa looked up from her lab notebook. "What's the matter now?"

"I just got some guy on a recording saying, 'The party you're calling is not connected . . .'"

"Yeah, so?"

"He just answered the damned thing thirty seconds ago."

"Hey, didn't you just tell me a couple days ago how this boyfriend of yours hates cell phones? Never turns them on 'less he has to?"

"Yeah, but—"

"So he's got it turned off, just like the man says. You just dialed the wrong number last time, that's all."

"I've got to talk to Colin . . . find out what this is all about," Jody said in a whispery, shaken voice. Her face was still just as pale as when she'd first looked at the evidence tag with Bobby Dawson's name in the victim block and Colin Cellars's signature at the bottom.

" 'Course you do, girl, but you're not gonna find out anything by running all over the county screaming and yelling like that."

"What would you suggest I do?" Jody demanded through clenched teeth.

"You just let your girlfriend here handle this," Melissa said as she picked up the phone and reached for the Jasper County phone book.

"Who are you going to call?"

"The county morgue."

"What? You can't just—"

"Hush, now." Melissa waved her away. "Hello, is this the Jasper County Morgue? How are you doin' this fine morning? What's that? You say it's getting fixed t' rain on y'all *again*? Well, don't that beat all. Listen, hon, I don't mean to bother you, but this is Alsalya June, N'awlins City Police, and Ah'm callin' 'cus we just got this here teletype from you-all sayin' that one of our fine upstanding citizens name of Ro-bert Dawson was killed in your county and transported to your morgue"—Melissa leaned over her desk to read one of the evidence tags that had nearly put Jody Catlin into shock—"this last Monday. Thass' right, Dawson, D-A-W-S-O-N, first name Ro-bert. But the thing is, sugar, we jes' don't see how thass' possible, seein's how one of our officers jes' made a traffic stop on that bad boy not fifteen minutes ago. Uh-huh, yes, ma'am, I certainly will wait." Melissa stared up at the ceiling, ignoring Jody's frantic hand motions. "What's that, hon? Well thass' jes' 'xactly what we figured. Thank you, sugar. Bye, now."

Melissa hung up the phone with a satisfied smile on her face.

"That's . . . that's criminal," Jody whispered, her eyes wide with shock.

"What, my genuine New-Awlins' accent?" Melissa grinned. "I don't know. I thought it was pretty good myself. Maybe not as good as my deep-down south Georgia accent, but what the hey." The forensic scientist's dark eyes gleamed with amusement.

"No, you just . . . I mean, what are you going to say if they trace that call back here?" Jody demanded.

"Now how are they gonna do that?"

"I don't know, caller ID, something like that?"

"Doesn't work when you use the government line, sugar. I know. I already tried it."

"But—"

"Hey, now, don't you worry 'bout a thing," Melissa said soothingly. "I told you I'd take care of it. And besides," she added, the self-satisfied smile back on her face, "don't you want to hear the good news?"

"What good news?" Jody came upright in her chair, her eyes widening.

"The nice lady just checked her central computer files, and guess what? There's no record of any body by the name of Robert Dawson, dead or otherwise, being delivered to the Jasper County Morgue. Not this week. Not ever."

"But—" Jody Catlin shook her head in confusion. "But what's *that* all about then?" she demanded, pointing at the offending evidence tag.

"This here?" Melissa held up the evidence envelope in her hand. "You want to know what I think?"

"Yes, tell me."

"I think maybe your boyfriends really did get back together after all these years, probably sat around drinking beer and talking about old times, and decided to play a little joke on you."

"A joke? You call that"—Jody seemed at a loss for words— "*funny?*"

"No," she said, "I can't say as I do. But I'm not the one who's had two grown men going at each other's throats over her little own self for the last fifteen years," Melissa reminded pointedly.

"You think it's *my* fault they're acting like this?" Jody seemed stunned.

"No, sugar, I'm just trying to think like a man. Not pleasant, I'll grant you. But what did you expect? You ever see the kind of games they play on each other?"

"Yeah, sure, but—"

"Girl, all you got here is a little piece of paper, and some weird-shit DNA that's making us tear our hair out. The first sample comes from boyfriend number one, and the second one here has boyfriend number one and boyfriend number two's names all over it. Now just what kind of person do you think it would take to rig up something biochemically tricky like this?"

"A . . . forensic scientist?" Jody said hesitantly.

"And just what did this boyfriend number two of yours do for a living before he came down here, all hot and in love, and found himself lecturing about crime scenes to a bunch of them alien-loving Alliance of Believers people?"

"Alliance of who?"

"Believers. You trying to tell me you don't know about them folks?"

"I have no idea what you're talking about," Jody said emphatically.

"Lordy, girl, I knew it was trouble the moment you told me that your two boyfriends were supposed to meet at the Jasper County Auditorium at eight o'clock on a Sunday night. Everybody—and I do mean everybody—around this part of Oregon knows all about those meetings. Never even occurred to me that you might not."

"*Alien*-loving? You mean, as in . . ."

"That's right." Melissa grinned widely.

Jody Catlin shook her head in confusion. "I don't even begin to—"

Then her head snapped up. "Hey, wait a minute; that's right. Colin used to work in the Portland crime lab, which means he could have cooked this up with one of their molecular biologists. Shit!"

"Uh-huh." Melissa nodded knowingly.

"If they really did this, I'm . . . I'm going to kill them myself!"

"I heard that, honey. But before you get yourself all worked up again, why don't we put our heads together and see if we can figure out what this weird-shit DNA-like stuff really is. Then we can decide what we're gonna do about it."

———

Cellars and Talbert were still standing in the morgue parking lot, trying to make sense of what they knew—or thought they knew—when Kathy Buckhouse came running out the door.

"Here's a copy of the videotape," she said breathlessly as she handed Cellars a black plastic cassette holder. "Also, I wanted to tell you that we just got an interesting call from the New Orleans Police Department, asking about a Robert Dawson."

Cellars and Talbert looked at each other in confusion.

"What did they want to know?" Talbert demanded.

"I'm not sure. They mentioned something about a teletype, and the fact that it couldn't be their Robert Dawson because they just pulled him over on a traffic stop. Does that make any sense?" the lab assistant asked.

"No, it doesn't," Cellars said. "Not at all."

"What did you tell them?" Talbert asked.

"The truth," Kathy Buckhouse shrugged. "That we don't have any record of a Robert Dawson in our computer files, and never have had. And if they wanted to know anything else, they'd have to contact my boss or the OSP."

"And what did they say to that?"

"Nothing," the lab assistant said. "Fact is, I don't think they even cared all that much. They just seemed to think it was kind of funny, that we made a mistake."

"Okay, thanks, Bucky, appreciate the information," Talbert said, then waited until the lab assistant went back into the morgue building before he turned to Cellars again.

"You send out a teletype on your victim?" he asked.

"No, I never got around to it."

"So what was all that about, then?"

"Somebody checking in to see if Dawson really is dead?" Cellars suggested.

"Meaning somebody who would have a good reason to think he's dead."

"Right."

Talbert nodded. "I don't like this," he said after a moment. "I don't like this one little bit."

"Me neither," Cellars agreed. "But I don't know what to do about it."

Talbert stared down at the two purple-capped blood tubes in his hand. "You sure you want me to do this?"

"What, the tox screen? Yeah, sure, why not? I just lost track of thirty hours of my life. I'd like to know what happened, and why . . . and I assume you would, too."

"I'd like to know more about this Allesandra woman," Talbert said. "You say the first time you saw her was at this Alliance of Believers lecture?"

"That's right."

"Then she shows up at the station later that night asking for you, but you're still up on the mountain looking for evidence and shooting at shadows, so she goes home. Only someone's been in her house, and she's scared, so she goes to a friend's house, where she stays until you find her on your porch Monday afternoon."

Cellars remained silent, watching Talbert's expression.

"She's still afraid to be alone," the watch commander went on, "and you've got shadows wandering around outside your house—which you don't shoot at this time."

"I figured you'd like that part," Cellars said dryly.

"Oh, believe me, I do," Talbert replied with no apparent trace of sarcasm. "So instead, you take this terrified but beautiful young woman—who looks amazingly like Jody Catlin, the girl you and your buddy Dawson had a fight over fifteen years ago—to the Windmill Inn. Have I got it right so far?"

Cellars nodded glumly.

"The two of you check into a single room . . . you both take showers, separately, I believe you mentioned . . . and sometime later that night you have sex, presumably with each other."

"I *think* we had sex . . . with each other," Cellars corrected.

"You don't know?" Talbert stared at his CSI officer incredulously.

"I—I'm not sure what I know anymore," Cellars admitted. "I remember taking a shower. And I remember crawling into bed, and my head hitting the pillow. After that—I have no clear idea of what went on . . . if anything," he added.

"None whatsoever?" Talbert looked understandably skeptical.

"I've got some interesting memories that might make more sense if I was still in high school learning about sex the old-fashioned way. Whether or not they have any basis in reality is something else entirely. If it turns out they do, then you probably ought to know that I'm going to be thinking real seriously about turning in my badge and running off to some deserted island with this lady."

"That good, huh?" This time the sarcasm was definitely there.

"No, better," Cellars said seriously. "Infinitely better . . . which is exactly why I asked Sutta to draw my blood. If I *was* drugged—which makes a hell of a lot more sense to me right now than what may or may not be my memories of last night—then there ought to be some residue or metabolite evidence of whatever they used in one of those tubes. And if none of the above are true," he added, "then it probably means I've got some other kind of problem that at least one of us ought to be really concerned about."

"Such as?"

"Beats the hell out of me," Cellars admitted. "I'm just the roving CSI officer around here."

"Seems to me that you're turning out to be a whole lot more than that," Talbert observed.

"You mean like number one suspect in the disappearance of four Jasper County deputies, not to mention the death of my buddy Dawson?"

"Whose death has never been documented—because, among other things, you don't have any scene photos—and whose body no longer seems to exist," the watch commander reminded. "Except, perhaps, in the minds of the New Orleans Police Department."

"You left out 'if it ever did,' " Cellars noted.

"Oh, I still believe you," Talbert said. "And you said you're going to show me that laser scanner file, or whatever the hell it is, which will presumably show a body of someone. But that isn't the issue here . . . yet," he added pointedly.

"Which is why you called Sutta to check on Dawson's body this morning. Because you've got complete faith in me, right?" Cellars smiled.

"No," Talbert replied after a moment, "I called him because I had a couple of interesting visitors this morning. Special Agents from the DEA."

"Internal Affairs types? Asking about Dawson and his helicopter accident?"

"About that." Talbert nodded. "And you."

"Me?" Cellars blinked in surprise. "What do I have to do with a missing DEA helicopter?"

"That's what they'd like to know."

CHAPTER THIRTY

CELLARS DROVE OUT OF THE JASPER COUNTY MORGUE PARKING lot after promising Talbert that he'd be back at the station with the laser scanner equipment as soon as he dropped the twisted piece of metal off at the OSP crime lab.

He was still heading in that direction, lost in his thoughts—of Allesandra, and her incredibly warm and sensuous hand sliding down the side of his face—when some discordant image caught his attention. He turned his head to see what it was, and almost lost control of his car.

What the hell . . . ?

Cellars immediately pulled off the road and doubled back, pulling into the shopping mall parking lot and coming to a stop in front of the photo shop.

Or what was left of it.

There wasn't much. Mostly a twisted and blackened pile of

aluminum studs, conduit, pipes, machinery, and water-soaked carpet. The distinctive smell of burned insulation hung in the air.

There was a man in overalls in the center of the mess, working with a rake to sort through the debris.

"Excuse me, I'm Detective-Sergeant Cellars, from the Oregon State Patrol. Do you mind if I ask you some questions?" Cellars called out, holding up his badge as he approached the man.

"Sure, why not," the man shrugged. "I'm just standing around waiting for the insurance rep to show up."

"Are you the owner?"

"I was," the man replied glumly. "Not sure who owns what anymore. Guess that's what I'm waiting to find out."

"When did it happen?"

"Last night. I got a call from the alarm company about one in the morning, said the fire department was responding, and to get down here right away. But by the time I got here"—the man sighed, looking around his soot-covered boots—"this is pretty much all that was left. Nothing much anybody could do except watch it burn."

"So you didn't manage to save anything? Photos? Negatives?"

The man shook his head. "Not a damned thing. Which I guess isn't the end of the world, but you know how people are about their photos. Every underexposed negative is a once-in-a-lifetime shot. Can't blame them for feeling that way, but hell, we had two sets of wedding photos in the files waiting to be picked up when the people got back from their honeymoons. Negatives, prints, and everything." The man shook his head sadly. "I sure don't look forward to seeing those folks show up here next week."

"No, I guess not," Cellars said as he stared numbly down at the twisted and blackened remains of what had once been the COMPLETED RUSH basket.

There was a long silence as both men continued to stare glumly at the wreckage.

"I almost hate to ask," the owner finally spoke, "but I get the feeling you didn't just come here to ask me questions about the fire."

Cellars shook his head. "No, I didn't."

"You lost something here too? Not wedding pictures, I hope."

"No," Cellars said quietly, "nothing like that. Just one of those underexposed, once-in-a-lifetime shots. The kind you really hate to lose."

———

Evidence technician Linda Grey looked up from her desk, and her face fell when she recognized Cellars standing at the evidence counter window.

"I guess you heard about the photo shop last night?" she asked hesitantly.

"Yeah, I was just by there a few minutes ago," he said as he placed a tagged and sealed manila envelope on the stainless-steel countertop.

The evidence tech read the expression on his face.

"Oh, no, don't tell me . . ."

"Yep," Cellars nodded. "They were going to make an enlargement for me yesterday afternoon, as soon as I got there, but I . . . got distracted."

The evidence clerk winced sympathetically.

"That's okay," Cellars said. "We've got other evidence . . . including this here." He gestured at the manila envelope.

"Same case?"

Cellars nodded. "Zero-nine-zero-zero-six-six-six-six."

"Easy number to remember," Grey commented as she typed the number into her computer and waited for the case file history and evidence list to pop up.

"Yeah, it's getting to be," Cellars agreed.

"So what's this one?" she asked over her shoulder, still staring at the monitor.

"I have no idea. That's what I want someone here to tell me."

Linda Grey rolled her chair over to the counter window, picked up the envelope, and read the tag. "Piece of torn metal with possible bloodstains."

"I picked it up from the Jasper County Morgue this morning," Cellars said. "A lab assistant named Kathy Buckhouse found it in one of the cold storage drawers. She gave it to me in a plastic bag. I transferred it to a manila envelope. Bag's in the envelope."

"Ol' Bucky, huh?"

"You know her?"

"Oh sure, we see her all the time when we go over to the morgue to pick up or return victims' clothing. She's always forgetting that bloody clothes have to go in paper bags instead of plastic after they're dry. Is this item related to your victim"—she looked back at the monitor—"Dawson?"

"I don't know," Cellars replied. "It could have something to do with the case, or it may just be something left over from a previous body."

"Well, we'll see what we can tell you," Grey said as she began entering the data on her keyboard. "Criminalistics exam, serology, the works?"

"Sure." Cellars nodded agreeably.

"You got it," the evidence tech said as she pulled the computer-generated chain-of-custody receipt out of the printer, signed it, and handed it to Cellars—who looked as if he was daydreaming. "Anything else we can do for you today?"

"What time does FedEx pick up around here?"

Grey looked at her watch. "Not for a couple of hours."

"Could you send something out for me?"

"Sure, what have you got?"

He handed her the black plastic video cassette holder that was now tagged and wrapped in tamper-proof evidence tape. "Here's the address." He reached into his shirt pocket and handed her a business card.

"We send evidence to these guys?" she asked, her eyes opening wide when she read the address.

"Not usually," he acknowledged.

"I guess not," she said as she quickly copied the name and address into her notebook. "Anything else?" she asked, looking up as she handed him back the business card.

Cellars hesitated.

Building fires happen all the time, and for lots of reasons, he thought. *But how many happen in photo shops? And what are the odds that one would happen in this particular photo shop, on this particular day, in the middle of a goddamned rainstorm?*

Cellars didn't like the obvious answer.

"As a matter of fact, there is." He hesitated. "I'd like to talk to Jack Wilson, if he's around. Talk to him about some of the evidence, and see if I can borrow a camera. But before I get around to that, do you have an extra computer around here that can read a PCMCIA memory card? One that's hooked up to the Internet for outside e-mail traffic?"

"Sure, a lot of them. And I know for sure there's one in photo-video that's not being used right now, because the guy who uses it is on vacation. Want me to tell them you're on your way?"

"That would be great."

"You've got it."

Not yet, Cellars thought. *But I'm going to.*

As promised, Linda Grey quickly had Cellars sitting in front of a desktop computer equipped with a fast modem and a PCMCIA slot.

He thanked the cheerful evidence technician again, waited until she closed the door behind her, then reached into his pocket, pulled out the memory card that he hadn't turned over to the lab, and slipped it into the computer's PCMCIA slot. Smiling grimly to himself, he quickly called up the resident e-mail program. Entering the code ~INTERNET allowed him to enter Malcolm Byzor's e-mail address again.

Then he started to type.

MALCOLM,

HOPE YOU GOT MY MESSAGE ABOUT BOBBY. THINGS ARE REALLY CONFUSED NOW. HIS BODY IS MISSING . . . STOLEN FROM THE COUNTY MORGUE, AND ALL RECORDS—INCLUDING THEIR SECURITY MONITORING TAPES—ALTERED. I DON'T KNOW WHAT'S GOING ON, BUT I NEED YOUR HELP. SPECIF-ICALLY, I NEED YOU TO LOOK AT THE VIDEOTAPE, TELL ME WHAT YOU SEE. I'M HAVING IT SENT TO YOU AT YOUR WORK ADDRESS BY FEDEX. IT SHOULD GET THERE TOMOR-ROW MORNING.

IN THE MEANTIME, THIS IS EXTREMELY IMPORTANT: I'M AT-TACHING A COPY OF A PHOTO FILE FROM A PCMCIA MEMORY CARD TO THIS MESSAGE. I ACCIDENTALLY TOOK THE PHOTO AT THE SCENE. THE CAMERA WAS DAMAGED . . . AND THEN STOLEN BY THE SUSPECTS AT THE SCENE AFTER I TOOK THE MEMORY CARD OUT. I HAVE NO IDEA WHY THEY'D BOTHER TO STEAL A BROKEN CAMERA. ONLY THING THAT MAKES SENSE IS THEY THINK THERE'S SOMETHING ON THE MEMORY CARD THEY DON'T WANT ME TO SEE. PROBABLY NOTHING, BUT SEE WHAT YOU CAN DO WITH IT . . . AND KEEP WHAT-EVER YOU FIND TO YOURSELF! I'LL TALK TO YOU ABOUT IT LATER.

ONE MORE THING: IS THERE ANYTHING ABOUT YOUR LASER SCANNER SYSTEM—THE ENERGY OUTPUT OR WHATEVER—THAT WOULD MAKE A ROCK OR SOME PIECES OF BROKEN GLASS MOVE? I KNOW THIS SOUNDS NUTS, BUT I THINK IT HAPPENED. OR MAYBE I'M JUST SEEING THINGS. GET BACK TO ME AS SOON AS YOU CAN, PLEASE.

BTW (YOU'LL LOVE THIS PART): THERE'S A YOUNG WOMAN IN-
VOLVED IN ALL THIS NAMED ALLESANDRA. PROBABLY ONE OF
BOBBY'S EX-GIRLFRIENDS. I THINK SHE'S IN DANGER TOO.
LOOKS A LOT LIKE JODY. BIZARRE DEAL. I'LL TELL YOU MORE
ABOUT HER LATER TOO.

COLIN

PS: WAS GOING TO ATTACH A COPY OF THE SCANNER FILE
TOO, BUT THIS IS A PC SO I'LL HAVE TO SEND IT LATER WITH
THE MAC.

Cellars paused to reread the message. Then, satisfied for the moment, he accessed the PCMCIA memory, attached the photo data
file to the message, and hit the SEND tab. Moments later, the computer confirmed that the message was in cyberspace.

Ok Malcolm, do your stuff. All I want is a lead. Anything at all.

Finally starting to feel like he had things under control, Colin
Cellars carefully removed all evidence of his message to Malcolm
Byzor from the OSP computer. He was reaching forward to shut off
the computer when he heard a familiar voice behind his back.

"So this is where you've been hiding," Jack Wilson said. "What's
this about you needing to borrow one of our cameras?"

CHAPTER THIRTY-ONE

"YOU KNOW," OSP SUPERVISORY SEROLOGIST JACK WILSON SAID as he and Cellars sat down at the crime lab's main examination table, which was covered with items of evidence from the Dawson cabin shooting scene, "I think I'm really going to enjoy having you working CSI down here in Region Nine."

"Oh yeah, why's that?" Cellars asked suspiciously.

"You always did collect the weirdest shit at crime scenes."

"Something tells me I'm not going to like this conversation."

"Probably not." Jack Wilson nodded sympathetically. "How about if I start by telling you that your TOD device went belly up on you out there at the scene?"

"You're kidding."

"No, I don't think so." Wilson looked down at his notes. "LAB-twenty, your item CC-twenty-three. One Model Four Byzor Time of Death device, serial number zero-zero-zero-one. Total number of data sets: two. First data set: body of malamute, recorded for forty-two minutes. Second data set: body of victim Dawson comma Robert, recorded for one hundred and twenty minutes before device automatically shut off." Wilson looked up from his notes. "Interesting set of priorities. You decided to determine the time of death for a dead dog before you started working a dead human?"

"It's a long story."

"I'll bet it is." Wilson smiled and shook his head as he went back to his notebook. "Anyway, the device calculated a time of death on the dog at approximately five-oh-five P.M. relative to the day of your reading. And that's plus or minus fifteen," he added, "because the closest thing we had for a correlation factor on a malamute was a German shepherd."

"Five-oh-five, plus or minus, would make sense, I guess," Cellars said, remembering that Dawson had promised to meet him at the County auditorium at sometime around seven that Sunday evening. An hour before the lecture. "What about the victim?"

"That calculation turns out to be a little more interesting." Wilson hesitated.

"Oh yeah? Why so?"

"Well, according to your buddy Malcolm's clever little device, your human victim never did die."

Cellars blinked. "What?"

"Or at least not all the way," Wilson corrected. "Probably a matter of definition, more than anything else."

"You care to elaborate on that?"

"Sure. It's real simple." Wilson smiled. "The thigh temperature data starts out reading three degrees Celsius above ambient air temperature. Nothing unusual about that. Fairly typical starting point for a body that's been cooling for a while. But two hours later, the thigh temperature of your victim is still showing three degrees Celsius above ambient. And that *is* unusual."

"Not to mention impossible," Cellars noted.

"Well, yeah, that too."

"So what you're really saying," Cellars went on, "is that the victim had been dead for a while, and that the TOD device simply hung up—for whatever reason—when it first registered a body temperature of three degrees above room temperature?"

"That would be a nice explanation. Unfortunately, however, the ambient temperature data indicates that you had some temperature fluctuations inside that basement during the recording time. No more than a two- or three-degree drop below the mean at any one time; but the ambient temperature probes definitely detected and recorded the shift."

"Probably when I opened the door to the outside a couple of times," Cellars said.

"That would be a nice explanation too," Wilson responded, "except for the minor little problem that the body temperature of your victim didn't fluctuate accordingly. Straight line across for the entire one hundred and twenty minutes—same exact reading for both probes. No apparent impact from the dropping ambient room temperature whatsoever."

"So the body acts as a more efficient heat loss buffer than a room full of air with the door opening and closing," Cellars suggested. "Either that or the probes measuring the body temperature malfunctioned."

"Right, makes sense, even if the probes are wired and programmed separately to eliminate exactly this sort of situation." Wilson nodded agreeably. "But just to see if that really was the source of your problem, I slapped your little device on a volunteer test subject: one hot-out-of-the-package Wendy's hamburger, double patty, no pickle or sauce. Basically sacrificed my lunch for the good of your investigation."

"Probably did you some good," Cellars commented, glancing pointedly down at his serologist buddy's ample waistline. "And?"

"I didn't learn anything useful about the time of death of my hamburger," Wilson said, "but I can tell you that all probes on your little device seemed to function just fine. Nice steady drop to ambient over a period of twenty-seven minutes. Just like with the dog."

"So what does that mean?"

"Other than the whole TOD situation being yet another fine example of Murphy's Law in action, I have no idea," Wilson confessed. "Probably means you should have started with the human first."

"Thanks a lot," Cellars said sarcastically. "What's next?"

"Well, let's see, why don't we just skip right over to my personal favorite bit of weirdness involving this case. LAB item eighteen . . . your item CC-twenty-one. The evidence package that—how did you put it in your little side note that I have locked away in my safe and fully intend to keep for my memoirs?—*might* have moved while you were busy marking and packaging your other evidence? That was what you meant to say, correct?" Wilson looked up at Cellars with a pleasant and expectant smile on his face. "Not fell off the table or anything like that? Actually moved, all by itself?"

"It was a fleeting impression," Cellars said evenly. "I can't say for sure that's what I saw."

"On behalf of OSP employees across the state, I can't tell you how glad I am to hear you say that," Wilson said seriously, "because all I found in that sealed envelope was a bunch of glass fragments and a small rock. And there's nothing unusual at all about that rock as far as I can see . . . other than the fact that it looks a lot like the rock necklace in the painting."

"A lot like?"

"Well, I assume we're talking about an artist's rendition here, so you'd expect some minor inconsistencies," Wilson said as he picked up the stone and held it up next to the painting. "Even so, you can still see a couple of obvious differences . . . here and here." He pointed with his finger. "But, in any case, it's just a rock. Kind of pretty in its own unique way, I suppose, but still a rock. And since rocks, in my experience, generally don't move unless you either kick them or pick them up and throw them," Wilson went on, "I have to assume you were either hallucinating or having a very bad day. Which, I might add, after reading your narrative report, really doesn't sound like all that bad an explanation."

"This is your idea of being helpful?" Cellars inquired.

"No, not really." Wilson shrugged. "But look at the material I have to work with." He gestured with his hand across the table.

"Yeah, I know. Don't remind me," Cellars said tiredly. "What else have you got?"

"Oh, several interesting things. Let's start with the blood samples." Wilson looked at his notes again. "First of all, you've got a pretty even division between human and nonhuman blood at this scene."

"Yeah, I figured the dog was probably killed inside the house and dumped out on the road." Cellars nodded.

"Well, that probably accounts for part of it," Wilson said. "The blood in your item numbers CC-ten, CC-eleven, CC-thirteen, and CC-twenty-two all screened negative for human and positive for canine. CC-nine screened positive for both human and canine."

Cellars looked at his own set of scene notes. "Okay, matted blood and hair on the rug, blood/water/mud mix out on the road, and blood on the easel that was lying on the rug. And whoever moved the dog out the doorway was either bleeding or stepped in some human blood on the way out. That would all make sense."

"And the blood in your item numbers CC-five, CC-six, CC-twelve, CC-fourteen, and CC-fifteen all screened positive for human, but we don't have a blood sample from the victim for exclusion purposes, so we're holding off on the DNA comparison work until it comes in from the autopsy. We're still working on the bone samples . . ." Wilson looked down at his watch, and frowned. "Hmm, that's odd, we should have gotten the autopsy specimens in by now."

"Don't hold your breath," Cellars said quietly.

Wilson caught the edge in Cellars's voice immediately. "Is there something about the autopsy I ought to know about?" he asked cautiously.

Cellars nodded his head slowly. "Among other things, it apparently hasn't happened yet, and probably won't. That's what I wanted to talk to you about. I just stopped by the morgue a little while ago." He hesitated.

"And?"

"And they have no record of ever receiving the body of my victim."

Wilson blinked. "You mean the body of the victim"—he glanced down at his case file notes—"that *you* delivered to the morgue Monday morning?"

"That's right."

"Oh." Wilson was silent for a moment as he stared down at his case file. "I assume you have a signed receipt for the body?"

"Oh yeah. But the trouble is, it was signed by a young morgue attendant who's somewhere in California on vacation for a week, and they can't reach him. And I didn't have a case number at the time, so he probably didn't log it into their computer system before he left."

"All of which is pretty much irrelevant—at least in terms of our need for exclusion samples—if they can't find the body in the first place," Wilson noted.

"Right."

"I take it you helped them look?"

"Every drawer and every table."

"Ah." Wilson was silent for a moment. "Just offhand," he finally said, "how do you suppose a county morgue goes about losing an entire body?"

"I don't have any idea," Cellars said. "And to tell you the truth, I'm trying real hard not to think about it."

"Okay, so much for the victim's blood," Wilson mumbled as he made some notes in his case file, then looked up as another white-coated figure entered the serological examination area. "Which brings us to some good news."

"It's about time."

"Yes, indeed," Wilson agreed as he gestured toward the newcomer. "Terry, come on over and grab a chair. Detective-Sergeant Colin Cellars, Firearms Examiner Terry Danielson. Colin's the one who brought that relic in from the morgue," Wilson explained as the two shook hands.

"Yeah, nice to meet you. Cool stuff," the firearms examiner said cheerfully as he sat down at the examination table and tossed the manila envelope onto the chemical-resistant surface. "Not often we get in evidence of a chain-fire for analysis."

"Chain—what?" Colin blinked in confusion.

"Chain-fire. One of the problems people used to have with the old nineteenth-century cap-and-ball revolvers," Danielson explained. "Manufacturing tolerances were pretty loose in those days, so there was usually a pretty decent gap between the front end of the cylinder and the back end of the barrel. That was usually fine in terms of the revolver not jamming up from dirt or mud, but there was one major drawback. If you weren't careful to seal off the front end of the cylinder chambers with grease, the flame and burning powder from one detonation could ignite the powder in one or more of the other five chambers. At best, the shooter had one hell of a surprise on his hands."

"And at worst?" Cellars asked.

"One dead or severely injured shooter from the exploding frame and cylinder fragments, plus torn-up lead balls flying in all directions . . . which is probably what you had here," Danielson said, gesturing at the manila evidence package. "Fact is, I'm almost positive this torn piece of metal is from the top frame strap on a .44 Remington New Army Model, cap-and-ball revolver. And based on the upward direction of the twisting and fracturing, not to mention the blood, I'd say whoever fired it last probably experienced a classic chain-fire: all six chambers going off at the same time, resulting in the cylinder blowing loose from the frame."

"How do you like that for an on-the-spot firearms examination?" Wilson asked, smiling.

"I'm impressed," Cellars said truthfully. "You guys always work cases this fast around here?"

"My hobby." Danielson shrugged. "I happened to be walking by when Jack here was logging it into his notebook, and spotted it right off. Otherwise, I wouldn't have had the slightest idea what it was either."

"Tell him about the chemistry," Wilson reminded.

"Oh yeah. Since I'd already stuck my nose into the case, I figured I ought to just keep on going. So I took your metal fragment over to the SEM, and came up with classic gunshot residues from black powder and the old nipple-cap primers," Danielson said. "Which were consistent with the loads in the other three cap-and-ball revolvers you collected. I had Susan help me collect the blood splatters. She's going to take it over to Ashland," he added as he picked up the evidence package and stood up. "Anything else I can do for you?"

"What about that Colt Dragoon?" Cellars asked.

"Oh, you mean the 'can it go off half-cocked' question?"

"I don't think that's quite how I put it, but—"

Danielson put up his hand apologetically. "Sorry, I'm just trying to prepare myself for the grand jury this afternoon. To give you a straight answer, no, a Colt Dragoon will not go off accidentally from a half-cock position. Fact of the matter is, that particular weapon doesn't go off all that easily from a full-cock position. Definitely could use some polishing on the trigger sear."

"So, in other words, if that gun did go off—let's say at a crime scene, for example—you're telling me that someone absolutely had to pull the trigger, right?" Cellars pressed.

"Either that or set it off with some kind of remote device, I suppose," Danielson said. "In fact, as I recall, someone apparently did fire it." He looked down at his notes. "Yep. That was the cap-and-ball that had one round fired from the cylinder." He looked back up at Cellars. "I take it this is a problem?"

"I was kind of hoping you'd tell me a raccoon could have set it off," Cellars said.

"A raccoon?"

"Uh-huh."

"Have to be one hell of a raccoon. Nothing you'd want to run into on a dark night . . . especially if it was armed." Danielson grinned. "Hey, I'd like to stay around and hear more about this raccoon, but I've really got to go. Anything else I can answer real quick?"

Cellars shook his head.

"Okay, see you two later."

Wilson waited until Danielson disappeared out the door. Then he turned to stare at Cellars. "Do I even want to know about this raccoon business?" he asked.

"Not unless you really want to start worrying about my sanity," Cellars replied, glaring at his former Portland crime lab associate.

"You think I'm not worried already?"

Cellars suddenly blinked in confusion. "Hey, wait a minute, did he say you guys sent those blood samples over to Ashland?"

"Now we're back to the bad news," Wilson said.

"Oh yeah, what's that?"

"The bloodstain on the twisted piece of metal."

"You've got something on it already?" Cellars's eyebrows rose in amazement as he looked down at his watch. "How can that be? I just brought it in a half hour ago."

"We usually do our initial screening with antisera, but we've also got a limited capability to look for species-defining hemogloblins using a thermospray LC/mass spec now," Wilson explained. "Dilute the sample with distilled water, inject, go get a cup of coffee, and be back in ten minutes to read the results."

Cellars shook his head. "Absolutely amazing. You're making me feel like some kind of forensic dinosaur."

"Yeah, well, stand by to be even more amazed," Wilson said. "The blood on that piece of metal?"

"Yeah?"

"It screened negative for human *and* canine hemoglobins . . . not to mention negative for all the other hemoglobins in our database . . . which isn't a lot," he admitted.

"What?"

"Just like the bloodstains from your item numbers CC-three, CC-four, CC-seven, CC-eight, CC-forty-two, CC-fifty-five, and CC-fifty-six," Wilson added as he referred to his notes again.

Cellars was following along with his open field notebook. "Wall and wood floor by the entrance to the kitchen where I found the body, wall and wood floor by the broken window, lead bullet in the north wall by the refrigerator, and blood from the seats of the Explorer?" He looked up at Wilson. "How the hell can that be?" he demanded.

"I don't know." Wilson shrugged. "You were at the scene. You tell me."

"I shot at . . . something"—Cellars hesitated—"going through that basement window. Whatever it was, the hole in the window was definitely too small for a human, but . . ."

"Maybe your gun-wielding raccoon? Or a bobcat?" Wilson smiled. "Neither of those would show up on our antisera or hemoglobin runs."

"What about a small monkey?" Cellars asked.

"In southern Oregon?"

"I know, the whole thing sounds crazy," Cellars agreed. "But I could swear I saw a long arm—and a small hand—reaching for a gun hanging on the wall. It was dark, and all I saw was a shadow, but—"

"You think you might have been shooting at a couple of small monkeys . . . who fired a shot back at you with a cap-and-ball revolver, and then took off with your vehicle?" Wilson stared at Cellars in disbelief.

"But monkey blood would have shown up as positive on your human antisera runs," Cellars said, ignoring the stunned expression on his friend's face. "So that can't be it, unless—"

"Unless what?" Wilson asked suspiciously.

"Your antisera's getting old?"

"You may be getting old . . . not to mention senile. Our antisera is fine," Wilson said firmly.

"Maybe a bad batch?" Cellars suggested.

"Are you telling me you want us to rerun everything with a new batch of antisera?" Wilson stared at his friend as if he'd lost his mind.

Cellars held his hands out in supplication.

"You know, Colin," Wilson said after a long moment, "if it was any other CSI officer in the state of Oregon—anybody at all, for that matter—I'd tell them to hang it in their ear," Wilson said seriously.

"But you owe me," Cellars smiled.

"Yes I do," Wilson admitted. "And I do believe in paying my debts, which is why I'm delighted to be able to tell you that we can't possibly rerun your nonhuman and noncanine bloodstains."

Cellars blinked. "Why not?" he demanded.

"Because, we just sent them over to the Fish and Wildlife lab in Ashland."

"Ashland?"

"That's right." Wilson smiled. "Maybe the federal bunnies and guppies folks can tell you what kind of long-armed shadowy critter you were shooting at."

CHAPTER THIRTY-TWO

THE INTERCOM BUILT INTO THE PHONE ON THE NEAR WALL OF THE Wildlife Forensic Lab's PCR room beeped twice before a familiar voice queried: "Jody, are you in there?"

"I'm here," Jody Catlin called out from her workbench.

"Somebody from OSP is out here at the front desk to see you."

Jody blinked in surprise as Melissa Washington grinned broadly. "See, what'd I tell you? Stay low-key, pay them no attention at all, and they'll come running to your door, faster than you can spit."

Jody rolled her eyes at her lab partner, and called out, "Okay, I'll be right there," as she got up from the bench.

"How long's it been since you've actually seen this boyfriend of yours?" Melissa asked as she watched Jody check her hair in the reflective surface of one of the instruments.

"Fifteen years. Something like that." Jody shrugged with feigned indifference.

"I don't know, girl." Melissa Washington shook her head solemnly. "The way you're looking right now, I got a feeling I'm not gonna be seeing you for the rest of the day."

It was an idea that caused Jody to smile as she hurried down the corridor. But when she got to the reception area, the man standing beside the receptionist's desk in the familiar Oregon State Patrol uniform wasn't Colin Cellars.

"Dr. Catlin," the uniformed officer said, as he stepped forward with his hand extended, "I'm Lieutenant Don Talbert, OSP Region Nine."

"Oh, uh, nice to meet you, Lieutenant," Jody Catlin stuttered, then recovered quickly. "How can I help you?"

"Well, if you don't mind," Talbert said as he took note of Catlin's efforts to mask the disappointment on her face, "I'd like to ask you a few questions."

"Certainly. Does this involve a specific case?" She hesitated as she started to direct the uniformed officer toward the lab's lunchroom. "If so, I'll pull the file."

"In a way," he said as he continued to watch the expression on her face. "The investigator is Detective-Sergeant Colin Cellars . . . and the victim is a man named Robert Dawson."

————

"So you don't really know for sure if Bobby's dead?"

They were sitting at one of the round tables in the lunchroom of the National Fish and Wildlife Forensics Lab.

Talbert shook his head. "Detective-Sergeant Cellars has reason to believe the body he transported to the morgue last Monday belonged to Robert Dawson—his friend, and yours, too, I understand?"

Jody Catlin nodded silently as the inconceivable images flashed through her numbed mind. Then the import of his words hit her.

"You said . . . 'has reason to believe.' I don't understand."

"The face of the victim was severely damaged, enough so that . . .

Detective-Sergeant Cellars couldn't be sure. I gather they haven't seen each other for a while?"

"No, it's been a long time. Fifteen years," she whispered.

"That's a long time for good friends to be separated," Talbert suggested. Little by little, he drew the story out of her. The childhood and college friendship torn apart by her and Bobby Dawson's innocent decision to carry on with their plans for an overnight hike around Lake Shasta after learning, at the last minute, from Colin and Malcolm separately that both had to cancel out. The casual bantering over the absurdity of setting up tents when the weather was warm and not a cloud in sight . . . that led to their laying their sleeping bags next to each other under a beautiful starlit sky. The tumble of emotions far more intense than either expected that led to the predictable intimacy . . . and a shared sense of guilt that neither had been able to conceal from Colin or Malcolm. And how the four of them had gone their separate ways for all these years . . . until Bobby's mysterious helicopter crash ultimately brought all of them together again.

Talbert listened patiently as Jody Catlin described her persistent efforts to bring the two long-estranged friends back together again, culminating in the agreed-to meet at the Alliance of Believers lecture where Bobby intended to ask Colin for help. But then Bobby didn't show.

"Do you know what kind of help Dawson wanted?" Talbert asked.

Jody Catlin shook her head. "No, he never said. Just that it had something to do with his crash, and that Colin was the only one who could figure it all out. He had to talk to Colin. I don't know why. It never made much sense . . . but you have to know Bobby. He can be . . . intense like that."

Talbert stared silently into his coffee cup as he considered his next question.

"Would you say that either of them is hot-tempered?" he finally asked.

"You mean Bobby and Colin? No, hot-tempered isn't the right word. More like thickheaded and stubborn."

"In other words, if both of them wanted . . . something very much, perhaps more than anything else, it isn't likely that either of them would give up easily?"

"Give up? Bobby or Colin?" Jody Catlin started to laugh, but then she saw the expression on Talbert's face. "What are you saying?" she asked in a hoarse whisper.

Talbert frowned. "I'm sorry," he said, "but what I'm trying to ask you, Dr. Catlin, in as gentle and roundabout way I can, if you think Detective-Sergeant Cellars might want you back badly enough that he'd be willing to kill his friend Dawson—and four Jasper County deputies who might have gotten in his way," Talbert added. "And after that, use his considerable forensic and crime scene skills to hide or confuse the evidence, specifically including the bodies of all five victims?"

"My God, no," she whispered, her face infused with shock and horror. "How can you possibly . . . suggest such a thing?"

"Almost thirty years in law enforcement tends to make you very cynical about the supposed limits of what any individual—even someone you know and trust—might do in a moment of stress or desperation. Also, I have the distinct advantage of not being emotionally involved."

Jody Catlin visibly recoiled from the cold and determined expression on Talbert's face . . . a reaction that was not lost on the veteran supervisor.

"You need to understand something, Dr. Catlin," Talbert said as he continued to stare directly into Jody Catlin's shocked eyes. "I think very highly of Detective-Sergeant Cellars. In fact," he added with a half smile, "you might even say that I hold some of his demonstrated talents dear to my heart."

"But—"

"However"—Talbert held up his hand—"you also need to understand that I'm facing a situation in which four Jasper County deputies

who were sent out to investigate a shooting scene are now all missing. As is the body of the victim who—at the very least—seems to
closely resemble this Bobby Dawson friend of yours. The DEA is
also looking for Bobby Dawson . . . something about a missing helicopter, and some kind of physical assault on two of their agents. And
every direction *I* look, the common factor seems to be Detective-
Sergeant Colin Cellars of the OSP. A man I'm responsible for."

"But—"

"When's the last time you heard from either one of them," Talbert interrupted again. "Dawson or Cellars?"

"I talked with both of them by phone last Sunday. Bobby on
Sunday morning, and Colin later on that evening—when he was
waiting for Bobby to meet him at the lecture."

"And not since then?"

"No."

"How would you describe Cellars's mood that evening?"

"I don't know, frustrated, I guess." She shrugged. "He didn't
want to be there. I guess he thought Bobby and I still had a thing
going."

"But you didn't?"

She hesitated, then frowned. "Is that any of your business?"

"I'd like to say no, but—"

"Never mind, I understand." Jody Catlin shook her head in irritation. "Bobby and I had a relationship several years ago. It . . .
caused everybody a lot of grief. We broke it off six months later,
and never saw any good reason to start it up again."

"Does Cellars know that?"

"I . . . don't know. It wasn't a topic that he was ever willing to
discuss with me."

"Which presumably brings us back to the thickheaded and
stubborn part."

"Right."

"Who would he discuss such a topic with?" Talbert asked.
"Dawson?"

"I don't know, but I'd say definitely not Bobby. Malcolm, I suppose."

"Malcolm being your mutual friend who works at the National Security Agency?"

"That's what he tells us. Actually, we have no idea where Malcolm works," Jody Catlin said with a slight smile. "We're not even sure he knows. If you ever find out, please tell us."

"Do you have a home or work number where I can contact him?"

"Sure, I'll get them for you." She started to get up, but Talbert waved her back.

"A couple more questions first, if you don't mind."

She sat back down warily.

"Does the name Allesandra mean anything to you?"

"Allesandra?" Jody Catlin's eyebrows furrowed in confusion. "No, I don't believe so."

"You don't recall Dawson or Cellars ever mentioning someone by that name?"

"No, I'm sure they didn't—at least not to me."

"How can you be so sure?" Talbert pressed.

"Because I would have definitely remembered the name of . . . another woman," Jody Catlin replied evenly, meeting Talbert's gaze. "Especially if she was involved with either Bobby or Colin."

Talbert smiled briefly. "Yes, I suppose that you would." Then he stood up. "I know you're busy, and I apologize for taking up so much of your time."

"That's all right. Anytime that I can help . . ." She let the words trail off as she escorted the uniformed commander back out to the lobby.

"Thank you very much for your cooperation, Dr. Catlin," Talbert said at the front entrance to the lab as he shook her hand briefly. "I realize this was upsetting to you, and I want you to know that I share your sense of disbelief."

"But you're not convinced, are you?"

"I beg your pardon?"

"You're not convinced that Colin had nothing to do with Bobby's . . . disappearance, and the missing deputies."

Talbert hesitated. "Dr. Catlin, if Detective-Sergeant Cellars had nothing to do with the disappearance of these people, as I sincerely want to believe, then I'm going to do everything I can to find out who did. But if it turns out that I'm wrong, and he was involved"—he looked squarely into Jody Catlin's eyes again—"then somebody needs to convince him to turn himself in immediately . . . before I find myself hunting him down."

CHAPTER THIRTY-THREE

CHRIST, OF ALL PLACES TO SEND THE EVIDENCE, THE FISH AND *Wildlife Lab in Ashland,* Colin Cellars thought numbly as he drove the Expedition aimlessly through the rain-drenched streets, twice driving past turn signs that would have taken him to the I-5 freeway . . . and south to Ashland. It was a repetitive argument, and he wasn't getting anywhere.

They sent the evidence there, so now you've got to go see her. Tell her about Bobby face-to-face.

Yeah, but she probably already knows by now.

Of course she does. It was right there on the evidence tags. Victim: Robert Dawson. Investigator: Colin Cellars. Dumb shit. You should have called her Monday, before you hopped into bed with Allesandra.

Allesandra. The mere thought of her name instantly sent a rush of incredibly erotic and sensuous images flooding through Cellars's mind. It was all he could do to keep his attention focused on the slippery roadway.

I didn't hop . . .

Yes, you did.

The rain was starting to fall harder, forcing the wipers to sweep against heavy volumes of water in both directions as they sought to keep the windshield clear. Even so, Cellars could just make out the freeway access sign a block ahead.

Okay, take this one, he told himself. *You need to—*

Shit!

The object hit the Expedition hard from the left side, just below his side window, causing Cellars instinctively to jerk the steering wheel away from the jarring impact, and sending the heavy utility vehicle sliding sideways on the slippery asphalt in the direction of a huge Douglas fir.

His subsequent reactions were the direct result of numerous practice runs on the OSP's pursuit driving course: He immediately turned the steering wheel farther in the direction of the slide, and used light taps on the accelerator in an attempt to regain some degree of traction first . . . and then control. A useful and potentially lifesaving procedure if you had plenty of room to spare. But the blurred image of a tree was coming up much too fast.

He hit the accelerator once more, felt the tire treads start to dig into the asphalt, then yanked the steering wheel away from the oncoming tree. The Expedition lunged forward, and he immediately brought the steering wheel back around to his right, trying to swing the back end clear. But he felt the jarring impact all the way up his spine as the right end of the rear bumper ricocheted off the soft bark.

For a brief moment, he thought the desperately squealing rear tires might break loose from the road surface completely, the momentum sending him spinning backward into the flow of traffic. But the deep rubberized treads finally responded to the on-off-on acceleration and caught again; an instant later, he had the

Expedition back on the road and accelerating forward in the right direction.

It was only then that Cellars realized he'd been holding his breath the entire time—which hadn't been more than a few seconds at the most. He released the pent-up air and quickly took in a couple of deep, steadying breaths.

Damn, that was close. Almost . . .

Another hard, jarring impact—this time against the right side of the vehicle—rattled the front passenger-side window and caused Cellars to jerk his head away, sending the Expedition careening head-on into the opposite flow of traffic. Tires squealed and horns blared in loud protest as startled drivers swerved to avoid the Expedition, and Cellars fought to regain control of his vehicle again.

But this time he saw it through the rain-blurred windshield.

The flickering shadow as it streaked parallel to the right side of the road . . . then disappeared up ahead, around the trunk of a thick redwood.

Cellars didn't even stop to think as he hit the gas pedal, launching the Expedition at a sixty-degree angle across the two-lane asphalt road and into a sideways-sliding stop in the soft gravel, wild rosebushes, and mud.

The heavy utility vehicle was still rocking back and forth on its springs when Cellars, cursing furiously, flung the door open and stumbled out into the mud. He was still screaming at his unseen assailant as he thrust the SIG-Sauer through the gap between the opened door and doorframe, then fired two .40-caliber hollow-points at the thin slide of dark shadow barely visible along the right edge of the massive tree trunk.

Chunks of redwood bark were still flying from the tree when Cellars spotted movement to the left of the trunk, shifted his aim, and sent two more high-velocity rounds streaking into the shadowy gloom.

Then he sensed—rather than saw—rapid and furtive movement behind the big redwood.

A delayed sense of caution caused Cellars to hesitate. His training instructors had always been emphatic on such matters: In a
shooting situation where you can't see what your suspect is doing,
the smart decision is to remain in your barricaded position and call
for immediate backup. All very fine, but Cellars's survival instincts
told him he had his assailant on the run, and this was no time to
stop. Having learned long ago to trust those instincts, Cellars shoved
himself away from the open door of the Expedition and ran directly
toward the huge redwood, with the SIG-Sauer held up at a point
shoulder position in both hands—ready to fire the instant he had a
target.

He reached the tree in ten strides and flung himself up tight
against the spongy bark. Then, before his sense of caution caused
him to hesitate again, he immediately swung his extended arms
around the tree to his right, using the massive trunk for protection
as he searched for a target through the rapidly falling rain.

Nothing.

What the—?

It was the chilling sensation racing up his spine that caused him
to whip around just in time to see the pair of shadowy figures pull
the front passenger-side door of the Expedition open.

His eyes widened in rage and disbelief. But the intense training
that the Oregon State Patrol gave all their officers came through
once again. The familiar and comforting sights of the SIG-Sauer
appeared and aligned themselves before his eyes . . . and he smiled
as his forefinger tightened against the trigger.

Yes.

He led the first shadowy figure, anticipating where it would be
in the next tenth of a second, and then sent the .40-caliber round
bursting through the front windshield of the Expedition about six
inches to the right of the rubberized gasket holding it in place. He
heard—or at least thought he heard—a shrill scream over the sharp
ringing in his ears.

The second shadowy figure ducked away instantly, then seemed to disappear into the misty gloom as Cellars sent two more hollow-point bullets streaking through the gap between the door and doorframe.

Then there was nothing to be seen . . . except for the pickup truck that had come to a screeching halt in the middle of the road and the driver who was peeking his head over the hood, looking like he was about ready to bolt at any second.

Cellars approached the Expedition cautiously, the SIG-Sauer out and ready, but the shadowy figures were gone. Both of them.

Where the hell—?

"Hey, Officer, you okay?" the man in the pickup yelled.

"Yeah, I'm fine, but why don't you stay back for a second," Cellars acknowledged as he continued to sweep the surrounding woods with his eyes, watching for the first shadowy movement. But there was still nothing to be seen. Then he realized that the man in the pickup was dangerously exposed out there in the middle of the road, so he directed him to pull the pickup over to the side of the road in front of the Expedition.

"Oh, boy," the man said in a shaky voice as he cautiously stepped out of his truck and walked over to where Cellars was standing. "I stopped because I thought you might need some help, but I never could see what you were shooting at. Damned near scared me to death, too."

Cellars looked over at his would-be rescuer—a tall, slender man who looked to be in his mid-seventies dressed in old and faded bib overalls and a down jacket—and noticed for the first time that he was holding what looked like a breech-loading single-barreled shotgun in his trembling hands.

"Yeah, I know what you mean," Cellars agreed.

"What the hell *were* you shooting at?" the man asked. If anything, his trembling was getting worse, and Cellars noticed that other cars were starting to drift by slowly, the drivers gawking curiously as they maneuvered around the pickup.

Christ, I'd better get out of here before I cause an accident.

But then he thought of something else.

"Escaped fugitive," Cellars said. "I think he's long gone, but I'm going to call for some backup and take a look around just to be sure. You mind standing by for a minute until they get here?"

"No, uh, glad to, Officer," the man said, looking around uneasily.

"Hold on just a second," Cellars said as he reached into the Expedition and came back out with the radio mike.

"Oregon-Nine-Echo-One to OMARR-Nine."

The response was immediate.

"OMARR-Nine to Oregon-Nine-Echo-One, go ahead."

"OMARR-Nine, is Oregon-Nine-Alpha-Two on the air?"

"Nine-Alpha-Two to Nine-Echo-One," a familiar voice responded, "go to channel five."

Talbert.

Cellars breathed a sigh of relief as he reached into the cab of the Expedition and switched the console channel setting to five.

"Nine-Alpha-Two, go ahead."

"I'm out on Timberline Road, heading north, about a half mile from the I-Five interchange," Cellars said, ignoring radio code now that they were on a secure frequency. "I need to talk with you, right now."

"What's the matter?"

Cellars hesitated, remembering that there was still one Jasper County scout car missing. A scout car equipped with an all-regional-channels radio.

"I need to talk to you in person," he spoke into the microphone.

There was a brief pause.

"I'll be there in five," Talbert responded.

———

The uniformed watch commander pulled up alongside Cellars's new Expedition in a brand-new, shiny white OSP scout car four-and-a-half minutes later, stepped out of the car, then stopped dead still when he saw the Expedition's windshield.

He was still staring at the starred and bullet-hole-pocked

windshield, the mostly blown-out rear window, and the huge dent in the side panel below the rear passenger-side window—seemingly at a loss for words—when Cellars came up beside him.

"Nice vehicle," Cellars commented. "Yours?"

"What?" Talbert blinked. He looked as if he was right on the edge of an apoplectic fit.

"Your new ride," Cellars said, gesturing with his head at Talbert's scout car. "I assume you liberated it from Hawkins?"

"He can find himself something else to drive," Talbert growled. "What the hell happened to my goddamned Search and Rescue vehicle?"

"Mr. Jonas Breem, here, is going to explain all that," Cellars said. He motioned with his head in the direction of the tall, slender figure standing a few feet away. "Mr. Breem, this is Lieutenant Talbert. I've asked him to come by here for a few minutes so that you could describe to him exactly what you saw happen out here a little while ago."

Talbert continued to stare wordlessly at Cellars for a long moment before turning his attention to the slender, elderly man in the muddy boots and worn bib overalls. "Go ahead, Mr. Breem," he said in a barely controlled voice. "I'm very interested in hearing what you have to say."

"Well, sir, I was driving home in my truck"—Breem pointed over at his pickup—"when I saw this OSP vehicle here"—he pointed at the damaged Expedition—"up ahead a-ways suddenly swerve to the right like the driver was trying to avoid hitting something. I never did see if there was anything in the road, but I mighta missed whatever it was on account I was watching his vehicle almost go into that tree back there," he added nervously. "Thought for sure it was gonna hit dead on. But then the officer here got it under control, and he was back on the road, maybe fifty feet ahead of me when he suddenly swerved again—this time to the left, right into oncoming traffic. Like to scared the very dickens out of me. Don't know how he missed hitting the people coming this way, but he did. Then, all of a sudden, this officer, he swerves off to the right again, right off the road, only this time he comes to a stop, jumps out . . . and starts shooting at something."

Talbert looked over at Cellars, who simply shrugged and gestured with his head in the direction of his visibly shaken witness.

"Did you ever actually see who or what Detective-Sergeant Cellars was shooting at?" Talbert asked.

"Uh, no, sir, I surely didn't. But I sure did slow down—almost to a stop, 'cause I was looking real hard, trying to see what he was shooting at, I mean. Then I saw him run right at that tree over there"—Breem pointed—"right where he's been shooting at before . . . and I remember thinking, oh boy, he's gonna get himself shot, sure enough. But then, all of a sudden," the elderly man added, his eyes wide with excitement, "this officer, he whirls around real quick-like and starts shooting at his own vehicle. I mean I couldn't hardly believe it, but you can see right there where he hit it."

"Yes, I certainly can," Talbert muttered. "Did you see anybody near his vehicle at that time?"

"No sir, I didn't see anybody then either. Guess I was kinda busy, trying to pull my old duck gun out of my pickup, thinking he might need some help. But I'll tell you what I did see."

"What was that?"

"Just before this officer shot his own car, somebody definitely opened the passenger-side door of that Expedition."

"Are you certain of that?" Talbert pressed.

"Yes sir, I surely am, 'cause when I saw that door come open, and the bullet hit that windshield, that's when I realized I didn't have any shells for my shotgun. So I turned around and started to run like hell . . . and just about got run over by a goddamned honey wagon. And wouldn't that have been a hell of a way to go?"

Talbert blinked.

"I wish I could tell you I saw that fellow, whoever this officer was shooting at," Breem added hesitantly, "but that wouldn't be the truth because I surely didn't. Never did see anything except for that passenger-side door opening."

Talbert finally found his voice.

"Thank you, Mr. Breem," he said, "for stopping to assist Detective-Sergeant Cellars . . . and for taking the time to report what you saw."

The elderly man smiled self-consciously. "Sure am glad I could do something useful. Uh, I suppose you want me to sign a statement, something like that?"

"We would very much appreciate it," Talbert said.

Breem hesitated. "Well sir, I'll be glad to—sure enough will. But I'm, uh, running a mite late right now. Would it be all right if I stopped by the station tomorrow morning, did it all then?"

"That would be fine," Talbert said as he escorted the elderly man back to his pickup and waited there until Breem drove off down the road. Then he walked back to where Cellars was standing beside his vehicle.

"Was that necessary?" he asked.

"Which part? The shooting or the witness statement?"

"Let's start with the witness."

Cellars shrugged. "All things considered, I figured you might like to hear about this from someone who could corroborate at least a part of my story for a change."

Talbert stared glumly at the crusted hole in the Expedition's starred windshield for a long moment before he said, "You want to add anything significant to his statement?"

"Not really . . . other than the fact that whatever it was that hit the side of the vehicle hit hard enough to create a spherical dent all the way to the inside panels on both sides."

Talbert walked over to the Expedition and examined the huge dents. His immediate impression was that the vehicle had been broadsided with a pair of high-velocity bowling balls, left and right.

"Did you see what did this?"

"No."

"And you searched the side of the road—both sides—and found nothing?"

Cellars nodded.

"Then what the hell were you shooting at?" Talbert asked as he ran his fingers along the smooth concave surface of the driver's side dent.

"Shadows."

Talbert turned and stared at Cellars.

"You're trying to tell me a fucking shadow threw some kind of cannonball at your car . . . correction, at both *sides* of your car . . . while you were driving down a goddamned public road?"

"No, I never saw what hit the car either time," Cellars repeated patiently. "What I am trying to tell you is that I saw two dark, shadowy figures. Both of them were about as tall as the Expedition, and they both looked like they weighed maybe a hundred and sixty pounds apiece. I saw the lead shadow pull open the front passenger-side door of this vehicle, and I fired at his upper body through the windshield just as he was starting to get into the cab. He screamed, and then—"

"He?" Talbert interrupted. "You think at least one of them was a male?"

"No, I have no idea," Cellars admitted. "I'm just saying 'he' because if I keep on saying 'it,' you're going to start worrying about my sanity, too."

"I'm long past that," Talbert replied. "I'm starting to worry about my own. Go on."

"He screamed," Cellars repeated. "Or at least I think he did. Then they both disappeared."

"You think you hit one of them?"

"No doubt about it." Cellars nodded. "I had him dead on in the sights, and there's blood on the front seat. Here, I'll show you."

They walked around to the passenger side of the Expedition. Cellars handed Talbert a flashlight, then stepped back so that the watch commander could examine the reddish stains splattered all across the front passenger seat.

"That's a hell of a lot of blood," Talbert commented. "So where's the body?"

"I have no idea."

"What about a blood trail?"

"No blood trail," Cellars said. "Or at least none that I could find."

"How do you explain that?"

"I don't. I'm just telling you the facts as I see them."

Talbert closed his eyes and sighed deeply. "So what's with the envelope?" he asked, pointing to the manila envelope lying on the floor next to the passenger seat.

"I wanted you to be here to watch me collect the blood."

"Since when do you need—" Talbert started to ask, and then shook his head. "Never mind," he said, "go ahead." Then his eyes widened in shock when he saw Cellars take a sharp folding knife out of his pocket, kneel, and place the knife blade against the edge of the seat.

"Hey, what the hell are you doing?" he demanded.

"I'm going to collect a sample of the blood for you to take back to the lab," Cellars said, looking back up at his stunned supervisor.

"Me?"

"Who else? You really want *me* to deliver the evidence on my own shooting incident to the lab? My second shooting incident in a period of four days," Cellars reminded, "when everybody there is already convinced I need a vacation . . . or a psychiatrist?"

"Okay, good point," Talbert acknowledged. "You probably do need a vacation . . . or at least some admin time off while we get this entire situation straightened out. But I'm short-handed enough as it is, and we've still got twenty-four missing Jasper County citizens out there somewhere. So until we find out what happened to them, and those deputies, you're staying on the job. Now what the hell's the deal with that knife? Why don't you use a swab or something?"

"There's not much DNA in a small bloodstain. I want to make

sure they have plenty to work with this time," Cellars explained patiently.

"So you're going to cut a goddamned hole right in the middle of a brand-new leather seat? *My* brand-new leather seat?"

"That's right."

"Bullshit! That's ridiculous. Why don't you just take the entire car over to the lab and leave it with them?" Talbert demanded.

"Because I need a vehicle to get around, and I'm not going to get much done on this case if I spend the entire day sitting around the lab."

Talbert hesitated, looked over at his new shiny white scout car, and then hesitated again.

"Where are you planning on going?" he finally asked.

"I was going to go see a friend of mine, to see if she could help me make some sense out of all this; but before I do that, I'm going back to the cabin."

Talbert blinked. "The cabin? You mean the crime scene?"

Cellars nodded.

"Why?"

"Because there's something inherently wrong with that entire setup," Cellars replied. "A lot of things that just don't make sense. I want to get out there while I've still got some daylight . . . and before anybody else messes up whatever's left of the scene."

"You're going back up there by yourself?"

Cellars shrugged. "Like you said, we're short-handed. If you can find a CSI officer who's not busy doing anything for a couple of hours, I wouldn't mind the company. But otherwise," he added firmly, "I'm going to go do my job."

"And what about these shadow figures you keep shooting at?"

"Yeah, I thought about that," Cellars admitted. "But whoever these idiots are, they're definitely on foot now. So I figure by the time they manage to hike all the way back up that mountain— assuming they're even headed back that way, which I doubt—I'll be long gone."

Talbert seemed to make up his mind.

"Okay, you take Hawkins's scout car up to the cabin. Transfer your gear. I'll drop the Expedition off at the lab, have somebody there take me back to the station. Then I'll see who I can find to give you a hand up there. And if I can't find anyone," Talbert added, "I'll go up there myself."

It took the two officers almost five minutes to transfer all of Cellars's CSI gear into the trunk and backseat of the new scout car.

"One more thing to remember," Talbert said as he stood beside the new scout car with his hand resting on the glistening white roof.

"What's that?" Cellars asked, looking up from the driver's seat.

"You start shooting at this one, you won't have to worry anymore about Hawkins gunning for you."

"Oh yeah, why is that?" Cellars cocked his head.

"Because I'll be the one looking for you," Talbert growled as he gently brushed his hand against the gleaming red-and-blue light bar. "Now get out of here before I change my mind."

CHAPTER THIRTY-FOUR

THE CABIN SEEMED DIFFERENT IN THE DAYLIGHT. SMALLER SOME-
how . . . or maybe it just looked that way in comparison to the surrounding firs, pines, and redwoods, Cellars thought as he leaned
back against his climbing belt and stared out through the trees at
the barely visible structure.

It was almost as if the forest had grown in some significant way
in the last few days, adding more protective vegetation in response
to the road crew who had apparently taken advantage of a brief
break in the weather to rescrape the rock, dirt, and mud border surrounding the cul-de-sac at the end of County Road 2255. And in
doing so, had completely obliterated any possible evidence at the
spot near the cul-de-sac where he'd found the dog carcass and the
tire tracks of the missing deputies' scout cars. The tracks he hadn't
been able to photograph because of his damaged cameras.

It was an impressive example of county government leaping into action at the first sign of a hazardous condition on one of their roads.

Except why would a repair crew come all the way out here—to the end of a remote and mostly uninhabited mountain road—when they've got all that storm damage out at the north end of the county to deal with?

It was a perfectly good question. But no one had given him a perfectly good answer yet. Which was why he was leaning back against the climbing belt and staring out over the trees, trying to figure out what, if anything, about the small, isolated cabin had changed. But in fact, he finally decided, it was really only his angle of view—twenty feet up in the air rather than down on the road—that was different. Although something about the incredible response time of the county road crew was still tugging at the back corner of his mind.

Cellars was still hanging there, lost in his increasingly skeptical perceptions of all the "whos" and "whys" and "hows" of the past few days, when he suddenly heard the sound of distant but rapidly approaching thunder . . . and immediately realized that the sky had started to darken.

Uh-oh, here we go again. Better get back to work.

He'd stopped by the local office for US West on the way back up the mountain, to see if he could get a lineman up to the cabin to reinstall the phone line. But the supervisor had explained to Cellars that the recent storm had done a lot of damage to utility lines at the northern end of the county . . . damage that his road crews were still trying to repair. And another storm was on its way, which was why he really couldn't send a truck out to repair a single-residence line up at the far end of an isolated mountain road. But the supervisor had come up with a useful option: two five-hundred-foot spools of insulated telephone line, a set of pulleys, a climbing belt, a repairman's phone, and a pair of climbing spikes. These items took up the front passenger seat and floor of Hawkins's increasingly cramped and overloaded scout car. A large dark green plastic tarp, his CSI kit, and the borrowed camera kit took up the backseat.

He'd located the first cut about a quarter mile down the road from the cul-de-sac, the point at which the fleeing suspects had apparently removed about two hundred and ninety feet of line between a pair of utility poles set about three hundred feet apart.

In theory, it had sounded like a reasonably easy task. Just strap on the spikes and belt, climb the pole, tie a couple of cable ends together with a square knot to keep them from pulling apart in the high winds, then strip the ends of the exposed wires, connect, and tape. What could be easier?

But, in fact, it had taken him almost half an hour to drag and winch the amazingly heavy three hundred feet of cable up to the top of the two poles and make the necessary ties and connections. The end result was a temporary fix, but Cellars figured it would probably last until a work crew could come and do it right.

All of which had brought him to pole number N3472—the third utility pole from the cabin—where he had first discovered the cut telephone lines. To start with, the pole proved far more difficult to climb because it was tilted at a fairly sharp and ominous angle. Which in turn forced Cellars to work his way up slowly and gave him plenty of time to wonder how the previous climber had managed to avoid leaving a fresh set of spike marks.

It was an interesting question that called for some further investigation. But the jarring sound of a lightning bolt ripping through the sky a few miles away quickly refocused Cellars's attention to the task at hand. It took him almost ten minutes to tie the first set of cable ends together with a square knot, then strip, connect, and tape the individual wires. By then, the sky had darkened considerably, and it had started to rain.

Man, I don't think I want to be up here this high and exposed much longer.

A second lightning bolt—this one much closer—ended any doubt on Cellars's part. He quickly scrambled down the pole to the ground in a flurry of rapid belt and spike movements, just as two more lightning bolts streaked across the sky in rapid succession.

Cellars stood there at the base of the pole, holding the other end of a three-hundred-foot length of cable. In order to reestablish a phone connection to the cabin, he still had to make a last tie and connection to the cable end dangling from the top of the next utility pole in line to the cabin. But in order to do that, he'd have to climb that pole.

And get my ass fried by the first lightning bolt that lines me up in its crosshairs? Yeah, right.

Then he smiled as a much better idea occurred to him.

Thirty minutes later, soaking wet, shivering, and covered with mud from the knees down, Cellars stood on the cabin's north-facing covered front porch with the end of the telephone cable in his gloved hand. But he was no longer smiling.

Twenty goddamned feet. I don't believe it.

Twenty more feet of cable was all he would have needed either to connect the end of the telephone line to the junction box mounted at the far end of the porch on the north cabin wall, or just work the line directly into the house. But he didn't have twenty more feet of cable. Both of the cable spools were now empty, and he'd already cut away as much of the line stretching from the cabin junction box to the first utility pole as he could without actually climbing up the pole. Which he wasn't about to do in any case.

Another lightning bolt crashed overhead, underlining the logic of his decision and causing him to wince and duck.

The only other option he could think of was to drag the seven hundred and eighty-some feet of cable all the way back to the third utility pole, then try to find a more direct line from the pole, through the trees, to the cabin. Assuming, of course, that such a shorter route actually existed. All for the purpose of having a working phone inside the cabin, where he could be warm and dry, instead of outside on the cabin porch, where he would undoubtedly be cold and wet.

But that meant another half hour or so of staggering around in the mud, rain, and treacherously concealed tree roots.

Forget warm and dry, he decided. *Not worth it.*

Still mumbling to himself, Cellars moved over to the near corner of the covered porch, pulled the cable tight, wrapped the end around the corner support post just above the railing . . . and tied it off with a quick clove hitch knot, leaving about two feet of cable dangling loose. It took him another couple of minutes to strip the wire ends and connect the repairman's phone.

To his absolute amazement, the soothing sound of a dial tone hummed in his ear.

Okay, Talbert, he thought with no little degree of satisfaction, *now let's find out what happened to that CSI officer of yours.*

———

"What do you mean you haven't seen him?" Cellars demanded, trying very hard not to yell into the phone. "He was supposed to have been there a couple of hours ago."

It was fifteen minutes later, and he was still standing on the exposed porch next to his stacked CSI, scanner, and borrowed camera kits; the folded dark green plastic tarp; a backpack containing food, water, and a toilet kit; a five-cell flashlight; and the 12-gauge Winchester 870 pump shotgun from Hawkins's scout car. Cold and shivering, and talking on the phone as he stared out at the windswept trees and the rapidly falling rain.

Just like he'd been doing five days ago, on the exposed porch of the Jasper County Civic Auditorium.

Jesus, is that all it's been. Five days?

It seemed like a lifetime ago.

"I'm sorry, Sergeant," Linda Grey, the OSP Crime Lab evidence technician said, "but I've been here all afternoon and I definitely haven't seen him."

"Could he have taken the vehicle somewhere else to have it processed?"

Grey hesitated. "No, I don't think so . . . and I can't imagine why he would. We've got an available garage bay right here in the back of the lab. That's the logical place to do the work. Plenty of light and out of the rain."

"Listen," he said, "could you please check with someone out there in the garage right now, just to be absolutely sure. It's very important."

"Sure, no problem."

She was back on the line a few minutes later.

"I'm sorry, but no one there's seen Lieutenant Talbert all afternoon either."

"And you definitely haven't logged in any additional blood evidence—I'm specifically talking about bloodstains from the front seat of a new OSP Expedition—on this case in the last three hours?"

"No, sir, not on your case or any other case for that matter. I just checked our computer files to make sure. The last item we have logged in on OSP-zero-nine-zero-zero-six-six-six-six is your item CC-sixty, which is the security videotape from the morgue."

"Okay, thanks, Linda. If he does stop by, would you please have him check in with OMARR-Nine ASAP?"

"Will do."

He said good-bye, disconnected the line, and quickly dialed the business number for OMARR-9.

"OMARR-Nine."

"This is Cellars again. OSP-Nine-Echo-One. Checking to see if Lieutenant Talbert might have checked in yet?"

"No, I'm sorry, we still haven't heard from him."

"And you've tried to reach him on the radio?"

"Three times so far. He's not responding to his calls, but he may be out at the north end, in one of the radio dead zones," she added. "We had a reported sighting of one of the missing Jasper County deputies about an hour ago."

Cellars closed his eyes in frustration. "Okay, listen, I'm going to be out here at the cabin for a while. You've got the number here, right?"

"Yes, of course. I wrote it down when you called last time."

"Okay, as soon as Talbert does check in, would you please have him contact me at this number immediately?"

"Absolutely."

"Okay, thank you," Cellars said as he disconnected the call.

It was starting to get seriously dark now, with the gathering storm, and he knew he really ought to get on with his search before he ran out of daylight altogether. But the inescapably erotic images flickering about in the back of his mind—of a cavorting and caressing and all-encompassing Allesandra—kept reminding him of another similar face, and of a heartfelt obligation.

He had a working phone now, he knew her private work number, and Talbert's CSI officer still hadn't shown up yet, so there weren't any more excuses.

Decide, he told himself. *Call her now, or walk away.*

CHAPTER THIRTY-FIVE

"HELLO?"

"Hi," he said softly. "How are you doing?"

"Colin?"

Only one word, but he was amazed to discover that he could still pick out the surprise, the delight, and the apprehension in her familiar husky voice.

"Yeah, it's me."

"What's . . . where are you? Your voice sounds different."

"Probably a lousy connection. I'm back up at Bobby's cabin, out on the porch."

"What? The cabin? My God, what are you doing up there again? I thought—"

He could sense the anguish now too, and it caused an ache deep in his heart.

"I'm not sure what I'm doing up here," he answered honestly. "Trying to make some sense out of it all, I guess."

"Bobby . . . is he really dead?"

Cellars took in a deep breath.

"I don't know."

"But you . . . they said you worked the scene, and . . . transported his body?"

"I transported *a* body," he corrected. "I don't know for sure that it was Bobby. The victim's face was . . . torn-up, and it's been a long time since I've seen Bobby. But all the circumstantial evidence—"

He told her about the partially finished portrait with Dawson's distinctive signature at the bottom, and the Custer-era guns, and the general description of the body—a description that caused Jody Catlin to emit an audible groan. He left out the part about the shadow figures. They were a separate problem. Nothing to do with her.

"So, yes, given all of that, and the fact that he never did show up at the lecture," he finished, "I guess I have to believe it really was him."

"But why?"

Cellars didn't respond for a few seconds. He was too busy reacting to the alarm bells in the back of his head, and the sudden chill up his spine.

The lecture. That's right. The first focal point. Me, Bobby, the DEA, and Allesandra.

So what did a nonsense lecture on alien contact to a bunch of fruitcakes have to do with all of this?

"Bobby was involved in something," Cellars finally said. "Something to do with DEA and that helicopter crash. I don't know, maybe it was drugs."

"Bobby? Involved with drugs? Are you serious? He wouldn't even take aspirin when his knee was swollen to twice its normal size."

"I know it doesn't make any sense," Cellars agreed. "But I know for a fact there are a bunch of people in the DEA who really want him bad. Maybe he caught one of them dirty . . . and they went after him to shut him up. Whatever it is, one way or another, somebody is definitely pissed off at him."

There was a long silence at the other end of the phone.

"I had a long talk with Lieutenant Talbert this afternoon," she finally whispered.

"Oh yeah, what did he want?"

"He knows that you were really upset at Bobby . . . for a long time . . . and he's probably about half-convinced that you killed him."

Cellars blinked, then continued to stare out into the darkening sky and wind-whipped rain as he considered this new bit of information. "Talbert's an ex-homicide investigator," he finally said. "His first instinct is to follow the evidence. Right now, a lot of the evidence doesn't make sense. And unfortunately, I'm the one, who collected it."

"Or . . . lost it," she reminded him. "Talbert said they can't find Bobby's body at the morgue."

"Yeah, that's another complication," Cellars acknowledged. And then, after a moment: "What does Talbert think, that I'm a good enough forensic scientist and crime scene investigator to completely fake a homicide scene?"

"I think the possibility really concerns him."

"Well, he should stop worrying about it. I told him I'd take a damned polygraph."

"You did?"

He tried to ignore the surprise in her voice. "Sure, why not? And besides," he added, "even if I was insane enough to go after Bobby and try to fake the scene—which I didn't—it's just not possible. You know that."

She hesitated again.

"It might be possible, if the people examining the evidence at the lab were involved . . . or if they didn't do their job," she finally said.

"Yeah, right. I'm going to work up a conspiracy to fake a homicide investigation with a bunch of forensic scientists at two separate state and federal crime labs, not having any idea who's going to get assigned the cases. And then somehow talk whoever does get the assignment into risking their careers—and only a life sentence in a federal prison, if they're lucky—to help me kill one of my best friends," Cellars said sarcastically, "all because he . . ."

A movement out of the corner of his eye caught Cellars's attention.

In the trees. A flickering, shadowy movement. Barely visible in the rapidly falling rain.

Oh, shit.

"Yes?"

"Never mind; none of that's important now," Cellars said as he reached down and picked up the 12-gauge pump shotgun, reflexively checked the exposed red button safety, and then shifted his position on the porch, watching the trees carefully now. "We were kids, and kids do stupid things. I just happened to excel in that particular category."

She must have sensed the sudden tension in his voice.

"Colin, what's the matter?"

"Nothing. I'm just standing on the porch getting cold and wet. Starting to lose daylight up here. Got to get back to work in a couple of minutes." Now that he was talking to her again, he didn't want to stop, but—

"Listen, before you go, there's something else you need to know," she said softly.

Another flickering shadowy movement. Definitely there this time, but farther away.

The sharp searing crackle of a nearby lightning strike made him wince, and he missed what she said.

"What was that?" he asked, distracted by the rapidly growing storm and the flickering shadows.

Clouds, he tried to tell himself. *I'm imagining things. Probably just clouds.*

"Talbert," she repeated. "He may be suspicious that you have inside help at one of the labs."

"Who? Jack Wilson?" Cellars almost laughed in spite of his uneasiness. "Talbert doesn't know Jack very well, does he?"

Still watching the trees, but he couldn't see any other movement. *I need to get off this porch. Too exposed.*

"No, not Jack. Me."

"You?" The idea caused Cellars to blink in confusion, and to momentarily forget about the shadowy figures. "What are you talking about?"

"Talbert found out I've been working some of the evidence on your case."

"You what?"

"I didn't know it at first," she said defensively. "I was working on . . . something else, something involving Bobby, and it matched up with some of your nonhuman bloodstain evidence that Melissa was working on."

The alarms were going off in his head again. Something about Bobby . . . no, there! Another flickering movement . . . off to the right this time and farther back. Hard to see. The rain was falling too fast, making everything blurry.

Retreating . . . or circling? Like they know the range of a 12-gauge three-ought shotgun round? Who are these shitheads?

He could feel the tingling starting up his spine again, and he suddenly remembered one of the first things his old training sergeant had told him.

Don't ever forget to listen to your instincts, son. You hear those alarm bells going off in the back of your head, or feel that chill going up your spine, you start paying attention to things around you real quick-like. Those are your survival instincts, trying to tell you something.

"Get out of the case right now, Jody," Cellars said emphatically. "You don't want to have any part of it. Believe me, you don't."

"It's too late, I already helped work some of the nonhuman blood evidence that the OSP lab sent us . . . before I knew you and

Bobby were . . . involved. The data's recorded in my lab notebook.
There's nothing I can do about it."

"Tell your boss you just discovered you've got a conflict of interest, and that somebody needs to reexamine the evidence. They'll
understand."

He had the short barrel of the shotgun raised halfway now . . .
finger across the trigger guard . . . ready to put the sights on a target.

"I know they would, but I . . . want to make sure—"

"Of what? That the people working the evidence do their job?"

"I suppose," she said hesitantly, but he could sense a dangerous
edge to her voice now.

Pay attention! He admonished himself. But it wasn't clear, even
to him, what or who he meant. He could feel himself starting to
shiver. *Got to get back inside.*

"So that someone like me . . . can't get away with faking a scene,
or getting rid of incriminating evidence? Is that what we're talking
about?"

Watch it.

Getting edgy, he realized. He hadn't meant to say that.

"Like the four deputies who might have gotten in your way?"
Catlin added forcefully.

Wonderful, now she's pissed too. Shit.

"Talbert said that?"

There was dead silence on the other end of the line.

"Is that what you think too?" he pressed. "That I could do
something like that? Kill Bobby . . . and four sheriff's deputies to
cover my tracks, all because . . ." He couldn't finish the sentence.

"Did you?" she whispered.

You've got to get your butt off this porch, right now, some entity in
the back of his mind warned.

"No," he said in a tense voice. "I didn't. I couldn't . . . not even
for you. Not even as much as I loved you then . . . or now."

He could hardly believe he'd spoken the words.

"Thank God."

The sound of heartfelt relief in her voice jarred at his senses.

My God, you really thought I could have done it, didn't you?

He tried to imagine the look on her face . . . but to his shock, all he could see—or imagine—was the face of Allesandra.

But then another flickering shadow moved . . . farther out to the right, but in closer now. Definitely circling . . . just out of effective range. Rain coming down in a deluge now. Concealing everything.

Shit, who are these guys? You'd think they were—

Cops?

Then it occurred to him.

Talbert.

Showed up very quickly after the shooting out on Timberline Road. Almost like he'd been nearby.

And why is he letting me run with this thing, when I've got a clear conflict of interest? Shit, talk about being emotionally involved.

"Jody, did Talbert say where he was going after he left your lab?"

"No, why?"

"There's somebody out here in the woods, watching me right now. I thought for a while it might be those DEA agents, but now I'm starting to think it may be Talbert."

"My God, Colin," she whispered. "Listen to yourself. You're starting to sound . . . paranoid."

"Me? At least I don't sleep with a goddamned .44 Magnum under my pillow."

Dead silence at the other end.

"What did you say?" she finally whispered.

"I said . . . oh shit, no." Cellars closed his eyes as the numbing realization hit. "Don't tell me. Bobby slept with a .44 Smith & Wesson under his pillow?"

"Always," she said with a catch in her voice. "One night, I almost—" Then she caught herself. "I'm sorry, I didn't mean—"

"No, it's all right," he said quickly, feeling his stomach churn. "I know you two slept together for . . . however long you did. It doesn't matter."

"Oh, yeah?" she said cautiously. "Since when?"

"Since I started growing up."

"Oh? When was that?"

"Kind of a recent event," he said in a hollow voice. "Probably started sometime this afternoon."

Then it occurred to her.

"Wait a minute," she said in a horrified voice, "you said . . . that must mean you found a—oh God."

"No, wait, it doesn't necessarily mean anything," Cellars said hurriedly. "This is Oregon. The whole state's wall-to-wall with paranoid types. A quarter of the male population probably sleep with .44 Magnums under their pillows."

"But—"

"Listen, you've seen Bobby recently, haven't you?"

Catlin hesitated.

"Look, forget about the sex. I don't care anymore. I honestly don't. All I want to know is, was he still weight lifting?"

"Was he . . . what?"

"Was he still lifting weights? You know, bodybuilding?"

"Well, yeah, sure . . . I mean, he never stopped. You know Bobby."

"So where are his weights then? And his gun safe? And his ammo stockpiles?" Cellars asked rhetorically. "I looked through every inch of this damned cabin. No weights. No gun safe. No thousand-round stocks of ammunition. So where are they? I mean they're not the kind of things that you can just casually pick up and hide. And no sketch pads or twelve-string guitars either. Just a bunch of old guns, a portrait that looks a lot like you . . . or maybe like somebody else . . . and a couple of goddamned shadows driving me—and everybody else who shows up at this scene—halfway crazy."

"Colin, what . . . are you talking about?"

"Never mind, it's not important. Just understand that there's something wrong with this whole goddamned scene. None of it makes any sense." Cellars paused to look around and take in a deep breath. He could feel the shivering getting worse.

"Listen, you said you and Melissa were trying to identify that nonhuman blood I collected, right?"

"Yes, that's right. We got it in from the OSP lab, but we couldn't ID it."

"Why not?"

"We got these really weird patterns with the sequencer. It's called a compression block. Like the program doesn't recognize what the restriction enzymes are cutting. We tried to rerun everything, but you know the problem. There isn't all that much DNA in blood to begin with. Then we started running out of sample."

The alarm bells and chills were back again, but he crouched behind the support pole with the shotgun clenched tight in his hand and ignored them.

"Not a problem," he said. "I'm right up here at the scene, and there's plenty of blood left. I'll get you more."

"I'm coming up there too," she said. "You need somebody there with you."

"No, that's okay, Talbert's sending—"

He blinked.

Somebody up here to help me.

Yeah, right.

"But—"

"No, you stay there at your lab," he said quickly. "I'm not going to be here very long. I'm just going to make another quick search around here, make sure I didn't miss anything the first time through, collect some more blood for you, then drive down and meet you at your lab."

"Colin, listen to me—"

Why is he letting me run with this thing, when I've got an obvious conflict of interest?

Because I'm useful? An obvious patsy? Somebody who's going to be perceived as trying to use his access to a scene and his CSI skills to resolve a personal problem?

But if that's the case, what would it take to get somebody like Tal-

bert to go sideways? Political pressure? Not likely. Big money? DEA-sized money?

Jesus.

"Look, I've got to go," he said as he came up to his feet quickly, holding the shotgun out one-handed, his index finger tight against the trigger.

"But—"

"I'll be there as soon as I can," he promised, and quickly disconnected the call.

———

The windows were shut, and the front and side doors were still sealed. He verified that quickly as he worked his way around to the west side of the cabin, leading with the barrel of the shotgun out and ready as he tried to shield his eyes against the rapidly falling rain.

Which left the back door to the south.

He'd used old-fashioned tamper-proof sealing tape to seal the doors. Good thing, he reminded himself, because he didn't trust Malcolm's electronic security devices anymore. Not after discovering that Allesandra had somehow managed to get through them back at the hotel without setting them off.

You must have given her the disarm and reset codes. You just don't remember, he'd tried to convince himself.

Which was true, he didn't remember any of that . . . and what he did remember hardly seemed believable.

He had to work to force the erotic and sensuous images back into the recesses of his mind, concentrating on something far less enticing.

Evidence tape. Red, sticky, tamper-proof evidence tape.

There weren't any arm or disarm codes with tamper-proof evidence tape. You either broke the fragile but incredibly adhesive tape, or you didn't. And the bright red, one-inch-wide, jagged-edged strips with his initials and date marked clearly on the nonerasable surface were still there, holding the jury-rigged door latch together.

Okay, that's more like it, he thought as he quickly put the CSI and scanner kits down beside the sealed door, covered them with the tarp, then ran back through the mud and rain for the borrowed camera kit and backpack. Then, after taking one more look around and seeing no sign of any shadowy figures, he quickly broke the seals and entered the basement, shotgun up and ready in both hands.

What the hell?

The cabin was clean.

No bloodstains inside the doorway.

No bloodstains in the middle of the carpet.

No broken easel fragments and palette, and scattered paint tubes.

No bloodstains on the floor at the east end of the utility wall.

Just the water dripping from his clothes, and the mud tracked in by his boots.

He moved forward into the middle of the cabin and carefully set the shotgun down against the woodstove. Then he drew the SIG-Sauer and flashlight from his belt holster and jacket and began a slow, methodical search through the darkened basement.

The first thing he discovered was that the phone by the bed and the second phone by the table were both gone . . . receivers, handsets, connecting wires, everything.

The broken window had been temporarily repaired with a piece of plastic wrap taped to the frame. *Probably to keep the rain out,* he decided. He hadn't noticed that from the outside. But he did find the four lead shot holes in the southeast corner, the three lead bullet holes in the middle of the north wall, and the three copper-jacketed hollow-point bullet holes in the middle of the west wall. A further search of the bathroom area revealed a small plastic bucket, a nearly empty bottle of bleach, a still-damp mop, and a still-damp pair of towels hanging in the shower.

Okay, so I'm not losing my mind after all. There really were at least two shooting incidents in this basement. So who the hell cleaned everything up?

And more to the point, how in the hell did they get in here?

He was still staring at the wood log wall beside the broken window, trying to make sense of it all, when he suddenly realized that something else was missing. Something that he'd completely overlooked during his initial search of the scene.

The two mushroomed copper-jacketed hollow-points on the floor. They had to hit something in order for them to have mushroomed like that. But there aren't any impact points on the log walls.

So what did they hit? The animal—raccoon, or whatever it was— that escaped through the window?

Cellars shook his head slowly.

No, that can't be it, because a spinning, high-velocity .40-caliber copper-jacketed hollow-point would have shredded skin, tissue, bone, and organs as it ripped right through something like a raccoon. Animal that small would have been torn apart. I would have found it right here . . . or right outside the window.

Cellars blinked.

The images that were forming in the back of his mind—causing chills to travel up his spine and into his neck and shoulders—had very little basis in reality. He tried to ignore them as he secured the south-side basement door from the inside. Then he holstered the SIG-Sauer, grabbed the shotgun, went up the stairs, through the mostly empty main bedroom, into the completely empty living room, then out the front door and onto the porch. Where he discovered as he reached for the phone that, if anything, the volume of water pouring from the sky and running down the mountain on either side of the cabin had increased significantly.

She answered on the second ring.

"Hello?"

"You said you needed tissue?"

"Colin? What are you—?"

"When they sent you the nonhuman evidence on my case," he interrupted, "did they include a pair of mushroomed .40-caliber copper-jacketed bullets? My CSI-numbers CC-forty-nine and CC-fifty?"

"I—I don't know. Hold on a second."

She was back in twenty, during which time the flickering shadow figure appeared again in the distance.

Still out of range, Cellars thought. *Afraid of the shotgun. Interesting reaction—assuming that they're even out there in the first place.* He was no longer convinced . . . and barely willing to believe his own eyes.

Got to get a picture, he reminded himself. *Got to get a picture.*

For reasons he couldn't even begin to comprehend, he wouldn't allow himself to think about what that picture might show.

"No, they didn't."

"Call the OSP lab. No, better yet," he corrected, "you stay there. I'll call them, explain the situation, and get somebody to send them over to you. And when they get there, check them out with a scope. They had to hit something solid enough to cause them to mushroom, and it definitely wasn't the log walls . . . so if it was some kind of animal, there ought to be small bits of tissue trapped under the peeled-back copper jacketing. Not sure I would have seen it when I collected or marked them, even if I'd been looking."

He felt the pager buzz against his belt. He quickly set the shotgun aside for a moment and checked the display screen.

Malcolm? What the hell does he want?

"Colin, I don't understand. What does any of this have to do—?" Catlin started to ask, but Cellars interrupted again.

"I've got to go," he said quickly. "Talk to you later. Bye."

CHAPTER THIRTY-SIX

THIS TIME THE PHONE RANG FOUR TIMES BEFORE SOMEONE FI-
nally answered it.

"Byzor."

"What do you want?"

"Colin, is that you? Where the hell are you?"

"Up at Bobby's cabin."

"Oh really?" There was a pause. "Whose phone are you using?"

"What do you mean, whose phone—? Wait a minute, you mean
you check up on who's calling you every time before you answer the
goddamned telephone?"

"Hell, yes, don't you?"

"No."

"So how do you know it's not your boss calling to check up on
you, if you keep on answering your phone blind like that?"

"Because the way things are going around here, if my boss wanted to check up on me—as opposed to just straight-out shooting me on sight—he'd probably just kick down my door," Cellars replied as he looked uneasily at the blurred trees through the surrounding downpour.

No shadowy figures.

"Colin, what the hell are you talking about?" Malcolm Byzor demanded.

Okay, guys, where are you now?

Cellars gently stroked the trigger guard of the pump shotgun with his index finger and kept his eyes on the trees as he quickly explained to his longtime and trusted friend the telephone line situation . . . and how he'd found the cabin.

"Everything's cleaned up?" Byzor asked when he'd finished.

"All the bloodstains. Took the phones away too. But they haven't tried to fill in the bullet holes in the log walls . . . yet."

"They?"

"Whoever."

The voice on the other end of the line paused. "Colin, where exactly are you right now, and what are you doing?"

"Right now?"

"Uh-huh."

"Right now, I'm sitting on the front porch of what may or may not be Bobby's cabin. I'm soaking wet, freezing to death. I'm holding a lineman's phone in one hand, because a couple of shadowy figures have been cutting the phone lines—and the lightning bolts around here are just waiting for me to climb the goddamned pole—so I had to string the telephone line on the ground through a goddamned forest full of trees and vines instead. And I'm holding a 12-gauge pump shotgun in my other hand because one of those shadowy bastards is watching me from the trees right now. Is that really what you wanted to know?"

"I see." There was a long pause.

"And no, I'm not nuts," Cellars went on. "I'm wet, cold, tired, confused, and pissed off, yes, but not crazy . . . or paranoid," he added, "in case you were wondering."

"Hey, it's like we always say around here, there's nothing wrong with being paranoid if people really are out to get you," Byzor offered philosophically. "After all, lots of people are paranoid about us."

"I'll bet."

"Of course, we really are out to get them, so it's a perfectly understandable reaction on their part. But while we're on the topic," Byzor went on smoothly, "mind if I ask what you're using as a reference point at the moment?"

"You mean for my sanity?"

"Uh-huh."

"Well, right now, instead of running around in the woods and capping off rounds at shadows and my official OSP crime scene vehicle—like I was doing a few days ago," Cellars said, "I'm sitting on a mountain cabin porch calmly talking on the phone to one of my three best friends in the world. A guy who would apparently rather spy on people with his electronic toys than chase his undeniably sexy wife around his bed. And, I would add, I am doing—or not doing—all of this less than fifteen minutes after having told one of my other three best friends in the world that I no longer care if she slept with Bobby."

"No shit?"

"None whatsoever."

"Okay, so it appears that you really have regained your sanity after a mere fifteen years," Byzor conceded. "So what's all this crap about my scanner moving pieces of glass and rocks?"

"Can it?"

"You mean the laser system, by itself?"

"Uh-huh."

"Not unless you use one of them like a stick . . . which you'd better not be doing," Byzor warned. "Those are expensive lasers, and the government doesn't actually know I lend them out to my fruitcake friends."

"So why do I still think I saw a manila evidence envelope—the one those glass fragments and that rock were in—move about eighteen inches across the top of a desk? Right after I accidentally turned the lasers on in the immediate proximity of the desk?" he added.

"Seriously?"

"That's right. Very seriously."

There was a much longer pause this time. And when Malcolm Byzor spoke again, there was a definite edge to his voice.

"Colin, listen to me. Those lasers I sent you are capable of generating some very narrowly focused energy beams at a very specific and unusual wavelength, and at an extremely low kinetic energy level. I could go into a lot of complicated math and physics to explain why, but I'd rather not. Take my word for it: Even if you had a thousand of those lasers hooked together and aimed at one spot, they could not possibly generate enough mechanical energy to make even a piece of paper move, much less a rock."

Christ, Cellars thought, *he sounds like he's scared.*

"You're not helping me much."

"Apparently not," Byzor said. "But assuming that you really are sane and scared and pissed, as opposed to merely playing some sort of devious little game with Bobby and Jody—which is what I honestly thought was going on when I tried to call you a few minutes ago—I would say that, all things considered, a moving rock is probably the least of your worries at the moment."

Cellars felt a familiar chill going up his spine.

"Malcolm," he said slowly, "what are you talking about?"

"You remember that memory card you sent me? The one from your electronic camera that you accidentally set off out at your crime scene?"

"Sure."

"Well, I've enhanced the image as far as I can . . . or at least as far as is practical, given that we are talking about individual pixels."

"Yeah, so?"

"I'm going to send you a copy of the image by e-mail to your OSP address," Byzor said. "It's going to be attached as an encrypted file with two keys. The name of the peak we climbed sixteen years ago, and the name of the route we took. Remember them?"

"Sure, but—"

"Don't say the names out loud," Byzor interrupted. "Just remember what they are and use them to unlock the file. Everything you need to do so will be there, and the message will explain it all very clearly. And when you do," Byzor went on, his voice definitely sounding shaky now, "I want you to look at that image very carefully, then call me right away and tell me exactly what it is you think we're both looking at."

"You know what, Malcolm," Cellars said seriously, "I think you're actually starting to scare me."

"Good, I'm glad to hear it . . . because right now, you are scaring the absolute shit out of—"

The phone went dead in Cellars's hand.

———

For a brief moment, it seemed as though the rain was about to stop. But a lightning bolt suddenly crashed overhead, causing the forest floor to vibrate and sending Cellars ducking down against a huge fir trunk for cover.

Then, as if the lightning bolt had been some kind of signal, the downpour began again in earnest, drenching Cellars to the skin as he quickly sat up and looked around with the shotgun in one hand.

If they were anywhere close, he couldn't see them.

Forget the shotgun, stick with the pistol, he thought as he set the weapon aside and pulled the SIG-Sauer from his holster.

He found the cut about fifty yards from the third utility pole from the cabin. This time, they'd only taken away about a hundred feet of the cable. But that didn't matter because Cellars didn't care about getting wet anymore. All he cared about was making one more call.

He'd taken everything with him that he absolutely had to have. The shotgun. The SIG-Sauer. The dark green plastic tarp. And the small backpack that now contained—instead of the food and water—the lineman's phone, a pair of wire cutters and strippers, an extra box of high-base three-ought buckshot rounds for the 12-gauge, and the notebook computer from Malcolm Byzor's crime scene scanner kit. Everything else he'd left inside the cabin, figuring he could come back for it later.

He'd used the tarp to cover the backpack, figuring rightly that he was already as wet as he was ever going to get. He was down on his knees in the middle of a stand of thick Douglas firs and pines— still muttering to himself as he quickly reconnected the lineman's phone to the far end of the cut cable—when a second overhead lightning bolt sent him diving to the ground again.

Shit, what am I doing, trying to talk on the phone in the middle of a lightning storm? I'm going to get myself fried.

But he had to make the phone call. Absolutely had to. So he found some rocks to brace the bright yellow utility phone against a tree, and a two-foot-long stick that he used to cautiously punch the numbers one at a time. Then he placed his head as near to the phone as he dared and listened for an answer, with the SIG-Sauer clenched tightly in his right hand as he tried to keep his eyes on the surrounding trees.

"OSP crime lab."

"This is Detective-Sergeant Colin Cellars. Can you please connect me to Jack Wilson?" Cellars spoke as softly as he could, trying not to let his words carry . . . but at the same time, trying to talk loud enough so that the receptionist wouldn't mistake him for a prank caller and hang up.

To his relief and amazement, she put the call through.

"Wilson."

"Jack, this is Colin Cellars. Can you hear me?"

"Yes, I can hear you, but you sound strange—like you're at the bottom of a well. What's going on?"

"I'm up in the mountains, at the cabin again. Only this time, I'm calling from a utility phone at the end of a grounded telephone line, because somebody cut and took away the rest of the line to the cabin. There's one hellacious thunderstorm going on up here, so I'm trying to stay as far away from the phone as I can."

"Doesn't sound like a good idea to me in any case, but I can hear you fine. Go ahead . . . but I suggest you talk fast."

"Yeah, no shit. Listen, two expended hollow-points on the Dawson shooting, my item numbers CC-forty-nine and CC-fifty. Can you have somebody hand-deliver them to Dr. Jody Catlin at the Ashland wildlife lab ASAP?"

"No problem. What's up?"

"I don't know, she said she was getting some weird results on her PCR runs, and needed more sample. There may be some tissue under the mushroomed jacketing."

"Good idea. We were getting some pretty strange PCR results on that case too," Wilson said. "I'll pick the bullets up and take them over myself."

Cellars suddenly remembered something.

"Hey, Jack, while we're on the subject, were you ever able to match all those bone fragments and blood from the cul-de-sac to that dog?"

"Uh, hold on just a second, let me go look at the case file. Susan's been working on that case." He was back on the line in a few moments. "Okay, I've got it," he said. "Do you remember the item numbers?"

Cellars already had his field notebook in his hand, holding it under his backpack to protect it from the rain.

"Yeah, my items CC-twelve through—"

A lightning bolt struck a tree a few hundred yards away, creating a horrendous boom and throwing sparks high into the air.

"What was that?" Wilson called out.

"Lightning hit a tree close by."

"Jesus. Are you okay?"

"Yeah, fine. Doesn't hardly bother me anymore," Cellars muttered. "That was CC-twelve through CC-seventeen."

"Okay, got it," Wilson said . . . then hesitated. "There must be some mistake."

"Why's that?"

"Except for one blood sample—your CC-thirteen, which did screen positive for canine—all the rest of the samples, blood and bone, came up human."

"Human? Are you sure?"

"Just a second." Another pause. "Yeah, no doubt about it. Two distinct PCR types."

"Two?"

"Yeah, that's kind of odd, isn't it? I thought you only had one victim up—" Then awareness apparently kicked in. "Oh, Christ."

"The missing deputies," Cellars said numbly. "Do you have known blood samples for them?"

"No."

"Maybe at least one of them's a blood donor," Cellars suggested.

"I should be so lucky," Wilson groused. "Listen, you stay where you are. It'll take me about an hour or so to put a team together and get up there. Then you and I will go over every bit of that road and cabin, inch by inch."

"Don't bother," Cellars said. "A road crew's already been up here. Completely rescraped the outer edge of the cul-de-sac. The entire scene's gone."

"What? Why would they do that?"

"I don't know, but we're going to find out. And you can forget about the cabin, too," Cellars added. "Somebody's already cleaned the place up. Looks like they did a complete bleach wash on the walls and floors."

"Somebody knew what they were doing."

"Yeah, looks that way. Listen, if you can get those samples to Jody right away, I'll meet you at her lab as soon as I can. I'm going to call OMARR-Nine, let them know, and then head on down there."

"Okay, I'm on my way. Take—"

The top of the third utility pole from the cabin—located less than fifty feet from Cellars's position in the trees—erupted in a brilliant white fireball as a huge lightning bolt ripped into the transformer. The concussion blew Cellars backward as the surge of electrical energy streaked down the wet outer insulation of the cable toward ground; and in doing so, instantly fused the circuit boards in the lineman's phone.

One glance at the smoldering remains of the utility phone told Cellars that he wouldn't be calling anybody until he got back down off the mountain.

Still muttering to himself, he pulled himself up out of the mud, reholstered the SIG-Sauer, picked up the shotgun and backpack, and was staggering back toward the cabin—intent on collecting the rest of his CSI and camera gear—when another glowing fire off to his right suddenly caught his attention.

It took him a moment to figure his bearings.

Oh, no.

Then he started running in the direction of the cul-de-sac.

———

It was Hawkins's scout car.

By the time he reached the newly scraped roadside edge of the cul-de-sac, the once shiny white patrol vehicle was completely engulfed in flames.

There was nothing he could do, so he just stood there and watched until the gas tank ignited, sending the fiercely burning vehicle tumbling high into the air. It reminded him of the OSP parking lot incident, and it occurred to him to wonder how Captain Rodney Hawkins was doing.

Probably a lot better than he would be if he knew what just happened to his new car, Cellars decided, which somehow seemed comforting in an odd sort of way.

He tried to remember if and when any one of the lightning bolts had hit near the cul-de-sac, but he'd been concentrating on the phone calls and hadn't been paying any attention to the actual location of the ground strikes. So he continued to stand there in the open roadway, watching patiently until the rain finally put the fire out.

As he did so, he took the box of triple-ought buck shotgun ammo out of his backpack, dumped the loose rounds into his soaking wet jacket pockets, and put the backpack bearing Malcolm Byzor's notebook computer and the folded tarp back over his shoulders.

Then, when the last glowing embers flickered out under the torrential downfall, he picked up the shotgun and started walking back through the mud and rain in the direction of the distant cabin.

CHAPTER THIRTY-SEVEN

THE WOOD WAS DRY, AND THERE WAS PLENTY OF KINDLING IN THE
box, so it only took Cellars a few minutes to get a fire going in
the woodstove.

The glow through the glass window on the stove filled the
southern portion of the basement with a warm, reddish orange
light. It was enough illumination for him to see reasonably well, so
he shut off the flashlight, figuring that he really ought to save his
batteries. The extra set—along with all the other extra equipment
he'd brought along for whatever unexpected situation might come
up—had been in the trunk of Hawkins's scout car.

The warmth of the fire helped. But he was still shivering when
he finally finished cleaning the mud off his boots, so he quickly got
out of his clothes and hung them around the stove. Then he dragged
the mattress, blanket, bedspread, and pillow from Dawson's bed
around to the front of the stove, and dried himself off with a towel

he'd found in the bathroom. Finally, he wrapped himself up in the blanket and bedspread and sat there staring into the fire.

Thinking.

It took his clothes over an hour to dry. But by then, he'd stopped shivering long enough to find some canned stew in the storage pantry and a cooking pot under the sink. He let the fire die down to coals long enough to warm—rather than burn—the stew, and get his still-wet boots in a little closer to the stove. In the meantime, he worked patiently with the flashlight, a ball of string, and several empty glass jars he'd found in the storage pantry to rig simple trip-wire alarms at the two exterior doors, the stairwell door, and the side window. The south-facing basement windows were securely locked and unbroken; but even so, he took the precaution of placing an additional series of glass jars in precarious positions along the windowsills.

During all of this activity, either the shotgun or the SIG-Sauer was never far from his grasp.

After his boots were finally dry, he filled the stove with firewood and closed the vent down to limit the flow of oxygen to the fire.

He was starting to yawn as he set the alarm on his watch for two hours, wrapped himself up in the bedspread and blanket, and placed the shotgun and SIG-Sauer on either side of the mattress within easy reach. He couldn't quite bring himself to put the SIG-Sauer under his pillow, deciding that he really wasn't that paranoid—yet.

Then, finally, he stretched out on the amazingly comfortable mattress, grateful for the comforting warmth of the bedspread against his naked body, intending only to rest for an hour or so.

Can't wait here too long, he thought sleepily. *Gotta get going as soon as the rain stops. Get to a phone, call the station, let them know what's going on.*

But outside the thick cabin walls, the lightning kept on crackling and striking in explosive bursts, and the wind and rain kept up their relentless pounding against the south-facing windows.

Within minutes, he was snoring loudly as the winter storm continued to rage.

———

Back in the serology section of the National Fish and Wildlife Forensics Lab, Jody Catlin, Melissa Washington, and Jack Wilson all sat in silence as they watched the graphics appear on the monitor.

They had been working at the evidence for several hours, ever since Wilson had arrived at the reception area with the two mushroomed semijacketed hollow-points. Jody had ushered him back to the serological prep area, where the two of them immediately began to examine one of the expended bullets under a dual-station stereomicroscope while Melissa worked to prepare the PCR gel.

Under 20x magnification, the bits of tissue had begun to appear as Wilson slowly bent the peeled-back sections of copper jacketing out of the way with two solvent-cleaned pairs of needle-nosed pliers. As he did so, Jody reached in with a pair of fine tweezers and carefully transferred each bit of tissue to a small capped plastic vial. After each transfer, she paused to clean the tweezers meticulously.

There would be no question of cross-contamination with this evidence, Jody Catlin resolved. At least not if she had anything to say about it.

By the time they had finished with the second bullet, twenty-four capped plastic vials were sitting in a rack, waiting to be extracted . . . and most of the other scientific, support, and administrative personnel in the lab were shutting down their instruments and computers, and getting ready to go home.

They selected eight of the tiny tissue samples at random—four from each bullet—and immediately transferred the remaining samples to one of the lab's ultra-freezers, which were set to maintain temperature down at the minus sixty degrees Celsius range.

Then it was Jack Wilson's turn to watch as the two wildlife geneticists first went through the meticulous and time-consuming steps to first extract and isolate the DNA from the macerated tissue cells, then cut and amplify the desired strands.

Three hours from the time Wilson first entered the serology prep room, Jody Catlin, Melissa Washington, and Jack Wilson all sat in silence as they watched the graphics appear on the monitor.

"It's the same pattern," Jody said in a hushed voice. "Exactly the same pattern."

"And I don't care what anybody around here says, we did clean extractions this time, no doubt about it," Melissa said to no one in particular.

"I'll be damned," Wilson whispered. "Just what exactly are we looking at?"

"I still don't know," Jody confessed. "But at least now we've got enough of a sample to figure it out."

———

The noise jarred Cellars out of his wondrous dreams. A faint knocking sound. Barely audible over the relentless pounding of the wind and rain against the double-paned windows, and the intermittent crackling of lightning bolts.

What? Where am I?

He reached out with his hand, seeking something solid. Something familiar.

His hand brushed across rough fibers.

What is it? A rug?

No, a bloodstained rug, his subconscious corrected. *The one in—*

He came awake immediately as the faint knocking sound came again. He could feel his heart pounding in his chest as he fumbled for the SIG-Sauer, knowing that no one should be outside Dawson's cabin in a rainstorm, in the middle of the night. No one except . . .

The image of the dark, flickering shadow figure reaching into the white Expedition filled his mind.

Oh, shit.

He approached the window first—buck naked, with the SIG-Sauer in both hands, ready to fire—and carefully pulled back the heavy curtains just a little bit, trying to see who or what was knocking against the south-facing basement door. But no matter how he positioned himself, he couldn't see anything at all in the complete darkness.

What did you expect? They're black shadows. Not going to be able to see a black shadow in the middle of the night.

But why would they be knocking?

He didn't have an answer for that.

Another faint knock. This time more insistent.

Before he could catch himself, Cellars stepped forward, released his jury-rigged door lock, and slowly pushed the door partway open.

The wind caught the door and flung it against the outer wall, causing the shadowy figure to stumble backward.

He was already starting to squeeze the trigger when he heard her voice.

"No, wait. Don't shoot! It's me."

Allesandra?

"What are you doing here?" he demanded as he shifted the pistol aside, lunged out into the chilling wind and rain, pulled her inside, then quickly resecured the door.

He turned to find her standing in the middle of the basement floor, dripping wet and shivering violently.

"What are you doing here?" he repeated as he set the SIG-Sauer down on the rug, then stepped forward and took her into his arms.

The familiar heat of her body seemed to envelop him, and he was immediately aware of his nakedness.

"I'm so afraid. Had to find you," she whispered, seemingly unable to control trembling that seemed more like violent seizures as she pressed herself tightly against his torso. "They said you came up here to Bobby's cabin, so I"—another seizure, this time less violent—"drove up here. Then I saw the car, or what's left of it, and I thought—" She sobbed. "I'm sorry, I thought you were dead."

"I'm not dead," he whispered. His rational mind was trying desperately to make sense of it all, but the heated points of her breasts were starting to burn twin holes into his chest.

"No, you're not," she whispered, her hands hot against his ribs . . . and hips . . . and thighs, as she slid them down his body.

"Please, help me."

He didn't remember taking off her clothes. The next thing he knew, they were naked together on the mattress, kissing, caressing, caught up in a swirl of lust and passion . . . that at once became three-dimensionally chromatic as he penetrated her—or she penetrated him, he couldn't even begin to tell which. Whereupon they became fused into a oneness that—in all meaningful senses of the term—completely blew his mind.

———

"Who are you?" he rasped when, finally, after some indeterminate passage of time that seemed to have no clear relationship to minutes or hours, they became two again.

"Hush," she whispered in his ear, the heat from her lips—and her breath—more soothing now than erotic. "You don't want to know."

"Yes, I do," he said insistently, but her hands became distracting again.

"Tell me about you," she whispered.

"What about me?"

Her hands were back up to his face now, sending thin ribbons of warmth swirling gently around the outside of his skull.

"What did you do when you were young?"

"I played . . . I climbed . . . I—"

She kissed him, slowly and gently above his eyes.

"What did you climb?"

"Mountains."

"By yourself?"

Her lips moved, slowly, gently down the side of his face, like a trail of simmering lava that warmed and glowed instead of burned.

"No, with my friends."

"Jody, Bobby, Malcolm?"

"Yes." Cellars smiled as her heated lips brushed against his ear. "Jody, Bobby, Malcolm."

"Where did you climb?"

"Lots of places."

He could feel the heat of her body again. Tendrils of heat that seemed to reach out for him from every possible direction.

"Sixteen years ago, where did you climb?" she whispered as she bit gently on his earlobe, sending the ribbons of warmth behind his eyes . . . and into his brain, where they diffused into a gentle, sensuous, and slowly rhythmic pleasure. A pleasure that had no apparent need to rise up in intensity to orgasm but, rather, seemed perfectly content simply to be.

"I don't know."

"Of course you do. You just blocked it away where I can't see it because you don't want to think about it right now. Where did you climb?" Like her hands, the question was soft, and gentle, and seductive . . . and impossible to ignore.

"Gravestone," he mumbled, feeling himself drift within the liquid warmth of her hands and arms and breasts and legs—that seemed to be everywhere now, throughout his body and into his mind.

"I don't understand. What about a gravestone?"

"Gravestone Peak. We climbed it. All four of us. Roped ourselves together. Nobody we knew had done that before." He smiled at the distant hazy memory.

"It looks like a beautiful place," she whispered, her warmth like an irresistible undertow now, drawing him in. "What does the sign say?"

"Windshear."

"What does that mean?" Her voice seemed to echo now, as if she had suddenly become large and distant.

"That's the route we took. The one nobody we knew had ever done before, because it was too dangerous," he heard himself answer as he felt his mind starting to drift away.

"We're in terrible danger right now," he heard her whisper from somewhere far away, even though the heat of her body continued to caress and comfort and envelop him. "We can't stay here much longer. We have to go."

And then he was gone.

The sudden clattering noise jarred Cellars out of his wondrously enticing dreams.

There was an immediate sensation of emptiness—as if he'd lost something that he desperately had to have back—that he couldn't understand. Couldn't even begin to comprehend.

Please help me.

We're in terrible danger.

We can't stay here much longer.

We have to go.

The words echoed through his mind, demanding his attention, but he continued to drift . . . searching for whatever it was that he no longer had. Whatever it was that he had to have back, no matter what it cost.

Where is she? Some deep, dark tangled recess of his mind demanded.

Who?

Jody?

Allesandra?

But that didn't make any sense either, because Jody wasn't there. And neither was Allesandra. Wherever he was, he was definitely alone.

Must have been dreaming, he decided. He was starting to drift away again, searching for the warm, enticing, distant place, when another clattering noise jarred him fully awake this time.

What?

Not alone . . . somebody here?

He twisted around in the bedcovers, desperately fumbling for the SIG-Sauer before some analytical portion of his terribly confused mind finally recognized the source of the noise.

It's okay. Piece of firewood . . . falling down inside the stove.

He became aware, then, that he was in Bobby Dawson's basement, and that the room was cold—much colder than when he'd fallen asleep—and that the storm was still raging outside. The wind was rattling the tightly sealed windows, but the rain seemed to have diminished in its intensity.

Maybe it's going to stop pretty soon, he thought dreamily. *Time is it?*

The softly glowing numerals on his watch read 20:57.

Nine o'clock?

He immediately sat upright and quickly looked around the darkened basement.

No wonder it's cold in here. Fire's starting to die down. Must have slept through the alarm. Probably didn't even hear it go off.

He got up, immediately started to shiver, then wrapped the bedspread around himself long enough to check the trip-wire alarms with the flashlight and fill the stove with another load of wood. Then he settled back down under the covers, only vaguely aware that he was responding to a subconscious urge to return as soon as possible to his incredibly enticing, incredibly addictive dreams.

Wonder why I'm so tired, he thought sleepily. *Can't stay here much longer. Too dangerous.*

Another huge lightning bolt flashed across the southern sky, but Cellars's eyes were already starting to close as he stared at the glow from the woodstove, so he didn't see the dark, horrifying shadow that suddenly appeared—ever so briefly—silhouetted against the drapes covering the south-facing windows.

Got to get going pretty soon.

His eyes closed. Moments later, he started snoring again, mercifully oblivious to the slow, methodical probing actions of the creature outside the cabin.

CHAPTER THIRTY-EIGHT

"LOOK AT THAT, IT'S ALMOST LIKE THEY'RE A BASE PAIR," MELISSA
Washington whispered in amazement.

"What are you talking about?" Jack Wilson protested. "That's
impossible."

They were in the instrument section of the laboratory now,
working at a larger monitor and keyboard linked to an array of in-
terconnected instruments that nearly filled the countertops along
one long wall of the room. Instruments capable of isolating and
identifying individual molecular structures, and displaying the results as a series of colorful three-dimensional images on the high-
density screen.

"No, I see what Melissa is saying," Jody Catlin said. "Look
there, when you rotate the first molecule like this—" She made an
adjustment with the mouse. "See how close the molecular structure
is to guanine, except for that extra amine group over there? And

when you rotate the second molecule through the y-axis to here . . . and turn it about thirty degrees through the z-axis to about here . . ."

"Cytosine?" Wilson whispered.

"Almost," Melissa agreed, "except that you've got a second amine substitution there too, which extends the whole molecule out on the x-y plane. And which also means," she went on, "if you rotate them around like this"—she reached over Jody's shoulder and made a couple of adjustments with the mouse—"you have the definite possibility of—"

"Four hydrogen bonds?" Jody scrunched up her face in amusement. "No way. That can't be. There's not enough room in the helix."

As the serologist and forensic scientists watched the monitor in stunned silence, the two molecular models slowly rotated opposite each other while the computer performed the innumerable mathematical calculations necessary to determine the angular impact of the molecular substitutions on the adjoining molecular bonds. Then, in one slow balletic-like movement, the computer brought the two molecules together . . . into a perfect three-dimensional fit.

"And oh-my-God . . . base-pairing," Melissa whispered.

Jody Calin stared at the monitor in silent and openmouthed fascination.

"We're deluding ourselves," Wilson objected. "Those are simple amine substitutions on a pair of purine and pyrimidine base structures that are thoroughly understood. If that sort of thing was possible with DNA, we would have known about it a long time ago."

"Hold on a minute," Jody said, her eyebrows furrowing in confusion as she pointed to a carbon atom in each of the six-ring portions of the two molecules. "Why is the computer showing these two carbons as being larger, and in a different color?"

"I don't know," Melissa said as she reached for the mouse. "The different color usually means a conflicting piece of data. Let's see what it says here."

Suddenly the monitor displayed a boxed message.

DATA CONFLICT ERROR: 344

DISPLAYED MOLECULAR STRUCTURE DOES NOT CONFORM

WITH INSTRUMENT DATA AND KNOWN REFERENCE DATA

SET

INSTRUMENT SOURCES: NMR AND LC3QPMS

MOST LIKELY ERROR: LC3QPMS

DO YOU WANT THE COMPUTER TO MAKE A BEST FIT

RESOLUTION? Y/N

"Yes, of course, we want you to resolve it," Melissa muttered. "You expect us to try to work something like that out with our puny human brains?"

The monitor blinked in acknowledgment, then redisplayed the pair of joined molecules . . . except in the two opposing positions where the monitor had displayed an off-color "C" there were now two larger atoms bearing the designation "Si."

"Silicon?" all three exclaimed at once.

"What the hell is this?" Jack Wilson was the first to speak. "One of Colin Cellars's little mind games?"

"There's no way in the world that Colin could come up with a silicon substitution for carbon in a paired set of purine and pyrimidine bases," Jody replied as she continued to stare at the monitor screen. "Nobody could . . . because it's impossible."

"What about that friend of his you're always talking about?" Melissa said. "The spook guy, whatever his name is?"

"You mean Malcolm? Malcolm Byzor?"

"That's the one."

"I have no idea what Malcolm or the people he works with can or can't do," Jody confessed. "But this kind of thing is way out there, even for them. It has to be."

"I almost hate to do this," Melissa said as she reached into her lab coat and pulled out a gray Zip disk, "but I'm going to designate those two molecules Jodine and Melissine, just for shits and grins. Which gives us a 'J' and an 'M' for codes." She went on mumbling to herself as she pushed the disk into the Zip drive slot of the computer, then quickly called up the sequencer files that had been driving them crazy for the past few days. "Which, in turn, might make sense to this hunk of transistors if it actually knew that . . ."

She hit the mouse key, then gasped as a slowly moving cursor proceeded to create a block display of sequential letters on the screen.

C-A-T-J-T-M-T-C-C-J-C-T-M-J-A-G-M-M-J-A-G-M-M-C-A-M-C-A-M-
C-A-M-T-A-T-A-T-A-T-J-T-J-A-G-M-C-A-M-A-T-A-T-J-J-A-T-C-C-
C-A-T-A-T . . .

"Oh Lord," she whispered in a deep south Georgia drawl that was no more of a put-on than her ashen face.

The three scientists stared at the monitor in stunned silence as the reenergized computer continued to spew out line after line of the bizarre code.

"Three base pairs instead of two? Is that really what we're talking about here?" Wilson asked when the computer finally stopped.

"My God, Malcolm," Jody Catlin whispered. "What have you people done?"

_____

"Think of the possibilities," Jack Wilson whispered, as if afraid that someone else would hear.

But it was almost midnight. And save for the three scientists in the lighted instrument room, the wildlife crime laboratory was dark and empty.

"The average DNA molecule is made up of approximately three billion base pairs . . . code units, whatever," Jody said, as much to herself as the other two. "Which gives us six possible codes instead of four at the first base-pair position; a total of thirty-six possibilities instead of sixteen in the first two positions; one hundred and ninety-eight possibilities instead of sixty-four in the first three . . ."

"Carry it out all the way to the end, and the number of additional coding possibilities is . . . huge," Wilson said, shaking his head in awe. "Unthinkably huge. And that's just with one chromosome."

"But what would you do with a DNA molecule like this?" Melissa asked, her dark eyes gleaming with excitement. "What *could* you do?"

"If this were human DNA, I'll bet you could change your shape at will," Jody Catlin ventured.

"Be serious," Jack Wilson scoffed uneasily. He was still having trouble accepting the idea that a third set of base-pair structures was real. The added possibility that someone at the National Security Agency might be responsible for both the synthesis *and* the application of such an enhanced DNA molecule was absolutely chilling.

"I am," Jody retorted. "Think about it. That much coding—almost limitless possibilities to construct new proteins—and the ability to incorporate silicon in the place of carbon. Why not? Who's to say what would or wouldn't be possible with tools like that?"

"Change your shape at will. Lordy," Melissa Washington whispered softly, looking down at what she often described as her full-on woman shape, "wouldn't that be something?"

"Are you sure this is a good idea?" Yvie Byzor asked uneasily as she pulled into the United Airlines passenger unloading zone at Washington, D.C.'s Dulles International Airport. "You know how you hate these red-eye flights."

Malcolm Byzor shrugged. "Colin said it was really important . . . something I had to see for myself."

"But do you really think it's going to explain what happened to Bobby . . . or that horrible picture you were working on last night?" Yvie Byzor shivered at the spine-chilling memory of the frightening creature that had just barely been visible on the monitor as a dark silhouette against a slightly less dark sky. She hated horror films.

Hated anything that even resembled one of the monsters that movie producers seemed to take so much delight in creating with their silicon rubber and fake blood. Give her a good old-fashioned romance movie any day . . . even if she did have to bribe her easily distracted husband into abandoning his cherished computers for a couple of hours.

"Both, with any luck," he said cryptically as he got out of the car, walked around to the opposite side of the car, opened the back door, and pulled his overnight case out of the backseat.

Yvie Byzor didn't even bother to ask what he was talking about. She had long since learned to ignore the fact that her brilliant and loving—but undeniably bizarre—husband frequently couldn't tell even his own wife what he was really working on.

"How can you say that?" She shivered again.

"Actually, I'm very anxious to see what this is all about," Byzor replied as he shut the door, set his luggage down on the pavement, and leaned in through the open driver's side window to give his ever-tolerant wife a good-bye kiss. "Colin had me very concerned there for a while, but perhaps this new evidence he's found will help explain things. Personally, I still find it very difficult to believe that Bobby Dawson is dead—especially if they can't find his body."

"You keep saying that, but—"

"There's always a rational explanation for these things, Yvie," Malcolm Byzor said as he gently brushed his fingers across his wife's worried face. "It's just a matter of working your way through the evidence, item by item, until all of the pieces fall into place. Patience and perseverance, and a little imagination, that's really all it takes."

"But—" she tried one last time.

"I'll be back soon," he said reassuringly as he winked, reached down to pick up his luggage, and turned toward the waiting terminal.

"Yeah, well, don't forget about the 'being careful' part!" Yvie Byzor yelled out as she watched her husband disappear into the darkened and mostly empty structure.

Then, as she pulled out of the unloading zone, she whispered to herself, "It's okay to perservere, and use your imagination, Malcolm . . . and Lord knows you always do. But being careful would be nice too."

CHAPTER THIRTY-NINE

"BLESS YOU. SO HOW DO YOU SUGGEST WE WORD OUR EXAMINA-
tion report?" Melissa Washington asked as she tapped her finger
impatiently on her lab notebook.

Jody Catlin blinked her watery eyes, sniffed, and reached for a
Kleenex as she shook her head. "I honestly have no idea."

"Probably 'cause that cold's going right to your brain."

"Thank you."

"You're welcome." Melissa grinned sympathetically.

In spite of their late hours the previous night, the two forensic
scientists were back at their lab bench at seven-forty-five in the
morning, anxious to dig deeper into the wondrous possibilities that
a third set of DNA base pairs might offer. But at the same time,
they were both increasingly uneasy as they considered some of the
more mind-boggling ramifications.

"So, you really think this new DNA coding is something the NSA came up with, then just let it get loose?" Melissa asked skeptically after a few moments.

"I don't know." Jody shrugged her shoulders helplessly. "I guess it's as good an explanation as any, but I still can't imagine how something like that could happen. I mean, Malcolm is one hell of a smart guy. As I recall, the teachers didn't even bother to give him those IQ tests anymore after the sixth grade. So I guess if anybody was going to come up with something like this"—Jody gestured with her hand at the display on her monitor—"it probably makes sense that it would be somebody like him . . . or one of his double-brained, superspook buddies.

"But even if they did work out the silicon substitution in one of their labs, and figured out a way to incorporate a third set of base pairs in the DNA helix," Jody went on, "then what did they do? Just synthesize a new segment of three-base-pair DNA pretty much at random, incorporate it into some kind of egg, and stand back and wait to see what hatches or pops out of its mother's womb? I mean, what kind of crazy sense does that make?"

"None whatsoever, in my way of thinking," Melissa admitted.

"And even if they did actually create—I don't know, what?—a survivable genetic mutation of whatever creature they were using, what in the world is it doing running around loose out here in Oregon? And at a crime scene, for God's sake?"

"You know what, this is beginning to sound like one of those movies where the bad guys find one of those ancient mummies in some old dusty tomb, take it to their lab, and zap it with lightning until it suddenly comes alive. And the next thing you know, all the people in white coats end up getting their eyes sucked right out of their heads," Melissa Washington commented.

Jody Catlin's eyebrows furrowed in dismay as she glared at her lab partner for a long moment before suddenly sneezing again. Melissa made a silent sign of the cross with her index finger.

"Thanks a lot," Jody said sarcastically as she reached for another tissue. "That's just the kind of image I need running around in the back of my head right about now."

"Girl, if an idea like that's gonna be runnin' round in the back of *my* head all day long, I figure I'm gonna want some company. 'Cept I'm not so sure I want company that's gonna be sneezing and honking all over the place," Melissa added thoughtfully.

"Yeah, well—"

At that moment, the phone rang. Jody Catlin continued to glare at her associate as she reached for the handset.

"Catlin."

"Hi, Jody, this is the front desk. I know you and Melissa said you didn't want to be disturbed for a while this morning, but I've got a call from a Lieutenant Talbert from the OSP. He says it's real important. You want me to connect him to your voice mail?"

"No, in fact, he's just the man I want to talk to," Jody said. "Patch him through."

"You got it."

"Dr. Catlin?"

"Lieutenant Talbert, it's nice to hear your voice," Jody responded, giving a skeptical-looking Melissa Washington a thumbs-up.

"Oh, really? Why am I suddenly suspicious?"

"It's nothing tricky or devious." Jody smiled. "It's just that we've had an interesting discovery out here that involves some of the evidence in one of your homicide cases, and I wanted to ask you for some advice."

"Amazing coincidence. That's exactly why I'm calling you."

"What, for advice?"

"No, not exactly, but it is about the Bob Dawson case. We've had some interesting developments of our own in the past eighteen hours. Some amazing revelations, actually, involving the NSA and the FBI. I can't discuss any of it over the phone, but I can tell you it's extremely important that we get you out here immediately . . .

along with any and all of the evidence that you've been given on the case."

"Are you serious?"

"Absolutely. We need you to bring all the evidence you have on this case with you, including all of the collected blood and tissue samples, as well as any DNA that you may have isolated from those samples."

"You want me to bring our DNA extracts to an investigation meeting?"

"Yes, the FBI definitely wants their lab people to take a look at all of the DNA you have on this case. Apparently a question of linkage to one of their other cases. Is that a problem?"

"Well, no, I suppose not," Jody said reluctantly. "I mean . . . there are some temperature considerations. But it's all stored in small vials, so I suppose we could transport them in a cooler with some dry ice. But you're going to want to get them back into an ultra-freezer or a low-temperature transport system as quickly as you can to prevent degradation," she warned.

"One of their lab people is here right now, and he has some kind of small electronic cooler plugged into a wall socket. Is that what we're talking about?"

"Yes, it sounds like it," Jody said hesitantly, "but—"

"In that case, we need to get you out here with your evidence right now."

"I'm sorry, I guess I'm . . . confused by all of this. I thought—"

"Listen, I'm sure I don't have an appreciation for all the technical difficulties involved in something like this. Would it help if I had you talk with Colin? He's in the other room talking with the FBI team right now."

Colin's there, with you? Thank God!

"Yes, please, that would be . . . wonderful."

"Hold on just a second."

There was a long pause that lasted for about fifteen seconds.

"Jody?"

"Colin! What's going on? Are you all right? I . . . I mean we were waiting for you to show up, but you never did . . . and we were starting to get worried about you, but then we made this incredible discovery that involves some of your evidence. I . . . I don't even know where to start."

"It's probably better if you don't even try. I've got a feeling what you're about to say involves something we're not supposed to be talking about. At least not over the phone, anyway."

"But—"

"Look, I know this all sounds horribly confusing. I should have gotten down there to your lab last night when I said I would, but it turned out to be one of those unbelievably bizarre evenings. First, right after I talked to you, a lightning bolt hit the transformer on the utility pole near where I was working and completely fried my utility phone. Then, a few minutes later, another lightning strike hit Captain Hawkins's new car, ignited the gas tank, and blew it all over the road."

"What?"

"Yeah, I think Talbert's kind of pissed about the car, but he says that's going to be Hawkins and my problem, not his."

"But—"

"Anyway, there's a radio dead zone that covers pretty much that whole mountain area. And after the first lightning strike, I didn't have a phone to call you back anyway, and it was raining too hard to try to hike out at night, so I just sacked out in Bobby's cabin. I started walking down this morning, and then got picked up by a Jasper County deputy in a scout car coming up to check on me. Sorry if I worried you, but . . . hey, I almost forgot what I was supposed to tell you. You remember you were telling me how Talbert seemed suspicious that I might have inside help at one of the labs?"

"Yes?"

"Well, it looks like you were right . . . but it wasn't anything like what we were thinking. I don't know all the details, but it looks like

Malcolm and his buddies are involved in this all the way up to their eyeballs."

"Malcolm?"

"Yeah, he's sitting here in the living room right now, along with a couple of real serious-looking suits from back East."

"Malcolm's here? In Oregon?"

"That's right, he just got in this morning on the red-eye from D.C."

"But why—"

"Listen, you're not going to believe this, but Bobby's alive."

"What? Are you kidding me?"

"Yes . . . I mean, no, I'm not kidding you. Listen, everything's going to be okay. Or at least it should be as soon as we can get all of this bureaucratic horseshit worked out. Can you believe it?"

"No . . . I can't. I guess I'm completely confused. I mean, how did you—?"

"Look, Jody, everything's kind of touchy and hush-hush around here right now, and like Talbert said, we really can't talk about it over the phone. But—hold it just a second." There was a long pause. "The lead FBI agent here asked me to tell you that the FBI is running the entire investigation now, and that it's very important we all do exactly what they say. Got that?"

"Yes, of course, but—"

"Okay, listen, I've really got to get back to what I was doing. I'll see you in a little bit. Hurry up and get out here, we're all waiting for you. Here's Talbert back."

"But—"

"Dr. Catlin?"

"Yes, I'm still here. Listen, Lieutenant, I'm sorry I seemed so skeptical a few minutes ago, but . . . is it true—I mean, about Bob Dawson being alive?"

"Like I said before, we're really not supposed to be discussing any of this on an unsecured phone. But I think it's fair to say that the four of you are about to have a very interesting reunion."

"Is . . . Malcolm in trouble?"

Another pause.

"I'm sure that Malcolm and his associates will have some serious explaining to do before this is all over with, but I really can't go into any details right now. I gather from Colin's side of the conversation that you may have some idea as to what this is all about."

"If you mean the—"

"Please, Dr. Catlin, not over the phone. Look, all I can tell you is that it's extremely important—for Malcolm, Colin, Bobby, you . . . and certainly for the OSP—that we turn everything over to the FBI right now before this entire situation gets any more complicated. Evidence, notebooks, photographs, charts, absolutely everything we have on this case . . . which specifically includes everything that was delivered to you by our lab staff. And if we do that, I think everything's going to work out fine for everyone involved. Do you understand what I'm saying?"

"In essence . . . we're talking about some kind of trade?"

"I think that would be a reasonable assumption."

Jody hesitated.

"Is there a problem?"

"No, it's just that I guess I thought . . . no, never mind what I thought." Jody shook her head. "The important thing is that everybody's okay. Let's get the legal issues resolved. We'll sort everything else out later."

"Good. I knew we could count on you. We're all at Colin's house right now. We need to get you here right away so that you can talk to these agents in person."

"Yes, of course. I'm sorry, I guess I'm just having a hard time absorbing this all at once."

"Perfectly understandable, Dr. Catlin. So if we send an officer by in, say, about a half hour, do you think you can have all your evidence and notebooks and everything else ready by then . . . out at the front entrance to your lab?"

"I—yes, of course."

"Okay, we'll have someone there waiting for you."

"Oh, wait, who should I be looking for?"

"Let's see, I think it's going to be someone from the Jasper County Sheriff's Department. Hold on a minute and I'll find out who they're sending."

Another much shorter pause.

"Dr. Catlin, a Jasper County patrol sergeant will meet you at the front entrance to your lab in exactly thirty minutes from now. He'll be in uniform and driving a marked scout car. He's going to pick you up and take you over to the OSP lab to collect the rest of the evidence that's over there. The people at the evidence unit will be expecting you."

"Fine," Jody replied. "I'll be ready."

"What was all that about?" Melissa Washington demanded, staring suspiciously at the stunned and pale expression on her lab partner's face.

"I'm not sure I really know," Jody Catlin said quietly. Her eyebrows were still furrowed in confusion, but her mouth had started to form a slight smile as she continued to shake her head slowly in amazement. "According to Colin, they found Bobby, and he's alive. And it looks like we were right about Malcolm, too. Colin says he's definitely involved in all of this, and from the sound of things, probably in some kind of trouble with the FBI. But they're all over at Colin's house right now, and I've got to—"

Jody Catlin's eyes widened as she looked down at her watch. "Oh, no," she exclaimed as she looked around wildly. "Melissa, you've got to help me!"

"Help you do what?"

"Gather up all the evidence and records we've got on the Dawson case. The FBI wants everything, including all the extracted DNA."

"What?"

"And I've got to get it all ready to go in"—she looked down at her watch again—"twenty-five minutes."

"Take everything with you? And give it all to the FBI? What in the world are you talking about?"

"I haven't got time to explain it all now," Jody called out as she ducked down under the counter and came up with a small ice chest. "Just help me!"

"I don't know," Melissa Washington said uneasily as she closed her lab notebook and got up from her chair. "You ask me, this is all starting to sound more and more like one of those eye-sucking, mummy-on-the-loose monster movies all the time."

CHAPTER FORTY

"WHAT THE HELL IS GOING ON AROUND HERE?"

Ruth Wilkinson, the day shift front desk clerk at the OSP Region 9 substation, jerked her head up in surprise.

"Captain . . . Hawkins?"

Her initial hesitation was perfectly understandable. The man standing at the front desk before her was so thoroughly bandaged—only his eyes, mouth, and the end of his nose were visible—that his own mother might have been excused for not recognizing him. But even so, Hawkins's voice was unmistakable.

"Of course it's Captain Hawkins," the bandaged man roared. "What do you think, that I'm some kind of goddamned impostor?"

"No sir, of course not. It's just that—" the veteran desk clerk stammered, unable to finish her sentence.

"I repeat. What's going on around here? Are you trying to tell me that I'm out of the office for only a couple of days, and, in the meantime, the whole damned place goes to hell?"

"Yes sir . . . I mean, no sir, but—"

"Never mind. Where's Talbert?" he demanded.

Wilkinson blinked in shock. "I, uh, don't know."

"What do you mean, you don't know? Do I have to remind you that it's your job to know where people at this station are at all times?"

"No sir." Wilkinson shook her head emphatically. "I know how to do my job. But the fact is, sir, no one seems to know where Lieutenant Talbert is right now."

"What?"

"The last radio contact we had with him was when he drove out to meet Detective-Sergeant Cellars on Timberline Road near the freeway."

"Cellars?" Hawkins's eyes widened as he took in a deep, hissing breath.

"Yes sir. It seems that Detective-Sergeant Cellars was involved in a shooting—"

"Yes, I know he was involved in a shooting," Hawkins interrupted. "He shot his own goddamned CSI vehicle. The man's a disgrace to the OSP uniform."

"Oh, no sir."

"What did you say?" Hawkins's eyes seemed to bulge out through his bandages.

"I mean, what I meant to say is, Detective-Sergeant Cellars was involved in . . . another shooting," Wilkinson explained hesitantly, realizing the moment the words left her mouth that she'd made a terrible mistake.

"Another shooting? What did that idiot do, shoot another OSP vehicle?"

"Well, uh, yes, sir."

"What?"

Ruth Wilkinson had the distinct impression that it was only

the tight bandages that prevented Hawkins's head from exploding in rage.

"As I understand the situation, sir," Wilkinson went on courageously, "Detective-Sergeant Cellars's vehicle was struck by some unknown object and run off the road out on Timberline near the I-Five on-ramp. Apparently by the same suspects involved in the mountain cabin shooting—or at least shadowy figures that looked an awful lot like those suspects," she added. "They attempted to steal his CSI vehicle again, just like last time. So he shot at them, and hit his vehicle again, just like last time. Which, I guess, is why Lieutenant Talbert responded to the scene right away, on his way back from the wildlife crime lab out in Ashland," she finished weakly.

The bandaged figure seemed completely stunned by this new information.

"Just what . . . the hell," Hawkins rasped when he finally found his voice again, "was Lieutenant Talbert doing out at the wildlife lab when he's supposed to be at his desk supervising this madhouse excuse for a police station?"

"I, uh, think he went over there to interview a Dr. Catlin," Wilkinson said as she glanced down at her notebook. "Yes, Dr. Jody Catlin. I believe it had something to do with Detective-Sergeant Cellars and the evidence on his, uh, first shooting."

"Cellars again." This time the drawn-in breath was more reptilian.

"Yes sir."

"I'm going to get to the bottom of this," Hawkins said, his voice now a menacing whisper.

"Yes sir, I'm sure you will," Wilkinson responded reflexively, but she was talking to empty space. Hawkins had already turned away and was heading out the front door.

———

Jody Catlin was just putting the last of her lab notebooks into a cardboard box when the phone rang.

"Catlin."

"Hi, Jody. Just wanted to let you know there's a Jasper County Sheriff's car parked outside the front door," the receptionist said. "And it's starting to rain hard again, so you'd better bring an umbrella."

"Okay, I'm on my way out there right now."

The sky was starting to darken again as Jody Catlin and Melissa Washington walked outside the front glass doors of the laboratory. They immediately saw a uniformed patrol sergeant in bright yellow rain gear waiting patiently for them at the curb with the trunk of his scout car already opened.

"Dr. Catlin?" the uniformed sergeant inquired.

"That's me," Catlin sniffed as she hurried to the car.

"Sergeant Paul Washburn." The almost-bald sergeant smiled reassuringly as he reached out to take the box. Then he noticed her red eyes.

"Are you okay, ma'am?"

"Just a head cold," she muttered.

"Can't hardly avoid catching those things in weather like this," he commented. "Is it okay to put all of this into the trunk?" He gestured with his head at the small cooler in Melissa Washington's hands.

"That would be perfect," Catlin said. "But I understand we're supposed to pick up some more evidence?"

"Yes ma'am. According to my orders, I'm supposed to pick you up, take you straight over the OSP lab to secure the rest of the evidence on this case, then take you directly to the home of a Detective-Sergeant Colin Cellars out on Willow Creek Road."

"Do you know how to get there?" Melissa Washington queried suspiciously as she handed over the ice chest to the helpful sergeant.

Washburn's eyes crinkled in amusement. "As a matter of fact, I used to live out on Willow Creek Road when I was a kid. I'm pretty sure I still remember the way."

"Good, it's about time things started going right for a change,"

Melissa muttered. "Too many people associated with this case wandering around getting themselves lost or killed. You make sure she gets there safe and sound, hear?" she added with a mock glare, her fists clenched on her ample hips.

"Believe me, I understand your concern," Washburn replied evenly. There was no indication that he was even slightly offended by Melissa Washington's aggressive stance. "Four of our deputies haven't been seen or heard from for several days now. And as far as I'm concerned," he added firmly, "that kind of nonsense is going to come to a stop right now, starting with Dr. Catlin here."

"Thank you, Sergeant, that's exactly what I wanted to hear." Melissa nodded and smiled cheerfully.

"If you two are finished discussing my welfare," Jody Catlin said, looking down at her watch pointedly, "we need to get going."

"Yes ma'am." Washburn glanced up to the sky as he reached for the front passenger-side door of his scout car. "Looks like it's getting ready to rain on us again, so let's get you going where you need to be before that cold gets any worse."

Moments later, as Melissa Washington stood at the door of the lab watching uneasily, the Jasper County Sheriff's scout car disappeared from view.

———

Thirty minutes later, Melissa Washington was still working to clean up the mess in the examination room left over from her frenzied effort to help Jody Catlin collect all the evidence on the Dawson case when she heard a ruckus outside in the hallway.

"Wait a minute, you can't—" a woman was saying as the hallway door to the examination room burst open and a bandaged figure appeared before Melissa's horrified eyes.

"Where is Doctor Catlin?" the mummylike figure yelled. "I demand—"

———

The high-pitched scream that reverberated throughout the small examination room caused Captain Rodney Hawkins to stop in his tracks and whirl his head back around toward the doorway, expecting to see something terrifying or threatening coming his way.

Unfortunately for Hawkins, it never occurred to him that the threat to his general welfare might come from the white-lab-coated source of that incredibly loud and penetrating scream. It was an understandable—albeit unfortunate—mistake that caused the OSP station commander to still be turning back in the direction of Melissa Washington when thirteen pounds of precision microscopy caught him a glancing blow just above his left eye.

Captain Rodney Hawkins dropped to the linoleum floor like the proverbial hundred-and-seventy-pound sack of rocks.

In a relative sense, fortune continued to smile on the OSP station commander. He was still trying to get to his feet—holding his head, cussing a threatening blue streak, and completely unaware that Melissa stood poised a few feet away with a twenty-thousand-dollar compound microscope in her upraised hand—when a US Fish and Wildlife Special Agent who happened to be in the lab dropping off a bald eagle for a necropsy exam intervened.

So instead of suffering a possibly life-threatening coup de grâce from a tough-minded young forensic scientist who had no intention whatsoever of having her eyes sucked out of her head, Hawkins found himself caught in an inescapable wrist lock that sent him plummeting facedown to the floor again—completely oblivious to the fact that the agent had placed his broad shoulders in the way of the threatening microscope.

Hawkins was still screaming threats of mass arrest and dismemberment when he felt and heard the handcuffs closing around his wrists.

"You can't do this!" he gasped in shock as the agent brought him up to a sitting position, pressing him back against a lab cabinet with one hand. "I'm a captain in the Oregon State Patrol. I'm here on official business. You can't . . ."

The unimpressed agent looked up at Hawkins's white-lab-coated assailant. "You know this guy?" he asked.

The wide-eyed forensic scientist shook her head, the microscope still up and ready.

"I'm telling you," Hawkins raged, "I'm Captain Hawkins of the—"

"Hawkins?" the agent interrupted. "*Rodney* Hawkins?"

"That's right." Hawkins's eyes gleamed maliciously. "And if you don't release me immediately, I'm going to—"

"Shussh, you're starting to give me a headache," the agent warned, pressing the fingers of one hand against Hawkins's mouth as he reached into his captive's jacket with the other to locate and extract a black leather badge case.

"Well, well, well," the agent smiled as he examined Hawkins's official photo, "Captain Hot-Rod himself. Doesn't look a whole lot like you," he noted as he slipped the badge case back into Hawkins's jacket. "No wonder people around here got confused. Probably ought to get that thing updated if you're going to run around looking like this." He looked up at Melissa again. "Did Captain Hawkins here identify himself before he burst in and scared you half to death?"

"No sir, he did not," Melissa said emphatically as she set the microscope back down on the workbench.

"I didn't—!" Hawkins started to exclaim.

"Shussh," the agent warned again.

"Goddamn it, you son of a bitch! I'm going to have your badge!" Hawkins screamed.

The agent looked around the examination room. "Could I borrow that roll of evidence tape?" he asked Melissa.

She quickly handed him the roll of two-inch-wide green-and-white tape.

"What the hell do you . . . uuuummff!" Hawkins's eyes bulged as the agent secured a couple of eight-inch-long strips of evidence tape across his exposed mouth and moustache.

"Thank you, that's much better," the agent said as he handed the tape roll back to the white-lab-coated scientist. Then he looked over at the receptionist and the other forensic scientists who had responded to Melissa's terrified scream. "How about the rest of you? Did this man identify himself as a police officer to any of you before he entered the laboratory and assaulted Miss Washington?"

Hawkins's eyes bulged again as the receptionist and the other lab staff all shook their heads.

"Anybody have any idea what he's doing here?"

"I think he said something about wanting to know where Jody was," Melissa Washington offered, "but I was too busy having a heart attack to pay much attention."

"He was asking for Dr. Catlin," the receptionist confirmed. "I told him she wasn't here, and I was trying to see if he wanted to leave a message when he just jumped over the counter and started heading toward the molecular biology lab."

"You sure this man's a real OSP captain?" Melissa asked suspiciously. "Seems to me he ought to know that Jody went to see Lieutenant Talbert."

"At the OSP station?" the agent asked.

"No, at Colin Cellars's house. Detective-Sergeant Colin Cellars, of the OSP," Washington added pointedly.

Hawkins's eyes bulged once again.

"Oh, he's an OSP captain, all right," the agent said. "Just not a very nice one . . . or a very smart one, for that matter," he added.

"But—"

"Don't worry, I'll take care of it," the agent promised. Then he looked down at his prisoner.

"Okay, Hawkins," he said as he pulled the still-furious but now mercifully silent station commander up to his feet, "why don't you and I go outside and discuss this situation like a couple of fellow law enforcement officers?"

Moments later, Captain Rodney Hawkins found himself sitting on the front steps of the National Fish and Wildlife Forensics Laboratory, his hands still handcuffed behind his back and his mouth still taped shut, as the broad-shouldered agent sat next to him writing in a field notebook.

Finally, the agent stopped writing and looked up.

"Okay, Hawkins," he said pleasantly as he put away his notebook, "this is the way it's going to go. I've got you down for breaking and entering a federal facility, failing to identify yourself as a police officer, and threatening a federal law enforcement forensic scientist while in the performance of her duties." Still smiling, the agent reached out with one hand and ripped the strips of tape away from Hawkins's mouth.

The OSP station commander screamed in agony.

"Don't worry, it'll grow back," the agent said reassuringly as he examined the numerous moustache hairs on the tape before he folded the sticky strips and placed them in his jacket pocket.

"If you think just because you're a goddamned federal agent you're going to get away with this—" Hawkins started in, but the agent held up a warning hand.

"Three names," he said in a soft voice.

It was the demeanor of the agent—quiet, calm, and confident, rather than aggressively defiant—that caused Hawkins's bureaucratic survival instincts to finally kick in. He remained silent.

"Ex–OSP Sergeant Tim Procter, Lieutenant Don Talbert, and Major Ralph Sorenson," the agent continued on. "You know them, they know you. None of them like you very much. You managed to run Tim out of the OSP. You do everything you can on a daily basis to try to make Don look bad. And you report to Ralph, making sure to kiss his ass while watching every move he makes. They view you as a climber who couldn't care less about the people who work for you. They also think you're an embarrassment to what is otherwise a top-notch state police agency. I happen to agree with them, but I don't work for you or with you, so I don't care quite as much."

Hawkins started to say something, then stopped.

"I'll bet you're wondering how I know all of this," the agent went on conversationally as he pulled Hawkins around by the shoulder, grabbed the cuffs with his left and reached for his handcuff key with his right.

"The thing is, Tim, Don, Ralph, and I all grew up together, so we see each other a lot. You know, play cards, fish, watch each other's kids. So that's how I happen to know that Ralph has been waiting for you to do something really stupid for a long time . . . kind of like what you just did back there," he said as he unlocked and removed the handcuffs.

"Or," he added with a hopeful smile as Hawkins lunged to his feet and whirled around, his eyes blazing with rage, "maybe even attempting to assault a federal agent?"

It was the word "attempting" that seemed to catch the station commander's attention. That, and perhaps the look of pleasant anticipation on the muscular agent's face.

Hawkins stood there on the concrete walkway staring at the still-seated agent as if he couldn't decide what to do. Then the expression on his mostly bandaged and concealed face changed . . . as if he'd suddenly remembered something.

"No, I didn't think so." The agent nodded sadly as he watched the OSP station commander suddenly turn and run toward his nearby car.

The front door to the laboratory opened as the agent continued to sit on the steps and watch the OSP scout car quickly back out of the visitor's parking space and accelerate out of the parking lot.

"What in the world was all that about?" Melissa Washington asked cautiously from the doorway.

"Oh, I don't know," the agent said with a slight smile as he stood up and stretched. "Maybe ol' Hot-Rod Hawkins finally managed to learn something useful for once in his sorry excuse for a life."

"Oh really? What's that?"

"Oh, I don't know. Maybe something along the line of a team always being stronger than the sum of its individual members," the agent replied, the slight satisfied smile still present on his suntanned and windburned face.

"Either that, or maybe just the idea that you never want to start poking and prodding and screwing around with people who grew up together, because you just never know when one of them's going to figure out how to return the favor."

CHAPTER FORTY-ONE

IT WAS THE WIND RATTLING AGAINST THE WINDOWS THAT FINALLY brought Cellars up into the realm of consciousness, leaving him with only a brief moment of time to grasp at the will-o'-the-wisp dreams (And what? Something else. Definitely something else, he was sure of it!) that instantly vanished into the deep, dark, and tangled recesses of his mind.

There was an immediate sensation of emptiness—as if he'd lost something that he desperately had to have back—that he couldn't understand. Couldn't even begin to comprehend.

Please help me.

We're in terrible danger.

We can't stay here much longer.

We have to go.

The words echoed through his mind, demanding his attention,

but he continued to drift . . . searching for whatever it was that he no longer had. Whatever it was that he had to have back, no matter what . . .

Danger?

What danger?

He sat upright—his eyes snapping wide open—and was immediately struck by how cold it was outside his blanket and bedspread cocoon. He was also astonished to realize that there was daylight streaming into the basement through small gaps in the heavy curtains. And that in spite of a full night's sleep, he felt exhausted.

How can that be? he asked himself, starting to shiver as he quickly looked around the barely illuminated but all-too-familiar basement for the source of the danger . . . and saw nothing.

He shook his head in confusion.

Don't understand. I slept all night. I can't be tired. Time is it?

He fumbled for his watch, and then couldn't believe his eyes: *09:55?*

Almost ten o'clock in the morning? What happened to—?

Then a stomach-wrenching memory suddenly flashed through his mind.

What day is it?

He looked down at his watch again.

Thursday. Thank God!

He saw his clothes hanging on the hooks by the woodstove, and the SIG-Sauer lying beside the mattress . . . and the memories instantly flooded back into his mind. His discoveries that someone had scraped the cul-de-sac, and cleaned the cabin, destroying any remaining evidence. And then the lightning . . . the telephone line . . . the transformer . . . and Hawkins's scout car, a fiery mass of metal tumbling away in the darkness. The car that Talbert had—

Cellars blinked.

Wait a minute. That's right. What happened to Talbert?

He tried to think back. What was it that Talbert had told him?

I'll drop the Expedition off at the lab, have somebody there take me back to the station. Then I'll see who I can find to give you a hand up there. And if I can't find anyone, I'll go up there myself.

Okay, Cellars thought, *so where are you? And what happened to my CSI officer? Somebody to help me collect and preserve the—?*

Cellars's mind suddenly went numb as he remembered the bloodstain on the car seat, and the dark shadowy figure reaching inside . . .

We're in terrible danger.

We can't stay here much longer.

We have to go.

The words flashed through his mind and he quickly looked around the basement again, ready to grab for the SIG-Sauer at the first sign of . . . what?

Danger?

What kind of danger?

But there was still nothing dangerous or out of the ordinary to be seen. Only the trip wires and glass-bottle alarms that he'd set the night before, still in place, waiting patiently to be jarred or disturbed.

No dark shadowy figures.

No . . . Allesandra?

The warning words—her words?—were only a distant echo in his mind now. Barely audible. Making no sense at all.

Why do I think she was here? She couldn't have been here. Must have been dreaming.

About Allesandra . . . or about Jody? he found himself wondering.

But to his utter dismay, he no longer had any idea.

He closed his eyes for a moment, numbed by the realization that nothing meaningful in his life had changed. If anything, it had only gotten worse. Among other things, he was still going to have to hike down the mountain to get any kind of help.

But he was starting to shiver more, so he stumbled to his feet, grabbed his clothes, and quickly looked out through the curtains. As he feared, the weather hadn't changed much. It had stopped raining, but the sky was still gray and gloomy, and it looked like the rain and lightning could start up again at any moment.

Wonderful, he thought. *Just wonderful.*

He dressed quickly, unable to shake an uneasy sense that something else was wrong. But he couldn't think of what, or why . . . only that it was terribly important.

So he ate a quick breakfast from Bobby Dawson's stock of supplies, cleaned up, wet down the coals in the woodstove, and used his pocketknife to fashion a makeshift poncho out of the plastic tarp. Trying, as he did so, to ignore the sense of emptiness and longing that seemed to fill every corner and recess of his troubled mind.

By the time he was finished with his self-imposed chores, the wind and rain had started to rattle against the south-facing windows once again.

Finally satisfied that he'd done everything he could to try to figure out what actually had happened at this remote and isolated cabin five days ago, Cellars snapped the SIG-Sauer into its hip holster, slipped on the backpack containing extra ammunition and Malcolm Byzor's notebook computer, and secured the makeshift poncho over his head and shoulders.

Then, after taking one last look around the basement, he picked up the 12-gauge pump shotgun and cautiously opened the south-facing door.

———

Jody Catlin sniffed as she stared dubiously out past the slowly sweeping windshield wipers of the Jasper County scout car.

There was one OSP scout car parked in front of the house. Other than that one vehicle, there was no sign of life anywhere around the house.

"Are you sure this is the place?" she asked as she pulled another tissue out of her purse.

The delay at the OSP crime lab, where the evidence technicians had worked feverishly to collect and log out all of the evidence items Colin Cellars had turned over to the lab for examination and analysis, had seemed interminable. And now that she was finally here, it was all she could do not to go running into the house where Colin and Bobby and Malcolm were waiting. But some sense of uneasiness—something that she couldn't quite define—was holding her back.

Jasper County Patrol Sergeant Paul Washburn consulted his notebook.

"Fifty-two-eleven Willow Creek?" He looked up at the address numbers on the house. "Yep, this is the address they gave me. Why, is there a problem?"

"No, I suppose not," she said hesitantly. "I've never been here before. I guess I was expecting to see a lot more official vehicles parked outside."

"Probably parked out in back behind the alley," Washburn suggested. "There's a big empty lot back there. That's probably where the FBI and everybody else parked all their cars, so as not to draw a lot of attention."

"I wonder why they parked that one out front?" Catlin pointed at the white OSP scout car.

"Yeah, that is a little strange," Washburn agreed.

He paused for a moment.

"Look," he finally said, "why don't you stay here in the car and let me check things out first . . . just in case. I'll leave the keys in the ignition."

Jody Catlin shook her head. "Oh no, that's not really necessary. I was just—"

"No, please, I understand completely . . . and I really don't mind," Washburn said as he quickly stepped outside the scout car into the falling rain. "Don't forget," he reminded as he briefly stuck his head back inside the door, "we've still got four of our deputies missing on this case. No point in any of us getting careless at this stage of the game."

Catlin continued to stare through the rain-splattered windshield as she watched the uniformed officer approach the front door, feeling comforted by the fact that he kept his gun hand draped loosely over the rubberized grip of the pistol that was sticking out through a side slit of his rain gear.

No, she thought as she watched him knock at the door, *I really don't mind either. You go ahead and double-check. Like you said, no sense in—*

She saw the door open, and Washburn keeping his hand on his gun as he appeared to be talking with someone in the darkened doorway. Then he stepped inside . . . and was gone for almost two minutes.

She breathed a sigh of relief when he finally reappeared on the front porch and waved her in.

"They're all in the study, back behind the kitchen," Washburn said as he walked past her on the wet driveway. "You go ahead and go on in. They're going to send a couple of the FBI guys around to help me with the evidence."

"You sure you don't want me to help?" Catlin asked, holding the small cooler in one hand.

"No, you go ahead. Get that DNA evidence in there." Washburn winked. "I get the impression there's a couple of guys in there real anxious to see you."

Colin and Bobby.

Jody Catlin smiled to herself as she grabbed up the small cooler and quickly headed up the walkway. She was inside the doorway and crossing the living room toward the kitchen when she had the first inkling that something might be wrong.

It was the silence.

Odd, she thought, *I ought to be able to hear them from here.*

She was still standing in the entryway to the kitchen when she heard Washburn's footsteps behind her.

"You know," she said as she started to turn toward the protective officer, "something doesn't seem—"

Then she stopped in mid-stride . . . and screamed.

A deep, dark, horrified scream.

CHAPTER FORTY-TWO

THE FOREST RANGER WHO PICKED CELLARS UP ABOUT A THIRD OF the way down the mountain road clearly liked to talk, and didn't seem the least bit put off by the fact that his drenched passenger sat silent all the way to the OSP substation.

"Hey, you sure you don't want me to wait for you? Give you a ride home?" the ranger asked, as Cellars pulled the backpack and the shotgun out of the back of the green-painted truck.

"No, this is fine. Thanks for picking me up. I really appreciate it," Cellars said, then waited until the truck disappeared around the corner of the building before he started walking toward the front door.

The ride down the mountain had given him a chance to think . . . and he wasn't the least bit happy about the conclusions he'd come to so far.

On the other hand, from all outward appearances, Ruth Wilkinson couldn't have been more pleased by Detective-Sergeant Colin Cellars's unexpected arrival.

"Sergeant Cellars! Am I glad to see you!" the front desk clerk exclaimed as Cellars came into the foyer. "Everybody's been looking for you and Lieutenant Talbert."

Cellars stopped with his hand on the entryway to the back of the station.

"Talbert's still missing?"

"I don't know that he's missing, exactly," Wilkinson said hesitantly. "We just don't know where he is right now. But a Mr. Breem came by this morning wanting to talk with him—something about giving a statement—and Captain Hawkins is definitely looking for him . . . and you too," she added with a sympathetic wince. "Or at least I think he is."

Cellars sighed heavily. "Is he around?"

"Who?"

"Hawkins."

"No, that's just it," Wilkinson said, her eyes wide with excitement, "he was so upset, he just stormed out of here, swearing that he was going to get to the bottom of all this. And that's the last we've seen of him, too."

"What?" Cellars blinked in disbelief.

Wilkinson shrugged. "Talk to OMARR-Nine. He doesn't answer his radio. I'm telling you, it's really getting strange around here," she added, but she was talking to herself. Cellars had already disappeared down the main corridor of the station.

———

It took Cellars less than five minutes to determine that, aside from Wilkinson and a couple of records clerks, the OSP Region 9 station was empty.

Accordingly, he went right out the door to the back parking lot. There he found an unmarked detective car with no apparent owner, used his Region 9 master vehicle key to open the doors, tossed his backpack and the 12-gauge shotgun in the backseat, and jumped into the front seat. He had just turned out of the parking lot and was accelerating down the road when he reached for the radio mike.

"Oregon-Nine-Echo-One to OMARR-Nine."

The response was immediate.

"OMARR-Nine to Oregon-Nine-Echo-One, go ahead."

"OMARR-Nine, be advised I have transferred to an unmarked detective car, OSP vehicle nine-four-seven," he read the numbers off the console.

"OMARR-Nine to Oregon-Nine-Echo-One, copy your new vehicle is OSP nine-four-seven."

"Affirmative. Is Oregon-Nine-Alpha-Two or Nine-Alpha-One on the air?"

"Negative, Nine-Echo-One, we're still trying to make contact with both of them."

"Ten-four," Cellars acknowledged. "Be advised that I'm en route to the OSP lab. I'll be out of my vehicle for a few, but please contact me at the lab by land line the moment that Nine-Alpha-Two or Nine-Alpha-One checks in."

"Ten-four."

———

It took Cellars almost twenty minutes to reach the OSP lab. When he got there, and signed in at the front desk, the first person he met was Jack Wilson.

"Where the hell have you been?" Wilson demanded.

"A long story," Cellars said. "I'm trying to find Lieutenant Talbert. He was supposed to have dropped my CSI vehicle off here yesterday afternoon, so you folks could collect some blood samples, but I'm told he never showed."

"He definitely never showed up here. And you're about the fifth or sixth person who's come by here looking for him . . . *and* you," the serology supervisor added pointedly. "What's the matter with you field guys? Can't you keep track of each other?"

"Tell you what, as soon as I figure out what's going on around here, I'll be happy to fill you in."

"Yeah, well, in the meantime, you might give your buddy Malcolm a call. He's been trying to reach you all morning." Wilson reached into his lab-coat pocket and handed Cellars a handwritten note.

Cellars glanced down at the note. "Area code three-oh-three? What's he doing in Colorado?"

"Don't ask me." Wilson shrugged. "But you'd better call him right now. He sounded pretty upset."

"Got a phone I can use?"

"Right over there." Wilson pointed him to a nearby desk.

Cellars sat down at the desk, dialed the number, then listened to an automated voice assure him that his call was important, so please stay on the—

"Hotel Sheffield. How may I direct your call?"

"Extension two-three-two-three."

"Thank you, just a moment."

The line only rang once before someone at the other end picked up.

"Hello?"

"Malcolm?"

"Colin? Jesus, where the hell have you been? And why don't you answer your goddamned pager?"

Cellars blinked in confusion, then reached back behind his holster. Nothing.

"Shit. I must have lost it up at the cabin when I was sliding around in the mud."

"Yeah, right," Malcolm Byzor said skeptically. "So, did you get my message?"

"What message?"

"You know, Colin, some days I really think you are hopeless." Byzor sighed heavily. "The message I left on your voice mail telling you not to pick me up at the Rogue Valley International Airport this morning like we planned because I'm stuck here in Denver. They closed down the runways about ten minutes after we landed on account of snow buildup, and they're estimating now that—"

"Malcolm," Cellars interrupted, "what the hell are you talking about?"

There was a long pause at the other end of the line.

"I was really hoping we wouldn't have to go back over our conversation from the other day . . . you know, the one regarding your reference points?"

"What?"

"Last time we talked, you were telling me about how you've been running around in the woods and capping off rounds at shadows and at your official OSP crime scene vehicle. So, keeping all that in mind, I was just wondering how things might be going lately?"

"Other than capping off more rounds at my brand new CSI vehicle, not to mention another pair of shadows who tried to break into the thing when I wasn't looking, everything's going just fine," Cellars replied sarcastically. "Of course, I actually managed to hit one of them this time—the shadows, that is, not the vehicle— which may say more for my improved aim than my sanity. Now I repeat, what the hell are you talking about?"

"You were going to pick me up at the Rogue Valley Airport this morning, remember?"

"No, I don't remember," Cellars replied. "Why was I going to pick you up at the airport?"

There was another shorter pause.

"Because yesterday evening, right after we got cut off, you called me back and asked me to fly out to Medford with all of the evidence you sent me on Bobby's investigation, that's why."

Cellars felt a cold chill starting up his spine.

"Malcolm, listen to what I'm saying. I called you last night on a utility phone that I connected directly to a downed phone line near Bobby's cabin. It was in the middle of a thunderstorm and there were lightning strikes hitting all over the place. Yours was the fifth call I made that evening. One to the OSP lab, one to OMARR-Nine, two to Jody, and the one to you. When we got cut off, I called Jack Wilson at the OSP, and was trying to tell him to get some blood and tissue evidence over to Jody when lightning hit the transformer and absolutely fried my phone. I couldn't have called you a second time. I didn't have anything to call anybody with."

"Yes, you did," Byzor said insistently. "I recognized your voice, and I know damn well you were using your cell phone because I could read its signature."

This time the chills surged across Cellars's neck and down his arms.

"Malcolm," he whispered in a hoarse voice, "listen to me very carefully. My cell phone was stolen four days ago—the first night I was up at the cabin—when those shadows I was shooting at took off with my car. I haven't had a cell phone, much less talked on one, since that night."

There was another long pause.

"What about your e-mail?"

"What about it?"

"When did you read it?"

"You mean that message you sent? No, I haven't yet."

"You haven't accessed your e-mail, or used those two keys I gave you to unzip the file?"

"No, of course not. How could I? I just told you, I was stuck up at Bobby's cabin all night because another lightning strike blew up my boss's damned car, and I didn't have any way to make a modem connection up there anyway. Probably isn't even a phone line up there now after that transformer blew," he added. "And besides, I had to hike down the damned mountain this morning, so I never had the chance to try—"

He hesitated. There was something in the dark, tangled recesses of his mind trying to poke through, but he had no idea what it was.

"Colin?"

Cellars shook his head. "Sorry, I got distracted for a moment. I just—"

"Where are you calling from?" Byzor interrupted.

"The OSP lab in Medford."

"What extension?"

"Uh, two-four-three-five."

"Hang up the phone and stay where you are. Don't move," Byzor ordered.

The phone went dead in Cellars's hand.

"What was that all about?" Wilson asked.

"I have no idea," Cellars confessed.

"Anybody ever tell you that you've got some really weird friends?"

"You don't want to get me started on that topic."

They were still talking about weird friends—and how an inordinate number of them seemed to be drawn to law enforcement careers—three minutes later when the phone rang again.

"Hello?"

"No names," Byzor said. "Who are you with right now?"

"A buddy of mine. The chief serologist around here."

"Anyone else?"

"No."

"Do you trust him?"

Cellars hesitated. "Yeah, sure I do."

"Do you still have my CSI Scanner notebook computer? The Mac?"

"Right here in my backpack."

"Okay, keep it with you for the moment." A pause. "You remember that desktop computer you used to contact me the last time? The one at the lab?"

"Uh-huh."

"Get to it . . . the same computer, same connections, no substitutes. And while you're doing that, put your buddy on."

Ten minutes later, Cellars was sitting in front of a computer keyboard and monitor waiting for the OSP Crime Lab's electronics engineer to finish connecting a cable between the OSP computer and Byzor's CSI Scanner notebook computer. He'd already connected an oddly shaped bright red telephone to the second of two modem lines in the small room.

"Okay, you're connected," the electronics engineer said as he handed Cellars a pair of small electronic devices. "Your new cell phone and your new pager. They're basically the same models as the last one, except that they're encrypted . . . and this time only you, your buddy, and I will know the access codes."

Cellars hooked the pager to his belt behind his hip holster and stuck the small cell phone in his jacket pocket.

"About the red phone," the electronics engineer went on. He pointed to an oddly shaped red phone set on the table next to the monitor. "You should have a pair of clean lines all the way across, but if anyone does try to break in, you'll know about it because this green light will start flashing." He pointed to a small green diode on the red receiver. "Shouldn't matter anyway because we're running PGP encryption at both ends, but why take a chance? Oh yeah, one more thing: Don't forget to tell your friend that we don't have any conversion software for the Mac, but he probably already knows that."

"Hello?" Cellars spoke cautiously into the phone when the electronics engineer shut the door.

"Are you alone?" Malcolm Byzor asked.

"Yeah . . . but the engineer said to tell you that they don't have any conversion software for—"

"I heard him," Byzor interrupted. "Not a problem. And by the way, I'm taking over the computers, so try not to touch the keyboard for a minute or so. We're going to make use of something a little more powerful than PGP for encryption."

As Cellars watched in fascination, the monitor in front of his eyes began to flash a series of text codes and graphics that had no apparent meaning or relation to each other. Finally, after this went on for almost three minutes, Byzor came back on the line.

"You still there?"

"Yeah, I'm still here," Cellars acknowledged. "But I'd like to know what's going on. To start with, what's the big deal about that e-mail message?"

"Someone accessed it, and erased it," Byzor said. "Completely. Even reformatted the sectors on the drive."

"So?"

"It's not easy to do something like that. Especially the access and retrieval part. It was a protected file—actually, a very carefully protected file—in a protected system. Which means no one except you and I should have been able to do that, period. Did you give anyone else your access code, or the keys to unzip the file?"

"No."

"Then we've got a problem . . . but not an insurmountable one because I kept a copy of the file," he added. "Stand by for a second. I'm going to put something up on your screen. Tell me what you see."

For about five seconds, nothing happened. Then, all of a sudden, the monitor shifted from a seemingly random pattern of bright colors to a mostly black image. Cellars instinctively recoiled from the screen.

"Christ, Malcolm," he whispered. "What the hell is that?"

"You tell me."

"I've never seen anything like it before. It looks like a creature out of somebody's worst nightmare. Either that, or one of those monsters you computer geeks are always dreaming up for your shoot-'em-up games."

"As it happens, I'm rather grateful to be able to say that I don't know a single game designer—or any other computer geek, for that matter—with an imagination like that," Byzor responded over the encrypted phone line.

"No shit?"

"None whatsoever. Trust me on that."

Cellars took in a deep breath and released it slowly.

"Okay," he finally said. "I stand corrected. So what is it?"

"I have no idea. But whatever it is, or was, my guess is that you were about fifteen or twenty feet away from it when you triggered that electronic camera of yours."

Cellars felt his stomach twist and his entire body go numb and cold.

"Are you trying to tell me . . . that thing's for real?" Cellars tried to laugh, but the sound stuck in his throat.

"You're the one who collected the image in the field," Byzor reminded him. "I'm just processing the data."

"Well, reprocess it then. Come up with something that doesn't make me want to hide under a bed."

"Are you telling me that you've never seen anything like it . . . out there at the cabin, or anywhere else?"

"Christ, no," Cellars whispered, shaken and chilled by the very thought. "You think I'd forget something like that?"

"Those dark shadowy figures you keep talking about," Byzor pressed. "What exactly did they look like?"

"I don't know, but nothing like this thing, that's for damned sure," Cellars said emphatically. "If they did, I'd have locked myself in a jail cell with a gun and flamethrower a long time ago."

"Curious."

"No, terrifying," Cellars corrected. "Curious is a very different sensation, believe me."

There was a long pause at the other end of the line.

"Malcolm," Cellars said, "are you still there?" He was working very hard at trying to keep his growing sense of panic under control.

"Yes, I'm here. I'm just working on something," Byzor replied in a distracted voice.

"Tell me something. How is a creature like this even . . . possible?"

"I'm . . . not sure," he said hesitantly. "I called Jody earlier this morning, and she mentioned something . . . interesting about the DNA in some of the tissue samples you collected at the cabin."

"What do you mean by interesting?"

"An extra set of base pairs."

"What?"

"Which, if possible, offers some rather incredible genetic coding possibilities, among other things," Byzor answered, a sense of distraction still very evident in his voice. "Ah, here we go. Take a look at this."

The horrifying blackish creature mercifully disappeared from the monitor, replaced by what was now—to Cellars—a very familiar image. The basement of Bobby Dawson's mountain cabin.

"Can you see it?" Byzor queried.

"Yeah, I see it just fine," Cellars responded. The sight of Bobby Dawson's torn body lying on the basement floor—even in black-and-white graphic form—still made his stomach churn.

"Look over at the northwest corner," Byzor directed.

"Okay, I'm looking."

"Now tell me what you see."

The graphic image disappeared from the scene . . . then a moment later, reappeared—except the lines were much lighter.

"The same thing."

"Okay, now watch."

As Cellars watched, the entire graphic image shifted to a light gold color. Then the monitor flickered again as a darker blue—but otherwise seemingly identical—graphic appeared as a three-dimensional overlay.

As Cellars continued to watch in fascination, the two images merged, forming one bright green graphic. All except for a small area in the northwest corner, where two small objects continued to glow gold and blue approximately three scaled feet apart.

"The gold image recording was initiated at oh-oh-thirteen-twenty-two hours, and lasted for a total of fourteen-point-two seconds, whereupon the recording was terminated . . . my guess, because you probably forgot to charge the batteries," Byzor said over the encrypted phone. "The blue image recording was initiated approximately fifty-four minutes later, at oh-one-oh-seven-thirty-seven hours—probably after you figured out how to recharge the batteries—and lasted for the full fifteen minutes. Tell me, did you enter the room between those two recording times?"

The rock.

"No," Cellars answered, the familiar chill starting up his spine again.

"Did anyone else . . . or anything else enter that room?"

"What do you mean, anything else?" Cellars demanded.

"I don't know. Animal, plant, shadow, whatever. Anything at all that could have moved that rock about three feet."

"No."

"Are you certain?"

"Yes, I'm certain. I sealed the room—all the doors and all the windows—with evidence tape before I went out to my CSI vehicle to recharge the batteries. No one—man *or* beast—got in there while I was gone. That's one thing I am certain of."

"Well, in that case," Byzor went on in what Cellars considered to be an amazingly controlled voice under the circumstances, "the answer to the question you asked me yesterday—whether or not my lasers could actually cause an inanimate object, like a rock, to move—appears to be yes."

"But how—" Cellars started to ask when suddenly the small green diode on the bright red receiver started to flash.

"Later," Byzor said quickly.

Then, before Cellars could think or say anything else, the computer screen went blank and the phone went dead in his hand.

———

Cellars waited for ten minutes for Byzor to call back. When the computer screen and encrypted phone line remained dead, he stepped outside the small room to get a drink of water . . . and to try to steady nerves that were now thoroughly shaken.

He was still standing next to the drinking fountain, lost in thought, when Linda Grey, the young OSP evidence technician, came running up with an envelope in her hand.

"Sergeant Cellars, thank goodness you haven't left yet," Grey said as she handed Cellars the envelope. "Jack said you might still be here."

"What's this?" Cellars asked, staring at the envelope in confusion.

"It's a photograph I took of the portrait you dropped off the other day," the evidence technician said, looking chagrined. "I'm really sorry. I know I shouldn't have done it, but I'm a real fan of modern Baroque painting, and there's something about this portrait that just caught my eye. I was going to take it home to show my instructors, but when Dr. Catlin came by to pick up all the evidence on this case, I started to get worried that I might have done something really stupid, so I thought maybe you could take it to her."

"Dr. Jody Catlin picked up all the evidence on this case? What are you talking about?"

The chagrined look on Linda Grey's face immediately shifted to one of uncertainty and confusion.

"The Dawson homicide case. You know, you directed us to release everything we had here at the lab to her."

"I did?"

"Uh, yes, sir, you did." Grey blinked uncertainly. "I, uh, took the call . . . and I'm sure it was you. I mean, I definitely recognized your voice."

The sensation of having cold chills running up and down his spine was getting to be so familiar that Cellars hardly noticed it anymore.

"Oh, right, of course it was me," he said, shaking his head ruefully. "The Dawson case. I'm sorry, I was thinking about another case and I just got confused for a moment."

The young evidence technician looked like she was about to faint from relief.

"Oh wow, you really had me going there for a moment." She smiled. "I mean I know we're supposed to get approval before we do something like that, but I guess I figured no one would care about a photo. That wasn't really evidence. I hope I didn't do anything wrong."

"No, not at all. In fact, you may have helped us tremendously," Cellars assured the young evidence technician as he quickly examined the familiar photograph and then slid it back into the envelope. "Uh, one more thing. Do you remember exactly when Dr. Catlin checked the evidence out?"

"Oh, let's see," Grey quickly checked her watch, "I guess it's been a couple of hours . . . which is why I was surprised to see you here in the first place," she added.

"Why do you say that?"

"Oh, because when I told Dr. Catlin that I was a little uncomfortable not having a written authorization from you to release the evidence—you know, something to put in the case file—she confirmed what you'd told me on the phone."

"Which was?"

The evidence technician smiled. "That she was going to be taking everything directly over to your house."

CHAPTER FORTY-THREE

EVEN WITH THE PORTABLE EMERGENCY LIGHT AND SIREN FLASH-
ing and screaming over his head, it still took Cellars almost twenty
minutes to work his way through the wet streets and traffic to his
new residence.

He saw the white-and-brown Jasper County scout car in the
driveway, and was momentarily relieved because the first thing that
occurred to him was the backup he'd requested from OMARR-9
had gotten there first. As he pulled into the driveway and came to a
stop next to the other vehicle, he reached for the console mike.

"Nine-Echo-One to the Jasper County deputy responding to
my backup request at Fifty-two-eleven Willow Creek. I'm at my
residence now. Where are you at?"

There was a pause of about five seconds before a voice finally
crackled over the console speaker.

"Nine-Charlie-Five to Nine-Echo-One, be advised, there are no

Jasper units responding to your call. Repeat, no Jasper units. Far as
I know, I'm it . . . and I'm still about two minutes out from your
location."

"Echo-One to Charlie-Five, I copy your transmission, but I'm
looking at an empty Jasper cruiser parked in my driveway right now."

Another brief pause.

"Charlie-Five to Echo-One, what's the plate on that cruiser?"

"Hold on."

Cellars quickly jammed the gear selector of the detective unit
into reverse, accelerated backward, then immediately hit the brake.

"Charlie-Five, I'm looking at an E-Plate, Juliet-Alpha-two-five-
seven-seven."

This time the response was immediate. "Echo-One, be advised,
that's the plate number for Sergeant Downs's vehicle, the one we've
been looking for all week!"

Cellars cursed.

"Charlie-Five, step on it, I'm going in now."

"Echo-One, wait—!"

But Cellars was already out of the detective car and running up
his driveway with the SIG-Sauer in his gloved hand.

He could hear the siren starting up in the distance as he hit the
door running, lunging forward and turning his shoulder into it at
the last second. The entire doorframe tore loose from the wall and
hit the living room floor in an explosion of plaster dust and wood
splinters. Cellars landed on top of the doorframe, rolled to his left,
and twisted around in the general direction of his kitchen and hallway with the SIG-Sauer extended in both hands, searching for a
target.

But as far as he could see or tell, the entire house was dark and
silent.

That was when the all-too-familiar smell hit him.

Oh, no.

Cellars lunged to his feet. He was halfway to the kitchen when
he saw the blood . . . and stopped dead still.

It was everywhere. Across the floor . . . the walls . . . the countertops . . . the refrigerator and stove.

Some distant analytical portion of Cellars's brain began to interpret the angles and velocities of the overlapping blood splatters. But he immediately gave that idea up because the interpretation didn't make any sense. It was like someone had put a couple quarts of blood in an open blender and then turned it on high.

Or like . . .

The horrible black image on the computer monitor flashed before Cellars's eyes. The image of a creature that actually looked—if you allowed your imagination the slightest leeway—like a bright-violet-eyed, flesh-and-keratin blender had come to life. A creature perfectly capable of tearing a human body apart and leaving blood all over the kitchen walls in the process.

The approaching siren was much closer now, but Cellars was hardly aware of it. For the second time in almost fifteen years of crime scene work, he thought he was going to vomit.

Why . . . her?

Cellars's brain had gone numb, and he was only vaguely aware of the fact that the increasingly loud siren had suddenly shut off outside the house. Moments later, as he squatted to examine more closely something embedded in a large mass of congealing blood on the linoleum floor, the sound of boots stumbling over the remains of a shattered door and frame echoed through the room.

"What the—oh my God!" the uniformed OSP officer exclaimed as he stopped dead a few feet from Cellars and stared over his shoulders in disbelief at the kitchen.

It was the torn corner of an OSP evidence tag. Cellars immediately recognized the last four inked letters of his last name and badge number. And something else too, he realized, now that he was much closer to the floor. Small fragments of bone, tissue, and—and what else?—some kind of wide-mesh fabric scattered and mixed throughout the slowly decomposing reddish brown mess.

"What the hell happened here?" the uniformed officer whispered.

Cellars shook his head wordlessly.

"But where's the body?"

Colin Cellars's head came up slowly. His eyes silently followed the heavy drag marks leading to the back door. Then, without saying anything at all, he stepped forward, instinctively stepping around the larger pools of congealing blood as he slowly moved toward the back door. He was aware—in some vague, distant sense—that the uniformed officer was following closely behind him, but he didn't care. All he wanted to do was put the sights of the SIG-Sauer between those bright violet orbs and keep squeezing the trigger until they were no longer identifiable as eyes. After that, he'd worry about what it was he'd shot.

But the drag marks crossed over the left-side imprint of a matched set of tire tracks running down the middle of the mud-and-gravel alleyway and turned left in the direction of the vehicle before they suddenly stopped.

"In the trunk?" the uniformed officer spoke in a hushed voice.

Cellars nodded silently.

They were back in the house, searching the back bedrooms to no avail, when the new pager on Cellars's belt began to vibrate. The message was brief and cryptic:

COLIN,

GO TO THE DOUBLETREE INN RIGHT NOW. TRY NOT TO BE FOLLOWED IF YOU CAN. CHECK IN UNDER THE NAME OF OUR OLD HIGH SCHOOL TRACK COACH, PAY CASH, THEN GO TO YOUR ROOM AND WAIT FOR MY CALL. HURRY!

MALCOLM

"What is it?" the uniformed officer asked.

"I've got to go," Cellars replied as he reattached the pager to his belt.

"But what about"—the officer hesitated, not quite sure what to say—"all this?" He gestured with a gloved hand to indicate the entire crime scene in general. "I can't even begin to work—"

"I can't either," Cellars said in a tight voice, barely able to get the words out. "My house; my girlfriend. Somebody else has got to do it. Seal off the house and the back alley where the tire tracks stopped, then get somebody from the lab out here right away."

"But—"

"Do it now," Cellars whispered in a deadly cold voice as he started walking toward the shattered doorway.

———

The desk clerk at the Doubletree Inn was clearly expecting him.

"Is there anything else I can do for you, Mr. Baker?" the clerk asked as he counted out three dollars in change.

"No, not right now," Cellars said. "Which way do I go?"

"Down the hallway to your right, third floor, all the way to the end of the hall."

"Thank you," he responded, but his mind was already far away. His cell phone rang within minutes of his closing the door.

"Hello?"

"Colin?"

"Yeah, it's me."

"What's the matter?" Byzor acted as if he'd immediately sensed his friend's dispirited mood.

"Jody's dead." He was barely able to get the words out.

"What? Are you sure?"

"I—" Cellars hesitated, his voice still shaky. "No, not completely, I guess; but I don't think there's much doubt about it." He described the identification of Sergeant Jim Downs's scout car and the scene at his house in short, terse sentences.

There was a long period of silence at the other end of the line. Then:

"I don't mean to question your expertise at a crime scene, Colin, but I really don't think she's dead."

Cellars blinked, then shook his head in a futile effort to clear his head. Nothing was making sense anymore. Not even his old, reliable computer-chip-minded friend.

"What are you talking about, Malcolm? I just told you, they sent her to my house with all the evidence on Bobby's murder. And when I got there, my kitchen looked like a slaughterhouse. Also, I found a torn piece from one of my evidence tags stuck in the blood."

"Yes, I understand all that," Byzor said patiently, "but did you actually see a body?"

"No, like I said, just blood everywhere . . . like somebody went ape-shit with a chain saw."

"Colin, I hear what you're saying, but it still doesn't make any sense. Think about it. Why in the world would they kill her?"

Cellars had the sudden feeling that his entire consciousness was being caught up in the undertow of a huge wave.

"Look, first of all, I don't know who 'they' are. And secondly, how the hell would I know what they're thinking?"

"You probably know a lot more than you realize," Byzor suggested. "How long has Sergeant Downs been missing?"

"I don't know. A few days. What difference does it make?"

"I need these details to clarify a few things," Byzor said. "Tell me how long."

"Since last Sunday."

"Has anyone else turned up missing?"

"Besides Downs? Sure. Three other Jasper County deputies, my lieutenant, and my captain."

"No one else?"

"Not that I know of, unless you count a young morgue attendant who's supposedly on vacation down in California . . . and Bobby's missing body . . . and the twenty-four people who've disappeared in Jasper County during the past eleven months," Cellars added after a moment. "Is that what this is all about?"

Byzor ignored Cellars's question. "Speaking of that young morgue attendant, that security videotape from the Jasper County Morgue you sent me was altered—a reasonably decent job, but nothing out of the ordinary for a professional electronics lab. But you already knew that."

"Knew what?"

"That it was altered. Forget about the tape. It's not important right now," Byzor said impatiently. "Is there anyone else you've talked with about all this? Anybody at all?"

"Sure, Jack Wilson at the OSP lab, and those DEA agents who gave me a bad time right after Bobby had his helicopter crash. Come to think of it, I haven't seen any of them around since last Sunday either."

"Not surprising. There's an eyes-only teletype going around federal law enforcement right now asking everyone to be on the lookout for a team of Internal Affairs–type DEA agents who turned up missing in southern Oregon last weekend."

"What?"

"Don't worry about it. That's the DEA's problem. Anyone else?" Byzor pressed.

Cellars hesitated.

"Just Allesandra."

"Who's she?"

"I don't know. One of Bobby's old girlfriends, I think," Cellars said evasively, suddenly unnerved by the realization that—in spite of all the evidence suggesting Jody Catlin's recent and violent death— he still felt an inescapable sense of emptiness and longing every time he even thought about Allesandra.

He described to Malcolm Byzor how he'd met her at the Alliance of Believers lecture, and about the partially completed portrait he'd found on the floor of the cabin.

"As far as you know, did any of these people have any direct link to Jody?"

"No, I don't think so." Cellars took in a deep steadying breath. "Look, as far as I know, the only reason Jody got involved in this at all was because the OSP lab took some of the blood samples that came up nonhuman over to her lab . . . and she got assigned the case. Then somebody worked things out so that she went over to the OSP lab and picked up all the evidence I collected at Bobby's cabin. Even made it seem like I authorized the transfer."

"Somebody called the lab using your name . . . and voice?" Byzor clarified.

"Yeah, I suppose so."

"Okay, I guess that makes sense if they wanted to scoop up all the evidence on this investigation in one quick move," Byzor said. "But even so, killing Jody would have been an incredibly stupid and thoughtless mistake on their part. They had to have realized—or at least suspected—by now that you weren't likely to be very coopera-tive unless they had something or someone of value to use as a bargain-ing chip. And there's certainly no reason to think these . . . people are even remotely stupid—much less thoughtless," he added.

"What do you mean, bargaining chip? What are you talking about?" Cellars demanded.

"Think about it, Colin. These people—whoever they are, what-ever they are—they definitely want something from you, right?"

Whatever they are?

"Want something from *me?*"

"Of course. Why else would they be playing you like a puppet for the last five days, unless they were trying to force you to do something for them that you don't want to do? And when you stop to think about it, who better to talk you into something you don't want to do than Jody, right?"

Jody . . . or Allesandra, he thought guiltily. Then it occurred to him. *Christ, what if they think they don't need Jody anymore because now they know they've got Allesandra?*

"Which brings me back to my original argument," Byzor went on. "Why in the world would they decide to kill her—and effec-tively discard the most powerful and effective twist they could possibly ever have on you—if they didn't have to? And even if they did have a good reason to kill her, why go to the risk of transporting her body when they could have just as easily left her there for you to discover?"

"But—"

"Face it, Colin, if all they wanted to do was kill you, they could have done that days ago . . . when you were first up at the cabin. One officer, at night, all by himself, with two or three killers—presumably professionals—moving in on him out of the darkness? If they'd been serious about putting you down, you wouldn't have stood a chance out there, and you know it. They were after something, no doubt about it . . . but it wasn't you.

"And don't forget about that walking nightmare, whatever it is or was," Byzor reminded before Cellars could respond. "What was it, fifteen or twenty feet away from your back when you set off that strobe? Think about it. If that thing had really intended to tear you limb from limb, do you really believe you would have frightened it off with a goddamned strobe flash?"

"You're suggesting that thing's . . . real? Not some kind of electronic trick or illusion somebody's using to mess with my head?"

Two minutes earlier, Cellars had been absolutely convinced that a treasured friend had been brutally murdered as a result of one of his crime scene investigations and that the people responsible were playing with his mind to keep him from figuring out the evidence. But now, instead of feeling elated by the logic of Malcolm Byzor's arguments, he was starting to feel the familiar chills running up and down his spine again.

"No, not necessarily. What I'm saying is: If it is a trick, it's not one of ours."

"Well, in that case, then who the hell's doing all this?" Cellars demanded.

"I don't know," Byzor admitted. "That's what we want to find out."

"Who's we?"

"That's a little too complicated to explain right now," Byzor said evasively.

"Bullshit!" There was an audible—and dangerous—edge to Cellars's voice now. "Listen, Malcolm, if you know something about all of this, and you're holding back, I—"

"Colin, if Jody really is alive, then what you want to do—more than anything else—is try to keep her that way, right?" Byzor interrupted.

Cellars started to say something, then hesitated.

"Exactly, so kindly shut up and start thinking instead of just reacting. Right now, if I assume for the moment that I really do have some vague understanding of what's going on right now—which I believe I do. And if I also assume correctly that Jody really is still alive—which I personally think is a really good bet, for the reasons I just explained—then it's equally probable that you're the only real chance she has right now."

"You want to go through all that again, only this time with a few more details . . . and a lot more clarity?"

"I can't right now."

"Why not?"

"Because . . . I just can't."

Cellars remained silent for a long moment.

"Tell me something, Malcolm," he finally said. "Why do I keep on getting the distinct impression that this entire situation has something to do with your current employers?"

"It's nothing we did," Byzor responded quickly. "But it may very well involve something that Bobby did—or more likely, didn't do."

"What the hell kind of sense is that supposed to make?"

"From your perspective, probably not much," Byzor conceded.

"So tell me something," Cellars said after a long moment, "all things considered—and I specifically include the apparent fact that somebody out there is very good at mimicking *my* voice—how am I supposed to know who I'm really talking to right now?"

"That's more like it," Byzor said approvingly. "You keep on thinking that way and we all just might get out of this alive after all."

"We?"

"We're all in danger," Byzor said cryptically. "But right now, probably you more than anyone else . . . and I specifically include Jody in that assessment."

"In that case, all they need to do is come looking for me. I'm easy to find, and I can't hardly wait," Cellars replied, the cold edge back in his voice. "And speaking of which, how do I find you if I need to get hold of you all of a sudden?"

"You don't."

"What?"

"Look, I'm going to be moving around a lot in the next couple of days, and I'm not going to be easy to find, so don't worry about it, okay?"

"So give me your cell phone number."

"I can't."

"Why the hell not?"

Byzor sighed heavily.

"Colin, has anyone ever explained the concept of a cut-out to you?"

"I have a general idea of how the process works," Cellars answered.

"I'm glad to hear that, because as far as you are concerned right now, that's exactly what I am. Your cut-out. Someone to keep all the people you're linked to right now as separate and isolated as possible. And in that sense, right at this moment, I'm probably the best chance *you* have to stay alive."

"You know, Malcolm, you really are starting to scare me."

"Good. I can only hope that means you're finally starting to pay attention."

"But if Jody really is still alive," Cellars went on, "and you're my only link to whatever it is you're doing to try to keep us that way, how do we stay connected?"

"Try not to worry about that part of the problem," Byzor advised. "Like I told you a long time ago, I can always find you if I really need to."

"But—"

"Look, Colin, just trust me for a couple more days, okay? That's all I need. Just a couple of days. And in the meantime, stay alert, and whatever you do, don't lose that new pager and cell phone."

The phone went dead in Cellars's hand.

CHAPTER FORTY-FOUR

I CAN'T STAY LONG.

I'm in terrible danger.

Please help me.

The very same words that continued, day after day, to echo through the deep, dark, tangled recesses of Colin Cellars's fevered mind.

Except that this time, the words weren't in the same order . . . and the focus was definitely singular now.

Not us. Just her.

He could feel his heart starting to pound in his chest. An emotional reaction to the possibility that his deep sense of longing and emptiness was about to be fulfilled once again? Or just a physical reaction to an unexpected shock? Cellars didn't know. And he wasn't sure he wanted to know.

"How did you find me?" he asked in a raspy whisper.

He was standing in the doorway of his hotel room, staring into her tear-filled eyes as he felt the familiar sensation of heat radiating from her full and enticing torso. Every survival instinct he possessed was screaming at him to slam the door shut, throw the bolt, and lunge for his pistol while he still had a chance.

But he couldn't.

Not after seeing the bloody parallel slashes across the right side of her face . . . and the dark purple bruising that surrounded her tearful right eye.

And all that blood in my kitchen, he reminded himself, fighting internally to maintain a tight grip on his emotions.

"They told me where you'd be," she responded with a choked sob.

But it was difficult. Terribly difficult.

"They?"

The computerized image of a violet-eyed beast—a black creature outlined against a slightly less black background—immediately leaped into his consciousness, sending the cold chills racing down his spine and straight into his heart.

She nodded.

"Please, can I come in?" she pleaded in a whispery voice as she quickly looked back over her shoulder. "I'm so scared."

Before he realized what he was doing—and certainly before he seriously *thought* about what he was doing—Cellars grabbed her upper arm, pulled her inside the room, and quickly shut the door.

"What happened to you?" he asked as he brought the fingers of his left hand up to the side of her face, feeling the radiating warmth flow into his hand and arm as he soothed and caressed the ugly-looking slashes and bruises.

"They hurt me."

Who are they? he wanted to ask. That and another equally important question.

What are they?

But he couldn't. Not now. Not yet. So he asked the one question that he thought might give him a chance.

"Why would they want to hurt you?"

The incredibly seductive, incredibly erotic warmth from her body was flowing into his shoulders and chest now, and he knew he was lost . . . but he didn't care.

She's like a physical addiction, he told himself. *Only worse . . . or better.* He couldn't even begin to decide which.

"You have something they want," she went on in her soft and ever-so-enticing voice. "Something they must have before they leave . . . and they're running out of time."

"So they sent you to get it from me?"

She nodded, her eyes filling with tears again.

"What is it?" he asked.

"Not now," she whispered. "Later."

And the liquid warmth of her body became a surging wave that caught him up and took him helplessly away.

CHAPTER FORTY-FIVE

"I HAVE TO ASK YOU SOMETHING," HE WHISPERED AS HE LAY there beside her, trying to recover his senses, and to extract himself from the sense of being caught in a warm and sensuous and soothing undertow that was no longer moving. "Something that's very difficult for me to ask."

"You've been my savior. You can ask me anything you want." She smiled with her mouth and her eyes, and he immediately experienced the sensation that his heart was actually melting into his body. As a result, he knew that it would take every bit of willpower he still possessed to force the words past his throat. Like deliberately cutting himself loose from a lifeline.

There would be no going back.

He took a deep breath, held it for a moment, and then said, "I have to know. What are you?"

He had a sense of feeling her reaction in every cell and fiber of his body . . . as if the two of them were still one.

But they weren't, and the change was immediately apparent. As if some portion of her thermal core had instinctively started to retreat, but then changed its mind.

"You know what I am," she finally said in a soft, distant voice. "You've known for a long time."

"You're not like me . . . not like us," he said hesitantly. "Beyond that, I'm not sure what I know."

"You know a great deal . . . but you understand very little."

"So humor me. Educate me."

She smiled at that.

"You . . . humans have such a wonderful sense of irony. It's one of your more interesting characteristics."

In that moment, time—like his heart—seemed to stop.

But to Cellars's absolute amazement, the expected chills running up his spine failed to appear.

For some indeterminate expanse of time, as the realization—and all of the ramifications that necessarily followed—began to fall into place in his stunned mind, the two of them simply stared at each other. Each observing the other with a new sense of fascination.

"How amazing," she finally said. "You really aren't afraid, are you?"

Cellars shook his head slowly as he kept his eyes fixed on hers.

"Why not?"

"It's very difficult," he said after a moment, "to be afraid of something you love."

Her soft and full lips opened up into a wide smile. A warm, enticing, and almost overwhelmingly seductive smile. It was all he could do not to reach for her, then.

"On the other hand," he forced himself to go on, "it's very easy to be afraid of something you don't know . . . or understand . . . or that you hate." He paused for a moment. "As you probably realize by now, we . . . humans are very good at that sort of thing."

Her eyes flickered.

"So tell me, please," he said, "while I'm still in love with you . . . and before I begin to hate you for all the reasons that I should." He paused again. "Who are you?"

"Why would you hate me?"

"You know why."

She nodded at that. "Yes, I suppose I do."

Then, after a long moment:

"You might describe me as an explorer and a teacher . . . or perhaps an anthropologist," she suggested.

"You explore other places . . . other worlds . . . and then teach others about them?"

"Yes, that's . . . a close approximation." She nodded. "Like you, we like to watch . . . and to experience. But also like you, we can't watch or experience whenever or however we wish. We have rules we are required to follow. In our case, very important rules."

"Such as?"

"First of all, we can't stay long."

"Why not?"

"Would you accept it if I told you it's much too difficult to explain, because you lack the necessary . . . context."

"You sound like my friend Malcolm."

She smiled. "Yes, I suppose I do in a way."

The alarm bells began going off in the back of his head. All the more chilling because he knew, somehow, that she could hear them too, but didn't seem to care.

"Okay." He shrugged. "Go on."

"Secondly, we can't use our advanced technologies while we're here."

"Same question. Why not?"

"Because of the third—and most important—rule, which is: We

cannot, under any circumstances, leave evidence of our presence here."

"That's funny," Cellars said after a moment.

"Why so?"

"I was remembering my lecture to the Alliance of Believers. The one you attended."

"Oh, yes." She smiled. "Your sense of irony again."

"But you did, didn't you?"

She cocked her head, and her eyes flickered again . . . but her expression didn't change.

"Leave evidence," Cellars finished. "Lost it, whatever."

She hesitated for several seconds, and then nodded.

"And Bobby found it."

She nodded again.

"So you killed him in an attempt to get it back . . . and Jody too," he added.

"No, that's not . . . correct," she whispered. "I didn't kill either of them."

"Why should I believe you?"

She smiled. A soft, gentle, and almost overwhelmingly enticing smile.

"Because you want to."

"That's my problem," he agreed. "It's not an answer."

"No, it's not." She stared off into the distance for a few moments, as if trying to make up her mind.

"First of all," she finally said, "you misunderstand my . . . role. I would never harm you or your friends. I couldn't."

"No?"

She shook her head. "No, my role as a teacher would absolutely prevent that. However," she added solemnly, "I would also tell you that my protectors would not hesitate—to harm, to kill, or to destroy any or all of you—if it became necessary."

"Your protectors?"

"The greater Universe is a dangerous place to explore, as you might expect. So they always travel with us, to protect us while we do our work . . . and to make certain that we always follow the rules. But they're not as fearsome as some would have you believe," she added cryptically.

"The shadows?" he whispered. "The ones I've been . . . shooting at?"

"Yes."

"I don't understand."

"No," she agreed. "You don't."

"Because I . . . lack context?"

"In essence," she said softly, sympathetically, as she stared deeply into his eyes, "yes."

He nodded slowly in acceptance again.

"But if you don't?" he said.

She cocked her head questioningly.

"Follow the rules?"

"Then I will be destroyed. Not killed, destroyed."

"I don't understand the difference."

"As I said before, it's a matter of context. Our concept of death is . . . different than yours."

"Whereas ours is simple," Cellars pointed out. "Dead is dead."

"That is your concept," she agreed. "It doesn't necessarily represent a full understanding of the possibilities."

Cellars blinked. "What do you mean by that?"

"Let me put it this way. What if I told you that both of your friends are—in your sense—retrievable?"

"Bobby and Jody?"

"Yes."

"I would be . . . extremely happy, and probably very distrustful."

"Because you don't believe me?"

"No, because I believe you'd tell me whatever I wanted to hear if it suited your purposes."

"Why do you say that?"

"The evidence," he said.

She cocked her head again.

"You've been perfectly willing to seduce me in order to get your evidence back."

"Ah, yes." Her eyes seemed to twinkle with delight. "Your irony again."

"Why so?"

"You have what I need—what I desperately need," she emphasized. "But you don't know where it is."

"You know that for a fact?"

She nodded. "We know that Bobby had it, and that he intended to give it to you," she said. "We have reason to believe that you took it, but—"

"I don't seem to know where I put it?" he finished.

She nodded.

"Which is presumably why I haven't been killed—or destroyed—yet? Or don't I understand the context?"

Her eyes flickered again . . . dangerously, this time, Cellars sensed, although he didn't know why.

"Why do you say that?"

"Black humor," he said, feeling his heart starting to pound in his chest again. "Something we humans resort to every now and then, to keep from crying . . . or losing our minds."

She smiled. "You are interesting, Colin Cellars. You really are. But your lack of understanding is very dangerous to you . . . especially now."

"I am trying to understand, but you've got to help me. Otherwise, how can I help you?"

She nodded in what Cellars took to be agreement.

"To begin with," she said, "you must understand that these protectors are—at least within our context—very simple and yet very adaptable organisms. An essential factor when you consider the huge variety of dangers that we might encounter in our work . . . and our travels. In effect, and within your context, we simply program them to perform a wide range of specific functions in a manner that you would probably describe as very adaptive, fearless, and unrelenting."

"But, at the same time, they are vulnerable," Cellars noted.

"In what way?"

"If I understand what you're saying, I believe I've wounded at least one . . . and possibly killed at least one."

"You killed them, yes, but you didn't destroy them."

"I still don't understand the difference."

"When you kill one of these 'creatures,' as you call them, they revert . . . to a much lower and more stable energy state. A state of preservation, if you will, that they can remain in for a very long time—hundreds of your years if necessary—until we have an opportunity to retrieve them. What you would call a rock."

"The rock that moved," Cellars whispered.

"Yes . . . because your ingenious friend, Malcolm, happened to choose a frequency for his scanners that we use to reenergize these rocks—so that they can be located and retrieved. There are technical differences that aren't important to what we're talking about, but that's the essence of the system."

"But if that's the case, why don't you just . . . do that?" he asked. "Use your scanners or whatever, and locate your missing rock?"

"Because our expedition lost that capability when we had an unfortunate mishap with your friend Bobby and his helicopter."

"You crashed into his helicopter?"

"We had an accident." She nodded. "A great deal of effort on our part was necessary in those first few minutes to conceal the evidence of that accident."

"Bobby's helicopter. The one that nobody can find."

"Yes, exactly. And by the time we did so, your friend Bobby and one of our stabilized protectors who had been killed in the accident were gone. The details aren't important. Suffice it to say that a well-known principle—what you call your Murphy's Law—does apply to the greater Universe."

"Malcolm will be happy to hear that."

"I'm sure he will." She smiled agreeably. "I would like to meet your Malcolm someday."

"That would probably be hard to arrange. I think he's afraid of you right now."

"Yes, I'm sure he is." Her eyes flickered dangerously again. "Perhaps someday we can meet, as friends, and enjoy the ironies. But not right now, because our time is running out. We must leave soon, and we must take the evidence of our visit—our stabilized protectors—with us when we do. If we fail in any of this, I will be destroyed. Not killed. Destroyed. And others will come to make the retrieval."

"Others?"

"Others . . . possessing far greater powers to seek, and find and destroy. Others who will display far less compassion for other life-forms."

"You mean hunters? Soldiers? Warriors?"

"Yes, all of that . . . and much more that you don't wish ever to understand, believe me."

"What can I do?"

"You are the key. I don't know why, or how, but you are. So if you wish to save the lives of your friends . . . and me . . . and many, many others of your kind in the very near future, you must find and return our evidence."

"How much time do I have?"

"Not long."

"Will they leave me alone?"

"Who?"

"Your protectors?"

She hesitated. "Yes, for a while. But—"

"I know, time is running out."

"Faster than you may think," she said as she abruptly slid out of the bed and reached for her clothes.

"But if I find it," he said as he sat on the bed and watched her dress, the sense of longing tempered now by a fierce determination to protect and survive, "how do I find you?"

"Find them," she corrected.

"Them?"

"Two of the stones are missing. You must find them both."

"Two? But—"

Then he remembered.

"The necklace in the portrait Bobby was painting."

"Yes, exactly." She nodded approvingly. "The portrait he was painting is a key to at least one of the stones. You are also a key. I don't know why, but you are. So you must figure it out. And you still must hurry. Time is running out very rapidly now."

"But—"

"And don't worry," she added. "When the time does come, I will always be able to find you."

"Funny," he whispered mostly to himself. "That's what Malcolm always says."

"You should listen to him more. He understands things—out of context."

"But you know what he'll want—Malcolm, if you ever do meet."

She stopped at the door and cocked her head curiously.

"Your technology. How you adapt. How you travel. How you obtained that third set of base pairs."

Her eyes flashed again, but this time with amusement.

"Don't you see, that's the greatest irony of them all," she said. "You already have everything you need, just as we did, but you are careless as a species. You lose things. Things that you can never replace. It's a very dangerous trait—and perhaps, if you stop to think about it, even a fatal one."

With that, she disappeared out the door.

CHAPTER FORTY-SIX

"I'M TELLING YOU, JODY TOOK EVERY ITEM OF EVIDENCE WE GOT in on that case with her, including all the DNA extracts," Melissa Washington said as she watched Cellars searching frantically through Jody Catlin's assigned evidence storage lockers. "If the kidnappers managed to steal all that, then they've got everything we had."

"That may be, but they're insisting they don't have them, and that I must have taken them away from the crime scene."

"How would they know that?"

"I don't know, from what they said over the phone, I guess they were watching me the whole time I was out there," Cellars said evasively. He hadn't told Melissa Washington—or anyone else, for that matter—about his incredible conversation with Allesandra.

And for good reason, too, he reminded himself. He wouldn't be of much help to Jody if the OSP decided to lock him up for a seventy-two-hour observation in the local mental health ward. "So there has

to be something I just didn't see," he went on. "Maybe there was a
hidden compartment in one of the items I picked up at the scene,
and the stone fell out when you folks here or the people at the OSP
lab were examining the items."

"But if that was the case, wouldn't one of us have noticed it if
something like a rock fell out of an evidence package and landed on
a countertop or the floor?" Washington reasoned.

"You'd think so," Cellars acknowledged. "That's why we've been
searching through all the evidence lockers, too, just in case it fell
out there . . . during the logging-in process, or maybe during one of
the transfers. A rock isn't something you'd normally think of as evidence if you saw it lying on the floor."

"Did you search that Jasper County scout car Jody was in?"

"Twice."

"What about your CSI vehicle?"

"That's a more difficult problem." He told her about the explosions that had destroyed two of his vehicles, and the OSP Expedition that was still missing with Talbert.

Melissa shook her head in amazement.

"What does the FBI have to say about all this?" she asked after a
moment.

"They want me to keep looking while they try to find some
kind of lead to the kidnappers," he lied. "I've already gone through
every examination room and evidence locker at the OSP lab, so the
only logical possibilities I can think of—other than my burned or
missing CSI vehicles, which I'm trying not to think about right
now—are the evidence items they transferred over here . . . and the
original crime scene."

"Let me see that photo again."

Cellars pulled the photograph of the stone necklace from Dawson's partially finished portrait out of the manila envelope and
showed it to her.

"Well, even if they did send it out here, I don't know why anyone would give it to Jody or me," Melissa said. "Ain't no way we're going to get DNA out of a stone."

Cellars started to say something, then shook his head and went back to his searching.

"Unless . . ."

"Unless what?" Cellars's head came back up.

"I was just thinking." Melissa shrugged. "What if our own evidence control people didn't give us everything?"

Five minutes later, the two of them were in the alarmed storage area of the wildlife forensic lab's evidence control unit, searching through rows of blue metal shelves . . . but again to no avail.

"I'm sorry," the evidence clerk said as she showed Cellars the red case file. "Everything we got in on the Dawson case is accounted for in the chain-of-custody log."

A white-coated Asian woman walking down the hallway past the evidence window suddenly stopped, came back, and stuck her head inside the window.

"Did I hear somebody mention the name Dawson?" she asked.

"Yes, I did," the evidence technician said. "Why?"

"Some fellow from the Jasper County Coroner's Office stopped by last Monday with a dog carcass. Wanted to know if we could hold it here for a few days because he wasn't supposed to be keeping dogs in the morgue freezers. I told him sure, just put it in our walk-in freezer. He promised he'd get us a case number, but I haven't heard anything from him since. I was going to log it in anyway, just to keep our records straight, but I can't because the only information I've got is a toe tag with the name Dawson on it."

"That dog—was it a malamute?" Cellars asked.

The white-coated scientist blinked in amazement.

"Yes, as a matter of fact, it is. Do you happen to know—?"

Cellars quickly stepped forward to the evidence window. "I'm Detective-Sergeant Colin Cellars, OSP," he said as he extended his hand.

"Ann Tsuda."

"Ann's our resident veterinary pathologist," Melissa explained.

"Dr. Tsuda, do you think we could take a look at that dog?" Cellars asked.

"Sure, why not," the veterinary pathologist shrugged. "Sounds like you know a whole lot more about it than I do anyway. Follow me."

————

The expression on the malamute's face hadn't changed, Cellars realized as he looked down at the horribly torn animal lying frozen and stiff-legged on the stainless-steel necropsy table. He still looked like he'd been scared to death rather than gutted.

"What is it you want to know?" Tsuda asked as she too stared down in amazement at the massive chest wound.

"Firs of all, what could have caused that wound?" Cellars said.

"My first reaction would be either a wide-bladed chain saw, or some kind of bear—a grizzly or a Kodiak," Tsuda replied, "but you said you're sure it was killed up on the mountain?"

"That's right."

"Well, there haven't been any grizzlies or Kodiaks up there for several hundred years, as far as I know."

"What about a black bear?"

The veterinary pathologist shook her head. "Black bears maul. What we're looking at here is slashing—by an extremely powerful animal."

"What about a cougar?"

"Not with wounds like that. A cat would go for the throat and head." Tsuda shook her head slowly as she bent to examine the torn ribs more closely. "Actually, what this really looks like—"

"Yes?" Cellars pressed as the veterinary pathologist remained silent.

"I was going to say these wounds look exactly like what you'd expect from one of those medium-sized dinosaurs in the move *Jurassic Park*. You know, the smart ones with those long sharp single claws who chased those kids around the kitchen. What did they call them? Velociraptors? Something like that.

"But that's not exactly the kind of diagnosis you wanted to hear, is it?" The veterinary pathologist looked up at Cellars and smiled.

"No, not really," he said truthfully, trying not to think about the image of the violet-eyed creature on the computer monitor.

"So what was it you said you were looking for? Some kind of rock?"

Cellars showed her the photograph.

"Well, if this fellow swallowed something like that, we aren't going to find it until we thaw him out. But what we can do right now is get an x-ray," Dr. Tsuda said as she wheeled the portable necropsy table over to the x-ray machine. She quickly transferred the dog onto the x-ray table, inserted a film magazine into the left-hand slot, then brought the illuminated crosshairs of the x-ray head around to center on the rear third of the frozen animal.

"If you folks want to step over there, this will take just a few seconds."

Cellars and Melissa Washington waited outside while the veterinary pathologist quickly took three partial-body x-rays, dropped the film magazines into the automatic developer, and came back out into the necropsy examination area.

"How long do you think this will take?" Cellars asked.

"To thaw him out so we can do some cutting? I'd say at least twenty-four hours."

Cellars closed his eyes in frustration.

"Is that going to be a problem?"

"I . . . don't know," Cellars said hesitantly.

"Can we tell her?" Melissa asked.

Cellars hesitated again, then said: "We don't want this information to get out, but Jody Catlin was kidnapped a few hours ago."

Dr. Ann Tsuda's eyes widened with shock. "What?"

"The people who took her are demanding that we find and return these rocks. We don't know why, but—"

A buzzer in the back room went off.

"Hold on a second." Tsuda said as she quickly disappeared into the adjoining darkroom and then came back out with a set of x-rays. She quickly snapped the first two up on the illuminator.

"If I see something here," she said as she held the third x-ray up to the light, "we'll forget thawing and go directly to a power saw. I can—"

Then she blinked, and a slight smiled appeared on her face. Without saying another word, she set the x-ray down, walked over to the x-ray table, and dug her hands into the thick fur around the malamute's neck.

"Is this what you've been looking for?" she asked, holding a stone necklace up in her gloved hand.

CHAPTER FORTY-SEVEN

"WHERE ARE YOU?"

"I'm heading back up the mountain, to Bobby's cabin," Cellars said into the cell phone. He'd been watching his rearview mirror, trying to keep track of the cars through the falling rain, wondering what they'd do. Go for the one he had, or wait until he found the second one?

Assuming there is a second one, he reminded himself. *No reason for them not to cheat. We would.*

"Why go back up there?" Malcolm Byzor asked, suddenly sounding very concerned.

"I found one of the stones."

"Which one?"

"The one in the portrait."

"Are you sure?"

"Yeah, absolutely, unless there's two exactly alike. Bobby got every

edge and curve exactly right, including the mounting positions for
the chain and a small chip at one end."

"Where did you find it?"

"It was wrapped around the dog's neck. I guess Bobby figured
even an alien protector might hesitate at something like that."

"Bad guess."

"Yeah, no shit."

"So why go back to the cabin?"

"If there really is another stone, I figure it's got to be up there
somewhere. Maybe I hit one of them and didn't know it. It could
have rolled under the bed. And besides," he added, "I've looked
everywhere else."

"What did you do with the one you found?"

"I hid it."

"Good thinking," Byzor said approvingly. "You know they'll be
watching you."

"Oh yeah, no doubt about it."

"Do you have anyone with you?"

"No. I'm going there by myself."

"You think that's a good idea?"

"Probably not." Cellars shrugged. "But who would I trust without running a blood test first?"

"Yeah, good point."

Byzor was silent for a several seconds.

"Listen, Colin, when you get up there—"

"Yeah?"

"Pay attention to your instincts . . . and be careful."

———

*Pay attention to my instincts? What the hell is that supposed to
mean?* Cellars wondered as he slowly and carefully worked his way
down along the west side of the cabin with the SIG-Sauer in his
right hand.

The wind and rain had started up in full force again, sending flurries of raindrops into his eyes and making the downward-sloping ground under his feet slippery and treacherous.

Here we go again, he thought uneasily, tightening his grip on the SIG-Sauer as he approached the south-facing basement door.

But when he got to the door, he found the red evidence tape still in place.

Okay, that's more like it.

The first thing he did, once he was inside, was to lock the windows and the doors, taking special pains with the door that led into the stairwell. He had no intention of allowing anyone—or anything—to sneak up on him this time. After that, he made a quick, cursory search of the basement, to make absolutely certain that he was alone.

Then, finally, he began his search. He started under the bed (just in case his casual comment to Malcolm Byzor had been some kind of premonition) . . . then slowly and methodically worked his way through the kitchen and bathroom on his hands and knees, using his flashlight to look in and around every cubbyhole and corner.

But no stone.

He was still on his hands and knees in the southwest corner of the basement, the flashlight and SIG-Sauer set aside for the moment as he felt under the edges of the table with his bare hands, when a very familiar voice spoke up out of the darkness.

"You're wasting your time. You'll never find it."

CHAPTER FORTY-EIGHT

CELLARS SPUN AROUND ON HIS HANDS AND KNEES IN THE DARK-
ened basement, his hand automatically going for the SIG-Sauer.

"Don't," the familiar voice ordered.

It took Cellars a moment, but then he saw him. A darkened figure sitting in a chair across the room by the workbench . . . with an
old-fashioned pistol in his hand.

"Bobby?"

"How you doing, bud?"

Cellars started to come to his feet, and then halted immediately
as the pistol came up, the long barrel centered on his chest.

"Pretty shitty, all things considered. What's with the gun?" Cellars demanded.

"Sit down." The barrel of the pistol pointed him toward the
chair next to the table.

"I repeat," Cellars said in a tight voice, glaring at the darkened figure as he sat down in the chair and rested his right arm on the table. "What's with the gun?"

"Trust."

"You don't trust me?" Cellars blinked, incredulous.

"Think about it," the darkened figure said.

"That's what everybody's been telling me the last couple of days."

"Good advice. You ought to listen to it."

Cellars sat and stared at the darkened figure for several seconds. "The problem is," he finally said, "it's really kind of hard to think things out when you get to the point that you can't tell good information from bad."

"That's a definite problem in this case," the dark figure acknowledged. "What do you *think* you know?"

"Where do you want me to start?"

"Probably doesn't matter a whole hell of a lot. Take your pick."

"Okay," Cellars said agreeably, "when I arrived here last Sunday evening—as the result of a call-out to what I assume is your cabin—I met a couple of sheriff's deputies who acted like they were scared to death of shadows. It didn't make a lot of sense at the time, but I've gained a whole new outlook on shadows over the past few days. They've been missing since Sunday, along with a couple of other deputies who also showed up here on the first call. I'm assuming they're all dead and buried somewhere out in the woods around here."

"A reasonable assumption," the dark figure agreed.

"Then, after I checked out the dead dog in the cul-de-sac, and worked my way to your cabin through your goddamned tree maze, I figured you were dead too. Another reasonable assumption since a body that more or less looked like you was lying there in the middle of your basement floor with most of its face blown off. At least that's what I thought until I saw the bullet patterns in the wall. Then I didn't know what to think."

"Good," the dark figure nodded. "Keep going."

"Since then, I've been trying to figure the whole mess out. But every time I tried, I ended up shooting at shadows that kept trying to steal my vehicle and my evidence. And then finally, when I actually managed to hit one of the damned things—instead of my official police vehicles, which I seemed to be doing a lot—they'd either disappear or turn into stones that tried to run away when I wasn't looking. We'll skip the fact that these shadows may, in fact, turn out to look like something out of a teenager's chainsaw nightmare, because every time I think about that picture, I want to pull the covers over my head."

"Not exactly the kind of thing they warned you about at the Police Academy."

"No, it's been a little disconcerting. Especially when everybody I tried to work with ended up thinking I was either corrupt, jealously homicidal, or just flat out losing my mind. Especially after I hauled what I thought was my best friend's body down to the county morgue, where it ended up disappearing in thin air along with any and all evidence that I was ever there in the first place. Except, as it turns out, it probably wasn't your body after all, because according to Malcolm's wonderful little TOD device, it never did reach ambient room temperature."

"Interesting."

"I thought so."

"So *are* you?" the darkened figure inquired.

"Am I what?"

"Jealously homicidal?"

"Depends."

"On what?"

"Did you sleep with Allesandra?"

The darkened figure hesitated.

"As a matter of fact, yes, I did . . . not that it's necessarily any of your business."

"Jody wasn't any of my business," Cellars corrected. "But I think I can make a good argument on the Allesandra issue."

"I can't wait to hear that one," the darkened figure commented.

"But in any case," Cellars went on, "I just thought you'd like to know that as far as I'm concerned, shacking up with Allesandra definitely makes up for your shacking up with Jody when we were kids."

"Oh really? And just how do you figure that?"

"Simple. If you let Allesandra get into your head, like she got into mine, then you've got to be just as emotionally confused and paranoid and generally screwed-up as I am right about now."

"You find that amusing?"

"No, actually, to tell you the truth, it scares the living shit out of me," Cellars said honestly. "I'm just grateful for the company. But it also brings us to a very relevant question."

"The paranoia?"

"Right."

"Go on."

"These shadows or protectors—or whatever the hell they are—that I've shot and killed, whatever that means in their case," Cellars added, "turn out to have some very interesting DNA. Three sets of base pairs, and a couple of unlikely silicon substitutions, among other things, according to Jody's lab partner."

"Yeah, so?"

"I gather this means they can apparently shape-change pretty much however and whenever they want. Like into a dead body that looks just like you—or the late General Custer after his little afternoon excursion at Little Bighorn got out of hand—lying on the floor of this cabin," Cellars suggested.

"Or a live body that looks just like me—or a reanimated version of the good general you just slandered—sitting in a chair with a loaded SAA Colt in its hand."

"Exactly."

"And if they can do that," the dark figure commented, "I suppose it goes without saying that turning themselves into a crime scene investigator with delusions of riding in on a white horse to save the fair damsel would be a piece of cake, figuratively speaking."

"Exactly."

"So tell me, bud, how do we go about figuring this whole thing out—seeing as how the bitch has clearly gotten into both of our heads, and pretty much knows everything that we know. In other words, are both of us who we think we are? Or is one of us a fake, just waiting to catch the other off guard so it can find out where the other stone is at?"

"Does she really know everything we do?" Cellars said thoughtfully. "I guess that's got to be one of the critical questions."

"My guess would be yes, but I'm not a forensic scientist."

"You're expecting *me* to figure this thing out?"

"You or Malcolm, I'm not picky."

"Okay, so let's get hold of him, get his brain—or one of his mainframes—to work on this."

"I don't think we can," the darkened figure reminded. "He contacts us, we don't contact him, remember? That way, she can't find him by getting into our heads and tracking back on the numbers."

"Assuming, of course, that we've been actually talking to the real Malcolm all this time . . . just in case you were in the market for something else to get paranoid about." Cellars smiled grimly. "And it goes without saying, of course, that she knows this too."

"This is starting to make my head hurt."

"That's the whole idea. It's a circular argument. We've got to find a way out of it, or she's got us cold."

"Yeah, tell me about it. I've been driving myself crazy the last few days trying to figure this whole mess out."

"Is that why you didn't try to contact me before?"

"Exactly right. Trying to keep both of us alive. If they ever caught us together—"

"With all of the missing stones—" Cellars nodded in sudden understanding.

"Probably make the good general's problems on that round-topped ridge look like a stroll through an elementary school playground," the darkened figure commented.

"That's why you said I'd never find the other stone. You've got it."

"You bet. Caught one of them bastards flickering around the cabin all by his lonesome the other day. Lined him up with the Sharps, and dropped him like a rock, so to speak."

"But you don't have it here. Otherwise . . ."

"Little Bighorn all over again." The darkened figure nodded. "Which means, I assume, that the other one—the one you've presumably got—isn't here either."

"That's right."

"So we're thinking alike—just like we'd expect each other to think. Which means we're probably both who we think we are. Or at least who we hope we are."

"But if we're wrong—"

"Jody's a goner, not to mention at least one of us," the darkened figure finished.

"I hate even to say this," Cellars said, "but do we really know she's alive in the first place?" He described the scene at his house . . . and all of the blood on his kitchen floor and walls.

"It's not her blood."

"Are you sure about that?"

"Oh yeah, I'm sure all right. You know an OSP captain by the name of Hawkins?"

"My new boss," Cellars said indifferently. He was still reacting to the wonderful news that Jody was still alive. If he could believe the darkened figure sitting on the other side of the darkened basement holding the old-fashioned SAA Colt in his hand.

"You fond of him?"

"No, not particularly."

"Good thing. He showed up at the wrong time. My guess is that his missing body was supposed to be part of the twist the bitch has planned for you. Force you to cooperate and hand over the stones, otherwise you're left facing a couple hundred years in prison for presumably wiping out a goodly portion of Region Nine law enforcement. I think we can assume the evidence would all fit nicely. As we both know all too well, the bitch is smart."

"How do you know about all that?" Cellars asked suspiciously.

"I was watching your place with a spotting scope, hoping to catch you alone and off guard. I saw Jody go in your house, heard her scream, started to go in after her . . . and saw this big Jasper County deputy carry her out to the car and put her in the backseat of an OSP cruiser."

"The backseat? Not the trunk?" Cellars pressed.

"Right. A couple of heavy dark green trash bags went into the trunk. Presumably your captain, or the major parts thereof. But by the time I was able to get in close enough to try to do something about it, they were gone."

"Shit."

"Yeah, tell me about it. But sitting around here grumbling about missed chances isn't going to do her any good."

"At least we know she was alive then."

"Yeah, but we're also running out of time," the darkened figure muttered. "We've got to figure out how we're going to get Jody away from the bitch and her little protective shadows."

"We make a trade." Cellars shrugged. "Jody for the stones, just like they want."

"Hell of a plan, compadre, except for the fact that we're all dead—you, me, and Jody—about three seconds after we hand over the stones. They don't like to leave evidence, remember?"

"Yeah, maybe, but we're going to have to try. What other choice do we have?"

"I've been working on an idea," the darkened figure said hesitantly. "Couple of weak spots in it though."

"Like what?"

"Well, for starters, if everything goes right—which it probably won't—you get the girl and I get to save the day."

"I can live with that."

"Maybe not," the darkened figure said. "It also means you get to be the one who walks out to make the exchange while I stay back and try to cover you both."

"So what's the problem . . . other than the minor fact that we're dog meat if you miss?"

"It's a little more complicated than that."

"Yeah, I was afraid it might be."

"The thing is," the darkened figure continued on, "I think we can work it out so that the bitch will agree to let me cover the exchange—try to keep the whole thing honest—if I'm out in the open."

"You got a place in mind?"

"Yeah, a spot about a quarter mile from here. Nice big open meadow by the lake."

"What's our advantage?"

"That it actually makes sense from her part. She can see me, and how I'm armed, which means she knows how far she has to stay back out of range. And also, it puts me in a position so that I can see one of those shadowy bastards coming the moment it takes off from the trees."

"I still like it so far. Keep talking."

"The trouble is, once this all starts, and we're all out in the open, the bitch is not about to let you or me be anywhere near her with a modern firearm."

"Oh yeah, right."

"That leaves us with this genuine SAA Colt. Six rounds, short range, no chance to reload. And my old Sharps carbine. Medium range, single shot, no chance to reload in time if either of you is in serious trouble."

Cellars nodded thoughtfully.

"As long as I've got the Colt as a close-range backup, if Jody can get to me, I can keep the shadows off us . . . depending, of course, on how many of those protective bastards the bitch has got roaming around out here in the woods. But the thing is, you're almost certainly going to be out beyond the far edge of the Sharps's range . . . unarmed and ripe for the picking, 'cause we both also know the bitch is not about to put herself within lethal range of any firearm she lets me have out there."

"But will she actually know the effective ranges of—?" Cellars stopped and shook his head in irritation. "Never mind, I forgot. Stupid question."

"Hey, you could have resisted her charms too," the dark figure said defensively.

"Yeah, right." Cellars rolled his eyes. "So what it all boils down to—if our dear treacherous Allesandra tries to have it both ways, and sends her shadows after all three of us, which we both agree is better than an even bet—the best you're going to be able to do is try to keep her and her shadows away from Jody."

"As long as there's fewer than seven of them, she'll be fine," the darkened figure promised. "But that leaves you in deep shit, which most likely means I end up getting the girl," he added grimly.

"Which is what you were presumably talking about when you mentioned that the plan still had a few weak points?"

"Uh-huh."

"Yeah, well, I always figured the white-knight-to-the-rescue business wasn't anything like they make it out in the stories." Cellars shrugged. "Maybe I'll get lucky. Continue on with the plan. How do we force her to make the exchange?"

"You've got one stone, I've got the other. You and the bitch meet out in the middle of the meadow. You show her the stone. She shows us Jody. I show her my stone. You give her yours. She lets Jody walk to a point maybe a third of the way from you to me . . . where she'll be within the protective cover of the Sharps, but probably not the Colt. I use a sling to throw my stone to Jody. She turns, throws it to you, as far as she can. You go over, pick up the stone, and take it to the bitch while Jody starts walking toward me."

"And if either of us sees one of those shadows coming, we yell to Jody to start running toward you, fast as she can," Cellars added.

"Right."

"Not bad." Cellars nodded approvingly. "Our dear Allesandra might actually go for it."

"At least until she gets her hands on the stones. At that point, the way I see it, all bets are off. However, if the bitch does try to cheat us, I figure you've still got one decent chance."

"Yeah, what's that?"

"The instant you see one of those shadow figures coming for you—and as soon as Jody's at least half the distance to me—you take off running too, fast as you can, toward me. If you can get within medium range, and there's only one of them, and I've got time—"

The darkened figure shrugged, leaving the rest unsaid.

"What are we talking about . . . in terms of rough distances?"

"For a high parabolic shot with the Sharps, maximum outer range, with enough velocity left for the slug to punch through whatever those bastards use for skin? Maybe a hundred and fifty yards . . . if I've got time."

"And if not?"

"Then you'd better duck and pray, because at that point, all bets are definitely off."

"Yeah, well, maybe I'll get lucky," Cellars said.

"Don't count on it."

"I'm not."

Cellars sat there for a long moment in contemplation.

"Explain something to me," he finally said. "Why did they bother to leave a replica of your body in the cabin for me to find, when all they had to do was wait and catch me off guard when I was trying to find my way through your damned maze, bury me alongside those two deputies, then take their sweet time looking for the missing stone necklace you hung around the dog's neck?"

"I assume they wanted to keep you around to get to me," the darkened figure suggested. "Especially when they couldn't find the stone during their initial search of the cabin. But in any case, they probably didn't have much of a choice. That old Remington cap-and-ball of mine blew up right in that critter's face, but it didn't kill him. From what I know about them, I'm guessing they could easily

shape-change their buddy to make him look like anyone or anything they wanted, but they couldn't shift him into one of their
stones until he actually died. Which presumably didn't happen until sometime after you transported him down the mountain."

"So what you're saying is they ran into a time-factor problem?"

"That and some bad luck. What did you and Jody used to call
it? Murphy's Law? Anyway, their buddy was still flopping around
on the floor when I grabbed up the first Sharps I could reach—I
wanted the rifle, but it got knocked under the workbench and I
couldn't get to it in time—and lit out the door like my tail feathers
were on fire. I don't know how many of them were in or around the
cabin at that point, but I do know that at least two of them were
still looking for me when that first pair of deputies showed up.
Somebody must have heard the shots and called it in."

"An older woman," Cellars said. "Presumably one of your
neighbors?"

"Must have been Mary. She lives down the road a bit. Anybody
talk with her?"

"Far as I know, nobody's seen or heard from her since the call."

"Shit. She was a nice neighbor."

They were both silent for a long moment.

"So when the deputies showed up," Cellars went on, "the shadows left you alone to focus on the new problem?"

"Right. I was still circling around in the woods—trying to work
my way back into the cabin and grab that necklace off the dog—
when I heard some screams . . . and then dead silence. At that point,
I figured the deputies were dead meat; which turned out to be the
case because about twenty minutes later, I saw two of the shadow
critters take two bodies in their underwear out into the woods, toss
the dog out on the road, then drive off with the deputy's scout car."

"Rigging the scene?"

"Either that or putting the dog out for bait. But in either case,
they definitely screwed up my plans, because now I had to work my
way back out to the road to get to the necklace. I was still trying to

do that, moving a couple inches at a time, and trying to figure out how I was going to get to the dog without being seen, when the second pair of deputies showed up. So there I am, hunkered down and watching the damned shadows move in on the new pair, when you pop up and thoroughly confuse the situation."

"A couple of pertinent questions, if you don't mind."

"Shoot."

"First of all, why didn't you try to help the second pair of deputies . . . or me . . . when you had the chance?"

"Simple. At that point, I had no way to tell who was who . . . or what. Don't forget, they had at least two Jasper County Sheriff's uniforms that I knew about . . . and I already knew they could transform themselves into whoever or whatever they wanted."

"Including me."

"You bet. Especially when I knew you were supposed to be down at the county auditorium giving a lecture to my wacko friends. And you didn't help things any—my paranoia specifically included—when you started cranking off rounds in the cabin, then drove off with the dog and all the rest of my guns."

"Which presumably brings us back to the central problem," Cellars noted.

"Exactly."

"So setting that problem aside for the moment, let's go on to question two. Namely: Are you going to tell me how you managed to get in here without me seeing you?"

"Nope. Thought I'd save that conversation for the homecoming. Give you something to look forward to . . . just in case."

"And I assume the same answer applies to how you're planning on getting out to that meadow without Allesandra spotting you?"

"That's right."

"Fair enough." Cellars nodded. Then, after a moment: "Just so you don't get too excited, I'm going to reach down and pick up the SIG, left-handed."

"Okay," the darkened figure said agreeably.

"Then I'm going to place it in my lap, grip outward, barrel facing the stove."

He did so.

"You really think that's going to make any difference?" the darkened figure inquired.

"Humor me."

"Actually, I was thinking of painting a big fat target on your chest before I send you out there. Hate to have to see you suffer after all these years."

Cellars smiled.

Then he reached into his jacket pocket, took out the stone necklace, draped it around his neck, picked up the SIG-Sauer with his left hand—by the frame—stood up, and started walking toward the door.

"Colin."

Dawson's voice stopped him as he was about to reach for the doorknob.

"Yeah, Bobby?"

"How can you be so damned sure . . . that it really is me?"

"Easy," he said with a shrug. "Good old black humor. A very human trait."

Then he walked out the door into the falling rain.

CHAPTER FORTY-NINE

HE WALKED IN THE RAIN FOR ALMOST HALF AN HOUR. WORKING his way along the narrow trail in the gloomy half-light with the SIG-Sauer held tight in his right hand, and watching the surrounding trees every step of the way.

He was within sight of the lake, and the meadow, when he first became aware of the shadow's presence.

He stopped then, and stared at the gap in the two distant Douglas firs where he had spotted the dark, flickering movement out of the corner of his eye.

"You know, I have no idea what will happen if I fire a high-velocity hollow-point bullet point-blank at this piece of silicon," he called out as he tapped the stone necklace with his left hand. "But if any of you get within twenty-five yards of me, we're going to find out."

There wasn't any answer, but he really hadn't expected any. So he just kept on walking—and wondering if she really would be there—until he reached the middle of the meadow and found Bobby Dawson's reference point.

It was a wooden target frame, made out of six-inch-diameter logs and heavy lag bolts and set solidly into the ground. He stood at the center of the open target frame, stared out across the meadow, and immediately spotted the range markers. Smaller logs, each approximately three inches in diameter and standing about three feet tall. They had been set into the ground at regular intervals, and in a straight line that led out across the meadow to the edge of the surrounding forest.

From his position, Cellars was able to count twelve posts, each of which appeared to be about seventy-five feet apart from the next one. As he did so, he observed that the posts were weathered and had clearly been in the ground for some time. A beautiful set of twenty-five-yard markers.

In the opposite direction, approximately one marker distance from the target frame, was the shoreline of a large lake: a safe impact point and repository for what Cellars guessed were probably hundreds—if not thousands—of Bobby Dawson's carefully aimed bullets.

Nice. He nodded approvingly. *Very nice indeed.*

He thought about reaching for the cell phone in his jacket pocket. But he had no idea what number to call, and he didn't think that the name Allesandra would be listed in the operator's directory for residents of Jasper County. So he continued to stand there with his back to the lake, staring out across the line of markers, lost in his thoughts, until he heard the sound of approaching footsteps.

He turned then and saw her . . . coming out of the tree line and walking in his direction along the edge of the shoreline.

Saw two of her, actually. Two beautiful women, identical in every way—hair, features, and dress—except for the fact that one of them had her mouth taped shut with almost-transparent packing tape . . . and her hands secured behind her back.

I should have realized, he thought as he stared at the untaped and unbound member of the pair.

Allesandra.

You took the photo of Jody from Bobby's dresser and you made yourself look just like her. Only I didn't realize it because I haven't seen her for almost fifteen years.

Assuming, of course, Cellars reminded himself, *that this isn't another one of your tricks.*

It was a numbing series of thoughts that sent the chills running up Cellars's spine again. But he refused to pay them any attention. Bobby Dawson would come through, or he wouldn't.

Then it was just a question of what she would do.

He still had the SIG-Sauer in his right hand, aiming down at the ground, but he never even considered the idea of trying to bring it up. They were walking too close together, this *doppelgänger* pair of enticing women. And even if she did give him a moment of opportunity, and he was absolutely certain which one was which, he wasn't at all certain that he'd actually be able to squeeze the trigger. Not with Jody Catlin's face staring at him above the sights.

They stopped about thirty yards away, at the edge of the water.

"Do you have them?" Allesandra called out.

"One of them." He fingered the stone around his neck with his left hand.

"What about the other one?" He could hear the edge in her voice. Serious now. No longer enticing or seductive. He could also see the expression in Jody's eyes—frightened and furious above the restricting tape—but there was nothing he could do about it. He had no doubt about what would happen to her if he made any attempt at all.

"Bobby has it."

She nodded as if that was exactly what she had expected.

"Get rid of your pistol and tell him to come out," she directed.

He was careful to keep the barrel of the SIG-Sauer pointed away from the two women as he first released the magazine—allowing it to drop to the ground—then jacked the round out of the chamber whereupon it disappeared into the brown grass. Then he threw the handgun as far as he could in the opposite direction from the lake.

He turned and started to yell in the direction of the distant trees. But he stopped when he saw the familiar, blond-haired, muscular figure step out into the open with the old Sharps carbine in his hand.

They all stood there by the target frame and watched Dawson come forward, slowly and steadily, until he passed the fifth marker.

Then Allesandra spoke again.

"Tell him to stop, right there."

Cellars held up his hand, and Dawson stopped immediately.

Twenty-five yards beyond the maximum parabolic range of the Sharps carbine. Cellars grimaced. Twenty-five yards to run. Too far . . . he'd never make it. But that really didn't make any difference, he reminded himself, because he'd never intended to try.

"You both understand what will happen to her if he comes any closer?" Allesandra asked as she—and Jody—came up beside him. He could hear the amusement in her voice.

He nodded.

"Good, then give me the first stone."

He lifted the stone necklace over his head and handed it to her, trying not to look at Jody Catlin's frightened and furious eyes. It occurred to him to wonder what Allesandra had told her—what threats she'd made to keep her apparent identical twin close at her side. Then he realized it didn't matter. That dark flickering shadow was still out there in the trees somewhere. Probably where the forest came right up to within a few yards of the lake—the point at which Allesandra and Jody had appeared—which was no more than fifty yards away. Much too close.

"Thank you," she said with a dimpled smile that did nothing at all to mask the alert expression in her eyes. "Now then, what did the two of you come up with for the next stage?"

He told her.

She nodded agreeably, and leaned over to whisper something in Jody Catlin's ear.

"You understand?" she then asked in a cold voice.

It looked to Cellars, for a brief moment, as if the rage in Jody Catlin's eyes was about to overwhelm her fear. But the moment passed, and Jody nodded.

Allesandra smiled, reached behind Jody's back and did something that released her hands, then gestured with her head for her human twin to begin walking.

It was then that Cellars saw the thin nylon line that bound Jody Catlin's legs close together—so that she could walk, if she took a normal stride, but not run. He also realized that Allesandra had positioned herself so that she and Cellars were very close to each other with respect to Dawson's line of sight.

They both stood there and watched Jody Catlin stumble her way to the fourth pole from the target frame and stop.

As she did so, Cellars felt the familiar heat of Allesandra's hand as it slipped around his neck.

"I told her she has to leave the tape in place until I have the second stone in my hand. And that if she tries to communicate with you in any way before then, I'll kill you immediately. I wouldn't, of course," she added as she pressed her lips against the side of his neck. "But she doesn't know that."

He could feel the intense heat from her lips and hand, but there was no sense of passion or fusion now. Only a sense of gentle probing.

"And the answer to the question you want so badly to ask—but not if it means taking the chance of upsetting me—is yes, we were responsible for the twenty-four missing people. Only the number is actually higher than that. Much higher. You have to include those four DEA agents. And Mary, courageous soul that she was. And the four deputies, and your Captain Hawkins, of course. But not your Lieutenant Talbert . . . or the vials of your blood. Not yet."

Cellars felt his stomach churn as he watched Jody stand there, alone and waiting.

"Why?" he asked in a soft voice.

"Why did we dispose of them?"

Cellars nodded.

"I told you, we can't leave evidence."

"But you don't have everything."

"We have everything of importance," she corrected. "Your videotape, your crime scene scanning data, your electronic image of the protector, your supposed information on the third base pair . . . all that you have left is easily faked and therefore useless. As you said so emphatically at your lecture, you can't trust an investigator who is emotionally involved not to fake his evidence. And how can you possibly deny your emotional involvement? Yet another irony, yes?"

He could feel—and sense—her amusement through the warmth of her hand.

"What about Talbert?"

"We still may need him . . . and your blood sample."

Then he felt her hand slip away.

"You're a brave man, Colin Cellars," she whispered beside his ear as they both watched Bobby Dawson set the impotent Sharps carbine down, then pull what looked like a long looped cord out of his pocket. He took something else out of his pocket, placed it in the bottom of the loop, and then started the cord swinging over his head.

"Did you really think I'd try to run—put her at risk—to save my own life?"

"No, not really."

"Then maybe you're beginning to understand us," he said as he watched his longtime buddy sling the small stone high in the air. It landed a few feet away from Jody Catlin, who immediately walked over and picked it up.

"Your moment of truth," Allesandra whispered, but Cellars ignored her.

Then he watched in disbelief as Jody Catlin turned and began walking back toward them. She was supposed to have stopped at the next marker, but to Cellars's horror, she kept on walking.

"No, Jody, stop there, throw it to me," Cellars yelled. But she ignored him, walked right up to Allesandra, and dropped the stone in her open left hand.

Then she tore the tape away from her mouth.

"There, is that what you wanted?" Jody Catlin snarled defiantly.

"Yes, it is. Thank you." As Cellars and Jody Catlin watched, Allesandra reached into her dress pocket and pulled out four other stones that she placed into her left hand with the necklace and the one that Jody Catlin had just delivered.

"Then go away and leave us alone."

"Oh, I intend to," Allesandra replied. "But I have a problem."

Cellars's heart sank.

"As I told each of you, there is one rule we must follow that is more important than any of the others."

She paused significantly.

"We can't leave evidence."

She continued to stare at him, warm and soulful and caring, but something shifted in her expression—something in her eyes—that caused Cellars's survival instincts to start screaming.

Oh, my God.

At that moment, she shape-changed . . . into a terrifying bipedal creature more reptilian than human, and more shadowy than real. But he hardly noticed her body changes. He'd seen them before . . . on the computer monitor. He'd been watching her eyes, and they changed most of all. The orbits and pupils enlarging . . . and then extending out at the edges into elongated slits as the surrounding tissues shifted into an impossibly bright and glistening violet.

Some portion of Cellars's subconscious recognized the shapes and colors immediately. The primeval signs of focused predation . . . and their rapidly impending death.

Then, before his own horrified eyes, she shape-changed again. Only this time, more subtly. Only the right hand . . . into an impossibly sharp claw.

Oh Jesus. . . .

A last-ditch sense of survival, more than anything else, caused Cellars to grab at Jody Catlin, fling her away in the direction of Dawson, then bring his hands up into a defensive stance. A posture that immediately looked absurd and futile. The glistening claw edge looked capable of severing the bones of both his arms in a single swipe.

Then they all heard the familiar voice.

"BACK AWAY FROM THEM, YOU TRAITOROUS BITCH!"

Dawson?

Forcing the image of his horrible and imminent death out of his mind, Cellars turned and stared at the distant figure.

In an instant, the creature's eyes refocused—on Dawson first, then on the ancient weapon in his hands.

Then she laughed . . . although the sounds that actually issued from her slitted and curved mouth were only vaguely human and understandable.

"YOU ARE STILL OUT OF RANGE WITH YOUR FOOL-ISH WEAPON, ROBERT DAWSON. TWO HUNDRED AND TWENTY-FIVE YARDS. MUCH TOO FAR AWAY."

As Cellars watched in amazement, the distant figure of Bob Dawson brought the ancient rifle up to his shoulder, the short barrel pointing high over their heads as Dawson—in defiance of the creature's laughing taunt—appeared to be lining up the ancient flip-up barrel sight for a high-arcing parabolic shot.

Then, in spite of his numbed fear, Cellars blinked in confusion as Dawson—in a move that defied logic—suddenly dropped the barrel of the nineteenth-century carbine back down to an almost level position.

What are you doing, Dawson?

Then, at that moment, he understood.

"GO AHEAD, SHOOT! DISCHARGE YOUR FEEBLE WEAPON!" The chillingly inhuman voice laughed loudly again. "YOU ONLY HAVE ONE SHOT, AND I CAN DESTROY BOTH OF YOUR FRIENDS AND BE AT YOU BEFORE YOU CAN RELOAD."

"No, you can't," Cellars whispered, feeling the cold numbness being replaced by a slight flash of hope as he forced himself to turn around and stare at the fearsome and chilling creature whom, only hours ago—or was it eons, he didn't know anymore—he had loved and desired beyond all sense of understanding. "He's tricked you."

"What?" the creature hissed. Her slitted eyes refocused on him as she whipped her head around, the claw coming up in a striking motion.

"Look at him," Cellars whispered, forcing himself to stare into her terrifying eyes. "Look how he holds the rifle."

The vaguely scaled head turned back to stare intently at the distant unmoving figure, and in that instant, Cellars saw recognition in her terribly cold and merciless eyes.

The shape-shift, when it came, was mentally jarring. In one moment, she stood fearsome, defiant, and malicious. The ultimate predator, scaled muscles tensed and ready to strike. In the next, she was reaching out, her smooth arms extended above her full breasts, imploring her ex-lover with her sensuous eyes—

That disappeared in a burst of blood and tissues as her high-pitched scream and the sound wave from the distant rifle shot struck Cellars's ears simultaneously.

He stood there, transfixed in time, watching the six stones fly from her hand as her body tumbled backward from the impact, her shattered head striking the ground.

He continued to stand there, staring down as the bodily remains of the woman he had loved—and the creature he had feared—with

every fiber of his soul shape-changed one last time. Then, as he continued to stare at the ground, Bobby Dawson, his childhood friend
came up, helped a stunned and shaken Jody Catlin to her feet, then
walked over and stood beside him.

For a long moment they both stood silently beside each other,
staring at the desolate ground that was empty now . . . except for
the seven glistening stones.

Each distinct, but each very much alike.

"How . . . did you manage to do it?" Cellars finally asked, his
voice a raspy whisper.

"Reloaded the cartridge with smokeless powder," Bob Dawson
replied evenly. "Had all the gear in the caves underneath my cabin,
where I've been hiding the last few days. Even turned the entire
basement stairs into a hinged door hatch with a concealed release
mechanism. That's how I got in and out without anyone seeing me.
Built the whole thing after I split away from her, so there was no
way she could have known about the reload possibility. Upped the
feet per second by a factor of three. Made for a nice straight-on
shot, low arc. No problem."

Cellars shook his head, still staring down at the ground. Then
he turned to face his childhood friend. The right side of Dawson's
face was covered with blackened gunpowder residues, his right eye
was swollen almost shut, and his hands and face were bleeding in
several places. But he held his shattered rifle steady, and the expression on his battered and bleeding face was that of a man finally at
peace with himself. That was the part that Cellars still couldn't
understand. Couldn't comprehend.

"No, I mean . . . how could you put her in the sights like that,
and then pull the trigger? Didn't you . . ." Cellars hesitated, uncertain of how to say it. "Didn't you love her?"

Cellars could still feel the terrible sense of grief and loss in his
heart and soul, the emotions churning in concert with the equally
overwhelming sense of escape . . . and survival.

"Yeah, I guess in a way I did. And you're right, it wasn't easy," Dawson conceded. "But the thing is, see, I know she had it all figured out."

Cellars's eyebrows furrowed in confusion.

"I only had one shot."

Dawson held the Sharps out so Cellars could see where the force of the smokeless powder had ruptured the barrel right up to the edge of the carbine's reinforced chamber.

Cellars shook his head silently, closed his eyes, and sighed. Then, not knowing what else to say or do, he knelt and picked up one of the stones. The last one to fall to the ground.

He was still standing there, staring at the small stone in his hand and trying to make sense of it all, when he became aware that Jody Catlin had come up beside him.

"Well, make up your mind, Colin Cellars," she said in her characteristic husky voice. "Which is it going to be? A chunk of inert silicon, or me?"

Cellars took one last look at the small stone in his hand. Then he tossed it aside—where it clattered, came to rest, and effectively joined hundreds of thousands of like stones that comprised the lake shoreline—and reached for her.

———

Sometime later—it could have been minutes, or only seconds, Cellars had no idea—a cell phone rang. He started to reach into his jacket pocket, to heave the offending instrument into the lake, then he realized it wasn't his cell phone.

Cellars disengaged himself slightly from Jody Catlin and looked around in amazement as he watched Dawson pull a small cell phone out of his jacket pocket.

"*You* have a cell phone?"

Bobby Dawson shrugged in seeming embarrassment as he brought the small electronic device up to his ear.

"I don't believe it," Colin Cellars whispered. But then Jody Catlin firmly redirected his attention to more important matters, and the issue of cell phones completely disappeared from his tumbled mind.

"Hi, Malcolm," Dawson said, still grinning as he watched his two treasured friends hold each other tightly.

"Well, how'd it go?" the electronics engineer demanded.

"Oh, pretty much about the way we planned it. Couple of unexpected twists, but we managed to adapt to the situation."

"Well, are they back together again?" Malcolm Byzor asked impatiently.

"Oh, yeah, you might say that." Dawson grinned again.

"What are they doing?"

"Oh, you know, the standard stuff: hugging, kissing, and fondling each other. Fact is, if they keep it up, I'm probably going to start getting embarrassed standing around out here all by myself."

"Oh well, you've always got Allesandra," Malcolm Byzor said philosophically.

"Yeah, as a matter of fact, I do," Dawson agreed, looking down at the stone in his hand. The one he'd picked up off the ground.

"All those base pairs to draw on, and a delusional human with a hundred-year-old rifle still took her down."

"You think she appreciated the irony?" Dawson asked.

"I don't know," Malcolm Byzor replied, "You'll have to ask her some day."

Dawson looked down at the small stone in his hand. "Oh I intend to, just as soon as you get those laser frequencies figured out."

"Which will be sometime *after* we get the cage situation figured out," Byzor reminded.

"Oh yeah, no question about that," Dawson agreed.

"But you know," Byzor went on, "I think the irony she'll appreciate the most is the one about Colin."

"Oh, yeah, what's that?"

"It's like I told you all along," Malcolm Byzor said with a satisfied tone to his voice. "Who would have thought that when all else failed, we could count on a thickheaded Scots-Irish crime scene investigator to get emotional about his evidence?"

ABOUT THE AUTHOR

A former deputy sheriff, police forensic scientist, and crime lab director, Ken Goddard is currently the director of the National Fish and Wildlife Forensics Laboratory. His previous novels include *Balefire*, *The Alchemist*, *Prey*, *Wildfire*, *Cheater*, and *Double Blind*. Ken and his wife live in Ashland, Oregon.